BLOOD
RUBIES

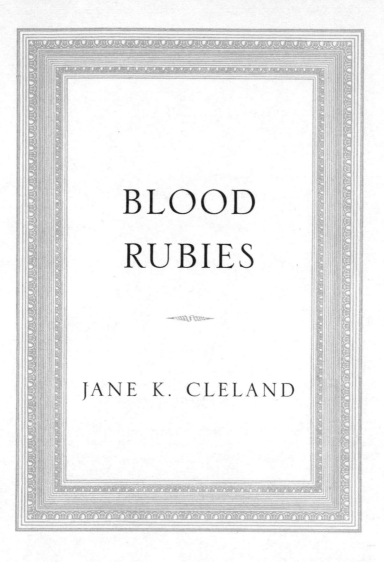

BLOOD RUBIES

JANE K. CLELAND

MINOTAUR BOOKS ⚜ NEW YORK

BLOOD RUBIES. Copyright © 2014 by Jane K. Cleland. All rights reserved. Printed in the United States of America. For information, address St. Martin's Press, 175 Fifth Avenue, New York, N.Y. 10010.

www.minotaurbooks.com

The Library of Congress Cataloging-in-Publication Data is available upon request.

ISBN 978-1-250-05413-5 (hardcover)
ISBN 978-1-4668-5715-5 (e-book)

Minotaur books may be purchased for educational, business, or promotional use. For information on bulk purchases, please contact Macmillan Corporate and Premium Sales Department at 1-800-221-7945, extension 5442, or write specialmarkets@macmillan.com.

First Edition: December 2014

10 9 8 7 6 5 4 3 2 1

This is for my niece Marci Gleason.
And of course, for Joe.

AUTHOR'S NOTE

This is a work of fiction. While there is a Seacoast Region in New Hampshire, there is no town called Rocky Point, and many other geographic liberties have been taken.

BLOOD
RUBIES

CHAPTER ONE

A na Yartsin stood beside one of her custom Fabergé-egg-shaped wedding cakes, unfazed by the frenetic activity swirling around her. The film crew was larger than I'd anticipated—I counted twenty-two people, including a uniformed security guard—and they all seemed to be doing things with frantic urgency. A young woman with pink hair and a star tattoo on her neck dabbed at Ana's cheek with a fluffy powder puff. Someone named Mack called to someone named Vinnie to check the light meter. The security guard, a big guy with a crew cut and a gun on his hip, stood near Ana, his eyes on the move. Timothy Brenin, the producer/director, dashed up to talk to a short man with spiky yellow hair carrying a clipboard, then called to Mack that we had another hour of good sun.

Timothy, tall and lean like a greyhound, dressed all in black like the New Yorker he was, approached Ana with a huge smile. I'd met Timothy briefly last week when I'd stopped by to order a cake for my office manager Gretchen's baby shower. He and Ana had asked me to come back and place the order again, this time on camera. They were in the early stages of filming a TV pilot for a reality show based on Ana's life, capitalizing on her dual role as a newly minted celebrity pastry chef with an ability to communicate Martha Stewartesque tips for gracious living and a recently divorced young woman ready for a fresh start.

Timothy spotted me, and his smile grew even broader. "Good to see you again, Josie!" He turned to Ana. "Why can't everyone be like her—on time and smiling?"

Ana laughed. "Because she's one of a kind. Lucky us!"

Timothy squeezed my arm affectionately, then turned toward Ana. "I just took a call from *People* wanting to know the skinny on the show."

"Oh, Timothy!" Ana exclaimed. "What a coup!"

"I knew your life would be perfect for a reality show!"

Ana laughed. "Talk about an upside-down compliment. My life is so chaotic, it's ideal for a prime-time exposé."

"True, true." Timothy flashed another grin, then flitted away calling something to Mack about moving cameras to catch the sun. Vinnie wheeled a camera to the left. "No, no! To the right. The *right*!"

Ana's eyes twinkled. "Survive a nasty divorce and a breach with your father, start to bake wedding and special occasion cakes based on Fabergé eggs, move to a small town on the rugged coast of New Hampshire where you don't know a soul, start a business on a wing and a prayer, and you, too, can have a reality TV show."

I chuckled. "I think the fact that you've won a gazillion awards for your pastries might have a little something to do with it, to say nothing of your charisma. Oh, let's not forget that your Fabergé egg cakes aren't just gorgeous, they're unbelievably delicious, too. "

"You're very sweet, Josie, but I cannot tell a lie—I've only won a couple of awards."

I waved her correction away. "You're destined for great success." I raised my chin and spoke in a tone of mock superiority. "Do not argue with me. I know these things."

She laughed, a pretty tinkling sound. "Thank you." She squeezed my hand. "You sure know how to puff a girl up."

Timothy stood in the center of the driveway and did a 180-degree survey, taking in the position of the ribbons of thick black cables and the pole-mounted overhead lights and reflective panels. He nodded and turned toward Ana. "All right, darling, get ready for your closing monologue."

The yellow-haired man hurried over to help Ana down from her canvas-backed director's chair and led her to a spot near the edge of her undulating lawn overlooking the serene sun-flecked ocean. She wore a lightweight baby blue buttoned-to-the-neck cashmere cardigan with a blue and tan floral-patterned swirly skirt and tan pumps. Her shoulder-length honey gold hair shone in the midday sun. She was my age, midthirties, but she looked younger. I moved off to the side, out of the way.

Timothy shouted, "Rolling!" A moment later he called, "Action!"

Ana smiled at the camera as if it were a friend. "Heather and Jason did exactly the right thing in talking to me at length about their dream wedding cake. They didn't use vague words like 'beautiful.' They were specific. They wanted a milk chocolate cake with gold-colored creamy frosting. They wanted the swan boats from Boston Public Garden, where Jason proposed, represented in the decorations." Ana paused for a second, letting her words sink in. "Here's the lesson: Everyone involved in helping you plan your wedding or special event wants nothing more than for you to be thrilled with the result—but they can't read your mind. You need to know what you want, and you need to communicate it clearly. Do that"—she paused again and smiled, a dazzler—"and your dreams will come true."

Three seconds later, Timothy yelled, "Cut! Fabulous, Ana, just perfect!"

My scene was scheduled next.

"Let me give you a quick once-over, Josie." The pink-haired woman appeared from the left and stared at my face.

"I just came from the makeup tent," I told her.

"And it shows. You look awesome! You just need a tiny de-shining."

Her feathery puff tickled, and I giggled.

Once I was sufficiently de-shined, I joined Ana, waiting for me by the lawn. "You're a hard act to follow, Ana. I hope I don't mess up."

"You'll do great."

"Just act naturally," Timothy instructed.

I laughed, "Right. Like it's an everyday occurrence that I'm filmed ordering a cake."

"Once you've completed your appraisal of the Fabergé Spring Egg snow globe, Timothy wants to record us discussing it."

"At least I'll be on comfortable ground. Compared to this, talking about antiques is easy. Speaking of which, are we still on schedule?"

Ana held up crossed fingers. "Dad checked in for his flight. He'll be here tomorrow, snow globe in hand."

"Is the egg as beautiful as Ana says?" Timothy asked, an anticipatory gleam in his eye.

"From the photos, oh my. Picture this: a huge, perfectly round snow globe. Visible through the glass is a baby pink enamel egg. On the egg is an enamel and emerald tree, dripping with diamond and rose quartz cherry blossoms. When the globe is gently shaken, silvery slivers create an illusion of rain. You push a spring-loaded latch and boom! The egg pops open. Inside is a gold-and silver-colored basket filled with five ruby red tulips."

Timothy rubbed his hands together and made a lip-smacking noise. "I can't wait to see it." Something in the background caught his eye, and he shouted to Mack. "Back up camera three for a long shot. I want to get Josie walking *up* the driveway toward the garage. *Up,* not down."

"It's a kitchen, not a garage!" Ana protested, laughing.

"Absolutely, darlin'! Josie, you start walking toward the structure that looks like a garage from the end of the driveway. You're excited. You're hopeful that Ana's cake will make Gretchen happy. Got it?"

"Got it," I said, feeling awkward, hoping I wouldn't get tongue-tied or stupidly giggly, wanting to do well for Ana. My mouth went dry. I hate being in the limelight.

"See ya in a sec," Ana said merrily. She walked to the office-cum-studio-cum-commercial-kitchen she'd built in her detached garage, a stopgap until her bakery business was large enough to justify a full-blown production facility, and disappeared inside.

Everyone was looking at me. My heart pounded against my ribs and my throat closed and my cheeks burned.

Timothy stood off to the side, near the pathway that led to the house. "Pretend we aren't here, Josie."

"Okay," I said, then started coughing. "Sorry about that."

"No prob!" Timothy said. "Take your time."

The yellow-haired man appeared with a glass of water, and after I'd sipped some, the pink-haired woman studied my lips, then nodded.

"Start again," Timothy said.

Fake it till you make it, my dad used to say. "Okay," I said, and this time my voice sounded like me, like a calm and controlled me. I started up the driveway toward the renovated garage.

"Rolling!" Timothy yelled. "Action!"

The sun was bright for March. A soft breeze rustled the tall grasses that grew along the property edge. I reminded myself to smile. I felt silly smiling at nothing, but I did it anyway.

Ana stepped out as if I'd called her. Her warm and welcoming smile reached her eyes and drew a more genuine smile in response from me.

"Josie! I'm so glad you're here."

"Thanks, Ana. What a beautiful location."

"Isn't it?" She gazed out over the ocean. "When I was a kid, this was where we spent summers. I'm delighted to be back in Rocky Point, to be a permanent resident." She turned to face me. "Come on in and tell me how I can help."

We stepped inside together. The walls and ceiling were painted snow white; the chairs were persimmon and cobalt. I could hear faint clinking and whirrs from the bakers at work in the rear.

"Oh, wow," I said, looking around. "It's so elegant."

A score of mahogany easels positioned in four diagonal rows showed two-part photos, fronts and backs, of various Fabergé-egg-shaped cakes, some large enough to serve a hundred people, most sized as individual portions. Just as each of the eggs Peter Carl Fabergé made for the Russian imperial family from 1885 to 1917 held at least one surprise, so too did Ana's cakes. From one side, the cakes appeared to be ornately decorated ovals. From the other side, the "surprise" was visible, positioned in a hollowed-out area reminiscent of an open-air theater. The surprises varied according to the occasion, the season, and Ana's whimsy; they included bouquets of flowers, a throne, a woodland scene, and a traditional bride and groom exchanging vows. All decorative elements were crafted out of frosting.

After I'd walked the aisles taking in all the options, Ana asked, "What's the occasion?"

"My office manager, Gretchen, is having a baby. I'm throwing a surprise Jack and Jill baby shower for her and her husband." I told her the date and grinned. "I expect about thirty people. I think Gretchen and Jack would love one of your Fabergé egg cakes."

"Wonderful! Do you have a theme in mind?"

"Hawaii. That's where Gretchen and her husband met and fell in love."

"How lovely. We could do a couple gazing at a baby in a lei-draped cradle with some palm trees and turquoise water in the background."

"That sounds perfect. Maybe with a rising moon."

"I love that idea!"

Ten minutes later, after I selected pineapple cake with orange-mango frosting, signed the order form, and left a deposit, Ana walked me out.

"Cut!" Timothy called. "We've got it. That's a wrap. Take fifteen and we'll pick up with Ana's Tips for Gracious Living." He squeezed Ana's hands. "Ana, you just keep getting better!" To me, he added, "Well done, Josie! Thanks."

I felt light-headed with relief that it was over. "You're welcome."

"Do you have a minute?" Ana asked me as I turned to leave. "I'd love to introduce you to my friend, Heather, and her fiancé, Jason. I've known Heather for years. Jason is an investment guy—Jason Ferris—do you know him? You might have seen him on TV."

"I don't think so."

"He's a pretty big deal in some circles."

"You sound skeptical."

Ana laughed. "Not so much skeptical as jealous. All the time they've been dating, a couple of years now, I've just been trying to cover the rent. Here he is, the building-personal-wealth guru. Having 'wealth' is a foreign concept."

"My gut tells me that's about to change for you."

"From your mouth to God's ears." I followed her across the driveway to the fieldstone path that led to the porch. "I don't mean to sound disingenuous." She laughed, half self-deprecating and half thrilled. "The last six months have been incredible. I have to remind myself that it's okay to celebrate a little."

"Is that why you started your snow globe collection?" I asked, thinking of the two snow globes she'd already delivered to us for appraisal, one a Victorian Christmas scene, the other featuring a winsome black-haired beauty ice-skating with a handsome cavalier on a glistening frozen pond.

She'd purchased both at a Midwest antiques store because she'd fallen in love with them, one of the joys of collecting. They were sold "as is," with no information provided or available about the objects' history or authenticity. From the lightbulb logo on the base, we were hopeful that the Christmas scene was an original Vienna Snow Globes creation. The other one remained a mystery.

"Yes, actually," Ana said. "A thousand dollars may not sound like much to some people, but to me, that I had an extra thousand dollars in the budget ... well, it's huge. If you tell me they're only worth two dollars each ..." She laughed. "Let's not go there."

I wished I could reassure her, but we never revealed partial information. It wasn't unusual for an antique that seemed promising at the start of the appraisal to turn out to be phony, and vice versa.

After a few seconds, I asked, "How do you know Heather?"

"We've been friends since we were kids—our families spent summers up here. She and I lived together in Boston for a couple of years after college, until she got serious with a guy and moved in with him—my brother, actually."

"That sounds as if it might be awkward."

"Not until Peter caught her in bed with Jason."

"Ouch."

"Luckily, civility and maturity prevailed."

We climbed onto the covered porch. Ana reached for the doorknob, then paused. She stood quietly for several seconds, looking down as if she were trying to figure out whether her shoes were too pointy. When she raised her eyes, I saw a complicated mix of emotions. Concern and apprehension, certainly, but there was more—in addition to worry, I saw anger.

"Are you all right?" I asked.

"I just fibbed. Civility and maturity didn't rule, at least not at first. Peter punched Jason so hard he broke his nose."

"Yikes."

"I know. Fortunately, Jason decided not to press charges." She shrugged. "To tell you the truth, I don't blame Jason. The media would have had a field day. A straight-arrow TV personality ends up on the losing end of a brawl over another man's live-in girlfriend. He'd be a laughingstock, which wouldn't suit Jason's view of himself at all."

"Definitely not good for business. How's Peter doing?"

"Fine, I guess. He sure dates a lot." Ana grinned. "They tend to have curvy figures and names like Trixie and Bambi, if you catch my drift."

"Not necessarily wife material, but an effective antidote to heartbreak?"

She chuckled. "That's one way to put it."

"What about you and Heather? Did it affect your relationship?"

"Totally. I didn't speak to her for a year. I'd trusted her completely. That she could do something like that shook me to my booties."

"Like an earthquake."

"Exactly. Ground I thought was stable wasn't."

"Yet here she is, helping you with your show."

Ana turned and stared out over the ocean. "She called me out of the blue last summer. I'd just split with my husband." She shrugged and turned back to face me. "Since Peter's doing all right, it's stupid for me to hold a grudge."

"Good for you. Not holding grudges is a sign of real maturity."

"Do you think so?" She smiled. "Let's go in so you can meet the guilty parties."

All change is hard, I thought. *Even when the change takes you back to familiar ground.*

CHAPTER TWO

A na's house was a surprising mix of traditional and contemporary design. The cottage itself was one of a dozen built by William Carlington between 1814 and 1833. Since that time, it had been completely overhauled. Walls had been removed to create an open layout. Recessed lighting and energy-efficient windows had been installed. Directly in front of the entrance, a fieldstone wall, original to the house, contained a fireplace large enough to roast an ox. All the furniture was ultramodern, mostly made of sleek white leather and steel.

Heather stood at a black granite kitchen island squeezing lemons into a pitcher. She was petite, even shorter than me. Her skin was super fair, and I wondered if she used whiter-than-her-skin-tone foundation or if this was her natural color. Her chin-length black hair was held off her face by a turquoise headband. Her eyes were hazel. Prisms from her huge—I guessed three karats—yellow diamond ring flicked along the counter. Jason was tall and classically handsome, with chiseled features and backswept brown hair. He leaned against a wall by the French doors that opened onto a slate patio, tapping into his smart phone. I guessed he was older than Heather by a dozen or so years.

"How did it go?" Heather asked Ana as we approached the counter.

"Fabulous, of course, since Josie was the guest." All signs of Ana's angst had vanished. "Josie, meet my good buddy Heather Walker. Jason? Let me drag you away from work for a moment. This is Josie—Josie Prescott. She owns a big-deal antiques auction house here in Rocky Point."

"Hi!" Heather said, smiling.

Jason looked up momentarily. "Hey."

"Hi," I said.

"Josie's doing the Fabergé Spring Egg appraisal, right?" Heather asked as she stirred in some simple syrup.

"Right. Timothy wants to use it in the pilot, so I figured I'd better get my insurance up to date. I'm embarrassed to admit that it hasn't been appraised in eighteen years."

Heather laughed. "You don't need insurance—your dad's house is a fortress!"

"True . . . still, eighteen years is a long time." She shrugged. "Anyway, since I was going to have that one appraised, I decided to have Josie look at them all."

"Have you seen the other two, the Christmas scene and the skaters?" I asked Heather.

"Are you kidding? I was the one who encouraged Ana to buy them. 'Live a little,' I told her. 'You're starting to make some money. Enjoy it!' For once she listened to me."

"What are you talking about!" Ana said, smiling at Heather. "I always listen to you."

Heather shot Jason a look I couldn't read. "As if. You're the smart one. If I have any brains at all, it shows in my talent for surrounding myself with people who are brighter than me." She dipped a spoon into the lemonade for a taste, then scrunched up her nose. "Tart." She ladled in some more simple syrup and stirred, then took a clean spoon for another taste. "Yum." She poured glasses and offered them around. "Lemonade, anyone?"

I reached for a glass. "Thanks!" The lemon flavor was bright and fresh. "What do you do, Heather?"

"I'm Jason's research assistant."

"We share that interest, then," I said. "A lot of my work involves research."

"Do you specialize?" Jason asked me without looking away from his device, making me wonder whether he'd been listening to our entire conversation or just happened to overhear that remark.

"No. We're a full-service house. I run monthly high-end themed auctions and weekly tag sales. Which means I need a lot of inventory, so I buy anything and we deal in everything."

I'd caught his interest, and he took a step toward us. "I collect chess sets. Just got a beauty—English boxwood."

"Nice!"

Jason cocked his head, reading my expression. "Not impressed?"

"I'm always impressed when a collector finds an object they love."

"But . . . ?"

"English boxwood chess sets aren't particularly rare."

"What is?"

"Decorative glass. Exotic woods, like rosewood. Anything from the eighteenth century or earlier."

"How much should I have paid?"

"There are too many variables for me to say without examining it—who made it, who owned it, who played with it, its condition, and so on."

"I like your style, Josie. I host a weekly investment show on cable and write a monthly newsletter, both called *Ferris Investor News*. We should talk. I'm always looking for expert investment advice I can pass on to my viewers and readers. When I get back from my honeymoon, let's brainstorm how we can work together."

"I'd love it," I said.

I extracted a business card from the sterling silver case my boyfriend, Ty, had given me for my last birthday and handed it to him. He pulled one from an inner pocket of his wallet for me.

"In the meantime, will you appraise my collection?"

I tucked his card away. "With pleasure!" I explained our procedures, and Jason said he'd stop by to sign the paperwork in the morning.

"More lemonade?" Heather asked.

"Thanks." I held out my glass for a refill. "Where are you going on your honeymoon?"

"Australia," Heather said.

"Bedarra Island," Jason said with a cocky grin.

"That's on the Great Barrier Reef, right?"

"You know it?" Jason asked, impressed.

"I read about it in *Travel & Leisure*."

"It's very chichi," Heather said, half embarrassed, half excited.

"I have a reputation to uphold," Jason said. "My audience expects me to live the good life, to live their dreams."

I couldn't tell if he was joking.

Heather placed her hand on her hip. "You're taking me to Bedarra to impress other people?"

I couldn't tell if she was joking, either.

"No. I'm taking you to Bedarra because you're the perfect woman I'd given up hope of finding. I want to impress *you*."

"You silver-tongued devil, you. You sure know how to make a girl feel special."

"That's the idea," he said, turning back to his phone.

She stirred the lemonade.

Ana stood off to the side, her eyes moving from Jason to Heather and back again.

"This lemonade is delish," I said to change the subject. "Do you share Ana's love of cooking?"

"God, no! In fact, I can barely boil a steak. Oh, wait, I just remembered! You don't boil steak."

I laughed. "Then I assume you're not having a do-it-yourself wedding. Who's your caterer?"

Jason wandered back to the window to catch the light and started reading something on his phone.

"Ana is taking care of the wedding cake and desserts, natch. Everything else is being handled by the Blue Dolphin."

"That's my favorite restaurant!"

"Me, too!" Ana said.

Heather giggled, her eyes beaming mischievously. "Josie's talking about the food, Ana, not the chef." She turned her gaze to me. "The executive chef, Ray, has been spending an awful lot of time going over the menu with Ana."

Ana laughed. "That's just because he's trying to placate his pastry chef, Maurice. Talk about temperamental! Jeesh!"

"Everybody's got attitude," Jason said, not looking up from his device. "Like this guy here." He tapped his screen. "He reads my investment newsletter, loses money, then has the gall to blame me."

"Aren't people supposed to follow your advice?" Ana asked. "Isn't that the point?"

"Hell, no. They're supposed to educate themselves, not follow the herd. It says so plainly at the top of each issue and at the start of each episode." He grinned at me. "Caveat emptor—right, Josie?"

"I don't know anything about your business. In mine, we warranty what we sell. Every antique or collectible's pedigree is set out in writing, or it's sold 'as is.' I don't want clients to misunderstand what they're buying."

He winked at me. "I knew I'd want to do business with you."

I couldn't think of a reply, so I stayed quiet. I wasn't so sure I wanted to do business with him.

"Enough work for today," Heather said, her tone issuing a challenge.

Jason didn't look up or reply.

"Jason? It's time for us to go. Chuck and Sara await." She smiled in my direction. "The wedding is in five days, this coming Saturday, and folks are starting to arrive. Chuck is Jason's best friend—his best man. He and his wife got in today, and like most of us, they're staying at the Pelican. Who wouldn't want to take an extra few days in Rocky Point, right?"

"At least March seems to going out like a lamb," Ana said. "Some years, people might be arriving in a blizzard. Or trudging through mud. I remember one year—"

Ana broke off as Heather gaped at something behind us. Her jaw hung open. She took a step back as her already pallid complexion turned paper white. Ana and I spun around.

A good-looking man about my age, maybe a few years older, strolled toward the island. I hadn't heard the porch door open or close. Seemingly, he just appeared out of thin air. It was eerie. He had light blue eyes and longish blond-brown hair, and he was shorter than Jason by half a foot, and far stockier. He didn't look fat, though; he looked strong.

"Hey, Ana!" he said, smiling. "Heather. Jason."

"Peter!" Ana said, rushing toward him.

He hugged her. "Hey, sis!"

"Peter," Heather said, turning the word into a plea.

"Nice to see you, Pete," Jason said, joining Heather at the island. "Let's go, babe." Jason touched her elbow, and she scurried from the room. He followed her with a swagger, pausing at the threshold to look back at Peter. "Quite a coincidence, your showing up this week."

"Didn't you think I'd come to cheer Ana on?" Peter asked. "Come on! It's not every day she films a pilot for a TV show."

Jason shook his head, communicating contempt. "You're not fooling anyone, Pete."

Peter spread his hands, palms up. "You've got it all wrong, friend. I'm here to celebrate."

"Bad idea, dude. Bad karma. It's time to be on your way."

"Thanks for the tip. I think I'll stay a few days, though." Peter said something that sounded like *Simyet blezh de cevyo* and grinned.

"Family above all," Ana translated, looking from Peter to me to Jason, then back to me. "Our family motto, inherited from our Russian forefathers."

"That's right," Peter said. "Words to live by." Peter placed his arm around Ana's shoulders, and squeezed.

When Jason didn't comment, Peter's grin broadened. "You're staying at the Pelican, right? Me, too. I'll probably see you around."

Jason glared at him for a few seconds, then marched out. The screen door slammed. No one spoke.

"Why are you staying at a hotel?" Ana asked. "I have room here."

"Too much activity going on, what with the TV shooting and all. Plus, they have a killer gym at the Pelican. You know me. I need my workouts." He squeezed her shoulder again and picked up a glass of lemonade. "I'll be here every day, though, clapping like a crazy man, watching my beautiful sister work."

Ana stared at him, trying to read between the lines, perhaps.

After a few seconds, I became uncomfortable witnessing their unbroken silence and walked to the French doors, looking past a small white-washed gazebo, past the rambling roses not yet in bud, past the feathery grass border, to the ocean, wishing I were somewhere else, anywhere else. I could faintly hear the waves crashing against the boulders. Ana's yard looked like it belonged in an article about dream locales, the ones that promise memory-laden lazy days and soul-searing romantic nights. Empty promises, usually.

"As you might have gathered, Josie," Ana said, "this is my brother, Peter, up from Boston."

I turned to face them. Ana was smiling, patting her brother's arm.

"This is Josie Prescott, Peter. I've told you about her."

Peter gave a two-finger semisalute. "Hey."

"Nice to meet you." I returned to the island and slid my empty glass onto the counter. "Thanks for the lemonade. I've got to get back to work." I headed for the living room. "See ya!"

As I stepped onto the porch, I heard Ana say, "Tell me the truth, Peter. What are you doing here?"

I closed the door, whispered, "Whew," and walked slowly to my car.

Timothy sat on a director's chair, drinking Coke from an old-fashioned small green bottle. The yellow-haired man pushed a large black crate up a ramp into an 18-wheeler. OSCAR'S MOVIE RENTALS was stenciled on the side.

"So what do you think of your first television role?" Timothy asked as I drew near.

"I think I'm lucky the star of the show and her director are so talented."

"You're too modest! You have a flair, Josie. The camera loves you."

Timothy was a diplomat. I'm old enough to know that the camera doesn't love me. It doesn't even like me much. I don't have good angles. I don't have a best side. I look like what I am—a pretty enough woman with a too-round face, chin-length nothing-special brown hair, a wide mouth, and big brown eyes. For Timothy's purpose, though, I didn't have to look good. My job was to help Ana shine, and if I excelled at that, from his perspective, I was a star.

I extended a hand for a shake. "Thanks, Timothy. I'm glad you got usable footage."

I was behind the wheel, latching my seat belt, when Peter strode down the driveway. Ana hurried after him, then stopped short of the street, letting him go, her eyes shadowed with uneasiness.

CHAPTER THREE

I peered under the photocopier and spotted the missing pink felt mouse right away. Hank, Prescott's Maine Coon cat, had batted it across the office, and when it disappeared under the machine, he got upset and started mewing and pacing, agitated.

"I see it, Hank!" I told him.

He meowed imperatively, unimpressed. He wanted his mouse and he wanted it now.

"Can you reach it?" Gretchen asked.

"I think so. Hank must have put some English on it—it's in the far corner and upside down. Let me try the yardstick."

She handed me the old wooden ruler we kept nearby for just this purpose. I waved it back and forth along the carpet. On my third pass, the mouse came flying out, and Hank leaped on it like a mountain lion attacks a deer. He picked it up in his mouth and shook his head so the little mouse rattled, then pranced away, his upset already forgotten.

"I could make a little skirt," Cara, our grandmotherly receptionist, said. Seeing our bewilderment, she pointed to the gap. "You know, for the bottom of the machine, to stop Hank's mice from running underneath. If you're all right with double-stick Velcro, Josie, I could attach it that way."

"You're a wonder woman, Cara! Sure, go for it! We'll have the best-dressed photocopier in Rocky Point."

The wind chimes Gretchen had hung on the front door years earlier jingled, and Ana walked in.

Seeing me kneeling on the floor, she laughed. "I bet there's a story here!"

I stood up and brushed a few dusty bits from my khakis. "Caught in the act of rescuing our cat's favorite toy." I introduced her to Cara and Gretchen. "What can we get you? Coffee? Tea?"

"Nothing, thanks. Do you have a minute to talk gifts?"

"Always. Have a seat. Or—if it's private, we can go to my office."

Ana sat down at the guest table, as stylish and put-together in jeans and a mint green sweater as she'd been earlier in the day in her on-air outfit. "It's not the least bit private. Or rather, it's top secret until Heather and Jason's wedding, then it's not. Here's the deal—I got them something from their registry, which is fine, but I've been racking my brain looking for a gift that's more, I don't know, personal. Hearing Jason talk about chess sets, well, it got me thinking. Any ideas on how to merge that interest with something art deco, which is Heather's style?"

"Maybe. Gretchen, would you see if we have any art deco chess sets in stock?"

She started tapping code words into the search function in our database.

Reacting to Ana's surprised expression, I added, "I told you we were a full-service house."

"That's great! I spoke to my dad, by the way, coordinating our schedules. If it's not too late, you can come by my house around five thirty tomorrow afternoon and pick up the Spring Egg snow globe."

"Perfect." I swiveled to face Cara. "Would you put that in my calendar?"

She nodded as the printer nearest Gretchen's desk whirred to life. Gretchen glanced at the one-page printout, then handed it over. I thanked her and scanned the list.

"It looks like we have two sets in stock, one decorative glass from France, circa 1928, and one Bakelite, circa 1935. If you'll wait here for just a minute, I'll get them."

Ana glanced at her watch, a gold and diamond bangle. "Oh, God! It's nearly four. I'll need to stop back tomorrow. I'm supposed to meet Ray about the dessert display for Heather and Jason's wedding at four-fifteen."

"That's fine. Anytime." I stood up. "I'm meeting my boyfriend, Ty, at the Blue Dolphin at six this evening. If you're still there, maybe you can join us for a drink."

She said she would, thanked me, said good-bye to us all, and left.

"She's so pretty," Gretchen said.

"Elegant," Cara agreed.

"Nice, too," I grinned, a cocky one, excitement bubbling to the surface. "And she owns a Fabergé egg that we get to appraise!"

•   •   •

I stood under the dome-shaped hammered-copper awning that shielded the Blue Dolphin's entryway waiting for Ty. I saw him as soon as he turned onto Bow Street, and I smiled. When he spotted me, he smiled back. I loved his rugged looks. He was tall, about six-two, and well-built, with broad shoulders and narrow hips. His brown hair was cut short. Since taking a job as a training supervisor with Homeland Security, he spent most of his time outdoors, and his skin had weathered to a warm nut brown. He was smart and wise and fun and funny. He was also compassionate and tender. I adored him.

"Hey, gorgeous," he said, leaning in for a kiss.

"Hey, handsome." I went up on tiptoe.

He opened the heavy wooden door, and we entered a special, rarified world. The Blue Dolphin was housed in a curved brick building that had been designed in 1740 to fit into the narrow rounded corner lot.

We greeted Frieda, the hostess, and waved hello to Suzanne, the manager.

"Is Ana Yartsin here?" I asked Frieda.

"No, she left about an hour ago. Sorry."

"That's okay," I said.

"Did you want to get seated now?"

"Thanks," Ty said. "We'll have a drink first."

We headed into the lounge, a cozy room with bay windows overlooking the Piscataqua River. On most days, you could see across to Maine. Jimmy, the bartender, was filling a silver-colored martini shaker with gin and chatting with a couple sitting at the bar. Ty and I made a beeline for my favorite table, in a corner by the window.

"Hey, Josie!" Jimmy called. "Hey, Ty. Be right with you."

Jimmy served the martinis, then came to us. He had red hair and freckles and a ready smile. He'd been one of the first people I'd met when I'd moved to Rocky Point nearly a decade ago, and one of the most welcoming.

"I'll take a watermelon martini," I said.

"And I'll try an Effinghamburgherbrau."

"You got it," Jimmy said, flipping cocktail napkins onto our table with his signature flair, as if he were skipping rocks.

When our drinks arrived, I clinked Ty's glass. "Here's to silver light in the dark of night."

"And to us."

"I love you, Ty."

"I love you, too, Josie."

I looked out the window. The river glittered as if someone had sprinkled sequins across the water. "Look what the sun is doing."

Ty followed my gaze. "Sparkly."

"Like me!"

He smiled, but before he could reply, a woman called my name. I spun around and saw Heather and Jason settling in at a table near the entry.

I waved hello. "Hi, there! Small world, right?" I introduced Ty.

Heather greeted him warmly. Jason looked bored, raising his eyes from his smart phone to say hello, then looking down again.

"Jason and I decided to sneak off for some one-on-one time."

Jimmy approached to take their order as Peter walked in.

"Uh-oh," I whispered. "Trouble's at the door."

Peter stood by the entrance surveying the lounge. He paused when he saw Heather, then continued his canvass. He smiled at me and nodded. I nodded back but didn't smile.

Ty took in the scene at a glance. Before he'd taken his big-cheese job at Homeland Security, he'd been Rocky Point's police chief. "Who is he?"

"Peter, Ana's brother." I repeated what Ana told me about his relationship with Heather, and their breakup, while surreptitiously watching the minidrama unfolding in the lounge. Peter slid onto a barstool at the far end of the bar, apparently ignoring everything and everyone except Jimmy, the bartender—except his eyes weren't on Jimmy; they were on the mirror, where he had a full view of the lounge. From the angle, I could tell he was watching Heather.

"I can't tell if he's a gnat or a stalker," I whispered.

"That distinction rests in his intention, whether he intends merely to irritate or to interfere."

"What should we do?"

"Nothing."

"What should Heather do?"

"Short term, leave. Long term, get an order of protection."

"Will that work?"

"Maybe."

"How could Peter possibly think Heather would find this behavior attractive?"

"I don't think he's doing it to attract her. I think he's doing it to piss off Jason." Ty nodded in Jason's direction. "Look."

Having realized Peter was in the lounge, Jason had turned his chair so he faced him. Peter swung his barstool around so he was facing the room, his elbows resting on the bar. The two men were locked in a silent battle. Heather leaned in toward Jason, talking animatedly, her expression earnest. Jason wholly ignored her.

"Peter's out for revenge," I said, thinking it through.

"Possibly."

"Or he's crazy."

"Or he's simply following a well-thought-out plan to get under Jason's skin." Ty nodded toward Jason again. "If so, it seems to be working nicely."

Heather touched Jason's forearm, and he shook her off like a flea.

"Ick," I said.

Ty turned to me. "Ick?"

"An official term for I don't want to see any part of this. Take me in to dinner, please."

Ty smiled, then leaned over and kissed me, a teasing brush of lip on lip. "With pleasure, ma'am."

I nodded at Peter as we passed his stool and did the same to Heather and Jason as we passed their table. I was glad to get away.

Frieda asked Suzanne, the general manager, to seat us, and we followed her into the dining room. Suzanne was tall and slender, like a model. She wore her auburn hair twisted into a high chignon. Her blue sheath fit her perfectly. Most women walked; Suzanne glided. I'd seen her frequently since she and my appraiser Fred had begun dating,* and the more I saw her, the more I liked her.

She led us to a nice table by the fireplace. Five-foot logs lay across giant brass andirons. A mishmash pile of kindling lay underneath, ready to be lit.

"We're having a big debate," she said. "Should we light the fire?"

"No," Ty said at the exact same moment as I said, "Yes."

We all laughed.

"It's not cold enough," he said.

"But it's so pretty," I said.

---

*Please see *Lethal Treasure*.

"We'll roast."

"True." I turned to Suzanne and smiled. "No."

A swarthy man in black-and-white-checked chef's pants and a tall chef's hat slammed open the swinging kitchen door as if he hoped to catapult it to Missouri, then stood by our table, his arms crossed and his chin jutting like a bull about to charge.

"Maurice," Suzanne said, surprised.

"We must talk," he said to her in strongly accented English. "You must listen."

"Of course."

"Are you the pastry chef?" I asked, smiling.

"Oui. Yes." He didn't smile.

"I love your vanilla crème brûlée. Best ever."

He lowered his arms, and his expression softened. "Merci."

"And your chocolate tower."

He bowed.

"I'll come to the kitchen in a moment," Suzanne said.

Maurice spun around and pushed through to the kitchen, sending the door furiously swinging.

Suzanne shook her head. "Maurice is a passionate man."

"He doesn't seem happy," Ty said.

"He's not." Her eyes sparked fiery daggers. You don't get to be a turn-around general manager star by taking guff, and I could see the steel in Suzanne's demeanor. "He objects to our including Ana's Fabergé egg cakes in our dessert offerings. We've had them on the menu for a week—they're selling well." She lowered her voice, talking to us as friends. "I hope he finds a way to deal with his anger. He's threatened to walk out if we don't cancel our order, and I told him we weren't canceling, and that if he wanted out, I wouldn't try to convince him to stay. I'm not sure he believed me."

"What does Chef Ray say?"

"That we need him." She raised her chin. Her eyes were as hard as iron, and unforgiving. "Everyone's replaceable."

After we'd finished our entrees. Suzanne stopped by our table. "How was dinner?"

I made a yum-yum smacking noise. "Wonderful. As always."

"Terrific," Ty said.

I glanced at Heather and Jason. They'd moved to the dining room for dinner and were seated by a window, along with another couple, maybe Jason's best friend, Chuck, and his wife, Sara. I was glad to see that Heather and Jason seemed calm and that although Jason's smart phone sat on the table beside his knife, he wasn't using it.

"Any dessert tonight?" Suzanne asked.

"I was telling Ty more about Ana's cakes. I was filmed today for her pilot, by the way."

"You're in the show?" Suzanne clapped softly. "How was it?"

"Nerve-racking. Ana was amazing, though. Polished and warm and engaging."

"I saw her on *Good Morning, New England* last fall sometime. She demonstrated how to convert doughnut holes into cute little apple treats using a red glaze, green frosting for the leaves, and black licorice bits for the stems. She made baskets of them as favors for a kid's party. I couldn't take my eyes off her demonstration—and I don't bake!"

"Even just hearing about it from you," I said, "I want to know how to do it. What a gift!"

She laughed and drifted away to the next table. Ty and I decided to try one of Ana's cakes. Ten seconds after our waiter disappeared into the kitchen, a plate shattered. I was about to say, "Oops," when a man began yelling.

"No more!" he shouted.

From his accent, I could tell it was Maurice.

Ty's brows shot up. "I'd say Maurice has anger issues."

"Narcissism. If I don't get my way I'm going to scream and pound my fists and heels on the floor until you give in."

"Amazing seeing adults behave that way. You'd think someone would have corrected his behavior by the time he reached puberty."

"Or killed him," I said.

Suzanne mouthed, "Sorry," as she hurried into the kitchen.

A moment later, the same man's voice yelled, "You should be ashamed. A cheap gimmick in a fine restaurant. And you want me to endorse it? Never!" A full minute of silence, then, "No. No. No."

"He sounds crazed," I whispered.

Suzanne reappeared, smiling around the dining room. She approached our table. "I'm so sorry you had to hear that. Your dessert will be right out, and of course, it's on the house."

"Is everything all right?" I asked.

She laughed without humor. "You know I don't have children, right? My brother does, though, so I know all about time-outs. In this case, taking a breather is a practical solution to what really is a complex problem. Maurice is incredibly talented and dedicated—but he doesn't play nicely with others."

We thanked her for comping the dessert, an unnecessary gesture, and she moved to the next table and repeated her apology.

We'd selected a cake that featured a woodland scene, and it was delightful—trees and wildflowers and a moss-covered rock, a miniature forest filled with enchanting details sculpted out of frosting in about five inches of hollowed-out cake. Amazing.

"Look at those violets," I said. "And those are lilies of the valley."

"I like the moss."

The cake was as tasty as I expected, rich and creamy and sweet, but not too sweet. I felt myself purr.

"Wow."

I took another bite. It was even better than the first.

"I want to tell Heather how good it is."

I turned toward the window where Heather and Jason and the other couple had been seated, but they'd already left. I glanced into the lounge. Peter was still at the bar, staring at the muted wall-mounted TV, eating a hamburger, a lonely man eating alone. I felt sorry for him, and sad.

I'd known a girl in college whose life was forever changed by a boyfriend's breakup. She'd been blindsided by his end-of-the-semester-I-need-some-space "Dear Jane" letter, weeping for days, unable to get out of bed. She missed her finals, didn't take the makeup exams, and flunked out. She wrote him daily missives pledging enduring love and promising to change in whatever ways he wanted. When he read her letters in open court, offering them as evidence in his petition to get a restraining order against her, she'd tried to kill herself, ending up in a mental institution. I'd felt stunned and horrified at her breathtakingly fast downward spiral, and helpless. I heard later that after a few months of hospital care, she'd recovered her equilibrium. She moved back in with her folks and went on to graduate from a different college. Four years later, she'd married a nice fellow from her hometown. Last I heard, they had three kids. What frightened me was how totally I'd misjudged her mental state. I'd known her pretty well, and it had never occurred to me that she was fragile.

Ty took my hand as we walked to the central garage.

"Peter is trying to spoil Heather's wedding. I wish I could do something."

He squeezed my hand. "You have a good heart, Josie, but you can't always fix things."

"I know."

"Talk to me about Fabergé eggs."

I laughed, surprised. "Now?"

"Yeah. Take your mind off Heather's troubles. How did Ana get the idea for those cakes?"

"Her family owns an important Fabergé original—or so the story goes."

"You don't believe it?"

"I'm reserving my opinion. Of the fifty Imperial eggs known to have been produced by Peter Carl Fabergé, forty two are extant. The Yartsin family believes theirs is the fifty-first produced, the forty-third extant. They're convinced that it's the real deal, the last egg commissioned by the tsar as his annual gift to his wife, Empress Alexandra, in 1917. Ana says that when the Bolsheviks seized the Fabergé workshops, this egg, the Spring Egg, was one of the few treasures that Fabergé was able to save as he fled. Afraid that it would be confiscated like everything else in his workshops, Fabergé crafted a unique hiding place: He hid the egg in plain sight, inserting it in a snow globe, certain that to a layman's eye, it would appear to be a cheap fake, a novelty knock-off sold as a souvenir."

"That sounds like a movie, doesn't it? The master craftsman escaping one step ahead of the marauding bad guys, then working by candlelight to fabricate a hiding place for a treasure."

"It gets better. According to the story passed down through the Yartsin family, Fabergé gave the Spring Egg snow globe to his wife, Augusta, for safekeeping. Augusta and their eldest son, Eugène, escaped Russia by sleigh and on foot, making their way through snow-covered forests until they reached Finland. Fabergé escaped separately, alone. His ruse worked, and the egg went undetected. Augusta sold the snow globe to a Swiss art dealer shortly after her husband's 1920 death. Ana's great-grandfather, Serge Yartsin, bought it as an Easter gift for his wife in 1922, and it has been bequeathed from mother to eldest daughter ever since."

"How much is it worth?"

"Ana gave me a copy of the last appraisal. Eighteen years ago it was valued at four million dollars."

Ty stopped short under a streetlamp. "In today's dollars, that's worth about what? Five and a half?"

"Five point eight, according to my calculations. Giving the current market for high-end antiques, though, and assuming I can confirm provenance, I think it's worth at least twenty million dollars, possibly much more."

"Who on earth would pay that kind of money?"

"Many museums. People who are proud of their Russian heritage. Status seekers. Investors. Lots of folks."

We climbed the parking garage stairs to the second level and walked up the incline to my car. Ty opened my door, and after I got behind the wheel, he closed it. I waited for him to drive by, then backed out and exited after him. We drove to Ty's house in separate cars, together.

CHAPTER FOUR

At ten of nine the next morning, Tuesday, as Cara and Gretchen were settling in for the day, Sasha, my chief antiques appraiser, said, "I just got off the phone with an account rep in Austria, Hans Micher. The Vienna Snow Globe company didn't produce Victorian Christmas scenes."

I picked up Ana's snow globe from Sasha's desk and shook it lightly, then placed it on her blotter and watched as silvery speckles whirled to the bottom. The scene showed Christmas on a quiet late nineteenth-century London street. "Couldn't it be a special order? Vienna Snow Globe is known for their custom work."

"Maybe, but if so, their account rep couldn't find any record of it."

"The company was founded in the late eighteen hundreds, right? I wouldn't be surprised to learn that some order forms have been lost."

She tucked her lank brown hair behind her ear, a sure sign she was feeling anxious.

"So what's worrying you?" I asked.

She turned over the globe revealing the Vienna Snow Globe mark, a lightbulb. "Maybe someone faked the company's logo."

I considered how it might have worked. "So some guy in the early nineteen hundreds gets his girlfriend a cheap Christmas present and slyly applies the lightbulb logo to trick her into thinking it's a pricey gift from a posh store. It's possible, I suppose."

I picked up the globe again. It felt heavy, substantive, a good sign. I brought it to the guest table, where I used a loupe under the strong light to examine the scene closely. Small-scale row houses ranged along one side of a cobblestone street. Each house was decorated for Christmas in a different way. There were evergreen garlands, boughs of holly, red bows, and wreaths ornately embellished with pine cones and tiny glass birds. Gas streetlamps lined the sidewalk. Gold-flecked bulbs seemed to flicker when the light hit them in a certain way. Several rooms were visible through the itty-bitty windows. In one, a young girl held a ball of yarn for her cat to swat. In another, a couple placed presents under their Christmas tree. Overall, the construction appeared flawless, the level of detail remarkable. It didn't look like a fake.

"It's beautiful, isn't it?" Gretchen asked.

"Very," I said. I shook it again, holding it at eye level so Gretchen could see. After a moment, I raised my eyes to Sasha's. "We're going to have to open it up."

"I know."

I set the globe down. "Let's call Dr. Grayman and see if she'll take a look at it." Elizabeth Grayman was the curator of decorative arts at the New England Museum of Contemporary Art in Durham, and an expert on eighteenth- and nineteenth-century European decorative artifacts. "Do you want to go, Sasha? Or would you rather work on the ice-skating snow globe?"

"Either way."

"You stay, then. I'll go." I turned to Cara. "Would you call and ask if Dr. Grayman can see me today? Then ask Eric to pack it up."

While Cara called the museum, I picked up the second snow globe and shook it gently, creating the illusion that I was watching the couple skate in a brisk snowstorm. The figures were beautifully rendered in what appeared to be porcelain. The young woman had an aristocratic cast to her face; her chin was held high, and she looked down her nose. Her hair was light brown, shoulder length, and wavy. Her eyes were celestial blue. She wore a traditional midthigh-length red skating dress. White lace at the chest and sleeves glittered thanks to the clever placement of crystal-embedded red beads. The fluttering flare of her skirt showed the craftsman's ability. The man was handsome, with thick brown hair and dark brown eyes under bushy eyebrows. He was half-smiling, pleased at his own skating, perhaps, or glad to be with such a beautiful woman. His outfit was as traditional as hers, loose-fitting blue slacks and a red and blue cropped jacket. I shook the globe again. They were both full-figured—not fat, even by today's twig-thin standards, but well-fed, a symbol of affluence in seventeenth- and eighteenth-century art; in an age when most people survived on a subsistence diet, only the rich got plump.

I looked at Sasha. "The couple is not skinny."

She smiled. "I had the same thought. Maybe eighteenth century."

"Do you recognize the maker?"

"No. I'll need to take it apart to look for a mark under the skaters. If we're right in dating it, obviously, the globe was added after the fact."

"What makes you so certain?" Gretchen asked, fascinated.

"Snow globes weren't invented until about 1900," Sasha explained, "when a surgical instrument repairman named Edward Perzy set out to invent a brighter light for operating rooms. His idea was to use glass balls filled with water and semolina. It didn't work, but seeing the semolina float and spin in the water gave him an idea for a novelty—and presto, snow globes were born. His company, Vienna Snow Globes, won the first patent for one."

Gretchen nodded, understanding the implications. "So if the skaters were sculpted earlier than 1900 . . . got it."

Cara swiveled toward me. "You're all set, Josie. Dr. Grayman can see you at eleven."

"Thanks, Cara." I glanced at the clock. It was just after nine. I'd need to leave by ten thirty. I was half-listening as Cara called Eric to explain the packing job when the door opened, setting the wind chimes jangling.

Jason stepped in, smart phone in hand. He wore a navy blue sport coat, gray slacks, and a crisply ironed and starched blue shirt. I could picture him on a billboard in an ad for a luxury car or expensive cruise. The modern man of distinction. I wondered how much of his facade was an act.

"Am I too early to do that paperwork?" he asked after I introduced him around. "It seems Timothy isn't quite done with us. I need to get over to the film site by ten."

"Oh, no! Did something go wrong with what he shot yesterday?"

"No, they just want to add in some romantic bits. It's the same on my show—everything is staged." He smiled, a good-natured one. "I heard rumblings about walking hand in hand on the beach, that sort of thing. Heather and Ana are already putting their heads together with Timothy about how best to communicate romance."

"I'm sure it will end up looking natural." I asked Gretchen to print out a copy of our appraisal agreement. Jason read the document carefully, then signed it.

"Here you go," he said, handing back my copy. His phone buzzed, and he glanced at it. "Business. I've got to take this. I'll have my assistant contact you about shipping and so on. Thanks again."

He strode across the parking lot to his SUV, gesticulating angrily as he talked on his phone. *He's got an edge,* I thought, *a real edge.*

"Are you going to be a good boy, Hank?" I asked, petting under his chin. He mewed and nuzzled my neck. "I won't be long, baby." He raised a paw and patted my cheek. "You're such a love bunny, aren't you!" Another mew.

The door opened, and Ana stepped inside, saw me cuddling Hank, and burst out laughing. "I'm noticing a theme!"

I kissed Hank on the top of his furry little head. "Caught in the act!" I let him down, and he rubbed my calf before sauntering off to the warehouse door. I opened it for him, and he disappeared inside. "As you can tell, I'm at his beck and call."

"Anyone would be. Hello, everyone!"

Gretchen and Cara said hello. I was familiar with the nuances of their greetings, and I could tell they had both warmed to her.

Sasha murmured hello, a coolish welcome, which didn't imply anything negative. Unless she was talking about art or antiques, Sasha was both shy and reserved. Only when discussing an object she knew about was she confident and animated. Sasha was brilliant, kind, honest, and skillful. The only thing she lacked was confidence.

"I only have about a minute and a half, but I thought I'd pop in to see those chess sets."

"I'm on my way out, but Sasha will take care of you."

As if a switch had been flipped, Sasha's entire manner changed. She stood up, smiling, her eyes alight. Her voice, when she spoke, showed no hesitation. "I have them ready. They're both fabulous, in different ways. I can't wait to show them to you. I'll get them now."

Sasha pushed into the warehouse, and I leaned against the guest table.

I chuckled. "A whole minute and a half—wow! I didn't even think you had that long. Jason said you were deep in planning romantic add-in shots."

"Not I, my friend. That's Timothy's bailiwick and involves only Heather and Jason."

Eric, my jack-of-all-trades helper, stepped into the front office, a sturdy box and bubble wrap in hand. Although he was now in his midtwenties, he was still teenage thin. Eric had started working for Prescott's part-time when he was in high school, going full-time right after graduation. Recently, I'd promoted him to operations manager, his second major promotion in three years. Deciding who should be responsible for what was one of the biggest challenges of my job.

"You're packing up my snow globe," Ana said.

"I'm taking it for an outside expert consultation. Research. We do whatever is necessary to learn the truth."

Ana smiled, a sad one. "I wish more people valued the truth."

I wondered what she was referring to, what memory my innocuous comment roused. I wanted to ask but didn't. Instead, I watched Eric wrap the snow globe.

"What makes the snowstorm?" she asked, also watching him work.

"Glycerin," I said. "Or mineral oil. Both are heavier than water, so the dots and slivers of silver or white metal move more slowly than they would in water."

"Will you take it apart?"

"Yes. There's no other way to examine it properly." I smiled at her. "We're as careful as possible."

"But losing some of the oil is inevitable, right?"

"Right," I said as Sasha reappeared wheeling a cart holding the two sets of chessmen, one made of ivory and black glass with sterling silver embellishments, the other made of cherry-colored and black Bakelite.

"Aren't they beautiful?" Sasha asked, her tone reverential.

Ana leaned over to look. "Totally."

"Notice the art deco influence," Sasha said, holding up a black glass knight whose shape evoked the lines and structure of the Chrysler Building in New York City.

I accepted the box Eric handed me, thanked him, and said, "Good seeing you, Ana. Sasha, I'll leave you to it."

I doubted that Ana would buy either set. Both were distinctive and rare, and therefore pricey, more than most people would want to spend for a wedding gift. The decorative glass set Sasha was showing her now was priced at $1,200; the Bakelite set, $850.

    •   •   •

When I was three miles away from the museum, I hit a detour. The police had cordoned off a section of Route 108. Turning onto Washington, I caught a glimpse of Timothy checking a camera angle and shouting directions. That stretch of Route 108 led to a bed-and-breakfast known for its lovingly nurtured grounds featuring rare plants, formal flower gardens, and Italianate fountains, and I suspected that he'd selected it as one of his romantic settings.

Despite the detour, I arrived a few minutes early. I used the time to stretch my legs along a portion of the museum's well-maintained five-mile-long nature trail. The museum sat in thirty-five acres of donated land. Positioned high on a plateau, the sprawling glass and stone contemporary building overlooked low hills of hardwood and conifer forests, a stream that meandered over and around granite outcroppings, and sweeping meadows and marsh set aside as preservation land. Ty and I often walked the entire trail.

I paused to admire a mossy rock, and my thoughts drifted to Ana. When listing all the life events that made her a likely candidate for a reality TV show, she'd spoken of a breach with her father. Yet while we were planning my role in the pilot, Ana had mentioned that her dad was going to be featured in a scene expressing his pride in her entrepreneurial accomplishments. I was glad to think their rift had been repaired. I'd asked whether her mom would be in the pilot, too, and Ana's mood changed. She became subdued, explaining that her mother had died of breast cancer when she, Ana, was nineteen, describing it as an unspeakably devastating loss. She'd been inconsolable, she said, adding bitterly that her grief was made worse when her father had turned almost overnight into a tyrant. Losing beloved mothers to cancer when we were young was an experience we shared. My mom had died a ghastly cancer death when I was thirteen. Unlike Ana, though, her death brought my dad and me closer. We'd circled the wagons, solidifying our tight-knit family of two. I know that everyone grieves differently, but I couldn't imagine how much harder my loss would have been had my dad not been loving and supportive.

I set off again, passing a black cherry tree, its delicate white blossoms just beginning to show, circled back along the short route, and popped out by the museum's outdoor patio. I went inside, told the receptionist why I was there, and took a seat in the lobby, as directed.

I hadn't seen Dr. Elizabeth Grayman, a no-nonsense woman who'd been in the job forty years, since she'd been awarded emerita status, three years earlier. I sat on a long backless leather bench facing a wall of windows, watching three small gray birds peck at something on the ground.

Ten minutes later, a young woman wearing black leggings and a peach silk tunic called my name. I followed her down a long hallway that led to the administrative offices. Dr. Grayman's corner office had six oversized windows. Bookcases covered two walls, one filled with exhibit catalogues and catalogues raisonnés, the other with books. Her desk was bare except for a laptop computer, a telephone, and a framed photograph of her accepting an award. A printer and a fax machine sat on a credenza positioned against the wall in back of her desk.

She came out from behind her desk to shake hands and led me to an oval conference table by the windows. She was short and stout, with curly gray hair and light blue eyes. She wore a gray tweed suit I'd find too warm for March.

"Good to see you, Josie. It's been a while. Sorry to keep you waiting."

"I appreciate your squeezing me in last-minute."

I unwrapped the snow globe and placed it on the table, explaining what Sasha had discovered and why we were concerned about its authenticity. She leaned over the table, peering through the glass.

"Whom did she talk to?"

"Hans Micher. An account manager at the company."

"Did she call the museum?"

"No. I didn't know they had one."

"They do, and it's a good one. Even if the curator doesn't know this object in particular, he should be able to help identify the materials. They maintain a careful accounting of materials and processes used for historical purposes." She turned the snow globe around slowly, then lifted it to examine the bottom. She gave it a shake and watched the silvery bits spin and settle. She raised her eyes and smiled. "It's precious, isn't it?"

I smiled back. "Yes."

Using a loupe and a high-wattage work light attached to the table by a clamp, she examined the snow globe methodically, quarter-inch turn by quarter-inch turn. When she finished, she removed the loupe, turned off the lamp, and sat back. "My gut tells me it's real. The level of detail and craftsmanship is noteworthy." She pointed to a town house in the middle. "Take this as an example—the moldings on this unit's door are carved out, not nailed on. Look at the doorknobs. The metal hasn't tarnished. They might actually be gold."

"If it were you, would you open it?"

"You have to. Do it in a plastic tub to preserve the fluid. Wear gloves."

She stood as I repacked it, then walked me out. I thanked her again and left. I couldn't wait to tell Sasha the good news.

CHAPTER FIVE

I took the scenic route back, wending my way along the ocean. Dark clouds were blowing in, east to west. The ocean was seaweed green, the waves tipped with white. Just beyond the Rocky Point police station, a one-story building designed to fit in with the affluent community, not stand out, I came upon Timothy and the film crew and pulled to the curb to watch.

Ana, wearing navy slacks, a yellow and blue patterned blouse, a navy blazer, and black low-heeled boots, was walking next to Chef Ray close to the shoreline.

I smiled. "I guess it wasn't all about Heather and Jason after all," I whispered to the breeze.

Ray was a big man, and muscular, like a boxer, completely bald, with brown eyes and a crooked nose. I felt a sweet intimacy between them, picking it up solely from their body language since I couldn't hear their words. They weren't touching, but I got the sense they might at any moment. One camera was positioned ahead of them and rolled backward on some kind of wheeled platform, another loomed large on the side, standing on metal legs near the top of the dunes, and a third sat on a tractor rolling in from the rear. Timothy walked slowly alongside, as Ana and Ray did a good job of ignoring everything but one another.

Jason and Heather sat in director's chairs positioned under a canvas roof alongside the couple who'd shared their table at the Blue Dolphin. Jason was reading on a tablet, shielding the display with his forearm. Heather was staring dreamily or moodily, I couldn't tell which, out over the ocean. The other couple held hands and were talking quietly, their heads nearly touching.

"Cut!" Timothy called. "Ana, Ray, you're both fabulous." He turned toward the cluster of director's chairs. "Jason? Chuck? Let's get a quick shot of you two."

Jason left his tablet on his chair and slipped his phone into his pocket. Chuck shook out his pant legs before joining him. The two men walked toward Timothy.

Timothy got them positioned ten feet from the water. "You know what to do, right? You're going to walk along the beach talking about the wedding, then Chuck, you'll stop to congratulate Jason. Do it earnestly. Shake his hand. Tell him what a great gal Heather is. Make it look natural and spontaneous. Then continue walking down the beach, talking." The cameras rolled into place, and one of the crew told Timothy they were ready. "Ready?"

"Ready," Chuck said, looking embarrassed.

"Sure," Jason said, looking bored.

"Keep your energy up, both of you! This is an exciting moment. Men's friendship."

"Got it," Jason said, smiling a little.

"Good, good. Let's do it!" He gave a thumbs-up to each cameraman, received one in return, then looked back at Jason and Chuck. "Rolling! Action!"

"The weather's perfect for a wedding," Chuck said. "You must be living right to get an early spring this far north."

"Always, my friend. Always."

Chuck stopped, and when Jason turned to face him, he held out his hand.

"Heather's a great girl, Jason," Chuck said.

The two men shook.

"Really, pal. Big-time congrats." Chuck grasped Jason's elbow with his left hand, a touching tribute.

"Thanks, Chuck. I'm lucky as hell, and I know it."

The two men resumed their stroll, chatting about mutual friends who were coming to the wedding. I stood and watched, rapt, for several minutes, then headed back to work.

I arrived at Ana's cottage at the same time as she did, five minutes before our scheduled five-thirty appointment. The clouds had thickened, and the temperature had dropped. I pulled up behind her in the driveway and got out. An east wind, the coldest kind, swirled up stray leaves and blew my hair every which way.

I called hello.

She smiled. "You're right on time." She stepped out of her car holding a big bouquet of yellow and white tulips, the cellophane wrap rustling in the breeze.

"Beautiful flowers."

"I love tulips," she said. Her eyes went to a white SUV with Massachusetts plates parked off to the side. "That must be my dad's car, although . . . Never mind. Let's go inside before we freeze to death."

"Can you believe the change? It was just all sunny and warm—now this."

We walked along the side path. "You know what they say about New Hampshire," Ana said. "If you don't like the weather, wait five minutes."

"I've always wondered about that," I said. "Lots of places say the same thing."

"Funny, isn't it? We all think our world is unique." We climbed the porch steps and entered the living room. "Dad?" She raised her voice. "Dad? Where are you?" She turned to me and made a "beats me" face. "He'll turn up, I'm sure. Let me get some lights on. You know the cloud cover is thick when it's this dark in here. Looks like rain's a-comin'." She flipped a wall switch, and an overhead crystal chandelier lit up. "Come on in and—" She stopped short. "Oh, my God!" She dropped the tulips and pressed her fingers against her lips.

Startled, I followed her gaze. Jason lay on the hearth, his eyes open, staring at the ceiling. His head rested in a puddle of shiny dark red liquid. Spiderweb-shaped rivulets ran along and between the stones and into the cracks and crevices of the old oak-plank floor. Bits of glass and colored metal were strewn on him, over the stones, in the liquid mess, and across the floor.

I hurried toward him. "Call nine-one-one."

"That's blood," Ana whispered.

I dropped to my knees and slid my hands under his head gingerly, seeking out the wound. His skull was dented.

"He must have fallen and hit his head," she said, dazed. "The floor was just waxed."

I rolled him onto his side to see if he was still bleeding, to see if I could do something to stop the flow. As I turned him over, his right arm flung sideways, landing lifelessly on the wood floor. The indentation in his head was deep. No blood was oozing. I rolled him back and began chest compressions. Maybe I wasn't too late.

"Ana. Go. Call nine-one-one."

She ran to the kitchen.

Compress, release. Compress, release. As I worked, dread took hold of me. Compress, release. Out of the corner of my eye, I saw Ana standing by the kitchen island clutching a portable phone to her chest. Compress, release. His eyes were glassy, unseeing. He was dead. I knew it, but I didn't stop. I didn't want it to be true. I winked away an unexpected tear and glanced at Ana. Her eyes were also moist.

"The ambulance is on the way," she said. "I know CPR. I can spot you."

I heard a faint siren, a double whirr, a distant noise. "Okay."

"One of Heather's aunts is hosting a cocktail party tonight. I can't believe this. I just can't believe this is happening."

Compress, release. Compress, release. We stayed like that, me trying to bring a dead man back to life, Ana watching, for what seemed like hours. The sirens grew louder.

"Do you want me to take over?"

"I'm okay. How long has it been?"

She looked at her watch. "Four minutes."

Compress, release. The sirens exploded into a nearby blare, then help was here, two men moving swiftly, with confidence. I fell aside, stiff from squatting, my wrists throbbing. I crawled to a wall and stayed there, huddled in a ball, tears burning in my eyes for a man I'd tried and failed to save. After a minute, I stood up and rested against a window frame. I watched the paramedics work for a moment longer, then walked outside onto the porch. Leaning heavily on the railing, I stared out toward the horizon. The air was thick and smelled like rain. Waves thundered into shore, raging against the boulders a hundred feet below the precipice that marked the edge of Ana's property. Branches from the stand of birch that lined the property to the south swayed and rubbed, making a whooshing sound. Ana joined me.

"They've called the police. Routine, he said."

"It's so shocking."

"I texted my dad. If he's in town already, he can drive me to see Heather. I don't want to go alone."

"I can take you."

"Thanks." She gulped back tears. "I put the tulips in water. It's awful to worry about flowers at a time like this, but I couldn't just leave them there. I couldn't let them die."

"Of course not."

We faced the ocean, waiting, watching, worrying. A gust of wind chilled me and I shivered.

"It's cold," I said.

"It's going to rain."

The sky to the east was nearly black. "Yes, and soon."

We stood silently for a few seconds; then Ana asked, "Did you see the debris? It's the Spring Egg, isn't it?"

"Oh, God, Ana, I hope not."

"I can't think about it right now. Not with Jason just—"

I looked down at my bloody hands. "Life. It's so hard." I took in a breath and rolled my shoulders, willing the tension to ease. "Why was he here?"

"To drop off a check. For the wedding desserts."

"How did he get in?"

"I keep a key in a make-believe rock in the garden. I told him to use it if I wasn't home."

"Do you know what time he was supposed to arrive?" I asked, keeping my eyes on the mist-shrouded ocean.

"No. We left it loose. Why?"

"Because I don't think he tripped and fell. I think someone killed him."

She turned to face me, to look into my eyes. "Oh, God."

Police Chief Ellis Hunter mounted the porch steps. He was tall, with regular features that came together well. He had brown hair cut shorter than was fashionable and gray eyes that had seen it all. A jagged dark red scar ran from the corner of his right eye to midway down his cheek. I'd never asked him about it.

Ellis and I were friends, and had been since he'd moved here four years earlier, shortly after his wife, a dancer, had died from lung cancer. He'd retired from the New York City police force to take the police chief job here.

He wanted, he said, not joking one bit, to see if Norman Rockwell had it right about small towns. He was dating my landlady, neighbor, and best friend Zoë, and we often hung out as couples.

Today, he wore a glen plaid sport coat and brown slacks. His tie was honey brown with teeny blue dots. He introduced himself to Ana, confirming that she owned the cottage and that she was the person who'd placed the 911 call.

"Are you all right?" he asked her.

"More or less."

"How about you, Josie? You okay?"

I shrugged.

He turned around, taking in the ocean view. His eyes came back to Ana. "Do you know what happened?"

"No."

Detective Claire Brownley rounded the corner. She was a little older than me, with crow-black hair cut short and sapphire blue eyes. Her skin was so fair it was almost translucent. She rarely smiled. She missed nothing. She nodded at me, one up-and-down motion, then wiggled her fingers, beckoning Ellis. She said something I couldn't hear, opened her notebook, and pointed to something near the bottom of the page. He read for a moment, then said something only she could hear. They climbed the steps to rejoin us.

Ellis introduced her to Ana and took another look at the detective's notebook. "The white SUV is registered to a Jason Ferris with a Boston address. Do you know him?"

"That's him . . . the dead man. I thought it was my dad's rental." Ana's eyes filled and she blinked a few times. "Jason was in Rocky Point for his wedding. His fiancée, Heather, is my friend. A good friend. I need to tell her what's happened. She's at the Three Crows on Market Street, for a party in their honor. The party was called for six." She glanced at her bangle watch. "Now."

"I offered to drive her," I said.

"We'll take her," he told me. He glanced at Ana, then at me. When he spoke, his eyes moved back and forth between us. "Obviously, I have several questions for you. First, though, I need to go inside and talk to the paramedics. The medical examiner and crime scene technicians will be here shortly." He pointed to a cluster of four Adirondack rocking chairs at the end of the porch near a trellis thick with tangled wisteria vines. "Why don't you get settled there. I'll be with you shortly."

"Heather must be wondering where he is," Ana said.

"We'll go soon. Just hang tight for a minute."

Ellis and Detective Brownley went inside. Neither Ana nor I moved from where we stood. The crashing waves seemed louder, angrier. Evergreen branches swooshed and swished in the now-steady wind. I looked out to sea. The cloud cover was dense. Lines of windswept white-riffled waves rode into shore on the diagonal. Two minutes later, Ellis and Detective Brownley reappeared.

Ellis spoke to Ana. "Detective Brownley is going to take you to the party." He turned toward me. "If you're all right with following me to the station, Josie, we can get going on your statement."

"I need to wash my hands." I raised my blood-smeared hands. "I did CPR."

Ellis met my eyes, understanding resonating in his. "Sorry, but the house is off-limits for now."

I swallowed hard and looked down at the gray wood floor. "I can't wait."

"You two go on ahead," Ellis said to the detective.

"There's an outside faucet around the side," Ana said, "near the—"

She broke off as a tall man with salt-and-pepper hair and bushy eyebrows came around the corner, walking briskly, a stack of folded-up newspapers and magazines tucked under his arm. He looked about sixty. He wore khakis, a black flannel shirt with the cuffs rolled up, and casual tie-up shoes.

Ana shouted, "Dad!" and ran to hug him, a big one, filled with love and caring. He hugged her with his left arm, then, after a few seconds, dropped the publications so he could use both. I felt a stab of envy. My dad died a decade ago, but I still missed him every day. Ana stepped back.

"I was so worried. Where have you been?"

"Why were you worried, hon? I was at the library catching up on my reading." He picked up the magazines and newspapers. Jason's newsletter was on the top, his photo smiling out into the world. I recognized the paper on the bottom, *The Wall Street Journal*. Stefan noticed me and Ellis and the detective. He looked at Ana. "Why is there an ambulance here? Are you all right? What's going on?"

"Oh, Dad! It's awful. Jason is dead."

"Mr. Yartsin?" Ellis asked, stepping forward.

"Yes . . . I'm Stefan Yartsin, and you are?"

"Police Chief Ellis Hunter." He walked down the steps to join the pair on the pathway, extending his hand for a shake. "I'm hoping you can help me." Stefan patted Ana's shoulder and squeezed her arm. "Of course."

"We're at the very beginning of an investigation into a sudden death, with no time to lose. Anything you can do to help us understand the timeline would be invaluable. Do you live in Rocky Point?"

"No, no. I'm here to celebrate Ana's new TV show and attend Heather's wedding. I live in Detroit."

"When did you arrive?"

"Today—about three thirty."

Detective Brownley was taking notes.

"What did you do when you got here?"

"Ana's car wasn't here, but I rang the bell anyway, just in case. There was no answer. I got her spare key from the fake rock and came inside."

"Were there any cars here?"

"No."

"Was anyone inside?"

"No."

"What did you do next?"

"Ana sent me photos of the house just after she bought it, so I knew where the guest room was located. I brought my suitcase inside." He shrugged. "I left for the library. I'm a day trader, so I spend a lot of time keeping up with the news. I've been there ever since."

"What time did you leave for the library?"

"I don't know. I didn't look. I couldn't have been inside more than ten, fifteen minutes, though."

Evidently, Jason died sometime between three forty-five, when Stefan left for the library, and five thirty, when Ana and I arrived.

"What did you do in that ten or fifteen minutes?" Ellis asked.

Stefan scratched his cheek. "You're really putting my memory to the test here. I did a lot of nothing stuff, you know, the things you do when you reach a destination. I washed off the travel dust, not a shower, only hands and face. I got Ana's Spring Egg snow globe out and unpacked it. I placed it in the center of the coffee table where it would be safe and she'd see it first thing. I hung up some clothes, just a few. A pair of slacks. A couple of shirts. I'm a travel-light sort of guy. That's it."

"Where's the spare key?" Ellis asked.

"I put it back in the rock when I left."

Ellis turned to Ana. "Which rock?"

She pointed to a small, irregularly shaped gray resin stone tucked under a bush near the porch steps. From any distance, it was indistinguishable from the real rocks nearby.

Ellis snapped on plastic gloves, picked it up, and used the eraser end of a pencil to slide open the bottom panel. He wiggled his finger in the opening and extracted a gold-toned key. He dropped it into a clear plastic evidence bag he took from his jacket pocket, then slipped the fake rock into another. As he sealed them, a crime scene technician came up the pathway alongside an older police officer I knew named Griff. The technician carried a big square black case, the kind pilots use.

Ellis stood. "Good timing," he said, dangling the bag with the key, then the one with the rock. "This key was hidden in this fake rock. With rain coming, I need you to take care of the soil pronto in case there are any footprints or debris."

The technician, a slender young woman who looked more like a farm girl than a scientist, said, "Sure."

Ellis explained where the rock had been positioned, then rattled off orders to Griff to secure the scene and block the driveway. As he went on about how many officers he wanted on the case and what he wanted them to do, I stopped listening. I turned back toward the water. The ocean surface was darker and wilder now, closer to black than green and covered by roiling ridges of churning white froth.

The technician started taking photographs of dirt. Griff went to his car for a roll of yellow caution tape. Detective Brownley left with Ana and her dad. Ellis turned to me.

"You want to run your hands under water from the faucet? Or I have some moist towelettes in my vehicle."

"That's better." I followed him to his oversized black SUV.

He raised the rear hatch and dragged a black camera bag forward. "I want some photos of the blood before you clean up. In case it comes up for some reason."

I didn't argue. I didn't care. I held my hands up, turning them as he instructed while he snapped away. When he was done, he thanked me and pulled a handful of individually wrapped towelettes from a mesh pocket built into the vehicle's side panel. He ripped one open and handed it to me. I rubbed my hands, but it quickly ran out of juice. He had a plastic trash bag ready, and I tossed it in. He tore open another one. It took six towelettes to get the blood off. Between the harsh alcohol-based cleaner and my strenuous rubbing, my skin ended up chafed and red. It looked as if I had a rash.

"Are you okay to drive? To follow me to the police station?"

"Yes." I started walking to my car, then turned back. "Thanks for letting me clean up."

"Sure," he said, his expression somber.

I glanced in the rearview mirror as we pulled out of the driveway. Griff was placing orange cones along the sidewalk.

Once we were on the interstate, I slipped in my earpiece and called Ty. I got his voice mail. I couldn't think of how to explain all that had occurred, so I only said that I had bad news, that Jason had died, that I'd been with Ana when she found his corpse, and that I was en route to the police station to give a statement. And that I loved him.

CHAPTER SIX

Ellis asked me to wait in the lobby, promising not to be too long. I used the time to sit with my eyes closed, thinking, trying to shake off the deep sadness that had taken hold of me. My phone vibrated, startling me, and I dug it out of my tote bag. It was Wes Smith, the local reporter for the *Seacoast Star*. I knew he'd call. He always called. I knew I'd talk to him, too, since he always had information I had no other way of getting, but I didn't want to talk to him now. If there was one thing I could count on, it was that Wes would call back. I hit the IGNORE button and tossed the device back into my bag, leaned back against the unforgiving wood, and closed my eyes again.

After a while, ten minutes maybe, I stood up and stretched. Cathy, the civilian admin who'd been there since before Ty had the chief's job, sat at her computer, typing. Two uniformed officers, one named Daryl, the other one new to me, were reading over her shoulder.

"He's a finance guy?" Daryl asked rhetorically. "I thought they all were in New York."

"Nah," the other officer replied. "There's mega-money in Boston."

"Guys," Cathy said. "Give me a break, will ya? I don't need you two yapping in my ear."

They stepped away. I walked to the community bulletin board and was scanning a "Call for Volunteers" notice seeking help cleaning up the village green when the front door opened and a stream of people entered. Detective Brownley led the way. Officer F. Meade, a tall ice blonde I'd known for years, was last in line. I'd never heard her first name. In between were Heather, Chuck and Sara, a middle-aged couple, an older single woman, Ana, Peter, and Ana and Peter's dad, Stefan. No one paid any attention to me. Ana looked poised but worried. Heather looked sick. Her eyes were rimmed in red. Her nose was even redder and mottled.

Detective Brownley invited everyone to have a seat except Ana and Heather. She led Ana down a long hallway to the right. Officer Meade escorted Heather down a similarly long hallway that branched off to the left. Having been in the station before, I knew that interview rooms opened off both hallways.

Peter approached the front counter and waited for Cathy to look up from her typewriter. "Where are they taking them?"

"I wouldn't know, sir."

"Who would?" he said, his voice low and tight, as if he were exerting control.

"Someone will be out soon, sir."

"Let me talk to the police chief," he demanded.

Cathy's eyes widened. "He's not available."

Peter slapped the counter, startling us all. I jumped and scooted forward, braced to flee. The others looked every which way, then moved closer to one another. I was tempted to join them. If Peter, foiled in his efforts to find Heather and Ana, spun around, ready to lash out, I, the only person sitting alone, would be an easy target. He half-turned toward me, considering his next move.

Stefan, his expression wary, walked to the counter. Daryl and the other officer approached from the other side. Showdown at high noon.

Stefan placed his arm around Peter's shoulders. "What's the problem, Pete?"

"I want to know where Heather is. And Ana. I have a right to know. And this"—he broke off, staring down at Cathy as if she were dirt—"this *woman* won't tell me." He spoke the word "woman" the way I say "spider."

Cathy stepped back.

"I'll take it from here," Daryl told her.

She slipped away without another word, leaving the reception room, perhaps to alert Ellis to send in the cavalry.

Daryl moved closer to the counter. "Sir, if you'll just take a seat I'll get someone to come out and talk to you."

"Come on, Pete," Stefan said, patting his shoulder. "Let's sit down."

Peter shook off his dad's touch and grasped the edge of the counter as if he expected to be dragged away.

Stefan stood his ground. "Don't get excited for no reason."

"I'm not going anywhere, Dad."

Ellis appeared from his office. He scanned the group. "Thank you all for coming in. I appreciate your cooperation, especially during this difficult time."

Peter spun around. "Are you in charge here?"

"Yes. I'm Police Chief Ellis Hunter. And you are?"

"Peter Yartsin, a friend of Heather's and Ana's brother. I want to see Heather *now*."

"I understand. I'll find out where she is."

Peter took a step toward Ellis, an aggressive move, fueled perhaps by Ellis's seemingly imperturbable calm.

"When I say now," Peter said, "I mean *now*. This minute."

"Of course." He nodded at Stefan, turned to the others, and nodded at them all. "I appreciate your patience. We'll be as quick as we can." He looked at me. "Josie, if you'd follow me."

I walked across the room, uncomfortably aware that everyone was looking at me, thinking that Ellis was clever to disarm Peter by agreeing with him. I doubted if Ellis had any intention of allowing him anywhere near Heather or Ana until they'd both given official statements.

Ellis didn't speak until we were seated at the old wooden table in Room One with the door closed. I was familiar with the space, having been interviewed in it more than once. It was small and windowless, with two video cameras mounted on abutting walls and a one-way mirror taking up most of one side. As usual, I sat with my back to the human-sized cage positioned in the corner. Ty once told me it was for unruly guests, a chilling thought. I heard the steady patter of rain.

Ellis reached for the wall-mounted phone, telling me, "I'll be right with you." He pressed three buttons, waited a moment, then said, "Is everything under control out there? . . . Good . . . Okay, then . . . Keep a close eye on him, will you? . . . Thanks, Daryl." He replaced the receiver and sat at the head of the table. "I'll turn on the cameras in a minute and make it official, but first, let's talk informally. Off the record. Okay?"

"Sure," I said, wondering where he was heading.

"I need help here, Josie."

"Of course. Anything I can do."

"The technicians tell me they've recovered hundreds of pieces of metal, wood, and enamel from the crime scene, even some stones that appear to be jewels."

"Oh, God, Ellis, the thought of a Fabergé egg being destroyed makes me ill. Literally ill."

"I can only imagine. When they're done with their work, will you take a look for me?"

"Of course."

"Okay, then." He reached for the remote. "Let's make it official."

Ellis stated the logistical information for the record, then leaned back and laced his hands behind his head. "Tell me about Jason."

"What do you want to know?"

"Everything. Anything."

I stared at him, confused. "I don't know what I can tell you. I met him yesterday for the first time. I've spent a total of about fifteen minutes with him, during which he mostly ignored the rest of us."

"How come?"

"Work, I guess. He was on his phone, reading things, texting. I don't know exactly."

"How did Heather feel about that?"

"I don't know."

Ellis unlaced his hands and sat forward. "What was your impression of him?"

"He was apparently successful, a famous investment guru, selling a dream to plenty of eager dreamers with money to spare."

"I infer you didn't admire his business model."

"He was a caveat emptor sort of guy. Not my style."

"Slick?"

"Maybe. He came off as serious, not sleazy, but so do a lot of con men. I doubt he set out to con people, it's not that. He just misdirected them, legally. He bragged about skirting the law—can you imagine? His customers admired and envied his success and assumed that if they followed his advice, they would achieve the dream, too. He didn't care about them at all. He was all about number one. He built in deniability, and he was proud of it."

"What about Heather? Did she believe the dream, too?"

"I don't know. It's possible she's not very smart, that it didn't even occur to her to question his judgment. Or she's gullible. Or she's wildly in love and can see no wrong in him." I shrugged. "There's a chance that she's as sneaky-bad as he was. I met her for an even shorter time than him."

Ellis riffed a little tap-tap-tap on the tabletop, thinking. "What do you know about Peter? Was that performance typical?"

"From what little I've seen, maybe. When he showed up out of the blue, Heather fled."

"Does she have an order of protection against him? Has she ever pressed charges? Anything like that?"

"I don't know."

"What can you tell about the snow globe, the one that might have been broken?"

I explained about Imperial Fabergé eggs and their surprises, Ana's family's narrative about how they acquired the egg, and the complexity in calculating value.

"The last appraiser attached Polaroids to his write-up," I said. "They've faded some, but there's sufficient detail to be able to identify the design. Diamonds and rubies and emeralds, oh my."

He soft-whistled. "No wonder it's worth so much money." He lowered his eyes and tapped the table with his index fingers as if he were hunt-and-pecking on an old-fashioned typewriter, then looked up at me. "What else should I ask you?"

I shook my head. "I don't know."

Ellis thanked me and clicked off the recorders. "I'll be in touch."

The lobby was empty. Cathy was back at her computer. Two different patrolmen sat nearby. One was listening to someone on the phone, taking notes; the other one was reading from a legal pad.

Outside, wind-driven rain was blowing sideways. I ran for my car and was soaked by the time I got inside. I sat and scanned my messages, waiting for the heat to come up and take the bite off the raw chill. Wes had called again, and texted. Ty had called, too, telling me he was sorry to hear about Jason and that he was stuck in a situation in Maine and wouldn't be home until late. All in all, it was a bad night.

CHAPTER SEVEN

T he storm continued unabated, causing flash floods on low-lying roads and snapping off tree limbs. The twigs and branches that scraped against the windows kept jerking me awake. After endless hours of wearisome tossing and rolling and fretting about Ty, I finally got up and went downstairs. I made myself a pot of tea and curled up on the couch under a cable-knit afghan to read my current book, Rex Stout's *Gambit*. I was on my second cup of the tea, happily lost in the story, when the rain stopped. I looked at the mantel clock. It was three minutes after four, hours before dawn.

I walked to the window and pulled aside the drapes. A sliver of moon peeked through the clouds, stippling the lawn and street. I opened the window and breathed in the fresh, clean air. It was a beautiful night, warmer than when I'd come home. It gave me hope that my day would be better, too. Ty pulled into the driveway. *Perfect timing,* I thought.

I opened the front door and waved. He smiled.

"Why aren't you asleep?" he asked me as he climbed onto the porch.

"The storm. Are you okay?"

"Yeah . . . just a long day."

"Tell me about it—on the other hand, don't. Let's talk tomorrow. I mean later. I need to go to sleep, and you must be ready to collapse."

"Close." He kissed me, a soft one, then stretched, reaching for the ceiling. "I need to be out of here by seven. One meeting in Boston, then I'm heading back to my place for a long nap."

"I may join you. Have you eaten?"

"If you can call cold pizza eating. I'm too tired to tell if I'm hungry. I'll grab something before I leave. What I'm not skipping, though, is a shower."

Ty went for his shower, and I crawled back in bed. I was asleep within seconds, and I slept like I'd been drugged, awakening to the alarm at eight, late for me. Ty was long gone.

I opened the blinds, and conical beams of bright yellow light slanted across the old oak floor.

Ty had left a note on the kitchen counter, an *xo,* followed by "To hell with being tired. Let's go dancing tonight." I smiled, grabbed my phone, and texted, "Dancing sounds great. Burgers, too?" While I waited for his reply, I made coffee, then checked my voice mails. I had three new messages, all from Wes.

"Josie," Wes had whined at seven this morning, his most recent message. Whining was Wes's default I'll-make-you-feel-guilty-for-ignoring-me tone. "I can't believe you haven't called me back. I've got a shockeroonie you're gonna wanna hear."

He was right. I did want to hear what he had to say. Wes's web of contacts was both deep and wide. I called him back and agreed to meet him on our favorite sand dune at ten.

I got to the dune, a mile south of the police station, first. The still-wet sand was hard to navigate, but the view from the top was worth the effort. Standing on the shifting sand, I had an unobstructed view of the ocean. The sun cast golden starbursts across the dark blue expanse. Waves rolled gently into shore, then ebbed away. Watching the steady, rhythmic motion was hypnotic.

A car's engine cut off, and I looked down at the street. Wes was stepping out of a red Ford Focus. *A loaner,* I thought. Wes's car was a dingy, rusted-out maroon Dodge that had needed a new muffler five years earlier, and no doubt still did. Maybe he'd finally taken it in for service and the shop gave him the Focus for the day. He looked different, too. I hadn't seen him in several months, but even so, the change in his appearance was startling. He'd lost about thirty pounds. His normally pasty-white skin looked ruddier, healthier. He was wearing slacks with a collared shirt and tie and lace-up shoes, not a ripped T-shirt, jeans, and dirty sneakers.

"What happened to your car?" I called down.

"I got a new one. New to me, I mean."

It was shiny. "It looks good."

"Thanks."

"You look good, too."

He grinned and fingered his tie as he started up the sandy mound. "A new image. If I want to be taken seriously, I have to dress like a grown-up."

"You got that from a self-help book."

"No, I got it from my girlfriend."

I grinned. "You've got a girlfriend."

He blushed a little. "Six months now."

"I had no idea. I'm thrilled for you, Wes. Who is she?"

"Her name is Maggie. Margaret Campbell. She's assistant manager of Rocky Point Community Bank."

"That's my bank. Wait! Is she the one who sits at the first desk on the right? Brown hair cut short and freckles?"

"That's her."

"I've talked to her. She was both knowledgeable and quick, a great combination."

"She is all of that. Ambitious, too, a real go-getter."

"Sort of like you, Wes."

"You think?"

"Yes. How did you meet?"

"I got talking to her about a customer."

I stared at him, appalled to think that my banker would gossip with a reporter. "She's one of your sources."

"No. I tried hard, but she refused to tell me anything," he said as he reached the top of the dune.

I laughed, reassured. "You're something like nothing I've ever seen, Wes."

"Thanks." His cheeks reddened again, and he cleared his throat. "So tell me what you know about Jason's murder."

"Murder?" I asked, thinking that I was right, that I'd known it as soon as I'd touched the gaping hole in Jason's skull. "I thought it was a trip-and-fall accident."

"That's ruled out. That's my shockeroonie. According to the ME's preliminary report, Jason died from blunt force trauma consistent with hitting his head on the fieldstone rock hearth, but here's the kicker. They're keeping it all hush-hush, but the ME used an imaging gizmo to prove there were multiple blows."

I tried to push away the gruesome memory of my fingers prodding the wound, but couldn't. I could feel Wes waiting for my reaction.

"You're not surprised," he said. "How come?"

I swallowed hard. "I felt the back of Jason's head to assess the wound, you know, to see if I could do something to stop the bleeding. Oh, God, Wes. I couldn't do a thing." I gulped and choked and coughed as a wave of nausea washed over me. "There was a dent in his skull, closer to a gully, actually. It was horrific—really, really awful."

He pulled a small spiral-bound notebook from his pants pocket and used his index finger to push out a pen he'd stuffed through the wires. Before Maggie, he carried a single ratty piece of paper and a pencil stub. He jotted a note. "Gully . . . good one, Joz!"

"God, Wes! You're incredible—not in a good way. Don't even think about quoting me."

His eyes opened wide. "What are you talking about? 'Gully' is a great word."

"Feel free to use it. Just don't attribute it to me. Same deal as always, Wes."

He sighed, Wesian for disappointed. I kept my eyes on the horizon and waited for him to speak.

"All right," he said, drawing out the words petulantly, as if he were making a huge concession.

"How about Ana's neighbors?" I asked. "Did anyone see anything?"

"Not from the initial canvass," he said, back to normal. "Lots of the cottages on that stretch of ocean are summer homes, and those folks aren't here yet. All the natives were at work or shopping or whatever."

"What happened to the check Jason was bringing Ana?"

"The police found it in his shirt pocket. My source says you're going to look at the shattered thing, whatever it is, as soon as the forensic team is done with it. Take photos for me."

"If I can."

"Josie! I need a little quid for my pro quo, if you get my drift."

I patted his arm. "You know I always tell you everything as soon as I can."

"I know you *say* you do."

"Wes!"

"Give me something, Josie. I need *something*. I'm on deadline."

"I already did—the word 'gully.' What else do you have?"

"Nothing yet. There's a boatload of people in town for the wedding. The police are checking whether any of them had an issue with Jason. So far, nothing has come to light."

"Not even with Peter?"

"Who's he?"

I explained his relationship to Jason and described Peter's outburst at the police station.

"This might be something." He wrote in his notebook for a few seconds. "I'll check him out. Who else?"

"No one. Jason's death screws up the TV pilot. How can they use a tape of wedding plans when the groom is killed only days before the ceremony? That means no one with a vested interest in the show has a motive. Like Ana."

"Unless her motive is unrelated to the show."

"True, but it would take a heck of a motive to risk losing an opportunity like this—her own TV show. What about Heather? Is there anything there?"

"*Cherchez la femme*—good one, Joz! Why would she want him dead?"

"I can't imagine. She was about to marry him."

"Did you ever see them together?"

Jason's preoccupation with business and his gratuitous talk about choosing a honeymoon site based on its perceived prestige wouldn't endear him to me, yet I had no reason to think it bothered her, at least not enough to break up with him, let alone kill him. My dad once told me that if I married a man for his money, I'd earn every penny. I wondered if Heather was named in Jason's will, thinking maybe she'd taken a shortcut.

"No one knows the truth behind other people's relationships. They seemed happy together."

"There's a 'but' there."

"You're right. From what I saw, he was into business and she was into him. Still, there's no reason to think they weren't truly in love. It only makes sense, though, to check out his will."

"In the works. Did you meet anyone else here for the wedding?"

"Ana's dad, Stefan. The families are friends."

"What did you think of him?"

"He seemed kind, concerned about Ana, willing to step up to protect Peter." My throat tightened at a memory of my father, his devotion and love. I turned toward the ocean. A sailboat was skimming north, running parallel to the shore, its sails billowing. About a week after my mom's funeral, I'd come down with a miserable case of the flu, and Dad, who couldn't work a can opener before her death, had used her cookbook—the one she'd hand-written and illustrated for me as she lay dying—to make her scratch chicken soup. Love equals effort exerted. Stefan loved Peter, of that I was certain. I turned back to face Wes. "He reminded me a little of my dad. A good guy." I felt my brow furrow as a new thought came to me.

Wes, as observant as ever, asked, "What?"

"Ana mentioned a breach between them—between her and her dad—but I didn't see anything like that." I held up a hand. "Keep in mind, I saw him for a total of about two minutes, which includes about no more than thirty seconds with Ana, so what do I know? Maybe they were faking getting along."

"How can I check?"

A man far down the beach tossed a stick for his dog, a little mutt. The dog ran like his life depended on retrieving it. Once he did, he half carried, half dragged it back and was rewarded with a big, ruffling pat. He darted a few steps away, then scurried back, challenging his owner to do it again, do it again, do it again. The man did, and again the little fellow took off like a bullet.

I turned toward Wes. "How about talking to Heather's family? Maybe the breach occurred when Ana was younger. That wouldn't be unusual, would it? To have a fight with your dad when you're a teenager? If so, some-one in Heather's family might be aware of it. The two families have been friends for years."

"You rock, Josie!" Wes made a note.

The little dog barked, and Wes and I both looked up. The dog was play-ing tug-of-war, unwilling to relinquish his stick. His tail was wagging wildly. His owner was laughing, having a blast.

"Who else?" he asked.

"Jason's best friend, Chuck, and his wife, Sara. I saw them for even less time than everyone else. You know, Wes, it's possible that Jason's murderer is someone we know nothing about. A disgruntled investor, for instance, who followed Jason here, hot for revenge. Jason enters an isolated cottage. The killer follows. They argue. They tussle. Jason ends up dead." I paused, thinking. "Jason wasn't a money manager or financial adviser. He gave advice, but while he marketed his information to individual investors, he was not pro-consumer—that's a potentially deadly mix. Plus, who knows how much he inflated his success? Maybe he was all hot air and no money. Can you check out his net worth?"

Wes scribbled in his notebook. "Sure. The police are following up on one more lead—the Blue Dolphin pastry chef. A guy named Maurice who has it in for Ana."

"Are you serious?"

"Why are you surprised?"

"It seems like a stretch. Just because a man is jealous of Ana and temperamental . . . why would he kill Jason?"

"According to my police source, Maurice has made threats openly, things like if Ana thinks she can breeze into Rocky Point and take over his business, she'd better watch her back."

"Wow. That's not good. Or smart. But what does that have to do with Jason?"

"The police think maybe he went to her house to confront her or something and ran into Jason instead."

"Do we know if he has an alibi?"

"Not yet. I'm checking alibis for everyone." He paused for a moment. "How about opportunity? Who had access to Ana's house key?"

"Everyone. Anyone. Ana was quick to tell people where she hid it."

"So Jason uses Ana's spare key, replacing it after he opens the door. When the killer shows up, either Jason lets him in or the killer gets the key from the rock." Wes's eyes opened wide. "If that's what happened, the murderer put the key back after killing Jason. What kind of person would have the wherewithal to do that?"

"Someone who's good in a crunch. Someone who thinks straight in a crisis."

"Then that's the kind of person we're looking for." He glanced at his notes. "So that takes care of opportunity. We know means. That leaves motive."

"Wait a sec. Back to means. Jason was a big guy. Either the killer is bigger than he was, or he was caught unawares, or he was struck by something first, then pounded against the stones, or he fell, like Ana assumed, then was pounded against the stones."

"Good point," Wes said. "What else?"

"Nothing."

"What about motive?"

"Revenge, lust, greed, right? The big three."

Wes flipped his notebook closed and gave me a fierce look. "Get me photos."

"If I can," I said, starting down the dune, "I will." When I reached the bottom, I scraped clumps of sand off the soles of my boots, shielded my eyes from the sun with the flat of my hand, and looked up at him. "You look fab, Wes. For real. It's great news about you and Maggie."

He smiled like he meant it. "Thanks."

Ellis texted as I was driving to work. I pulled off to the side of the road to read it. "Call. Urgent." I punched in the numbers for his cell phone.

"What's wrong?" I asked when I had him.

"Nothing, why?"

I exhaled.

"Call me crazy, but when a police chief tells me to contact him immediately, I get, you know, a little anxious."

"Sounds like a guilty conscience to me. Are you withholding information relevant to the investigation?"

"No! And I don't have a guilty conscience."

"Good. Can I drop off the material the techs recovered at the crime scene? They're done—they found nothing useful. The only pieces big enough to take fingerprints don't have any. There's nothing significant forensically, except that they know the debris landed on Jason, not under him. You're our last hope."

"Is that why you texted?"

"Yes."

"I'll do my best."

"I'll be at your office in half an hour."

I felt a familiar rush of excitement. Starting an appraisal, even of broken pieces, represented the beginning of what might turn into an epic quest. "Hot diggity!"

"Hot diggity?"

"Don't you know that term? It's an official phrase in the antiques business. It means yippee."

He chuckled. "I'll see you in a few, Josie."

I pushed the END CALL button. "Hot diggity," I said aloud.

CHAPTER EIGHT

C ara was on the phone giving someone directions to the tag sale. Gretchen was on the phone with Rocky Point Interiors getting a quote on new carpet for the front office. Eric and Sasha were discussing a furniture pickup she'd scheduled for that afternoon. Fred was reading something on his monitor. Another busy day at Prescott's.

"Everyone?" I said.

They all looked up, even Cara and Gretchen.

"When you're off the phone," I mouthed.

While we waited for their calls to end, everyone's eyes were on my face.

"I don't know if any of you have heard the news about Jason . . . I'm certain Wes has already posted updates. If not, I'm afraid I'm the bearer of bad news." Cara frowned. Sasha began twirling her hair. Fred pushed up his glasses and cocked his head. Gretchen leaned forward, her eyes reflecting her concern. Eric pressed his lips together. "Ana's friend Jason is dead, and it looks like murder, but it's too soon to know anything definitive." Gretchen's hand flew to cover her mouth. Cara gasped. "It happened at Ana's house. There's nothing else I can tell you at this point." I took in air. "We've been asked to help the police with an antiques-related aspect of the investigation." I looked at Sasha, then Fred. "What are your schedules like today? I may need help re-creating an object from broken pieces."

"I'm open all day," Fred said, his tone subdued.

"I have a call with the director of the Vienna Snow Globe Museum at noon," Sasha said, her anxiety apparent. "Other than that, I can help. Or I could reschedule the call if you wanted me to."

"We'll see. The analysis may take all of us working together. The object is in so many minuscule pieces, it's unrecognizable."

Fred leaned back, intrigued. "Minuscule—all of it?"

"Some bits are microscopic."

"That's a challenge, all right."

"How is Ana holding up?" Cara asked kindly. "And her friend, Heather, wasn't it?"

"Ana was pretty shaken up, but her dad is in town, and he seems to be a real support for her. I haven't seen Heather since it happened, but you can imagine how she must be feeling." I paused. "Each of us has to process something like this in his or her own way. Take as much time as you need—I mean it. Take the rest of the day off if you want." I scanned their attentive faces. "You know me, so you know that in times of strife, work is my salvation. Just because that's how I cope, though, doesn't mean it should be your strategy. Do what's best for you."

"I'll stay," Fred said.

"Me, too," Sasha added.

"I have a pick-up," Eric said, "and two deliveries. I'm fine to go."

"I'm going to call Jack," Gretchen said. "If he can get off work for lunch . . . I think I'd like to be with him for a while."

"Good idea," I told her.

"I'd rather be here," Cara said, "with all of you, than home alone."

"All right, then." I turned to Sasha. "It's moot now, of course, but what did Ana think of those chess sets?"

As always, the moment the conversation turned to antiques or art, even in an atmosphere of uncertainty and fear, Sasha blossomed.

"She liked them, but said even the lowest price was more than she wanted to spend."

"As expected," I said. "What are you working on, Fred?"

He grinned and leaned to the side, placing his left elbow on his armrest and propping his chin on the back of his hand. He looked like he was posing for a high-end art photo.

Much to my enduring surprise, despite being, from all appearances, a quintessential New Yorker, Fred was happy in smaller, quieter Rocky Point. Nine years after moving to New Hampshire, he still wore the Italian suits and skinny ties in a place where most men wore flannel shirts and jeans, and he still visited New York City once a month or so, but Rocky Point was, to him, home. *Me, too,* I thought.

"You remember that mahogany side table we bought last week from Mrs. Malier," he said.

"Sure."

Did I ever. A woman walked in with two boxes of run-of-the-mill kitchenware and a 28" × 33" × 17" table, an odd size. She was downsizing, she explained, moving into a condo. She didn't know anything about the table's history, just that it came from her deceased husband's family, and, she confided, she'd never liked it. No one in the family did. She'd asked her husband's cousins if they wanted it; everyone declined. She didn't want it appraised even after I told her its low height suggested it came from an era where people were shorter, the nineteenth century, maybe even earlier. She just wanted it gone. It happened that way sometimes, when people were out of patience or energy or the objects brought back bad memories. We bought the lot for two hundred dollars.

"From your expression," I added, "I'm going to be happy."

"Maybe even ecstatic. It's an eighteenth-century game table. I'm not surprised she didn't know it—it's about as clever a design as I've ever seen. A leaf slides out revealing a chessboard, ebony inlaid with two tropical hardwoods, bloodwood and yellowheart. Using an ingenious double-jointed hinging system, obviously handcrafted, the leaf flips over onto the tabletop."

"How would anyone have got their hands on exotic hardwoods back then?"

"Booty from the rum trade?"

"Maybe." I crossed my fingers in front of my face. "Condition?"

Fred's grin broadened. "Pristine."

My eyes lit up. "Marks?"

He pushed up his black square-framed hipster glasses. "Are you braced?"

I grasped the rounded rim on his desk. "I'm ready."

His smile grew, and when he paused, heightening the drama, I felt my pulse quicken.

"WH. In script."

My mouth opened, then closed. I took in a deep breath. "Oh, my."

"Oh, yeah."

We'd recently researched that mark when we found it on a mahogany chest of drawers. In fact, we decided to organize an auction around that one piece. At first, we assumed that the WH identified the maker. We were wrong. Those ornately carved initials identified the man who commissioned the pieces, not the firm that made them or the craftsman who worked on them. They referred to Whitmell Hill, a wealthy North Carolinian who, in the late 1700s, ordered dozens of magnificently designed and expertly crafted pieces of furniture from the master house builder, William Seay of Roxobel, North Carolina. His work was coveted by collectors, and now we had two of his pieces for our upcoming auction, Southern Life.

"So we're looking at high four figures?" I asked.

"More. I've never seen anything like it. It's elegantly designed and perfectly constructed of rare-to-the-max wood. I'll be recommending an estimate in at least the thirteen- to fifteen-thousand-dollar range. I'm still researching rarity. I want to know how many game tables Seay made. If it's as rare as I suspect it may be, my recommendation will go up."

Rarity was one of the most important factors determining an antique's value—how many of an object were created in the first place. The fewer game tables Seay made, the more each one would be worth. Fabergé, for instance, only made one of each egg.

"Well done, Fred. I'm impressed. Seriously impressed."

"You're the one who did the heavy lifting identifying the mark in the first place."

"We're a good team."

I smiled, thinking how amazing it was that with all our different personalities, education levels, and interests, we fit together so well. Eric and Sasha had been born and reared in Rocky Point; the rest of us came from other worlds. Only Sasha, Fred, and I had any college. I had a bachelor's degree. Fred had earned his master's. Sasha held a PhD.

In recent years, Eric had become a tournament poker player, earning, he confided, a few extra thousand dollars a year. Gretchen lived for celebrity gossip. Sasha attended scholarly lectures on an eclectic array of topics. Fred haunted museums. I snorkeled. What we shared was commitment to Prescott's and mutual respect.

Lucky me, I thought.

"All right, then," I said. "I'm going to prep for my three-D jigsaw puzzle. Cara, when Chief Hunter arrives, let me know. I'll be at a workstation."

As I headed for the warehouse door, I glanced out the window and was surprised to see Heather. She was in the woods, poking her head out, looking around. She pushed aside a low-hanging branch and stepped onto the asphalt parking lot. *She must have come from the Congregational church a quarter mile away,* I thought. She looked around as if she were lost. She was wearing a black leather bomber jacket zipped to the neck and skinny dark blue jeans tucked into black leather midcalf tie-up boots.

"I'll be back in a sec," I told Cara.

I stepped into the blinding sun and took half a dozen steps toward Heather, blinking until my eyes adjusted.

"Heather?"

"Josie." She looked up at the PRESCOTT'S ANTIQUES AND AUCTIONS sign mounted on the roof, then looked back at me. "This is your place."

"Yes."

"I'm trespassing."

"You're welcome. I've been hoping I could see you to tell you how sorry I am for your loss."

"Thank you." She paused, her eyes still on my sign. "That's what I'm supposed to say, right?" She looked at me. "Thanks."

"I don't know that there's a 'supposed to' here. You can say whatever you want."

"Sorry." She pressed her index fingers against her eyebrows for a moment. "I'm not myself."

"Is there anything I can do?"

"Have any whiskey?"

"Sure."

Heather followed me inside. She didn't say anything to anyone. Maybe she didn't notice them. I led the way across to the warehouse door. Cara stood up, smiling, ready to offer tea or coffee. I shook my head a little, and she sat down. I could tell Heather wasn't in the mood to meet new people.

I paused with my hand on the knob to tell Cara I'd be upstairs, adding, "Send up a setup for some drinks, okay? I'll take lemonade. Add a nibble if we have anything."

"Right away," Cara said, standing again.

Heather and I crossed the concrete span, our heels clicking a tippita-tappita beat. We climbed the spiral staircase that led to my private office. Heather paused three steps in.

"Nice office."

"Thanks."

She pointed to the display case holding my rooster collection. "You collect roosters. How come?"

"I don't know. Why does anyone collect anything?"

"To show off."

I opened my mouth to protest, then closed it again. Anything I said would come off as defensive. Plus, I bet she was talking about Jason, not me.

Heather walked to one of the yellow Queen Anne wing chairs, then changed her mind and crossed to the love seat. She perched on the edge, loosened the laces on her boots, kicked them off, then sat back, crossing her legs Indian-style.

"I hope it's okay to take my boots off," she said after the fact.

"Sure."

Cara appeared, tray in hand. It held four cut-crystal glasses—two highballs, two rocks—a crystal and sterling silver bucket of ice with matching sterling silver tongs, individually wrapped cheese wedges, a bowl of crackers, another filled with Cara's homemade chocolate chip cookies, a little plate of preportioned clusters of champagne grapes, a small cut-crystal pitcher of lemonade, and four crisp white linen cocktail napkins. She slid the tray onto the butler's table.

"Thanks, Cara."

She smiled and left.

Heather reached for a cookie. "Do you have any single malt?"

I pulled a bottle of Macallan from the cabinet next to my rooster collection. My dad had always kept a bottle for his friend Buddy. This one, still a third full, had been his. Now both men were dead, and the bottle was mine. "How do you take it?"

"A little water, no ice."

I poured two inches of the honey brown whiskey into a rocks glass and placed it on a napkin in front of her. "Sparkling or still?"

"Still."

I took a small bottle from the minifridge beside my desk and gave it to her. I poured myself a lemonade over ice.

"Not a drinking girl?" she asked, raising her glass.

"Work awaits, so as much as I'd love to, I need to stick to lemonade. I'm with you in spirit, though."

She downed the whiskey in one gulp, winced a little, and shook her head, clearing it, or wanting it to clear.

"More?" I asked.

"Please."

I poured another two inches, then placed the bottle on the side table nearest her. "Help yourself."

"Thanks."

She sipped this one, then sighed. "I needed this."

"A lot going on?"

"It's not that. It's that I'm royally pissed off. Boot-kicking angry."

"At what?"

"I don't know. That's the worst of it." She tossed back the whiskey and poured herself another, a three-incher this time. "That's why I was in your woods." She laughed mirthlessly, self-deprecatingly. "Talking to God, I guess you could say." She shook her head as she refilled her glass again. "I went to that church to speak to the pastor, a nice enough man. Do you know him?"

"Ted Bauer, yes."

"I keep snapping at everyone from the man at the funeral parlor while I was making arrangements to ship Jason's body home and my mother to waitresses and hotel housekeepers. It's exhausting and frustrating and embarrassing. So being a gal of action, I got a list of nearby religious institutions from the front desk and starting calling. You know it's not so easy to find a pastor interested in talking to a stranger around here?"

"Really? That surprises me."

She shrugged. "I just said that to be mean. Do you see what I was saying? I'm acting out, and I know it, and I can't stop. I only called three places, a Jewish temple, a Catholic church, and the place next door, a Congressional church, I think it is. I went in alphabetical order. The rabbi at Beth Shalom is in Boston with a youth group. The priest from the Church of the Holy Family is at Rocky Point Hospital giving last rites to someone, then making rounds. Ted Bauer was available, so I jumped in the car and raced off to see him. He was great, actually. He didn't criticize me for being angry. He pointed out that I had a lot to be angry about, the loss of dreams, the end of hope."

"The end of hope? That seems a little extreme."

"Does it?" She unwrapped a cheese wedge and placed it on a soda cracker. She popped the bite in her mouth and chewed like she wanted to kill it. "Does it indeed?"

"Did he offer any advice?"

"He didn't say that thing about the end of hope. I did. Advice? Sure. Get some exercise. Fresh air. The anger will pass, he said. It's a natural stage of grieving. Which means it may not pass for years. You should see my mother. She's been a widow for a year and she's a mess." She flipped her hand backward, pushing air over her right shoulder, communicating a dismissive "whatever." She took a cluster of grapes and ate one. "That's why I went for a walk. The woods are pretty—but you know that. It's your woods, right? I like the shushing sound pine needles make when you walk on them." She paused to eat another grape. "I didn't care where it went. Then the path ended and poof, here I am. Like magic. He also said to keep talking." She shrugged again. "What is he going to say, right? 'Snap out of it'? 'Pull yourself together'? 'Time heals all wounds'? It's hopeless. I'm hopeless." She closed her eyes for a moment, the muscles along her jawline bullet hard. "Sorry. I'm not myself."

"No need to apologize. You can say anything you want to me."

"Really?" She opened her eyes and finished the grapes. "Now there's an offer I ought to take advantage of." She wrapped her arms around herself and leaned forward. "The Josie confessional." She sighed. "I'm not religious. Isn't that funny? I'm not religious, but when I wanted to talk to someone, I didn't think of a therapist . . . I thought of a pastor." She reached for her glass and finished the whiskey, then poured another portion. "I'm a mess."

"You're not a mess. Grief is messy."

She stared at her drink as if she were having trouble recognizing what it was, or perhaps she was hoping the amber liquid held the answer. After a few seconds, she raised her eyes to mine. "I don't miss Jason at all. Not even a teeny tiny bit. Isn't that odd?"

"Maybe you're missing him so much you're angry, and all you can feel at this point is the anger. Later, you'll feel sad."

"Do you think so?" she asked, sounding dubious.

"I don't know."

She sighed again, heavily, then swigged the whiskey, finishing it in one gulp. She coughed, a small one, then placed the glass neatly on the tray.

"Time to go." She unwrapped her legs and reached for a boot, nearly toppling off the couch. "Whoa. I better take it slow."

Her motions were methodical, as if she were thinking about each step first, then doing it. *Pull the boot toward me. Straighten it so the toes face out. Put my foot in. Tighten the laces. Tie a bow.* She got her boots on, then stood and clutched the sofa's back to steady herself. She experimented with walking, and when she didn't collapse, she smiled.

"All right, then," she said. "I'm on a roll. Thanks, Josie, for your above-and-beyond hospitality to a near stranger."

She was having trouble with sibilants. "Hospitality" sounded more like "hoshpitality," and "stranger" came out as "shranger."

"How about topping off that whiskey with a coffee before you go? We can make cappuccino or espresso, if you prefer."

"No, thanks. I have to go. My mother will be worried. I didn't tell her I was leaving the hotel. I just slammed out of the room. Chuck and Sara will be worried, too. I blew off lunch."

"No prob. I'll drive you."

"No need. I left my car at the church. I'll walk back and drive myself."

"Better not. Whiskey and steering wheels don't mix."

She glared at me. "You're so judgmental, Josie."

"Sorry about that . . . but I can't let you drive."

"It's none of your business!"

"It is, actually. Since I served you whiskey, there's a liability thing. I can't let you get behind the wheel."

She walked toward the door, stepping carefully, trying to hide her sway, keeping her chin up. "I'm fine."

"I'm sure you are. Regardless, let's agree to let me do the driving."

"No."

I suspected that trying to reason with someone in her condition was a waste of time. "Please . . . let me drive or call you a cab."

"Forget it."

"I can't."

She was not amused. She stomped down the spiral staircase. Two steps down, she slipped and flew outward, landing hard on her bottom three steps down, the backs of her calves slamming into the riser.

"Heather!" I ran to her, stepping around her and going down three more steps. I looked up at her. "Are you all right?"

Without saying a word, she stood up, grasped the iron railing and walked down the stairs one at a time, placing her feet carefully, consciously. She walked slowly across the warehouse. I trailed behind. When she reached the warehouse door, she ripped it open, sprinted across the office, and darted outside. I stayed close. She was running fast now, faster than I would have thought she could, heading for the woods. The strong midday sunlight penetrated the tall bare trees that stretched high above our heads, dappling the path, lighting the way.

When we reached the church parking lot, she was half a dozen steps ahead of me. She ran straight for her car, a Lexus. Her chest heaving from her exertion, she poked her car key at the lock, unable to fit it in, forgetting, perhaps, that all she had to do was push the unlock button on the remote.

When she spotted me coming up behind her, she spun sideways, hurled her key ring into the side garden, crossed her arms over her chest, and said, "Happy now?"

"It's okay," I said, breathing hard. I stood ten feet away from her and patted the air, hoping to reassure her, to communicate that I had no intention of attacking or trapping her.

She closed her eyes. "I'm sorry," she said so softly I had trouble hearing her. Tears streamed down her cheeks. "I'm sorry." Her voice lowered further until her words were indistinguishable, a shadow of a sound, a hint of intention. "I'm sorry," I think she said. "I'm sorry. I'm so sorry." She collapsed onto her car's hood, weeping, her sobs coming in big, gusty waves. A few seconds later, without warning, she began pounding the hood, the thuds echoing and reverberating in the still, dry air. She stopped as suddenly as she started and slid down the car, landing in a heap on the ground, her tears falling silently now. She slapped the pavement; then her fingers curled into fists and she pounded it.

Ted stepped out of the back door and smiled, glad to see me, unaware of the drama playing out behind the car. His hairline had receded some over the last year, and he'd gained another few pounds on his already comfortable frame. He looked cherubic.

"Josie!" he called. "What a nice surprise."

"It's Heather." I pointed to where she lay. "She's pretty upset."

His expression shifted from jovial to concerned, and he hurried across the lot to join me at Heather's car. When he saw her lying on the ground, her hands in loose fists now, still softly pounding the asphalt, he stopped short and looked at me, an unspoken question in his eyes.

"She walked through the woods to my place. She had a few drinks, enough so I thought she shouldn't drive. One thing led to another . . . I don't know what to do."

Ted made a tch-tch sound and reached for Heather's arms. "It's all right, my dear. Come inside."

Heather didn't resist him, but she didn't assist him either. She remained a deadweight. I took one arm while Ted took the other, and together we hoisted her upright and leaned her against the hood. Rivulets of mascara crisscrossed her cheeks. The three of us walked slowly toward the church. Inside, Ted led the way to the kitchen, a cheerful old-fashioned room.

As Ted got her situated at the round oak table, I said, "I'll get her keys. She tossed them in the bushes."

"Good idea," Ted said, squatting beside her. "I'm glad you came back, Heather."

"I'm sorry."

I slipped out of the room, relieved that Ted was there, knowing I was out of my depth.

I found the keys under a hydrangea bush and scooped them up, then hurried back to the kitchen. Heather wasn't there.

"Heather wanted to clean up," Ted explained. "I asked Pam to go with her."

"Good. I suspect Pam is just what the doctor ordered." Ted's secretary, Pam, was closer to seventy than sixty, a latter-day hippie. Her gray hair reached nearly to her waist, and she usually wore peasant dresses and Birkenstocks. She had a warm nonjudgmental smile. Heather couldn't be in better hands.

"I agree." Ted shook his head sadly. "Grief is a spiteful beast with sharp teeth and long claws."

I handed him her keys. "I'm glad she's here with you."

"Hopefully she'll agree to stay for a while, to rest and talk some more."

"She told me she was concerned about her mom, that she left the hotel without telling her she was going. And some friends. Jason's best friend and his wife. She said she blew off lunch with them."

"I'll ask if she'd like us to call them."

"When she's ready to go, I'll be glad to drive her."

"Thank you, Josie. We can see she gets back safely."

"You're a wonderful man, Ted."

His cheeks reddened at the compliment, and his eyes brightened. "I don't know about that. I just empathize. Losing someone you love suddenly—I think it's among the hardest things we have to endure."

Memories of loss pricked my heart. *Oh, Dad.*

"She'll be fine," Ted continued, and from his expression, I could tell he was trying to reassure me. "We all learn to cope. We all have a far greater capacity to cope than we realize."

"Coping takes such energy," I said.

Ted patted my arm. "It does, doesn't it? Have you ever noticed, though, how you cope and cope and cope, and then one day, you realize you're not coping anymore? You've pushed through the grief or whatever and you're on the other side, back in the land of the living."

"The land of the living—to be awake, to be aware, to care once again."

"To be with God. Psalm 27. If you'll wait just a moment, let me ask Heather if she'd prefer that you call her mother, not us. She might want her presence here to remain private. You can honestly say that she decided to spend a little time chatting with you."

"Of course." I smiled, amused at his earnest effort to stick to the truth. "And what will I say when her mom asks to speak to her?"

He smiled back. "That she asked you to call since she doesn't feel like explaining anything just yet."

"And her mom will be in the next cab across town."

"Where you can greet her with the news that Heather decided to go for a walk."

"You're a smooth talker for a preacher-man."

"Thanks," Ted said, smiling, pleased. "I'll leave you here while I check with her."

He went upstairs, and I sat at the table to wait, idly stroking the satiny, well-rubbed wood. The old-style white tiles that ran from the floor to the ceiling gleamed. The oak floor was covered here and there with cheerful multicolored rag rugs. The stainless steel tables and appliances—the only upgrades in the place—glistened.

Pam came in, smiling. "Heather's calmer now. She asked Ted to call her mom. Before you go, would you like a cup of tea?"

"No, thanks. I need to get back." I stood up. "How is she, really?"

"Jason's death hit her hard. She seems to think she should be able to carry on as usual with no break in her routine." Pam shook her head and sighed. "She just keeps saying she's sorry."

"She's lucky to be here with you and Ted."

We shook hands, and I made my way to the pathway, glad to have a little time to think, glad to smell the fresh new leaves and budding bushes, the scent of hope. As I walked, I wondered what exactly Heather was sorry about—her emotional meltdown, her unbridled anger, or something else.

CHAPTER NINE

I was still at the church when Ellis stopped by my office, and he didn't leave anything except a message—call him ASAP.

"I'm sorry I missed you," I told him and thought of Heather. Her apologies stood out because she repeated the words over and over again and because no one knew what she was referring to, but lots of people, especially women, use those words as filler, as accommodation. "Something came up. I'm here now."

"Great. I'm on my way."

Ten minutes later, Ellis delivered the shattered remains of what I feared was the Fabergé Spring Egg snow globe. He'd placed five one-gallon clear plastic evidence bags in a cardboard box large enough for boots, which he lowered onto the guest table in the front office. He held up one of the bags and read the label.

"Enamel."

He returned the bag to the box and picked up another.

"Metal."

He repeated the process with the other three bags: "Wood," followed by "Gems," ending with "Glass."

He slid the box toward me. "The techs asked me to tell you that while they tried to segregate the pieces by material, they're certain there are crossovers."

"Understood." I eyed the bags. "This is even worse than I expected."

"All you can do is the best you can do."

"So true. Any news about Ana's house key? Or the soil?"

"The technicians tell me they're working as quickly as they can."

"Any progress with the interviews?"

"Everyone is being cooperative."

Ellis had a gift for nonanswers.

"Even Peter?" I asked, smiling, teasing him.

He smiled back. "People get emotional. We understand that."

I couldn't think of a way to phrase a question so he'd answer it. Instead, I took photos of the bags and printed out a receipt.

Ellis sat to read it. He signed it and handed it over. "Are you going to be able to tell anything from this junk?"

I smiled, a cocky one this time. "Oh, yeah."

I started with the enamel. Wearing plastic gloves and using tweezers, I extracted the largest piece, about the size of my thumbnail. The topside was pink, and the reverse side was shiny gold. Using the faded photographs attached to the previous appraisal as a reference, I compared the color. It was impossible to tell if they matched. The enamel I was holding was a delicate seashell pink. The one in the photos had yellowed, as expected from eighteen-year-old Polaroids.

"What do you say, Hank?" I asked. "Shall I get right to the acid test?"

He'd flopped over in his basket and was lying on his back, with his four paws sticking up in the air. He was solidly asleep. I had to resist an impulse to give him a tummy rub.

I applied a drop of nitric acid to the gold back and watched it turn milky.

I gawked. "What?"

I tweezed out a second piece, this one the size of my pinky nail, and applied the nitric acid. It, too, turned an opaque cloudy white.

I leaned back in my chair, my mouth hanging open, stunned. The metal wasn't gold.

I opened the bag labeled WOOD. The cracked and split pieces were mostly the size of large splinters. Holding one sideways to view a cross-section, it was evident I wasn't looking at solid wood. A thin veneer of what appeared to be mahogany covered what I was certain was medium-density fiber-board.

"MDF?" I said aloud. "How can that be?"

It was possible that Fabergé used a base made of cheap wood to support the illusion that his egg was an inexpensive novelty, but there was no way he could have used a product that wasn't invented until the 1960s, more than forty years after his death.

I turned the splinter over, staring at it. It was possible that the base had been replaced. Why? Had someone broken it at some point over the years? I consulted the past appraisal. The base was listed as solid mahogany. How could the base have broken without damaging the glass dome and the egg? I shook my head. It didn't make any sense. I looked back at the enamel pieces. It seemed that the entire thing was a fake. *But why?* I shook my head. I didn't know enough to begin figuring out the why of the situation; what I needed to do was finish analyzing what I had in front of me. I needed information, not conjectures.

I picked up the phone and dialed Nate Blackmore, our first call for jewelry appraisals. He was in and could see me right away.

Blackmore's Jewelers, the finest jewelry store on the seacoast, bar none, had been in its current location, across from the village green, for ninety-four years. It was still owned and operated by the Blackmore family. Although they'd brought it up to date with recessed lighting and new, thick carpet, not much else had changed, not the cherrywood paneling, the comfortable plush seating, or the Bach sonatas playing softly in the background. Nate, the current owner's grandson, was about thirty. He looked older because of his professional grace and polished manners.

"Can we go in the back?" I asked, after exchanging greetings.

He pretended my request was routine. "Sure."

The back office at Blackmore's was a large room designed for work, not show. Tall file cabinets lined one wall; two computer stations ranged along another. Four blue upholstered chairs and a small round table were positioned off to the side, and an oversized cherry desk was littered with papers, folders, and sample books.

Once we were settled on guest chairs, I extracted the plastic bag labeled GEMS and placed it on the table between us. Shards of bloodred, iridescent pink, creamy white, and pale green stones jostled one another in the bag.

"Are any of these real?" I asked.

He lifted the bag and stared at the colorful, broken pieces, twirling the bag this way, then that way. The stones glimmered as they caught the light.

"I'll need some time. Not too long. I'll call you this afternoon."

I thanked him, accepted his receipt, and returned to work, eager to continue my examination, to see if I could figure out what I had. I was pretty sure I knew what I didn't have—a genuine Fabergé egg.

•   •   •

By the time Nate called around four to report that all of the gemstones were, in fact, colored glass, cheap crystals, and painted rocks, I'd found additional anomalies. Comparing the materials in my possession with those listed on the previous appraisal, I was able to confirm that the object I was assessing was different in every way, from the MDF and veneer used on the base to the glycerin inside the dome to the Harber clasp attached to the egg. I called Ellis and told him what I'd discovered.

"The oily substance found at the crime scene was glycerin, so now we know where it came from," he said. "Is there any way you can date the replica in your possession, assuming that's what you have?"

"Not any closer than post-2005, which was when the Harber Fastener Company opened its doors. The screws are modern, but impossible to date exactly. They adhere to the Unified Thread Standard, which came into play in the late 1940s, but obviously, that doesn't help us. The other materials are also modern, but even using the most scientifically advanced chemical dating technology, it's unlikely we can narrow it down further than 2005."

"So all we know is that we've dealing with a phony."

"Right, or rather, all we know is that I'm not looking at a Fabergé egg or a snow dome fabricated by Fabergé. It might be a replica of the Spring Egg snow globe—as you say, a phony—or it might be some other object. There's no way to know. I tried piecing together the dome and the egg, but I can't. Too many of the pieces are too small."

"How is this related to Jason's murder?"

"I don't know . . . but . . ." I paused, thinking how to express my hesitation. "Coincidences are funny things. I mean, I know they happen, but . . ."

"Yeah . . . 'but' is the right word. Obviously, I need to tell Ana about this, to get her take on it, to see if she has an explanation. I'm certain she'll have questions I can't answer. Stefan, too. Technical questions about how you verified the egg and snow globe weren't real, what the materials actually are, and so on. I'd prefer to interview them in a neutral environment, not the police station. I'm thinking the hotel might be a good choice. They've checked into the same hotel where the bridal party and most of the wedding guests are staying, the Pelican. If I set something up, will you join me there?"

"Of course."

He paused. "What do you think is going on?"

"I think someone created a replica of the Fabergé Spring Egg snow globe during the last nine years so they could sell the real egg or the jewels without anyone catching on. We should publicize the theft. This is major."

"How much are we talking?"

"A known Fabergé egg, and by known, I mean authenticated and with clear title, would sell for around twenty million dollars, maybe more."

"Seriously?"

"Yes."

"Twenty million?"

"Or more."

"I'll call the FBI giving you as a contact for further information about the object. Will you notify the appropriate antiques sites?"

"Yes. Listing you as the contact for details about the theft. I'll ask Nate Blackmore to post a listing of the jewels, too, on sites he knows about. They're unique."

"In case someone destroyed the egg to get to the jewels."

"Exactly."

"Twenty million?" he asked.

"Hard to imagine, isn't it?"

"Impossible, actually. You used the word 'known' before. Is Ana's egg known?"

"No. It comes with a great narrative, but there's no evidence it's true."

"What would someone be able to sell it for?"

"A few hundred thousand, maybe as much as a million."

"Who'd buy it?"

"Megarich people without ethics. Drug lords. Gangsters. Modern-era robber barons." I shrugged. "There are a lot of Russian megamillionaires who might be interested in repatriating it on the QT."

Ellis didn't speak for several seconds. "This is a mess." I could hear him breathing. "Shouldn't Stefan have noticed that it's a fake when he packed it up?"

"Only if he actually looked at it. You know what I mean, right? You see something every day for enough years, you simply don't notice it anymore. In a rush of packing, I can see how he might have placed a sheet of bubble wrap on top of it, taping it as he rolled it up, which means he might well have never actually looked at it."

"What a situation." Another pause. "It was on display in the family home . . . is that right?"

"So Ana told me. Heather described the house as a fortress."

"The family home . . . that sure points to Ana, Stefan, or Peter."

"Or any visitor who might have an opportunity to snatch it. Just 'cause you build a fortress doesn't mean it can't be breached. Maybe Stefan is as loosey-goosey in allowing access to his house as Ana is to her cottage. Whoever took it wouldn't need it for long. A day maybe, just enough time to allow a craftsman to take measurements and photographs. I'm guessing here, but I bet that when Heather was dating Peter, she visited his dad's home."

"Do you think Heather killed Jason?"

I'm sorry, she kept saying. *Sorry for what?* "No. Do you?"

"We're looking into all possibilities."

Another evasion, no surprise. "You're so forthcoming."

"It occurs to me that since we're going public about the snow globe, we should go all the way," he said, ignoring my comment. "Tips from the community can be very helpful."

"Are you going to release it to the media?"

"Not me. Too official. Some people get spooked when it's a police matter."

"Especially people who might have contacts in the black market."

"Especially those people."

"Those people won't talk to me either."

"They might. They might want to get their side of the story out there. Maybe whoever took it doesn't think they did anything wrong. It's possible they think it's unfair that the egg has been passed down from mother to daughter."

I understood his point. Sibling rivalry was part and parcel of my business. "Peter."

"Will you tell Wes?"

This wasn't the first time Ellis had drafted me as his amanuensis, and I was glad to do it. Telling Wes what was going on would go a long way toward satisfying his quid pro quo demands. "Yes."

"Okay."

"Thanks, Josie. I'll call you when I know about meeting at the Pelican."

I placed the receiver in the cradle and turned to Hank. He was purring in his sleep, his front paws twitching. He was dreaming, perhaps, of chasing a mouse.

"You're so beautiful, Hank," I whispered, not wanting to disturb him.

I posted notices of the missing egg on all three of the proprietary industry Web sites we subscribed to, one of which fed directly into a lost-art database maintained by Interpol, then called Nate.

"Tell me it ain't so," he said after I explained why I was calling.

"Isn't it awful to think about?" I sighed.

"Give me the list."

I rattled off jewel type, cut, karat, and all the other details the appraisal specified and gave him Ellis's number for the law enforcement contact. He agreed to send me the links once he'd uploaded the reports, and we promised to stay in touch.

I squared up the Polaroids. The images were so faded, they weren't useful for identifying anything, but I wondered if an artisan could bring the colors back. Anyone can learn to use Photoshop and insert colors where none existed or change colors or textures at will, but it took a master craftsman to understand how colors changed over time and re-create a true rendition of the original. I called down to Gretchen.

"Who are we using for photo retouching these days?"

"Matthew Hughes."

"I'm going to scan in some old shots. He needs to repair the coloration. It's crucial he gets as close to the original as possible. Ask him to rush it, all right?"

Ten minutes later, she IM'd me that Matthew would have them back to me by ten Monday morning, the fastest he could manage. I okayed it, then called Wes and got him.

"You're a hot potato, Josie!" he said after I filled him in. "Fantastic."

"You said you wanted some quid for your pro quo. I'd say that after this exclusive, I've got a nice little credit balance going."

"I don't know about that."

Give a reporter a few bars and he wants a symphony.

I stood up and stretched, then went and sat cross-legged on the floor near Hank's basket watching him sleep. I stroked his tummy, down, then up. Down, then up. Down, then up. Still asleep, he rolled over, ready for me to rub his side.

I couldn't see how the counterfeit Fabergé Spring Egg snow globe could have led to Jason's murder, which meant either it hadn't or I lacked information.

I gave Hank a little kiss, pausing midsmooch, as a research idea came to me.

"Let's do it."

I told Hank he was a very good boy, then hurried upstairs to my private office. If my idea worked, I was about to learn more about the shattered snow globe.

CHAPTER TEN

I typed "snow globe" into our database and learned that we had twelve in stock. I wasn't surprised we had that many since they were steady sellers at our weekly tag sale.

Ellis called at five to ask me to meet him in the Pelican coffee shop at six. I agreed and called Ty to tell him I'd be home late. I got his voice mail and left a message. I glanced at the clock on my monitor. I had forty-five minutes before I'd need to leave.

Unless there's a good business reason to do otherwise, like covering the phones, or meeting with a client, or making a scheduled delivery, I let my staff set their own hours. Fred was a night owl, often coming into work around noon and staying late into the evening. Since he'd begun dating Suzanne, he joined her for an early dinner at the Blue Dolphin two or three times a week, arriving around four, before the after-work crowd flooded the lounge for drinks and the early-bird diners descended on the dining room for dinner. If today was one of those days, he wouldn't be in. I picked up the phone and dialed his extension.

He was in. I asked him to meet me at the worktable.

I held up the plastic bag of glass shards so Fred could see it. "I have a crazy idea, and I need your input. I want to figure out how large a snow dome this glass would make. If I take an existing dome and weigh it and then weigh this Baggie, am I comparing apples to apples?"

He stared at the bag. I could almost see the wheels in his brain turning. He raised his eyes to mine. "It depends on the thickness of the glass."

"Which we can measure. I've already measured several pieces in the bag and tagged them. They're uniform in thickness."

"Really?" Fred pushed up his glasses. "That's not good."

Given that antique glass was handblown, it was subject to vagaries of breath and heat and humidity and craftsmanship. It was never uniform.

"I know. I have so much evidence that both the egg and the snow globe—if that's what these are—are modern reproductions, I can't even tell you. And not very good repros, either."

He shook his head, commiserating at the loss.

"These have glycerin on them," I added. "We need to compensate for that, too."

"If you can live with a ballpark estimate, your idea should work. Shall I check if we have any cheap, modern snow globes in stock?"

"I already have." I explained what I'd found in the database, and he set off to gather a few samples, starting with the least expensive.

Removing a snow globe dome was a risk; we might be able to put it back into salable condition, but we might not. I got a plastic tub and canvas aprons from the supply cabinet. I was tying the apron when Fred came back with a souvenir snow globe from Tampa dated 1953. We'd priced it at twelve dollars. He put his apron on.

"All right, then," I said. "Here goes nothing."

I placed the snow globe in a tub, slid my fingers into plastic gloves, and eased a hard plastic chisel under the glass lip. I tapped it with a rubber mallet, one gentle tap. Nothing. I tapped a few more times, without loosening it at all.

"I think you'll need to use a metal one," Fred said.

"I agree." Wedging the metal tip under the glass overhang, I tapped the handle with the mallet, then switched to the flat end of a claw hammer, and the seal broke. Fred lifted the dome. Mineral oil poured into the tub. The innards—miniature palm trees, carefully arranged and glued-down sand, and stacked crates of oranges—were undamaged. All the plastic snowy bits were intact, floating in the oil. Fred laid the dome on a piece of wax paper and measured the thickness of the glass. It was about a sixty-fourth of an inch thicker than my shards.

"We can use it for reference, at least," I said.

"True." Fred placed it on the digital scale. "Just over six ounces."

I placed the plastic bag on the scale. "This is so inexact. Between the thickness of the glass, the glycerin coating some pieces, and the weight of the plastic bag, to say nothing of my certainty that there are plenty of pieces missing—" I broke off, my eyes on the scale's display. "Am I reading this right? Fourteen and a half ounces?"

"Yes . . . so the snow dome was, theoretically at least, more than twice as big as this little guy from Tampa."

"Which is consistent with the size required to cover an Imperial egg. Those were the big ones. Go get the largest snow globe we have."

While Fred went to the shelves, I retrieved a second plastic tub and put on a fresh pair of gloves.

"This one has some heft to it," he said, cupping the snow globe, a 1970s Christmas scene showing Santa Claus in his sleigh flying high above a nameless city's rooftops.

It was huge, about the size of a honeydew melon, but inexpertly made and painted. Santa's features were crudely rendered, and the paint was sloppily applied. We'd priced it at fifteen dollars, less than a third of what it would have fetched had it been more expertly crafted. I used the same tools and had the same happy result. Nothing broke. All the mineral oil and white flecks were salvaged.

Fred slid the dome onto the scale. "Twelve and a quarter ounces."

"So the broken one is even bigger than this."

"Right."

"Good. This is helpful. Let's weigh the oil, then I've got to scoot. Sorry to leave you to put the two Humpty Dumptys back together again."

"No problem."

We weighed an empty tub, then the two that contained varying amounts of oil and "snow," and deducted the tub's weight to learn the difference. The smaller one, from Tampa, weighed just over two ounces; Santa Claus came in at a full eight ounces.

"That's a lot of goo," Fred remarked.

I stared at the viscous liquid, implications sparking through my brain like live wires.

Fred said something else, but I didn't hear him.

"Josie?"

I peeled off the gloves, untied my apron, and dropped everything on the floor. "Sorry . . . I need to go."

I grabbed my tote bag and ran for the door.

•   •   •

I peeked through a plastic palm tree in the entryway to see into the Pelican's coffee shop. Ana, Stefan, and Peter sat next to one another along one side of a round table set for six, each in his or her own world. Ana, frowning, slid her knife closer to her teaspoon, lining them up, then moved them apart, aligning the tops, then the bottoms, as if she were working a geometry challenge. Stefan stared into the middle distance, a million miles away. His lips were puckered, the corners of his mouth pointed to the floor. Peter looked at nothing, then scanned the room. He crossed his arms over his chest and screwed his lips into a cynical smirk. He kept scanning the room, left to right, looking for I didn't know what.

Ellis wasn't at the table, a good thing. I needed to talk to him privately, urgently, before he confronted the Yartsins.

I backed out of the palm tree and returned to the lobby, texting Ellis as I walked. "In lobby by front door. I have news."

His reply came within seconds: "2 min."

While I was waiting, Wes called. I let it go to voice mail, then listened to his message. "Heather's mom won't talk to reporters, but maybe she'll talk to you. What do you think? Give me a call."

Ellis pushed through a revolving door, spotted me, and headed my way. "Are you all right?" he asked.

"Yes. I snuck a look in the dining room. The Yartsins are at a table already."

Heather and one of the older women I'd seen at the police station crossed the lobby from the elevator to the revolving door without seeing us. *Her mom,* I thought. Heather's eyes were red and puffy. Her mom cast worried looks at her. I toyed with saying hello to Heather, getting an introduction to her mother, but decided to skip it. I didn't know whether she'd told her mom about talking to me.

I looked up at Ellis. He was waiting for me to continue, as patient as ever.

"Stefan lied," I said.

Ellis cocked his head, surprised. "Stefan?"

"It may be nothing."

"What did he lie about?"

"Flying here with the snow globe. He couldn't have. It's too big." I described how Fred and I estimated its size, then added, "Only snow globes the size of tennis balls or smaller—deemed to contain less than three point four ounces of liquid—are allowed in carry-on luggage. Unless he took a private plane, Stefan didn't fly here from Detroit."

"How do you know he didn't check a bag?"

"He said he was a 'travel-light sort of guy,' so I assumed it. Maybe I'm wrong and he did." I shook my head. "No way. It would be foolhardy to send a Fabergé egg in checked luggage."

"What else?" Ellis asked.

"Nothing. But if you lie about one thing . . ."

"Anything more about the snow globe?"

"No."

He didn't speak for several seconds. "Wait here, will you? I need to make a call."

"Sure."

He pushed through the revolving door and disappeared to the left. I wondered who he was calling. Detective Brownley, I guessed, to get the investigation into how Stefan traveled to Rocky Point under way.

I people-watched while I waited. Most people seemed happy. A little girl about seven in a dark pink satin dress giggled and played with her long pink sash, holding the ends out like wands and twirling like a ballerina. A woman about my age, maybe her mom, wearing a glove-fit navy blue sheath, looked on, proud and pleased. Two men in suits joined them, and, chatting, they headed out. One man was about the woman's age, her husband, I figured. The other was older, her dad. A wedding. They were on their way to a wedding, and the little girl was a junior bridesmaid. One wedding canceled. Another on schedule. Two older women sat on club chairs, their heads close together, laughing so hard one of them was wiping her eyes. A middle-aged couple strolled from the coffee shop toward the elevator, holding hands. Chuck and Sara each wheeled a suitcase to the front desk. They'd planned to stay over one more night, I guessed, but changed their minds. Time to go home.

Life rolls on.

Ellis reappeared by my side. "All right, then. I'm not going to mention that Stefan couldn't have flown with the snow globe in this discussion. When we're done, I'll invite Stefan to the station house for some one-on-one conversation. Can you come? I want you in the observation room, in case antiques-related questions come up."

I glanced at the clocks mounted over the reception desk. There were five of them, set to different time zones, grandly implying that Rocky Point was akin to the other cities showcased. London. Tokyo. Sydney. Los Angeles. Rocky Point.

It was five after six. I had a feeling I wouldn't be dancing tonight.

"Sure," I said.

CHAPTER ELEVEN

Stefan stood as soon as he saw us walking through the dining room. Peter remained seated. Ana tried to smile, but it was a wan effort. She looked sad and stoic.

"Thanks for agreeing to meet with me," Ellis said to them, holding my chair. "You know Josie." They nodded and murmured, except Peter, who didn't react at all. Once I was situated, Ellis sat down. "I have news for you about the Fabergé egg snow globe. I asked Josie to join us in case you have questions about it I can't answer." He looked from one to the other of them. "The smashed pieces found on and around Jason's body—they're not from the Fabergé egg."

"What?" Ana exclaimed.

Ellis held up his hand like a traffic cop. "I know. I can't tell you what they are—but I can tell you what they're not. No insurance settlement will be forthcoming."

"What are you implying?" Ana asked. "I don't want the insurance. I want the egg."

Peter's eyes narrowed to slits. "He's implying you were trying to pull a fast one."

Ellis shrugged. "If you knew the real egg had been destroyed, this might appeal to you as an option for getting some compensation at least."

Ana shook her head. "If I knew it had been destroyed, I wouldn't need to pretend. I could simply submit a claim."

"She's right," Stefan said. "What am I missing?"

Ellis's tone was as calm as ever. "Nothing. I'm just considering all options. And one option is that for whatever reason, someone got a repro made specifically so Ana could submit an insurance claim." He opened his palms to the ceiling. "The real Fabergé egg snow globe may be intact. It's possible the plan was to sell it privately, while also submitting an insurance settlement."

"That's crazy," Ana said, sounding confused. "The insurance company would catch on."

"Perhaps the person who undertook this misadventure didn't think of that."

"Now he's calling you stupid," Peter said.

"Whether he's calling Ana names or not," Stefan said, "is beside the point. I brought the Fabergé Spring Egg snow globe to Rocky Point myself. I would have noticed if it was a fake. My God, how can you think I wouldn't have noticed?"

Ellis focused on Stefan. "Someone switched it out."

Stefan raised his chin. "I don't believe it."

"Do you want the technical details?"

"Yes."

Ellis turned toward me. "Josie?"

"The evidence is overwhelming. I'll be detailing it all in a formal report, of course, but here's the short version." I described the fake gemstones, the acid test, the MDF, and the modern-era latch. As I spoke, I watched their faces. Stefan's mouth fell open. Ana's eyes grew round. Peter's brow wrinkled.

Stefan leaned back, convinced yet incredulous. "I don't understand how it could have happened." He shook his head. "I have a state-of-the-art security system at home, and always have. I update it whenever new technology becomes available. I'm diligent about turning it on."

"How about workers?" Ellis asked.

"None."

Ana touched his arm. "You had the downstairs painted, Dad. When was that? Five years ago? Six?"

"So what? I cleared everything out. I relocated the snow globe to my bedroom."

"If a switch occurred, it happened post-Christmas," Peter said.

Everyone looked at him.

"I took it out over Christmas to show Toni and that friend of hers from out of town, what was her name? Carly, right? Carly Summers. She was in from Massachusetts to visit her old friend, Toni." He looked at Ellis. "Toni is a new neighbor. I may not have an artist's eye, but I guarantee I would have noticed peeling veneer and a cheesy latch." He shrugged. "Ask them. They'll remember."

Ellis made a note. "I will. Thanks." He gazed out the window, then turned back to the group. "How about a cleaning lady?"

"I clean the house myself," Stefan said.

"Other guests? Friends for dinner?"

"My friends aren't thieves," Stefan said, outraged.

Ellis exhaled. "With all respect . . . you're saying it couldn't have happened. I'm telling you it did."

Stefan shook his head and examined his knuckles. Peter pressed his lips together and didn't comment.

Ana said, "But—" She broke off, her muddled thoughts evident from her expression. "How—?"

Ellis waited.

After a few seconds, Peter pushed back his chair and stood up. He glared at Ellis. "This is bull. I looked at the snow globe last Christmas. It was real. I don't know what's going on, but I'll tell you what I think. Neither my dad nor my sister switched out a replica. Nor did I. So if it really is a fake, someone, not us, is pulling a fast one—or trying to."

"Who?" Ellis asked.

"How am I supposed to know?"

"You're the one throwing around the charges."

"Right—talk about blame the victim. Except I'm not the victim. Ana is." He turned to Ana. "I'm outta here. If you're smart, you'll call a lawyer before they end up charging you with murder." He strode toward the lobby.

"What?" Ana exclaimed. "Murder!" Ana watched until Peter was out of sight, then turned toward Ellis. "I can't think." She pressed her hands into her eyes. "Dad?"

Stefan raised his eyes to her face.

"What do I do now?" she asked.

"I don't know," he said, dropping his eyes again.

"Oh, God," she whispered as the reality began to sink in. "This is just too much. Too much." Her shoulders began to shake.

Stefan patted her back softly. "It'll all right, Ana. It'll be fine."

Ellis watched them for a moment, then said, "I know it's hard to—" He stopped talking and stood as Chef Ray approached the table. Ray looked serious but not stern. He stopped beside Ana, taking in that she was crying.

Ray glanced in our direction, then placed his hand on her shoulder. "Ana?"

She dropped her hands and looked up at him. "Oh, Ray!" She swallowed hard. "I'm so glad you're here."

"You're Chef Ray?" Ellis stood and extended his hand. "Ellis Hunter, Rocky Point police chief. Josie raves about your food."

Ray half-smiled at me, then shook Ellis's hand. He turned to Stefan. "Is everything all right?"

Stefan looked up. "No."

Ellis pointed to a chair next to Ana and Ray slid into it.

Ana leaned her head against his shoulder, tears shimmering on her lashes. "Thank you for coming." She looked at Ellis. "I called and asked him to meet me here. I was certain you were going to deliver bad news." She sighed. "I was right."

Ray took her hand in his.

Ellis stood up. "Ana, I'll leave you to explain what's going on. Stefan, do you have a minute? I want to show you something outside."

"Of course." He stood up. He turned to Ana. "Will you be all right if I leave you for a few minutes?"

"Yes." She smiled, a wavering one but a strong effort. She pressed her head deeper into the crook of Ray's shoulder. "Especially since Ray is here."

Ray leaned in to kiss her cheek.

Ana looked at me, swallowing tears. "Can you find it, Josie? Can you find out what happened?"

"Maybe. With luck. You know I'll do my best."

"About what?" Peter said, reappearing as abruptly as he'd left.

"Finding out what happened to the Fabergé egg," Ellis said.

Ana reached a hand toward me, then withdrew it. "Thank you, Josie."

I nodded, then followed Ellis and Stefan into the lobby. As we passed the plastic palm tree, I looked back. Ana's head was still nestled in Ray's shoulder.

CHAPTER TWELVE

The Rocky Point police station observation room is about twenty feet long and narrow, maybe eight feet across. There's a window at the rear overlooking the back parking lot. A beige sheer curtain blocks the view but not the light. Orange faux-granite Formica countertops stretch the length of the room on both sides under one-way windows that allow observers to see and/or hear the action in Interview Rooms One and Two, depending on which way they're facing.

Stefan sat alone in Room One. Either the lights weren't on in Room Two or drapes were drawn over the one-way window.

Ellis stood beside me. Officer Meade sat near the door in front of a built-in control panel. Ellis looked at the various audio and recording switches, confirming everything was off.

"Are you all right?" he asked me.

"Yes," I said even though I wasn't. I felt exhausted and hungry, and I was tired of thinking. It had been a long day, and it wasn't over yet.

"Officer Meade will stay with you. If you have any thoughts, if you want me to ask Stefan anything, or if you hear something you know is wrong, text me or tell her and she'll text me. Any questions?"

"No. I'm all set."

"Stefan won't know anyone is behind the window," Ellis said.

"Sure he will. He's not dumb."

"Let me rephrase that: He won't know you're here. He won't be able to see or hear you." He must have seen something in my expression—fatigue, I guessed, though I'd tried to hide it—because he added, "I appreciate your staying, Josie."

"Ty and I were going to go dancing tonight."

"How come?"

"We like dancing."

He smiled. "I mean, what's the occasion?"

"No occasion."

"So you can go tomorrow."

I nodded. "Or the next day."

"Do you need to call Ty? Or do you want me to call, to explain how you're helping us?"

"No need. Thanks, though. One advantage of dating a man who had your job is that he understands what's involved in it."

Ellis patted my shoulder, a friendly gesture. He turned to Officer Meade, standing off to the side. "You ready?"

"Yes, sir."

Ellis stepped out of the room, reappearing ten seconds later in Room One. Officer Meade flipped a switch, and the words AUDIO ON glowed in bright red.

I took a seat as far away from Officer Meade as I could, next to the window, and raised and lowered my shoulders several times, trying to relax. Stefan was drumming his fingers on the table, but looking at his face, I couldn't tell whether he was impatient or irritated or bored.

"Sorry to keep you waiting," Ellis told Stefan.

Stefan stopped drumming. "What's going on, Chief? You said you wanted to talk to me outside the Pelican, and the next thing I know I'm being interrogated by the police chief."

"This is an interview, not an interrogation. Let me just get the logistics out of the way and I'll fill you in." Ellis turned on the video recorders and stated the required information. He asked Stefan to sign a form indicating he'd received the Miranda warning, which he did. "You'll understand why I wanted to talk with you alone when I tell you that we know you didn't fly here from Detroit. We try to protect people's privacy as much as possible."

Stefan shifted in his seat. "I'm not sure I follow you."

"You said you flew in. No doubt you have a good reason for having misspoken. In case that reason is personal, I didn't want to ask you about it in front of your children."

Stefan frowned. "Let's back up a minute. What possible business is it of yours how I got here?"

"On the face of it, none. However, in a murder investigation, any anomaly must be accounted for. Please explain."

"No."

"Why didn't you fly?" Ellis asked again.

"What makes you think I didn't?"

"I've already submitted formal requests to the airlines to review their manifests."

"Doesn't that require a subpoena?"

"Yes."

"How could you get one?"

Ellis shrugged. "In a murder investigation, judges tend to cooperate."

Stefan began drumming his fingers again. "This is absurd. You're going fishing. You have no probable cause."

Ellis was getting annoyed. "Are you a lawyer?"

"No, but I know a good one."

"Is that a threat? Or a request for counsel?"

Stefan pulled himself together, breathing hard, pausing before speaking. "No. It's not a threat." He paused to take in a deep breath. "Nor is it a request for counsel. I don't like being blindsided, that's all. Who does, right? Why don't you try telling me what you told the judge? It's likely you'll find me cooperative."

"Fair enough. The snow globe was too large for carry-on. I don't think you checked a bag. I'm going to learn that you didn't fly, aren't I?"

Stefan didn't reply. From his bland expression, he could have been trying to decide whether he wanted pepperoni or sausage on his pizza.

"I ran the plates on your rental car," Ellis continued. "It's part of the Garrison Rental fleet—I spoke to a nice woman at the Detroit airport, very helpful. You rented it in Michigan and drove here. How come?"

Stefan took in a deep breath and half-smiled. "I felt like a road trip."

"Why did you say you flew?"

"I didn't want the hassle of explaining my change of plans."

"What hassle?"

"Do you have children?"

"No."

"Then you don't know. Kids are work from the minute they're born until forever. If I told Ana and Pete that I was going to drive, they'd have been on me like a tick. They'd want to know why and how come and where was I going to stop en route and did I want company and on and on and on. I chose to avoid all that, so I didn't tell anyone my plans."

"Where did you stop?"

"You want the hotel receipts?"

"Yes. Thank you."

Stefan looked at Ellis as if he thought he was as dim as a 10-watt bulb. "I was being facetious."

Ellis didn't blink. "I wasn't."

"This is unbelievable! Jesus! The first night I stayed at a Holiday Inn in Binghamton. The second night, a no-name place, somewhere near Albany. The receipts are in my room."

"Thank you. I appreciate your cooperation."

"Right," Stefan said, his tone sarcastic. He grasped the edge of the table, ready to stand. "Is that it? Are you done?"

Ellis cocked his head. "No."

Stefan dropped his hands and sat back.

Ellis crossed his right leg over his left knee, Mr. Casual. "If the real reason you drove is unrelated to a crime, I can keep it quiet. A poker game, maybe?"

Stefan stood up in one seamless motion. "What I did on my trip is none of your business." He headed for the door.

Ellis swung his leg down in no hurry and stood up. "I do appreciate your cooperation. Very much. I'll walk you out." He used the remote to turn off both recorders, then led the way out of the interview room.

Five minutes later, Ellis walked me out, too.

"Sorry for wasting your time," he said.

"It wasn't a waste. You had me in reserve in case I was needed."

Ellis smiled at me, and seeing the crinkling lines around his eyes, I realized he was as tired as I was, maybe more. He pushed open the door and took in a deep breath of cool, fresh air.

"Do you know Maurice Charpentier?" he asked out of the blue.

"Maurice? The pastry chef at the Blue Dolphin? I met him briefly. Why?"

"What did you think of him?"

"He seemed, um, I don't know . . . volatile."

Ellis nodded. "Thanks, Josie."

It was after seven by the time I got into my car. The temperature had dropped, and it felt more like winter than spring. I was famished, to-my-bones weary, cold, and cranky. I called Ty.

"Do you still want to go dancing?" I asked.

"Sure. Don't you?"

"No. I feel battered. I'm starving and freezing and I'm sad. I'm really, really sad. I want to change into my pink chenille bathrobe and my fuzzy slippers and have a watermelon martini, a hot bath, and eat. Then I want to go to bed."

"Okay, then. You have a rain check. I'll poke around the fridge and see what I can come up with, foodwise."

"You're wonderful."

"I'm glad you think so."

I felt my eyes well with unexpected tears. I pressed the heels of my hands against my eyes, but the tears kept coming.

"Josie?" Ty said, wondering about the too-long silence.

I gulped. "Sorry."

"You're crying. Do you need me to come get you?"

Yes, I thought. "No," I said. "I'm okay. I'll be home soon."

I listened to the local news as I drove. When I heard Wes's voice, I realized I hadn't returned his call and pulled off to the side of the road.

"You've been at the police station again," Wes said, as omnipresent as ever. "How come?"

"Never mind that now, Wes. I got your message. Do you think I should approach Heather's mom in the morning?"

"Yes. Get her talking about the family. What are Ana and Peter really like? You know . . . get the picture."

I stared out over the dune toward the horizon. The sinking sun cast orange and yellow glitter on the near-black water.

"Josie?"

"I'm here."

"What happened at the station? What's going on?"

"Nothing," I said, snapping out of my funk.

"Heather and her mom have developed a routine. They have breakfast every morning at eight in the Pelican coffee shop. Heather has a fruit plate. Mom has cereal. Maggie says I should eat more fruit and less bacon. What do you think?"

"She's right."

Wes sighed. "At nine, Heather heads to the gym, leaving her mom alone in their room. Guess who also goes to the gym at nine?"

It took me a moment. "Peter?"

"Bingo on that."

"And the hotel can't stop him because he's a registered guest."

"Double bingo, ring the bell! Heather told them this guy freaks her out, and they agreed to post a security guard in the gym from nine to ten. She must have some pull, huh?"

"More like risk mitigation. Once she reported her concern to the hotel, there's an implied liability. What's Peter's reaction to the guard?"

"From what I hear, he ignores the guard and is a perfect gentleman around Heather. Bring your gym clothes and sneak in. Take photos."

"God, Wes."

He chuckled. "They're in room five-twelve, but you should call up. The room is registered under the mom's name—Allison Walker. Hotels don't give out room information willy-nilly, so if you just show up at her door, she may freak out."

"Will do."

"Call me after."

I promised I would, and Wes ended the call with a brisk "Catch ya later." I slipped my phone back into my tote and eased back onto the road.

Talking to Wes helped me refocus. I had work to do. I needed to consider ways and means of tracing the Fabergé egg snow globe, and I needed to think how best to approach Heather's mom, Allison. Nothing might come from either initiative, but doing something was always better than doing nothing. If idleness was the devil's tool, inertia was one of his favorite weapons. I no longer felt like crying; instead, I felt like thinking, and for that I silently thanked Wes.

CHAPTER THIRTEEN

As soon as I pulled into my driveway, Ty stepped onto the porch and stood in the circle of golden light from the overhead fixture. He smiled and waved. I waved back, scrambled out of the car, and ran into his arms. He hugged me tight, then kissed me.

"You're feeling better," he said.

"'Tis true." I took his hand and led the way inside. "What's for dinner?"

"You have options. I pulled a London broil from the freezer—it's thawing in marinade now. Or there's leftover roast chicken."

"I could eat both, I'm so hungry. The roast chicken is ready, so let's go with that."

"Done. I made a salad, but you've got to make the dressing. I don't have your touch."

"It's my mother's secret." I put on a French accent. "And I will not tell you, my darling. To enjoy it, you must let me prepare it for you."

"That's the worst German accent I've ever heard."

"That wasn't German! That was French."

"Oh."

I started laughing, and soon Ty was laughing, too. After a minute, I caught my breath and said with what dignity I could muster, "I'm going to change into my robe." I reached the doorway and looked back over my shoulder with a sassy flair. "M'sieur."

Ty grinned and shook his head. "We're going to have to sign you up for some German lessons. Worst accent I ever heard."

Later, after we'd eaten, I sat on the bench that ran behind my kitchen table while Ty loaded the dishwasher. I was tucked in the far corner leaning against cushy orange and blue pillows. The bench stretched along all of one wall and part of two others to form a U.

"Do you think people can change?" I asked.

He shot me a glance. "Sure, don't you?"

"I don't know." I looked out into the blackness. Streaks of moonlight gave the trees and flowers a silvery luster. "Wes has a girlfriend."

"Who's trying to change him?"

"Who seemingly has changed him. He has a new car. He was wearing a tie. He's eating less bacon."

"That's all superficial stuff. Is he still Wes on the inside?"

I thought about that. "Yes."

"Then it sounds like she's bringing out the best in him, not changing him."

"That's a great way to look at it." I smiled. "You bring out the best in me."

Ty got the dishwasher started, then dried his hands on the linen towel my mom had embroidered with a strawberry pattern.

He sat on the short end of the bench, at right angles to me. "How so?"

"You help me see the best in people. You help me be more patient."

"You're forgetting that I also point out your flaws."

"What flaws?" I asked, feeling fussy. "You've told me you think I'm perfect."

"I think you're perfect for me. That doesn't mean you don't have flaws."

I narrowed my eyes, waiting for him to continue.

"Like your German accent," he said and starting laughing again.

I laughed, too. "You're so right. I admit it."

He stretched his hand toward me, and I took it in mine.

"I love you, Josie. You are perfect."

I kissed his palm. "You're perfect, too."

"We're so lucky," he said.

"What if we change?"

"Then we adapt."

"What if we can't?"

"We will." He squeezed my hand, a love-squeeze. "What's wrong, Josie?"

"I'm scared of change."

He slid along the bench until our shoulders touched. He put his arm around me.

"I'm not worried. You and I love one another. If one of us changes, the other one will adapt."

I laid my head on his shoulder and sighed. "I hope you're right."

● ● ●

At 9:05 A.M. the next morning, with a box of Mandy's Candies in hand, I used a house phone on a console table in the lobby and asked the operator to ring Heather's room. A woman, not Heather, answered. "Hello?"

"Hi. Is Heather there?"

"No, I'm sorry. May I help you? I'm her mother—Allison Walker."

"Oh, hi. I'm Josie Prescott. I met Heather the other day. Ana Yartsin introduced us. I wanted to pay my respects, to tell her how sorry I was about Jason."

"That's awfully nice of you. She'll be back in . . . well . . . I guess it will be an hour or so."

"Oh . . . darn! I should have called ahead. I'm downstairs in the lobby. I'm afraid I'm not going to be able to wait that long, and I really wanted to touch base. I'm wondering . . . would you have a minute? I brought a little something for her."

"Sure. Come on up. Room five-twelve."

I stepped out of the elevator onto the small fifth-floor landing. A sign told me room 512 was to the left, and I turned that way, pausing at a double-wide window that faced the back of the hotel. Through a thick stand of white pines and maples I could see Interstate 95 running parallel to the hotel about a quarter mile away. Straight down, I saw an uninviting pool area. The standard-issue rectangular pool was surrounded by concrete slabs and enclosed by an industrial chain-link fence. A blue plastic tarp, dotted with a winter's worth of bird droppings, twigs, and dead leaves, was lashed over the pool. A four-foot-high weathered picket fence enclosed a work area. I wondered if they set out big tubs of palm trees and strung colorful lights along the fence for the summer season or whether austere was the Pelican's style.

The hallway was austere, too. The carpet featured a kind of paisley pattern in shades of dull brown and dark green, no doubt selected because it hid dirt, and that was the only color in the place. The walls were painted off-white and devoid of artwork. The overhead light fixtures were simple white globes.

I knocked on room 512's door, standing directly in front of the peephole. The same woman I'd seen with Heather at the police station and in the lobby opened the door. She was in her midfifties, with gray hair cut short and skin my mom would have described as peaches and cream. She wore blue jeans and a black turtleneck with silver and turquoise earrings. She was barefoot.

"You're Josie Prescott," she said, smiling. "Stefan pointed you out at the police station. Please come in."

She turned to lead the way to a small table by the window, and I saw that her back pockets were decorated with sparkly crystals arranged in a chevron pattern.

"I was about to order a pot of coffee," she said as we got settled at the table. "Will you join me?"

"Yes, thank you." I handed her the box of chocolates. "I brought this for Heather. Mandy's Candies is Rocky Point's best."

"That's lovely of you," she said, placing the box on one of the two unmade double beds. "Heather will be very appreciative."

The room was as austere as the hallway. The walls were the same plain white. The one painting, a bowl of orangy-pink pears, hung on a wall over the TV. A bedside table stood between the two beds. Lamps on folding gold metal arms were mounted on the back wall.

She called room service and asked them to send up a basket of breakfast rolls with the coffee.

"It's awfully nice of you to stop by." She sat across from me and looked into my eyes. Hers were hazel, green flecked with gold. "Did you know Jason?"

"Not really. I only met him this week. He asked my firm to appraise his chess set collection."

"I didn't know he had one."

I paused. "How's Heather?"

"Not well." She looked at her hands resting on the table. Her fingernails were painted a glossy peach. "To be expected, of course." She raised her eyes and smiled. "I'm a widow. Just about a year now. I'm young, well, relatively young. I'm only fifty-six. Doesn't fifty-five seem young to be widowed?"

"Yes."

She sighed. "It's not. It's the average age a woman is widowed in America. I'm average." She shook her head, a private thought being cast off. "Of course, averages aren't medians. It doesn't take many twenty-year-old widows to shift the numbers."

"You weren't prepared to be a widow any more than Heather was prepared to lose her fiancé."

"That's right." She waved it away. "It's amazing what you can deal with if you have to. Women have great coping skills. More than men, I think."

"My dad was widowed in his forties. He did all right."

She held up her hand, signaling a mea culpa. "I withdraw my chauvinistic comment. Most people have great coping skills."

"Some do. Some don't. I suspect the ability to cope is very individual." I smiled again. "It seems to me that you're not giving yourself enough credit."

"That's kind of you to say."

A rat-a-tat-tat, shave-and-a-haircut knock sounded on the door, and she whip-turned, startled.

"My nerves are shot, still, after a year." She exhaled, smiled, and stood up. "I'm sure it's the coffee."

"Quick service," I said, just for something to say.

Allison let the room service waiter in. He placed a brown plastic tray on the table, had her sign the check, and left.

"Have you known Ana for a long time?" I asked, watching her pour the coffee.

"Oh, my, yes! Since she was a little girl."

The basket of rolls was covered with a cloth napkin. After she passed me a cup, she opened it. There were two croissants, two blueberry muffins, a huge cinnamon bun, and a cherry Danish. A tub of butter and one of strawberry jam were tucked in the middle.

She pointed to it. "Have one . . . or cut off a piece if you'd prefer." She paused for a moment. "Our families had summer houses on the same street on Strawberry Hill. The girls were inseparable, as if they were twins. They were the same age, and they shared interests. They both swam like fish, loved clamming, and would talk and talk and talk about I don't know what for hours on end. They were both readers, too. Such special girls, both of them. I think they were shocked to learn they weren't actually related."

I smiled. "Isn't it wonderful that they're still close. It doesn't always work out that way."

"I agree. Our families, too, are still friends," she said, taking a blueberry muffin from the basket and cutting it in quarters, "although we're not as close as we were when Maria was alive—that's Ana's mom." She ate one of the muffin bits. "Ana went through some rocky patches, of course. Nothing is all smooth sailing."

I tilted my head and opened my eyes a little wider, silently asking for details.

She laughed, a little embarrassed, and sipped her coffee. "I don't think I'm telling tales out of school if I tell you that Stefan can be a bit domineering. Maria mellowed him, and when she died . . . let's just say, I was thinking of Stefan when I said men didn't cope as well as women. After Maria's death, Stefan changed. He became snappish and quite controlling. He positively bullied Ana into going for her MBA. He wouldn't hear about culinary school, he just wouldn't listen, and she hadn't found her own strength yet."

"I didn't know. I thought she did go to culinary school."

"She did. But only after she finished business school and had a few years' experience under her belt." She laughed a little. "It sounds absurd, doesn't it? What a mean dad, encouraging his daughter to get an MBA. Especially now that she's running her own business. I suspect she's glad she has some business expertise in her pocket."

"Maybe, but a bully is a bully."

Allison sighed. "I know. I wondered if I should have tried to help her, to reason with Stefan on her behalf, maybe." She shrugged. "Shoulda, woulda, coulda."

"What happened that made Ana decide to go back to culinary school, do you know?"

"Not really. She was working for some company in upstate New York. She had a very good job in marketing. She liked the owner very much, but I don't think she liked the work. She got some unexpected money, a bonus, I think—enough to pay for culinary school. I don't recall exactly. I'm just glad she finally went for it."

"Did Stefan push Peter to be an engineer, or was that Peter's choice?"

"There was some arm-twisting. Peter wanted to be a photographer." She paused to eat another piece of muffin. "I hear Peter is very happy in his career."

I shook my head. "I'm so surprised to hear this. Never in a million years would I have pegged Stefan as a bully. I only met him briefly, but he seemed so kind and caring."

"You're right . . . he is. During the last several months, he's changed back into sweet Stefan." She laughed again, this one rueful. "It gives me hope that in a few years I, too, will regain my balance." She closed her eyes for a moment. When she opened them again, they were moist. "I loved my husband very much."

I thought of the grief I'd endured. "I don't know that you ever get over a loss, not really. It changes you."

"I appreciate your saying that. Most people talk in platitudes."

"They don't know what to say, so they fall back on clichés."

She sighed and inhaled deeply. She used a napkin to pat the corners of her eyes. "I hate that I get emotional. I hate it. Enough of that. Tell me about yourself. Are you a native of Rocky Point?"

"No. I grew up in Wenton, outside of Boston, then lived in New York City for almost ten years after college. When I decided to open my own antiques appraisal and auction house, I knew I wanted to stay on the East Coast and that I needed to be near a major airport and highways. Rocky Point has a lot of charm, so that was a plus. When I saw the abandoned factory building—I don't know if you know Prescott's, or if you remember the place before I bought it. It used to house a canvas goods manufacturer. Well, it was the building itself that sealed the deal. It was perfect for the business model I had in mind, with room for high-end auctions on one side and a big tag sale venue on the other and storage galore in the middle. It was near the interstate and priced to sell. I bought the place the first day I saw it."

"And a great tradition was born."

"Thank you." I stood up. "Thanks for the coffee, too. I need to go, but would you tell Heather I stopped by and pass along my sympathy?"

"Of course." She walked me to the door. "Life keeps on coming at us, right?"

"It does. It surely does."

I walked back toward the elevator and paused again in front of the big window. Wispy gray clouds hung low in a Delft blue sky. Traffic was steady along the interstate. A maintenance man in a navy blue jumpsuit was on his knees inside the pool work area looking at something on the ground.

Life does indeed keep coming at us.

I called Wes from the parking lot.

I repeated Allison's comments about the Yartsin family, then said, "There's nothing there, Wes. Just normal family angst and typical twists and turns . . . you know, life."

"Did you get a photo of her?"

"God, Wes! Of course not." I shook my head, constantly amazed at his seemingly unlimited chutzpah. "Did you hear anything about the soil from Ana's house or her key?"

"Yeah . . . nothing. No usable prints. No sign of nondirt material in the soil. No footprints. Nothing."

"How about Jason's finances? Any news there?"

"Not yet. I'm still working on it. It's complicated because he set up several trusts and seems to have offshore accounts."

"Shielding his assets from the IRS, probably."

"Jeesh! What a joker."

"How about alibis for the afternoon Jason was killed?"

"The police haven't finished, but here's what I have so far." I heard rustling and could picture him flipping through his notebook. "From two thirty on, Ana was at the Blue Dolphin having coffee with Chef Ray in the lounge, then consulting with him in the kitchen. Maurice arrived around four forty-five, saw Ana in his kitchen, and went ballistic. Maurice called her a publicity whore, an inexperienced baker of gimmicks with no soul or heart. Is that a great quote, or what?"

"What a nightmare. Then what happened?"

"Ana turned her back to Maurice and continued her conversation with Ray in a normal voice, as if he wasn't there, shunning him, and Maurice stormed out. Ray rushed after him, leaving Ana in the middle of the kitchen. Impatient with Ray's apparent sanctioning of Maurice's high-maintenance behavior and mindful of her five-thirty appointment with you, she left. She stopped at a grocery store to pick up some tulips, arriving home a few minutes early. They have her on security cameras both at the restaurant and the florist, so her story checks out. She could have got home a few minutes ahead of when she said, though. Early enough to kill Jason."

"I got to Ana's house at the same time as she did, which shows she's out of it."

Wes chuckled. "Oh, paleeeze. She could have bashed Jason's head in, then driven around the block, timing her arrival to match yours."

"We know there were no neighbors around to notice her—but she couldn't have known that."

"If the police ever asked her about it, all she'd have to say is that since she was a few minutes early, she drove around looking for landscaping ideas."

"You're right. Oh, God, Wes. It's so horrible to think about!" I sighed.

"At some point, she and Ray made up. I just saw them, and they were very sweet together, all lovey-dovey. He seemed especially solicitous."

"My police source says that Ray called her around five twenty that day, after he finished hunting for Maurice. He apologized and promised it would never happen again."

"What did she say?"

"Nothing until later. His call went to voice mail. She kept the message, so the police were able to verify it."

"What happened with Maurice?"

"Chef Ray says that he searched for Maurice everywhere he could think of, from a nearby bar that Maurice frequented to the central garage where he parked his car, without luck. Maurice's car was there, but he wasn't. After about half an hour, he returned to the Blue Dolphin to find Ana gone. It turns out that when Maurice left, he went straight to the beach, about a ten-minute walk, and sat on a dune watching the ocean. It calms him, he said. He saw no one, and evidently no one saw him. At least no one has come forward saying they did."

"Maurice would have had plenty of time to get to Ana's house."

"Why would he?"

"To have it out with her once and for all."

"As far as he knew, she was at the Blue Dolphin."

"Right, right. Oh, my . . . do you think he could have gone to her house not to confront her, but to do something to hurt her, to burn down the kitchen she built in her garage or something?"

"I can see that. He goes to Ana's place to do some damage. Jason was there to drop off the check. One thing led to another. They struggled. Jason died."

"I can't fathom it." I swallowed fear mixed with horror. "What about Peter?"

"He doesn't have an alibi. He says he was in his hotel's gym, working out, that he used the weights, then was in the steam room. The keycard records verify that he entered the gym at two forty-five, but there's no way to tell when he left. There is no attendant on duty, and none of the other guests using the facility reported noticing him come or go. The hotel is only a fifteen-minute drive from Ana's cottage."

"Security cameras?"

"Easy to avoid, if you want to."

"What was he doing at the gym?" I asked. "You told me Peter goes in the morning."

"Just because he goes in the morning doesn't mean he couldn't go again in the afternoon. If he was creating an alibi for himself, he could have left one minute after he got there anyway."

"True."

"Stefan was at the Rocky Point library, reading investment reports and so on. One of the day librarians remembers seeing him there as she was finishing up around five. The evening librarian didn't notice him. The library is twenty minutes from Ana's place. Heather was alone, walking along the beach near Ana's cottage. She said she was taking a break from the commotion, just spending a little 'me-time.'" Wes laughed, a tinny sound. "Have you ever noticed that girls seem to need a lot more me-time than guys? Why is that?"

"I don't know," I said, thinking it was true. Women succored themselves; men sucked it up.

"I was thinking of getting Maggie a gift card to Lavinia's Day Spa for her birthday. What do you think?"

"I think she'll love it."

"Thanks. So anyway, the police haven't found anyone who noticed Heather on the beach."

"Too bad she and Maurice went to different sections of the beach." Call waiting buzzed, and I asked Wes to hold on. It was Cara telling me that Ana had stopped by, hoping I might have time to talk. The dash clock read 10:40. I told Cara to let Ana know I would be back in ten minutes. I clicked back to Wes and asked if he had anything else, and when he said no, I thanked him for the info, said I had to go, and hung up.

Ana was standing by the front window staring at nothing. Ray stood close to her. She looked upset. Ray kept glancing at her as if he weren't sure what to do to help.

"I'm sorry to keep you waiting," I said.

"I should have called ahead," Ana said, stepping forward slowly, as if it took real effort to move. "Any chance we can talk for a few minutes?"

"Sure," I said. Something in Ana's tone, a tightness, a clipped quality, told me all was not well. "We can go to my office."

Hank meowed loudly as soon as we entered the warehouse, welcoming me back while also complaining about how long I'd been gone.

"Hi, Hank. Have you been a good boy?"

He scampered around my feet, wanting a cuddle.

"Sorry, Hank. Not now, baby."

He ignored me and climbed the spiral steps alongside me, meowing the entire way.

Ray and Ana sat close to one another on the love seat. I sat on the wing chair. Hank jumped into my lap and starting purring, a husky manly purr. I rubbed under his chin, and he circled around, getting himself situated just as he liked.

I scanned their faces and saw trouble. Ana's eyes showed confusion and anxiety. Ray kept his eyes on Ana.

"What's wrong?" I asked.

Ana leaned forward, her elbows resting on her thighs. "I spoke to the police chief. All of us did. We gave him every name we could think of, people who could have stolen the Fabergé egg snow globe since Christmas. We don't think the police will get anywhere, though. What is he going to do? Ask our neighbors if they stole it? They say no, then what? Once we have a solid lead to the buyer—a fence, I guess it's called—then the police can use our list to find evidence against a specific person, but until then . . ." She took in a breath and glanced at Ray. He nodded, encouraging her to continue. She looked at me. "Do you think Jason was involved? If so, that implicates Heather. I can't bear it. I just can't bear it."

I'd had the same question in my mind when I'd asked Wes to investigate Jason's financial status. "I don't know. Do you have any sense of his finances? Was he doing as well as he implied?"

"I've wondered. What's that old saying? He who talks the most does the least."

I turned to Ray. "What did you think of him?"

He looked momentarily flustered that I was consulting him. "You want the truth?"

"Yes."

A slow smile crossed his face and reached his eyes. "I thought he was an empty bag of wind."

I smiled. "And I bet you're a heck of a good judge of people."

"I'm not invincible, that's for sure, but I've got some experience."

"How many people work in your kitchen?"

"All told, with the part-timers, seasonal workers, and the extra hands we bring in for big catering jobs? Close to a hundred."

"How many let you down?"

He grinned. "Not many."

I smiled back. "I rest my case."

He patted Ana's hand. "Even when an employee is difficult, like Maurice, I can't say he let me down. I knew what I was getting when I hired him."

"Speaking of Maurice, how long has he been with you?"

"About six months. He came to us from a very high-profile position in Boston. He said he wanted a quieter environment, less stressful." Ray shook his head. "Instead of his calming down, we got revved up."

I looked at Ana. Her cheeks had sunk in a little. She didn't care about Maurice. "Is there any hope, Josie? Tell me the truth. Is there any chance the egg is still intact?"

"Honestly, I don't know. Certainly there's a chance."

"If they've destroyed the egg for the jewels," Ray asked, "how much would they get?"

"Oh, don't even suggest such a thing!" Ana said.

Ray slipped his arm around her shoulders and drew her closer to him. He kissed her forehead.

"We have to face facts," he said.

I shrugged. "I don't know. Not off the top of my head. Less than if the egg remained intact."

"But for less risk," Ray said.

"Maybe, maybe not. The gems are unique."

Ray gave Ana a final squeeze, then stood up. He extended a hand to help her, and she took it.

"When will you know something?" she asked.

"I don't know that, either. I'm sorry I can't be more specific. I'll call you as soon as I have news."

Hank leaped to the ground as I stood up. He yawned and stretched his bottom half, then his top half. He looked at me and meowed, then jumped onto the love seat and sniffed around before curling into a tight little ball.

"I know you will," Ana said as we headed down the stairs.

I waved good-bye at the front door and watched them walk across the parking lot hand in hand. From the questions Ray asked me, the answers he gave to the ones I asked him, the comments he made, and his overall calm and supportive presence, I could tell that he was a practical man, and confident. Watching him interact with Ana, I could see that he was also kind. Ana was in good hands.

CHAPTER FOURTEEN

T y left for North Conway the next morning, Friday, before I woke up. He was working on a new training exercise that involved tracking off-hour, unauthorized small plane landings at regional airports and private airfields. If everything went well, he would be home late Saturday.

I spoke to Wes that afternoon, and again on Saturday, and both times he told me he had no news. The police, he said, were playing it close to the vest. His own inquiries were leading nowhere. I was glad I had work to distract me.

Ty called around six Saturday evening, just as we were locking up after the tag sale.

"I've run into a snafu," he said.

"Oh, no," I said. I caught Gretchen's eye and mouthed "I'll be right back," then walked outside so I could talk privately.

The sun was low on the horizon. It would be dark in an hour or so. Slivers of sunlight filtered through the trees and dimpled the pavement with faint yellow streaks. I leaned against my car.

"Yeah," Ty said. "I've got to run one of the exercises again. Maybe more than once."

"You sound tired."

"You have no idea. I'm going to hit the hay early, as soon as I eat. Don't get jealous, by the way, at the thought of me eating in a fancy hotel. Dinner is a turkey sub from a local pizza joint."

"Poor baby."

"I miss you, Josie."

"I miss you, too, Ty. I hope the exercise goes well and you're home before noon."

"Me, too. I hate having to work on Sundays."

We blew kisses through the airwaves, then said good-bye.

The next morning, while I waited for Ty, I used my home computer to research Fabergé eggs. The last time a Fabergé egg sold at auction was in 2007, when the Rothschild egg sold for $18.5 million. Eighteen years earlier, in 1989, Joan Kroc, heir to the McDonald's fortune, bought one, also at auction, for $3.1 million. Based on past sales alone, the previous appraisal of $4 million was on the mark. But previous sales is only one indicator of value, by no means the sole determinant. In addition to sales records, you also had to assess rarity, scarcity, authenticity, provenance, condition, popular trends, and association. Assuming the Fabergé Spring Egg snow globe was authentic, some factors were evident, but others were not. Rarity, check. Scarcity, oh, yeah. Condition, unknown. Popular trends—the eggs' allure had only grown over time. Authenticity and provenance, not so much. Association, also uncertain. And of course, the underlying assumption of authenticity might be wrong.

I reached for my copy of the eighteen-year-old appraisal. The appraiser, Winston Mackley, who had worked for a company called Zinsser's Antiques in Chicago, had added a footnote disclaimer that read as if it had been written by a lawyer. I read it through twice slowly and concluded that he had attempted neither to authenticate the object nor to verify its provenance. The note explained that his valuation was based on the veracity of the owner's statements. In other words, he based his appraisal on undocumented facts, facts given to him by people with a vested interest in receiving a high appraisal. This approach was common and often unrevealed. At least Mackley included a footnote. I shook my head and wrinkled my nose. I found the practice, whether acknowledged or not, distasteful. It was not the way we did business at Prescott's.

I Googled Zinsser's, got the phone number, dialed, and promptly hit a temporary dead end. The business was closed on Sundays.

I gave up, reassuring myself that tomorrow was another day, and decided to cook, one of my favorite ways to relax. By the time Ty got home around two, I'd baked double fudge brownies, prepped mustard-thyme chicken, and put coated buffalo wings into the refrigerator to chill, the only way to set the spices.

·　　·　　·

On Monday morning, when I called Zinsser's again, the dead end became permanent. Winston Mackley had died eight years earlier. No one who worked there now had been there eighteen years before. There was no Zinsser, hadn't been for seventy-plus years. According to the CEO's assistant, a curt young woman named Lila, their pre-2003 documents weren't computerized.

"We keep them in a warehouse."

"I'm hoping to get a look at Winston Mackley's notes from a 1997 appraisal. Is that possible?"

"I don't know."

"How can I find out?"

"You'll need to send in a written request explaining what you need and why."

"How long will it take, do you think?"

"Maybe a couple of weeks if we can find the documents. Not everything is labeled right."

"It's police business."

"We do our best," she said, sounding half defensive and half indifferent.

I got her e-mail address, thanked her, and hung up. I typed up the request, stressing the urgency, reiterating that it was police business, and cc-ing Ellis.

"Do your job, Lila," I said aloud and pressed SEND.

Gretchen IM'd to alert me that Matthew had sent over his retouched scans.

Matthew's work was masterful. The Polaroids weren't changed, just enhanced. The dull yellow that had washed over everything was gone. The faded colors were brighter, the hues truer, the resolution crisper. The pink enamel I'd thought of as seashell was more opalescent, almost translucent. The gems were vivid: The red was closer to apple than cherry; the green was Kelly bold, not celery pale; the blue was more like cobalt than sky. Even the gold was truer to reality, appearing to be the darker, richer shade of 18 karat, not yellow, like cheap plate.

I uploaded the scans to our image-sharing site in case I needed them when I was away from my computer, sent the link to Fred and Nate and asked them to update our various call-for-sightings postings by replacing the photographs, and IM'd Gretchen to go ahead and pay Matthew's bill.

• • •

It occurred to me that I had been thinking only about the Fabergé egg, not the snow globe. Time for more research.

I searched for sales of rare snow globes and got twenty-six hits, none of which was relevant. *Now what?* I asked myself. I swiveled toward my window. I couldn't see the ocean past the birches and white pine and maples that ringed my property, but I knew it was there. Despite our being five miles inland, seagulls often circled overhead, and when the wind was strong and from the east, the air smelled as salty as if I were standing on the sand. *If I wanted to get money from a Fabergé egg encased in an antique snow dome, how would I do so?*

I might use it as collateral for a loan—but only if I had an appraisal the bank would accept. Thinking that an appraiser who been fortunate enough to work on a Fabergé egg might be eager to parlay his experience into another commission, I posted a call for appraisers on our proprietary Web sites, asking anyone who'd appraised a Fabergé egg in the last six months to contact me, giving no reason for the request.

"Okay, then," I said. "How else might I get money from the egg?"

We hadn't had any hits from Nate's jewelry postings, which, while a disappointment, wasn't a surprise. Less than reputable jewelers—the only ones that would buy rare jewels from a stranger for cash—probably didn't subscribe to pricey Web sites; even if they did, they wouldn't want to advertise they'd bought rare gems at a discount. No matter how good a story the seller told about falling on hard times and needing quick cash, any doofus would suspect that something was fishy. Receiving stolen goods was a serious crime.

My cell phone rang. I recognized the number. It was Shelley, my good buddy from my days at Frisco's in New York, before I got caught up in the price-fixing scandal, before I blew the whistle on my boss and lost my friends, my job, and life as I'd known it. Shelley was one of the few people from those dark lonely days who stayed in touch, who was still my friend.

"Shelley! You're calling because you've finally scheduled your New Hampshire visit."

"You're such a card, Josie. No, I'm calling because you have a question about a Fabergé egg, asking for people who've appraised them recently. You know me—Ms. Curiosity. What's your interest?"

"Hi, Shelley, I'm fine. How are you?"

"Cute, Josie. Deflecting a question. Very cute."

"I'm not deflecting anything. I'm awed. I posted that inquiry about five minutes ago."

"And a notice about a missing egg yesterday. What gives, my friend? Do you have it back already? Are you selling it?"

"I swear I can't believe you're calling me so fast. I exaggerated before. I posted the notice four minutes ago."

"And in that time, three people have run in here wanting to know if I've called you yet. If you're getting ready to sell a Fabergé egg, you need us, Josie. Prescott's is a wonderful house, but we can help maximize value."

"You can tell your coworkers that if Prescott's is going to auction off a Fabergé egg, I'll make certain they get invitations."

"One of those three people works in the Russian artifacts division. He has a client, a Russian oil mogul, on the line now—on an open line. I could hear the client begging for the opportunity to bid. I'm not joking, Josie. I know it's only been four minutes, but the hordes have crossed the moat and are pounding at the door. Talk to me."

A haunting memory of the bleak isolation I'd endured during those seemingly endless days a decade ago washed over me. Unquestionably, I'd been on the right side of the law and morality, yet I'd found myself battling for my job and my reputation. I'd spent hours locked in cheerless rooms while my boss's lawyers challenged my memory, my motivation, and my integrity. Shelley often surprised me by showing up outside the lawyer's midtown office during my lunch break, serving up pretzels or hot dogs fresh from a cart. We'd sit on the cold green slat-back chairs that fill the walkways in Bryant Park chatting about country music and line dancing and whether hem lengths would stay long and whether Pierre, her favorite masseuse at her favorite spa, was single. She'd helped make the nightmare bearable.

"You're such a good friend, Shelley."

"You, too, Joz. So talk to me."

"Have you ever heard of the Fabergé Spring Egg?"

"The Winter Egg, yes. The Spring Egg, no. Don't tell me you have your hands on a previously unknown Fabergé egg."

"Actually, I'm not going to tell you anything at all. Not now."

"Will you promise me that I'll be your first call?"

"I can promise you that if I call anyone, you'll be first."

"Why wouldn't you call?" she asked.

"Maybe I have a client who just wants an appraisal."

"You're planning on auctioning it yourself, aren't you?"

I chuckled.

"You can't do that on your own. It's too big. You can't do it in New Hampshire. Do you realize you'll have a thousand million people invading your sweet little country town? The natives will hate you. The police will bill you extra for security. Half the high rollers won't show up because they'll get lost en route. The other half will be on the phone, and you don't have that many lines. You'll never pull it off. You need us."

I bristled at the implication that my firm was small potatoes. "Thanks for the vote of confidence."

"Really, Josie. We can help."

"Prescott's isn't that small, Shelley. We can afford to pay for security. We have plenty of phone lines. New Hampshire isn't the backwater you seem to think it is. We even have highways and signs and airports. But thanks for the thought."

"Sorry, sorry. You know me . . . I get enthusiastic and speak without thinking. I'm so used to teasing you, I forgot we're having a for-real business conversation."

"Apology accepted. But I still have nothing to add at this point. If and when, I'll be in touch."

It took an additional five minutes to get her off the phone without offending her. As I replaced the receiver in the cradle, I couldn't help but smile. If I ever found myself with a Fabergé egg to auction, whooey, would we have fun!

Cara buzzed up just before five that a Drake Milner, a Boston antiques dealer, was on line two. So far, I'd received sixteen calls from dealers, curators, and collectors from within the U.S. and from Paris, Moscow, Riyadh, and Hong Kong wanting information about my inquiry, hoping I had a Fabergé egg to sell, but I was no closer to finding the Fabergé Spring Egg snow globe than I was before I'd posted my request to talk to appraisers who've worked on Fabergé eggs. I figured Milner would be more of the same.

After exchanging greetings, he said, "I saw your inquiry. Naturally, I was curious."

He sounded British, refined. "Have you worked on one, Mr. Milner?"

"May I ask about the nature of your interest?"

"I'm working on one and was hoping to be able to consult with an experienced appraiser."

"Smashing, then. I appraised an Imperial egg just a week ago, so perhaps I can be of assistance."

"Which one?" I asked, firing up Google.

Drake Milner hailed from Cambridge, England. He'd worked for the London Institute of Art and the Russian Historical Society before immigrating to the United States in 2008. He was now an appraiser with Marlborough Antiques in Boston.

"Perhaps you could tell me about your project."

I didn't find Drake's hesitation unusual. None of us volunteers information.

"I can do even better than that. I just Googled you. You're in Boston, is that right? May I come down to see you?"

"I'd welcome it. Did your search tell you I'm with Marlborough Antiques on Newbury Street?"

"Yes. In fact, I know your company. I worked with Edmond Marlborough, gosh, it must be ten years ago, when I was with Frisco's."

Quickly scanning a few of Marlborough's past catalogues, I saw that Milner was an expert on a wide range of Russian antiques, from paintings to soup tureens.

"It truly is a small world, isn't it? We work with Frisco's frequently. I'm afraid I'm the bearer of bad news, though. Mr. Marlborough passed on four years ago . . . no, it's five years, now."

"I'm sorry to hear that. He was a fine man. A real gentleman."

"Yes, indeed. His son took over. He's more business-oriented than antiques-oriented, which works out well for us all. He gives us free rein."

"That's great to hear. Many new managers feel the need to change things. You're Marlborough's Russian objects expert, is that correct?"

"Russian art and decorative objects, yes."

We made an appointment for ten o'clock the next morning.

Without question, Milner was a good choice to appraise a Fabergé egg. What was less evident was how anyone not immersed in Russian antiquities would have known to hire him.

If I was familiar with the antiques appraisal process, I might go to any of the various professional organizations' Web sites and do a search. Most sites allowed those of us in good standing to state up to three categories of specialization. But if I was unfamiliar with the antiques appraisal process, I might not know that such listings existed. Instead, I might simply conduct a standard search.

I Googled "Fabergé egg" and "appraisal," and more than three hundred thousand listings appeared. The first several were from major auction houses, places I'd want to steer clear of because of the potential notoriety. If I were a thief—a buyer or seller of stolen goods—I'd want someone reliable but way less famous. Neither Marlborough Antiques nor Drake Milner appeared in the first two pages of listings. I noted that many of the entries referred to Russian art, however, though not specifically Fabergé eggs. That was interesting. In Google's algorithm, Fabergé eggs led to Russia.

I tried a new search: "Russian art" and "appraisal." Poof, first up was a white paper posted on Marlborough Antiques' Web site about how to identify "Fauxbergé eggs," intentional fakes created in the twentieth century as decorative objects for the middle class. The article's author was Drake Milner.

I raised my brows as the implications rattled around in my head. Out the window, fast-moving clouds streaked across the twilight blue sky. Whoever hired Drake Milner thought of his object as Russian art, not as a Fabergé egg. That was, perhaps, telling.

I glanced at the time display on my monitor. It read 6:35. I texted Ty that I would be leaving within the next fifteen minutes, then called Ellis and got him in his office.

"I have news," I repeated my conversation with Drake Milner and explained my logic in Googling information about Russian artifacts.

"Great that you got an appointment. Should I go with you?"

"I don't think so. I think it would spook him. Right now, he's acting normally—he's a little reticent, but not overly so. He's in information-gathering mode, and he's discreet."

"You think so? The way you described that conversation, he seems cagey to me."

"Context is everything. High-end antiques dealers don't gab. Pretty much we keep secrets for a living."

"That's an interesting spin on your job."

"People trust us. If I sell something to a man, I can't be talking about it to his wife. What if it's not for his wife? And vice versa. I might learn that one sibling was favored over the others. Or that someone in gambling trouble has to sell his antiques. If we tell tales out of school, the next guy won't trust us, and we're screwed."

"As with everything important in life, the subtleties rule. So we're holding me in reserve?"

"Yes."

"All right. Call me the minute you're out of his shop."

I promised I would. I hung up, stretched like a cat, and headed downstairs to get Hank settled in for the night.

I was willing to bet I wouldn't get a wink of sleep. I was champing at the bit to get to Boston. With any luck, I'd learn enough from Drake to identify his client—and I was willing to bet that person was a thief, and probably a killer.

CHAPTER FIFTEEN

arlborough Antiques occupied a street-level shop on Boston's swanky Newbury Street. A search of public records showed that the company owned the building and that the business had operated out of that location for fifty-one years. Impressive. That kind of stability implied good things about the company—and its employees.

A young woman with chestnut-colored hair that hung to her shoulders greeted me as soon as I stepped into Marlborough Antiques. Looking at her and glancing around the super-refined shop, I felt excruciatingly underdressed. My khakis and maroon sweater set didn't hold a candle to her midthigh-length white silk shirt, black leggings, and ankle-high black leather stiletto-heeled boots. She looked like she worked on Newbury Street. I looked like I drove in from the country.

She smiled warmly. "Welcome. May I help you find something?"

"Thanks. I'm Josie Prescott, here to see Drake Milner."

"Oh, yes. He told me to expect you. This way."

I followed her on a serpentine trek around a pair of exquisite gold ormolu Regency tables and a six-foot-high leather giraffe and a tall double-wide display cabinet filled to the brim with Edwardian silver coffee and tea sets and shelves of eighteenth- and nineteenth-century red, brown, blue, and gold leather-bound books, the kind interior decorators buy by the foot based on color and size, and side tables and tallboys and chairs. At the back, we went through a heavy oak door and down a short corridor and paused at an open door on the right.

Drake Milner looked up from his laptop and stood. "Thank you, Julie."

Julie left.

"Come in, come in."

Drake Milner was short and portly with thin wisps of gray hair draped over his bald pate. He wore a lightweight wool suit, gray with faint blue stripes, a pale blue shirt with a white collar, and a blue tie that matched his eyes.

His office was pristine. His window probably overlooked an alley or a parking spot, but the hunter green velvet drapes created a wholly different impression. So did the walnut-paneled walls and the thick green carpet and the brass sconces and coordinating table lamps that cast a golden glow throughout the room. Behind his desk was a built-in wall of open shelving and walnut cupboards. Reference books filled the shelves. The only things on his desk were his laptop, a telephone, and two lamps. There were no papers, photographs, stacks of catalogues, or Post-it notes in sight. Evidently, his style of work was opposite to mine.

"Your office is beautiful," I said. "An inspirational place to work. My office is never this neat."

"I confess it's not usually this tidy. I cleaned up for you."

I laughed. "Why?"

"Please, have a seat." He waited for me to sit, then got himself settled in his high-back black leather chair. "It's not every day we get a visit from the owner of one of *Antiques Insights'* 'Small Houses to Watch.'"

"Is it that? Or is it that I'm interested in Fabergé eggs?"

"It's both . . . but touché. I am, of course, burning with curiosity." He smiled and leaned back. "Is yours one of the Imperial eggs?"

"This is a little awkward." I smiled and shrugged. "I can't tell you anything about the project."

He raised his brows. "That makes it a bit difficult to consult in a meaningful way, doesn't it?"

"You'd think so, but you'd be wrong. I need to know about the egg you appraised last week."

He shook his head. "We never reveal confidential dealings."

"I understand. I don't either." I paused. His expression communicated nothing but mild interest. "I need to trust you."

"You may."

"There's a Fabergé egg that's gone missing. It was replaced with a bad repro, presumably to delay the discovery of the theft. The real egg had been in a private collection for nearly a hundred years. It's called the Fabergé Spring Egg. Am I warm?"

Something on his laptop caught his eye. He tapped some buttons and extracted a flash drive, dropped it in his shirt pocket, and closed the laptop's lid. "Sorry . . . I'm paranoid about backups. One computer crash is all it took." He rubbed his nose, thinking. "I can't tell you whether I worked on that egg in particular since my client requested confidentiality and it's in a private collection."

"Please."

Milner shook his head.

"Can you tell me this? Was the egg you appraised genuine?"

"That I can answer—yes."

"If you appraised the Spring Egg, you were hired either by the thief or by a buyer of stolen goods. My client is the owner. How can you justify maintaining confidentiality about an illegal act?"

"First of all, I don't accept the premise of your question—I'm not acknowledging or disavowing that I appraised that particular egg. Second, even if I did appraise that egg, I have no reason, beyond your statement, to think anything illegal occurred." He shrugged and opened his palms. "Maybe the thief and the owner are one and the same."

I nodded slowly as the implications ricocheted through my brain. Was it possible that Ellis had been right all along, that someone—presumably Ana—had concocted this whole scam for the insurance money? Get a new appraisal, say the egg was stolen? Or get a new appraisal and a new fake egg, sell the real egg on the black market, and destroy the fake egg for the insurance payout? Maybe, except the insurance company would catch you dead to rights. Plus, that's not what happened. Unless Jason interfered with her plans. I shook my head. There was too much I didn't know.

I met Milner's eyes. He was waiting for my response.

I smiled at him and crossed my legs at the ankles. "I told Police Chief Hunter there was a better chance of you talking to me, professional to professional, than there was of you talking to him. You're going to have to talk to one of us, I think. It looks like the Fabergé Spring Egg is somehow involved in a murder case."

"Murder!" He sat forward. "Who was killed?"

"A Boston-based financial expert." I explained the situation, then added, "Now you see why I've been pushing."

"Of course. It's a terrible situation. And confusing. I'm empathetic, Ms. Prescott, I really am, and I'd like to cooperate, but the only way I'll talk is if I'm presented with a document signed by a judge."

"So you can tell your client you had no choice."

"Do you blame me?"

I shook my head. "No. In your position, I'd be tempted to do the same." I lowered my eyes to his desk, needing a moment to think. When I raised them again, his eyes met mine unwaveringly. I knew when I'd lost an argument. "Can you tell me how much you appraised it for?"

"Yes—I can talk about that. Five to eight million at auction."

"Why so low?"

"You're thinking of the Rothschild egg. I discounted from full value, which I assume would be somewhere in the twenty-one- to twenty-two-million-dollar range for two reasons—the Rothschild egg was a gift from the imperial family, adding value through association, and this egg, the one I appraised, did not have an undisputed provenance."

"Disputed or simply not provable?"

"There's no documentation of the egg itself, period. Not in the Fabergé archives or in any historical or scholarly records that I could find—and I'm confident that if any existed, I would have found them. Neither is there any record regarding the sale of the egg to its current owner. The owner had a credible explanation, but I couldn't verify it. The shop where it was purchased has been closed for nearly seventy years, and its records are long gone." He paused for a moment, perhaps considering whether he felt comfortable revealing additional details, then continued. "I concluded that it was an actual Fabergé egg based on my physical examination. All wreaths are hand-chased, for instance, not punched from a mold. All diamonds are rose-cut, not single-cut. The enamel colors are vibrant and consistent throughout, including on the inside, not speckled or spotty." He shrugged and flipped open his hands. "But without clear provenance . . . I would be leery of recommending its purchase to all but my most passionate clients, and even to them, I'd issue a serious warning."

"I bet the owner wasn't pleased with your assessment."

"My job is telling my client the truth."

"Always," I said. I needed to know if the egg he was referring to was the Spring Egg, and if so, I needed to know who his client was. I had one arrow left in my quiver, but given his deft deflections, I wasn't optimistic. I leaned back, relaxed, signaling that I was no threat, and smiled a little. "All things considered, you've been very helpful. One thing—was the egg you appraised encased in a snow dome?"

123

He smiled, a small one. "Are you trying to trick me into revealing more than I'm comfortable with?"

I opened my eyes wide. "Me? Never."

"I've been in the business a long time, Ms. Prescott."

"All right. I confess. Mr. Milner, please know that I truly understand and identify with your position. I wish I could let it go, but I can't. I'm an emissary for the police. If you won't tell me, I think they'll try to compel you to tell them."

"You mean ask a judge for a court order? If they do, I'll fight it."

"And you'd lose. Can't we just skip it?"

He pushed his lips out, thinking. "If you'll step out into the other room, I'll call my client. If I'm given permission to tell you, fine. If not, not."

My heart skipped three beats. "God, no! Don't do that. We can't risk revealing we're closing in."

"Then I'm stymied."

I stood up. "I suspect you'll be hearing from Police Chief Hunter soon."

Milner grasped the edge of his desk and rolled back. He stood up.

"He'll do what he needs to do, as will I."

He held the door for me, allowing me to go first.

As we approached the front of the shop, I heard Julie speaking to someone I couldn't see.

"Notice the uneven nail heads," she said.

I spotted her squatting next to a middle-aged woman in jeans and a flannel shirt, pointing to something on the underside of a cherrywood side table.

"That indicates they were hand-forged."

"Thank you," I said extending my hand to Milner. "I'm glad to have met you."

"Me, too." He shook, a good one, just firm enough, and not too long.

As I walked toward the garage under Boston Common where I'd left my car, I went over everything I'd said to see if there was anything I could have done differently to have inspired Milner to confide in me, and concluded no.

"Darn!" I said. "Double darn."

"I'm sorry, Ellis," I said after I recounted my conversation with Drake Milner.

"It sounds like I'm going to need a warrant."

"I think so."

"I may need your testimony. I'll keep you posted."

"Should we ask for public sightings? I mean, the thief doesn't know we got to Milner, and we don't have to reveal that. We can make it a broad request—has anyone seen this object, period. Not just to antiques experts. To everyone."

He paused for several seconds before replying. "It might even help, implying that we have no leads. Do you have an approach in mind?"

I smiled. "Yes."

As soon as Ellis and I had finished our conversation, I called Wes. He didn't answer, and I left a message. "Want to meet at the Portsmouth Diner at two thirty?"

I sat on a park bench in Boston Common near the entry to the parking lot to think. The sun was warm, and the air smelled clean. I watched a tall, too-thin man about thirty play Frisbee with his black lab. The dog wore a red bandanna. The man whip-spun the Frisbee, and the dog chased after it, spinning and leaping and catching it in his mouth. He ran back to the man and dropped it at his feet, then pranced backward, his tongue lolling, his tail wagging, eager for another go. It reminded me of the man throwing sticks on the beach for the little mutt. Men and their dogs—some things don't change. Once you know how people are likely to act, you have a good chance of predicting the future.

Milner's client selected him after researching and assessing Russian-antiques appraiser options, choosing him based on predetermined attributes he or she had identified as required for the job. The client would have sought out an appraiser known for the quality of his work, the integrity with which he conducted his business, and geographic proximity. The client also would have had to have the money to pay the invoice, which, I knew, would have been in the low four figures. The person we were looking for was methodical, educated, astute, and, seemingly at least, affluent.

Who among the suspects fit that bill? Heather and Ana for sure. Both women were smart and organized, and they earned enough to have discretionary funds—or enough credit to cover a four-figure expense. Ditto Heather's mom, not that she was a suspect. Stefan and Peter fit the profile, too. So did everyone even remotely connected to the situation, including Ray and Maurice. I might be gaining understanding about a thief, but I wasn't narrowing in on a killer. I sighed and was about to get up when my phone rang. It was Ana.

"I know these things take time," she said, "but I thought I'd call, just in case you have news."

"I don't. I thought I might, but I don't yet. I just met with a man I think might have appraised your egg, but he wouldn't confirm it."

"Oh, Josie!" she exclaimed, soaring into optimism. "That sounds like a real break. Why won't he help us? Is he afraid of being accused of being involved somehow in a crime?"

"No, not at all. He's being appropriately discreet. I just wish he weren't."

"What now?" she asked, her excitement dissipating.

"The police take it from here. If they can compel him to talk, they will."

"You mean they'll get a court order."

"Yes."

"I know you're doing everything you can."

"Thank you, Ana. It's true—I am. How's Heather?"

"About the same. Blue."

"Sounds like we're all doing the best we can."

"Yes." Ana sighed heavily. "I guess that's all we can do."

"I was glad to spend a little time with Ray. You and he seem great together."

"Can you see my smile?" she asked, with a small laugh. "It happens whenever I think of him."

I grinned. "Yes, I can—it's a big one. Can you see mine in response to yours?"

"Yes, indeed. Thanks, Josie."

I hung up, thinking as I walked slowly to the parking garage that funding her new life—an oceanfront cottage in Rocky Point, a commercial kitchen conversion in her garage, and a wardrobe fit for a television star—couldn't have come cheap, and it all happened in the last few months. I'd been assuming that everyone was affluent because that's the image they conveyed. Images, I knew, could be faked, and often were.

Not for the first time, I wondered where Ana got the money.

CHAPTER SIXTEEN

es called back as I was crossing the New Hampshire border.

"You bet I want to meet. Whatcha got?"

"News. You're going to be a happy man."

"Tell me now."

I laughed. Wes, too, was predictable. "I'll see you soon, Wes," I said, and hung up.

Wes was on the phone when I arrived at the diner, a glass of pink fizzy something in front of him. He ended his call with a brusque "Catch ya later," and sat back, grinning like the Cheshire Cat.

"Why are you looking like that?" I asked as I slid into the banquette across from him.

" 'Cause when I tell you I have rocket news, I'm not just whistling 'Dixie.' This ammo is gonna blow the top off the investigation. Whammo! I just got confirmation that all is not as it seems in moneyland."

"I'm all ears," I said.

The waitress breezed over. I ordered hot tea and a club sandwich. I waited for Wes to order bacon. He always ordered bacon; sometimes he placed a double order.

"Nothing else for me," Wes said.

"Don't you want bacon?" I asked.

"No." The waitress took the menus and left. "I'm cleaning up my act for real, Josie."

"Maggie must be happy to see her influence at work."

"I guess. But it's not just for Maggie. It's time I grew up."

"Then I'm impressed."

Wes sipped some of the pink liquid through a straw that bent at the top.

"What is that?" I asked, pointing at the glass.

"Sparkling water. Maggie said I should cut back on Coke."

"Why is it pink?"

"Maraschino cherries. Maggie said I could put fruit in it and it would still be healthy. I tried it with lime, but I like Maraschino cherries better."

I toyed with the idea of telling him that Maraschino cherries weren't what Maggie had in mind, healthwise, but decided against it. Let Maggie be the heavy, not me.

"So what's your rocket news?" I asked.

"Ana's broke. Busted flat. She's wiped out all her savings and maxed out all her credit cards."

"What?" I exclaimed, shocked. "That doesn't make any sense."

"Ana bought her house using money she got from her divorce settlement and by cashing in some stock options she'd received as part of a compensation package at an old job. She used a bonus she got at that job, plus the advance she got for the book, to renovate the garage and has been living on hope and mirrors for a couple of months. With the TV pilot on hold . . . well, bad news just got worse."

"I had no idea."

"Way more people are good liars than you expect, huh?"

"I met someone who appraised what I'm pretty sure is her Fabergé egg snow globe last week."

Wes's eyes fired up. "Do you think she sold it to raise money? And had the replica made to fool everyone? Like maybe she was embarrassed and didn't want her dad and brother to know." He leaned forward. "Jason found out and confronted her."

I met Wes's eyes. "She would have had to travel to Detroit to get it."

"Which means she would have left a trail. I can find out if she flew by commercial air during the last month."

"Maybe you can find out if she wasn't around here for a couple of days." I shook my head. "I can't believe it, Wes."

"Money, honey. It's the root of all evil."

"It's the *love* of money that's the root of all evil, not money per se."

"Personally, I think it's the lack of money that's the root of all evil."

"You and Mark Twain."

"Really?" Wes said, grinning. He sat up straighter and puffed out his chest a little. "I'm thinking like Mark Twain. You gotta admit . . . that's pretty cool." He sipped his drink, finishing it. "So whatcha got for me?"

I grinned. "Get your smile ready." I filled him in about the retouched photos and the eighteen-year-old appraisal and invited him to issue a call for sightings. "An exclusive—and you can quote me."

"Hot banana, Josie!"

I e-mailed him the link to the image-sharing site where he could retrieve the photographs. He opened it and downloaded one of the pictures.

"Will you read my copy for accuracy?"

"I'll be glad to."

"Thanks," he said, flashing a grin, a big one.

The waitress slid my sandwich and a bottle of mustard onto the table. "Here you go, hon."

"Thanks."

Wes extracted his notebook and wrote a few lines, then looked out the window. I followed his gaze. The parking lot was about a third full, with cars scattered here and there. I glanced at him. He wasn't looking at the cars. He was looking past them, past the service road that led to I-95, into the forest. I could almost see the wheels turning in his brain as he assessed and evaluated and prioritized. He jotted another note. I finished one of the triangular quarters of sandwich and was almost done with a second one before he was ready.

"The point is that it's gone missing, right?" Wes asked.

"Yes . . . and that it may still be intact."

"Got it." He wrote for another few minutes, then read the text to me, a paragraph maybe.

"That's good," I told him.

"Thanks! I'm off, then." Wes's eyes sank to my half-eaten sandwich. "I can stay. I'll keep you company."

"Thanks, but go ahead."

"Thanks," he said.

He double-tapped the table, slid out of the booth, and was gone. He strode out of the diner and across the parking lot to his car like a man on a mission.

I waved at the waitress and asked for more hot water. I was just as glad to be alone, to eat slowly and have another cup of tea, to sit quietly and think.

Ellis called as I was paying the bill.

"There's something called the Uniform Act to Secure the Attendance of Witnesses. A judge up here has to sign a certificate telling a Massachusetts judge that Drake Milner's testimony is material. Judge Rutherson has scheduled a hearing at nine thirty tomorrow morning. Milner and his lawyer will be present. Tell me you're available."

"I'm available."

"Good. The ADA—Rusty Barton—do you know him?"

"No. What's he like?"

"Humorless. By the book. Skeptical. He doesn't like New York."

"Well, to hell with him."

"I tell myself that no one's perfect. He has a sterling reputation. Plus, he's Frank Harson's handpicked choice for the case."

Ellis was communicating more than information. Frank Harson was New Hampshire's attorney general, and Ellis wanted me to know that he was taking a direct interest in the case.

"Mr. Barton must be honored."

Ellis chuckled. "Or ready to run for the hills. In any event, he wants to review your testimony before you talk to the judge. Can you meet him now?"

I glanced out the window. Long shadows striped the asphalt. The day was shot. "Sure."

"Good. He's in my office reviewing our files."

"I'll be there in fifteen minutes."

I got settled in my car, then called work to tell them I wouldn't be in. I checked e-mail, too. Lila from Zinsser's Antiques wrote to tell me they'd checked the warehouse, and no records relating to Winston Mackley's appraisal of a Fabergé egg existed. I forwarded the e-mail to Ellis, adding a note: "Another dead end."

Rusty Barton rose when I walked in. He glanced at Ellis entering behind me, then looked back at me and extended a hand. "Thanks for coming in on such short notice."

"Glad to help."

"Have a seat. Let me tell you what the judge is going to want to hear."

The round table near the window was covered with stacks of papers and manila folders. A yellow legal pad with several pages looped backward over the binding rested near his right hand. Ellis sat beside me.

Much to my surprise, Rusty Barton's hair wasn't red, reminding me never to jump to conclusions. His hair was black, slicked back in a leonine wave. His eyes were black, too, or maybe just a really dark brown. He wore a brown suit with a yellow shirt and a brown tie with tan diagonal stripes. He was younger than I expected, late twenties or early thirties.

Barton flipped back two sheets on his legal pad and scanned his notes. "First, the judge will want to know why we think learning about the Fabergé egg snow globe will help solve the murder." His eyes shifted to Ellis. "Chief Hunter will explain that part. Second, he'll want to know why we think Drake Milner has material knowledge about the object." He pinned me with his gaze. "That's where you come in." He leaned back in his chair. "If I say, 'Why do you think this man has knowledge of the Yartsin Fabergé Spring Egg snow globe?' what will you say?"

"Mr. Milner told me he appraised a Fabergé egg last week. I think it's this one."

"Why?"

"Because the Yartsin Spring Egg is missing. For two Fabergé eggs to be in play at the same time would be a nearly inconceivable coincidence."

"At this point Milner's lawyer will jump in. 'So, Ms. Prescott, let's be clear. You're saying that you have no actual evidence that Milner has material knowledge about the Yartsin Fabergé Spring Egg snow globe, is that correct?' He'll turn to the judge, righteous indignation written across his face. 'Your Honor, this is an outrage.' How can you confute him?"

I didn't know what to say.

"Ms. Prescott?" he prodded. "What will you say?"

I pressed my lips together, stymied.

Barton turned to Ellis. "We're in trouble. Big trouble."

CHAPTER SEVENTEEN

R ocky Point's new courthouse was built of wood, fieldstone, and glass. It was contemporary in feel, yet stately. I spotted Ellis and Barton by a soaring stone column in the lobby, just past security. Once I was through, I joined them.

Ellis smiled as I approached. "Hey, Josie."

ADA Barton's tension was evident. His brow was wrinkled, his shoulders stiff, and there were ash-colored smudges under his eyes.

"I'm ready," I told him. "I know I messed up yesterday. I won't mess up today. I promise."

A big man, both tall and wide, wearing a charcoal gray suit and a red and black striped tie, stopped short. "Rusty, you old dog. Don't tell me they've assigned you to this loser."

"Dale . . . how do you know which case I'm on?"

"I don't. But if you're on it, it's going to be a loser."

"Nice, nice. You're still Mr. Personality, I see. What are you doing here?"

"Up from Boston to protect the right to privacy. Rocky Point vs. Milner."

"Then we are going to be meeting up soon." Rusty leaned toward Dale and lowered his voice. "Except this time, you're going to be the loser."

Dale chuckled and wagged his index finger in Rusty's face. "You were always good for a laugh, Rusty. See you in chambers."

He strode across the lobby. Barton watched him until he turned the corner and disappeared from view.

"Dale Morrison," Rusty said staring after him, "epitomizes the worst of the law. He's both amoral and articulate, a dastardly combination." He turned to me. All signs of tension had disappeared. Now he looked angry. "He's a master at making witnesses feel foolish and look inept." He faced Ellis. "This applies to you, too."

"I'm a righteous man," Ellis said. "When it comes to telling the truth, I fear nothing."

Rusty nodded enthusiastically. "Yes, that's exactly the right approach. Take the high road." He looked at me. "Will you be all right?"

"Yes. I'm righteous, too."

"I hope so," he muttered, not believing it.

"Really," I assured him. "I'm prepared."

He looked at me straight on and lowered his voice. "Meaning you're ready to answer the question that stumped you yesterday?"

I spoke softly. "Yes. After I left, I went home and wrote out what my reply should have been, the one I should have been able to deliver with calm confidence instead of going completely blank." I shook my head, wincing at the memory. "I felt awful freezing like that. I went ahead and thought of every question I might be asked and prepared notes on my replies. After dinner, I read and reread them until I darn near memorized it all. I promise you that I won't forget the points I want to make."

"I wish we had time to go over it," Barton said. "Keep your answers responsive and short." He glanced at Ellis. "Both of you."

We nodded, then headed out, following the route Dale Morrison took. Our footsteps echoed on the stone flooring. Blinds blocked the view while allowing light. I wondered if the halls were wide and the ceilings high simply to make mere mortals feel small. It was working with me. We walked three abreast without filling half the corridor width.

Midway down the hall, Barton stopped and looked at me. "I'll do my best to keep the brunt of Dale's attack off of you, but no matter what, don't let him get to you. Stay cool. It's all right to take a few seconds to think."

"Okay," I said, swallowing hard.

"You, too, Ellis. Dale is going to try to bait you."

"Let him try. He won't succeed."

We took the elevator to the third floor and turned right, then right again. Rusty paused at the third door on the right. The top half of the door was frosted glass. JUDGE MATTHEW Q. RUTHERSON was lettered in gold, outlined in black. Barton opened the door and held it so Ellis and I could enter first.

A petite redhead older than me sat at the desk facing the door. To the right was a conference room with a long, narrow table covered with stacks of books, piles of file folders, and what seemed to be reams of paper. Some sheets had been crumpled and tossed aside. Three men and a woman, all in their early thirties, all in suits, sat around the table. They weren't talking. Two were reading; two were writing on legal pads. To the left was a hallway. At the end I could see an alcove containing a photocopier and a coffeemaker. Three doors ranged off the hall, all of them closed. Five blue upholstered chairs were positioned against the side wall.

Barton stepped up to the desk and greeted the receptionist by name, Ms. O'Neill.

At first I thought he'd been here before, but then I saw a brass plate affixed to a wooden stand on her desk. Her first name was Olive.

"I'm ADA Russell Barton. These are my witnesses."

"How do you do? Have a seat for a moment, please."

Barton turned away but didn't sit. I did. Ellis did a slow 360 taking in the scene. His scar looked darker under the fluorescent lighting than it did in natural or incandescent light.

Ms. O'Neill picked up the phone and pushed a button. "Mr. Barton and his witnesses are here . . . Yes, sir."

She stood up, smiling at us with practiced professionalism. "This way."

She led us behind her desk to a vestibule, opened a heavy wooden door, and announced, "ADA Barton."

"Sit, sit," the judge said.

Judge Rutherson was tall and thin, with the leathery brown skin of an outdoorsman. Four chairs were lined up in front of his desk. Barton stood in front of the chair closest to Morrison, then pointed at the most distant one and looked at me. I sat. Ellis sat between us. A court reporter sat off to the side in front of a metal wheeling table.

"This is going to be very informal," the judge said with some kind of drawl, Texas maybe. "I have to be in court in thirty minutes, and I'm giving you fifteen of them. Don't mess up. Here's my plan. I'll ask you a few questions, and you'll answer them simply and clearly. And quickly. We're not going to have a lot of posturing or pontificating. Do you understand that, Counselor Morrison?"

Morrison paused before answering. "I assume I'll have sufficient time to present my client's point of view, is that correct, sir?"

The judge flipped his palm at Morrison, irritated. "Of course, of course." He moved his eyes to Barton. "Do you understand it, too, Mr. Barton?"

"Yes, sir."

"I appreciate brevity," the judge said, sending his eyes around. He glanced over his shoulder. "You got that, Priscilla?"

The court reporter, an older woman with a thin face and curly brown hair, said, "Yes, sir."

"Good, good. State your names for the record." After we finished, the judge picked up a blue-covered document, then dropped it. "Let me summarize. You gentlemen don't agree on whether I should compel testimony from a Mr. Drake Milner, a Russian artifacts expert from Boston."

"That's right." Morrison crossed his legs and smiled, man to man. "Your Honor, we've both read this absurd application, and I'd like to say—"

"Be quiet, Dale," Judge Rutherson said, his tone stern but not hostile. He looked from one of us to the next, starting with me, meeting each person's eyes for a good three-count before moving on to the next person. At the end, he moved back to Barton. "What is it you think this man Milner knows?"

"Chief Hunter will address that, Your Honor."

"Mr. Milner appraised a Fabergé egg that we believe is relevant to a murder investigation." Ellis described the connection, then added, "I don't think Milner has guilty knowledge. I think he's simply protecting a client."

"He wants to be able to tell his client he had no choice," the judge said.

"Yes, sir."

"Your Honor!" Morrison said. "This is outrageous! They're going on a fishing expedition."

"Maybe," the judge said. He turned to Barton. "Give me one reason I should grant this application, why I should believe that you have evidence, that you're not just throwing toddlers into the swimming hole to see who makes it out. Do it now. Do it quick."

"There are too many coincidences for it to be anything other than cause and effect."

"Good answer. Explain."

"Your Honor!" Morrison objected.

"Be quiet!" the judge said, raising intensity, not volume. He turned back to Barton. "Continue."

Barton leaned forward and turned toward me. He smiled, the first time I'd seen him do so. He looked back at the judge.

"Josie Prescott is an antiques expert. She spoke to Drake Milner about his appraisal. I've asked her to describe the many coincidences she noted and tie it all together for us."

"I read your statement about Ms. Prescott's qualifications and am ready to certify her as an antiques expert," the judge said.

Morrison sat forward. "Your Honor! Ms. Prescott is neither a Russian decorative arts nor a Fabergé egg expert. You can't certify her."

"I'm an antiques appraisal *process* expert," I said, "and that's what's relevant here."

"I agree," Judge Rutherson said. Morrison expelled air, a sharp hissy sound of disapproval. "Proceed."

"I've been asked to appraise a previously undocumented Fabergé egg, an extraordinary occurrence." I explained about the rarity of Imperial eggs and Fabergé's escape using the snow globe ruse. The judge's eyes never wavered from my face. "The egg I examined was a fake. The real egg is missing. Drake Milner appraised a Fabergé egg last week. His egg was also undocumented and lacked provenance. That, Your Honor, is, in my expert opinion, impossible."

Morrison smiled at me, a nasty one. "Didn't I read an article in the *Seacoast Star* about an undocumented Van Gogh you located?" He turned to the judge and shrugged. "Finding rare, previously unknown masterpieces happens."

"That's right, but those two situations aren't analogous. Van Gogh was so poor, he often traded paintings for food. He kept no work records. Contrast that with Fabergé. He worked for the Russian tzar and was paid top dollar. He kept meticulous work records. For two previously unknown Fabergé eggs to surface at the same time stretches credibility. There's more." I continued talking without pause, ignoring Morrison. "Both Milner's egg and mine were purchased from stores that closed about seventy years ago. Both owners have an appealing, though wholly anecdotal, narrative to explain their acquisitions." I shook my head. "It's not a coincidence. It's a pattern. They're the same egg."

"If I may?" Morrison asked the judge.

Judge Rutherson made a circling motion with his index finger.

"Thank you." Morrison smiled at me. This one was smarmy. "Ms. Prescott, my understanding is that fewer than ten percent of antiques come with clear provenance. Is that correct?"

"Yes, but—"

He cut me off. "If you please." He turned to the judge. "Your Honor—how can we possibly think Milner's testimony is material with that kind of a statistic? That both eggs share a lack of provenance isn't a coincidence. It's the way of the world."

"You're mistaken," I said to Morrison. I smiled at the judge. "It's an example of an accurate statistic leading to an inaccurate conclusion, and if I recall correctly, that's called sophistry. That ten percent statistic encompasses everything from two-dollar collectibles to multimillion-dollar antiques. If Mr. Morrison asked me what percentage of multimillion-dollar antiques come with clear provenance, the statistics reverse—nearly ninety percent do. Few people would risk paying that kind of money if they didn't have absolute knowledge about an object's pedigree. Consider all the elements my egg and Milner's egg share." I ticked off my points by raising fingers on my left hand. "One: Two Fabergé eggs brought in for appraisal within a week of each other. Two: There's no record of either one, whereas no undocumented Fabergé egg has ever before been validated. Three: Neither comes with clear provenance. Four: Neither comes with a sales receipt." I raised my left thumb. "Five: Both were purchased from stores that closed more than seventy years ago." I started on my right hand. "Six: Both owners provide a charming explanation of the eggs' histories. And you're to believe this is a series of coincidences? Hogwash. No one element may be sufficiently persuasive on its own, but look at the six together and the pattern becomes clear."

"I said it was absurd at the start," Morrison said, bridling with amused contempt, "and I'll say it again now. This is all creative fiction, pure speculation based on minor and commonly found elements."

"No, counselor, I agree with Ms. Prescott. I know cause and effect when I see it." Judge Rutherson signed the certificate and handed it across the desk to Barton, then stood up. "I'm late. We're done."

The judge hurried out, leaving the door open. Two seconds later, Ms. O'Neill appeared at the doorway.

"This way, please," she said, and we filed out.

Morrison paused in the lobby to extend a hand to Barton. Barton shook it without comment.

"Well played, Rusty, old boy. My client instructed me to inform you that in this eventuality, he will not be appealing the judge's decision."

"Good. We'll be in touch."

I was surprised Barton didn't call him a loser. Morrison left. We stepped toward the guest chairs, out of the way.

"Well done, both of you," Barton said. "Now if you'll excuse me, I want to get this certificate to Massachusetts."

Barton marched down a hallway to the left. Ellis and I went out the way we'd come.

"Now what happens?" I asked when we reached the street.

"I'll ask you to join the meeting once it's set up—now that you're a certified expert." He smiled. "Thank you, Josie. We wouldn't have been able to do it without you."

CHAPTER EIGHTEEN

W es called me at seven in the morning, just as I was scooping cornflakes for breakfast. I had an eight o'clock appointment with a woman thinking of consigning her collection of antique gentleman's gadget canes and a ten o'clock appointment at the Rocky Point police station to listen in to Ellis's interview with Drake Milner, and I was running late. A spring snowstorm had sprung up overnight, catching me by surprise. Driving would be slow going. Already there was a thick coating, two inches deep, maybe three.

"I only have a sec," I told him as I sliced a banana onto the cornflakes. "I saw your article online. The photos look good, huh?"

"That's why I'm calling. I just got off the phone with Peter Yartsin. He's going to sue the paper—and me."

"Why?"

"I'm not sure exactly. I don't think he knows exactly. He was ranting something about privacy, then something about obstruction of justice."

"Peter has anger issues. Once he thinks it through and talks to Chief Hunter, he'll calm down."

"He says he's going to sue him, too."

"I don't think you can sue a police official."

"He also said he was going to sue you. That the photos you sent me were his sister's property and you had no right to allow them to be published without her permission."

My mouth went dry. I coughed.

"What did he—" I broke off, coughing again. I couldn't speak. I couldn't think.

I poured a glass of water and sank onto the bench behind my kitchen table. I looked out the window past my patio, over the meadow, to the forest beyond as I drank. The grasslands were solidly white, the pines dotted with snow.

When I didn't say anything, Wes added, "I've already spoken to the paper's lawyer. He says we're clear, but you may not be." He cleared his throat. "That's why I'm calling. To give you a heads-up."

A robin landed on the flagstone patio, which was protected by an overhang, pecked at something, then flew away.

"Thanks," I said. I drank some more water. "Are you going to write about Peter's threats?"

"If he actually files suit, or if Ana does, that's news, and we'll report it. Until then, no."

"Okay. Thanks, Wes." I hung up.

I found my lawyer's home phone number in an old-fashioned address book I keep in a drawer of my eighteenth-century lady's writing desk, and dialed. Max's wife, Babs, answered, said a cheery hello when she heard my name, and told me to hang on.

"Josie," Max said, sounding as friendly as ever. "What's the trouble?"

I could hear his daughter, Penny, griping about having to eat breakfast. "I'm not hungry," she said. I couldn't hear Babs's reply.

I repeated what Wes told me, then asked, "What should I do?"

"Do you know how Ana feels about it?"

"No."

"Why did you do it?"

I leaned forward, resting my forehead on my hand. "It never entered my mind that Ana might not want them released, or that I ought to ask permission. She talked about the previous appraisal—including those photos—on the set, for instance, and in front of Heather and Jason. The simple truth is that the only thing I was thinking about was that if you don't tell people you're looking for something, how do they know to tell you if they know where it is?"

"What's the downside? Why is Peter so upset?"

"Maybe he's worried that thieves will take notice. If you have one valuable object, a thief might assume you have others."

"Why else?"

"I don't know. Ana planned on using the egg on her TV show. She's not antipublicity, by any means."

"She's not anti-*good*-publicity."

"True." I sat up. "I don't know, Max. If it was my oldest friend's fiancé who had been murdered, I wouldn't hesitate to allow the photos to be used."

"And we have no reason to think she will." He paused for a moment. "Why don't we ask to meet to discuss Peter's threats? She can bring him, if she'd like. It's illegal for a man with no legal standing to threaten people, and he should know that."

I smiled and exhaled, relieved. No matter what issue I threw at Max, his counsel was always wise. "The best defense is a good offense."

"Indeed. In the course of our conversation, I'll make certain Ana understands your good intentions."

"If Peter comes along, brace yourself."

"I've had many dealings with hotheads. He doesn't concern me at all."

"I'm so glad you're my lawyer."

"I'm so glad you're my client. Do you want to ask Ana to meet you at my office, or would you prefer that I make the call?"

"I'll do it. If you're available at noon, I can position it as a quick chat, then let's go to lunch."

"Excellent idea. Kill 'em with kindness. Let me check my schedule."

Tips of purple crocuses poked through the snow, a symbol of hope and renewal and progress. Funny that I hadn't noticed them before.

"All right," Max said. "I'm open. Noon it is. Call my office to confirm as soon as you reach Ana."

I promised I would and punched the END CALL button. I looked up Ana's number and dialed.

She answered on the fifth ring, sounding sleepy and anxious.

"It's Josie," I said. "I'm sorry to call so early, but it's important. Do you want to take a minute to wake up?"

"No, no. I should be up already. What's wrong?"

"Nothing, I hope. It's just a time crunch/scheduling thing." I closed my eyes and crossed my fingers. "I was wondering if you're available at noon to go over where we are with the appraisal and the search for the missing egg. Afterward, maybe we could go to lunch."

"That sounds great. Thanks, Josie. Should I come to your office?"

I opened my eyes, but I kept my fingers crossed. "Have you spoken to Peter?"

"No. Why?"

"He's making some pretty out-there statements."

"Oh, no. Tell me."

"We'll talk at noon. Do you have a pen? I'll give you the address of where we should meet."

"Give me a sec." I closed my eyes again for the three seconds she was gone. "Shoot." I rattled off Max's firm's name and location, and she added, "A lawyer? Am I in trouble?"

"I'm hoping none of us is."

"You sure know how to wake a girl up."

"I'll see you at noon."

"Okay," Ana said, sounding scared.

I got into work two minutes before Marianna Albert arrived with a photo album tucked under her arm. The storm had slowed to flurries, a relief. I'd worn a spring coat, a sure sign of optimism.

"Come in, come in," I told her.

While she got settled at the guest table, I hung up her leather duster, an unusual choice for a woman her age, which I pegged as closer to eighty than seventy. Otherwise, she was conventionally dressed in a brown tweed skirt, a green cardigan over a white silk blouse, and cordovan-colored knee-high boots. The skirt had green flecks in it. Her gray-white hair was cut short. Her jade earrings matched the flower-shaped pendant that hung just below her collarbone.

I pushed aside the panicky fear that had come over me as soon as Wes told me about Peter's threats and offered her coffee or tea. I was doing what I could, what I should. I was carrying on.

"Thanks, no. I'm off to a hair appointment," she said, "so I can only stay a minute. Since we spoke, I've checked you out. You have a very good reputation."

"I'm glad to hear that. Do you have any questions about the consignment process?"

"A thousand," she said, smiling. She placed her photo album on the table in front of her, lowered her eyes, her expression softening, and patted the navy blue leather cover. She looked up at me. "Walter . . . that's my husband, I told you on the phone how he passed away last year . . . Walter loved his canes. He collected them for more than fifty years. I've tried to keep everything the same, but—" She lowered her eyes to the photo album again but didn't resume talking.

"But then you realized that everything isn't the same."

She shook her head, resigned, not sad. "Nor should it be. I'm moving to St. John." She grinned. "You know why?"

"Because it has perfect weather and the drinks come with cute little umbrellas in them?"

She laughed. "No. Because I like to snorkel, and I want to live somewhere where I can snorkel every day."

"Wonderful! I love snorkeling, too. Why St. John?"

"I saw a seahorse there once. I'd never seen one before, and I've never seen once since." She took in a deep breath. "Walter and I never had children. It's time to let the walking sticks go."

I nodded. "How many are there?"

"Eighty-seven."

"Eighty-seven! Wow. That's a huge collection."

She slid the album across the table toward me. "Take a look and see if you're interested. If so, you can come out to the house and examine them, and then we can discuss terms and see if we want to work with one another."

I opened the album. Each plastic sleeve held six photos, three shots per cane. The first shot showed the full-length cane on a white background. The second showed the decorative head. The third showed some aspect of the gadget or an abditory.

"Is this silver?" I asked, pointing to the filigreed embellishment near the grip in the first photograph.

She leaned over to look. "Yes, with ebony. That was the first walking stick Walter ever purchased." She raised her eyes. "I have complete records. All receipts, appraisals, and the catalogue entries Walter wrote."

I smiled. "That's very good news indeed." I studied the third photo. "Is this aperture for cigarettes?"

"Yes. It doesn't show in this photo, but there's a second opening on the other side for matches."

"Fabulous. Which one was Walter's favorite?"

"Ooh, that's a tough one. He loved the violin walking stick made by

Augustus Johnson because it was so rare, but I think he was proudest of his binocular cane. It's made of perfectly matched bird's-eye maple, with professional quality, full-sized binoculars tucked in so cleverly you'd never see them if you didn't know they were there."

My pulse speeded up, a sure sign I had a winner on my hands. "I know you're in a hurry, and I don't need to look in detail to know I want to see the collection. Even at a quick glance, I'm impressed and excited."

"Wonderful. How's this afternoon?"

My stomach sank as I recalled my noon appointment. Even if Ana didn't intend to sue me, it was certain to be an angst-filled time. Once again, I forced myself to ignore that and concentrate only on what was within my immediate control.

"This afternoon is perfect. Where do you live?"

"In Durham."

I did some mental calculations on how long it would take to drive to Durham after lunch. "Will three thirty work for you?"

"Perfect," she said, standing. "I'll make tea."

Drake Milner didn't show up. He didn't answer his phone. He didn't respond to texts or e-mails.

At ten forty-five, Ellis called Marlborough Antiques and spoke to Julie. He put her on speakerphone so I could listen in.

"He's not there?" Julie asked, surprised.

I could picture her elegant demeanor and her reddish hair.

"Do you know when he left Boston?" Ellis asked.

"He called around eight this morning. His message said that he was en route to New Hampshire and that he expected to be back to the shop after lunch, somewhere around three. He should be there by now." Julie's surprise changed in a flash to worry. "He should have been there an hour ago."

"That's true. If you hear from him, ask him to call me right away."

"All right."

Ellis tapped the button to end the call and looked at me. "Where is he?"

"Maybe his client got to him and bribed him to keep him quiet."

Ellis shook his head. "He would have invented facts to avoid talking to us. A variation on 'the dog ate my paper,' like the records got put through the shredder by mistake or the computer crashed and there was no backup, something like that."

I gazed out the window. The sky had brightened into a soft dove gray.

"Drake's left town," I said. "Either his client threatened him or he's been involved in the fraud from the start."

He raised his brows.

"Yup," I said. "I betcha—he's on the lam."

"You seem very positive."

"What else could it be? If he had a flat tire or something, he would have called. He's at the airport and checked in for his flight, either because he's terrified to talk to you or because he planned it this way all along."

"Where is he flying to?"

"Somewhere without extradition." I shook my head as pieces of the puzzle fell neatly into place. "He's the scammer, Ellis. I can't believe it didn't occur to us until now, but look at it. Someone delivers the Fabergé Spring Egg snow globe to him for appraisal. He replicates it, gives them an appraisal showing a high value, and hands over the fake egg. Based on the inflated appraisal the person can get a secured loan. He sells the genuine egg to a collector and disappears. It's slick."

"If he knew we were working on a subpoena, why would he stick around? Why wouldn't he have left the country the minute I filed the paperwork?"

"He didn't think he'd lose. And maybe he didn't call from the highway at eight this morning. Maybe when he agreed to this appointment, he was zipping up his suitcase, eager to make the night flight to Croatia."

Ellis pursed his lips, thinking. "Croatia has no extradition treaty with the U.S. It has a stable government, cheap prices, and gorgeous scenery. He could do worse." He paused. "You've almost got me convinced. Is it realistic to think that he sold the egg to a collector? I mean, I know we've talked about it. But if it's black market, would he have those contacts?"

"Yes. When you deal in high-end antiques, you meet lots of people with lots of money. Not all of them acquired their money legally. He could have sold it for several million dollars, which has already been deposited in a Croatian bank account."

"I need to check it out."

"We've been snookered."

"Why would he call you and offer his services?"

"Greed. He thought that if he could pull off a switcheroonie once, he could do it twice."

Ellis grinned. "He didn't know you."

"He still doesn't. I don't like being snookered."

"Leave it to me, Josie."

I stood up, anger that had been simmering just below the surface beginning to boil. I marched to the window, spun around, stomped back to the table, then repeated the trek. Ellis watched me silently.

"I'm mad," I said.

"Yeah." He reached for the phone. "Pace if you want to, but stay quiet. I need to make some calls."

I paced, half-listening as Ellis called the FBI, Interpol, and someone called Rocco. I kept my smart phone in my hand, waiting for Drake's callback or text. I felt foolish, like a mark choused out of her life savings by a fast-talking con man.

At eleven forty-five, Ellis got a call, listened for a full minute, then thanked the caller and hung up.

He looked at me. "Drake Milner didn't fly out of the country under his own name."

"If I were him, I wouldn't either. I'd pick an all-new name, one no one knew about." I glanced at my smart phone. "I have to go. I have an appointment at noon."

"Who brought him that egg?"

"Ana. She wanted it appraised, maybe for insurance like she said, or maybe so she'd have collateral for a loan, like we've been speculating. She hired Drake because her father thought anyone who wasn't a Russian artifacts expert was Mickey Mouse. She was going to let me appraise it, too, because she'd already signed a deal with me. Ana and her father have a complicated relationship. They had a falling-out because he didn't approve of her choice of career. You were there when she saw her dad round the corner of her house—she looked at him like he was her total hope and comfort, her rock. No way would she risk his disapproval, not at this stage of their relationship. He tells her to go to Drake, she goes. What does she care? So she double pays. If she can win back a little more of her dad's love, I bet she'd count it cheap at double the price."

"You're making this up."

"Yes, but not on impulse. Something Drake said—that maybe the owner and the thief were the same person—stayed with me. At first I couldn't see how the scam could work. Now I can." I held up a palm. "There's still too much we don't know. I don't know who replicated the Fabergé egg and snow globe. I haven't got a clue who killed Jason, or why. I don't know whether the egg is related to the murder or not—but I know it's possible that I'm right because I know a lot about how women interact with their dads."

"If you were me, what would you do next?"

I glanced at my phone again. I was going to be late. "I'd ask me to call you after my lunch with Ana."

Ellis leaned back in his chair. "Will you call me after you have lunch with Ana?"

"Sure."

He stood up and walked toward me until he was standing only inches away. He looked down at me.

"I have a better idea . . . May I join you?"

I gazed into his eyes but learned nothing. "How come?"

"Curiosity."

I met his eyes. They didn't look intrigued. They looked worried. "You think I might be in danger."

"In a public place? Unlikely."

"Yet you want to join me."

"Excess of caution."

"I'll learn more if I'm alone."

Ellis shook his head. "Don't question her, Josie. Your job isn't to learn anything. Chat about the weather."

"The situation is bound to come up."

"Don't let it." He raised a hand to stop me from replying. "Ana might be a killer."

I paused, trying to picture Ana bashing Jason's head against the field-stone hearth. The image did not compute. Ana was reserved, pleasant, pol-ished, elegant, and calm. I'd seen her sad and anxious and angry, but I'd never seen her lose control. No matter how bad her financial situation was, I couldn't envision Ana as a murderer. A thief, possibly. A killer, no.

"Do you suspect her more than anyone else?" I asked.

"No."

"Me either. I was just talking."

"Don't do anything stupid, Josie."

"Me? Never." When he didn't respond right away, I touched his upper arm. "Really, Ellis, I'm a scaredy cat. I'd never do anything stupid."

Outside, streaks of pale blue sky showed through the dense gray cloud cover. The storm had passed. I walked across crunchy snow to my car. *Ana,* I thought.

CHAPTER NINETEEN

Max Bixby's small law firm was housed in a big white house on Brook Street, just outside Rocky Point's main shopping area. He owned the building, which used to be a private residence, and rented out suites to other professionals. His current tenants included an independent insurance agent, two psychotherapists, a title company, and a nutritionist. Max kept the sprawling ground floor for his company.

Max was just what a lawyer should be: smart and knowledgeable, objective and fair, protective and flexible. Today he wore a blue and brown tweed jacket with brown slacks and shoes, a yellow shirt, and a blue bow tie with brown polka dots. He was tall and thin, and his eyes twinkled when he said something he thought was funny, which happened a lot.

He opened his office door in response to his secretary's buzz. I didn't recognize her. I wondered what happened to his longtime assistant, Gloria.

"Josie!" Max said.

He extended a hand. We shook. He stepped back and waved me in.

His office was as modern as I recalled, an odd variance to his courtly old-world appearance and manners. His desk had been created from a slab of black granite. Smallish diamond-shaped glass-topped tables were positioned on either side of the black leather and chrome sofa. A glass-topped conference table stood near the windows. The iron gray curtains had gold and silver threads running vertically through the fabric. The rug was charcoal gray. The walls were light gray, a sort of pale blueberry color. Abstract paintings, mostly geometric shapes, hung on every wall. Some contained slashes of red or purple.

Max led the way to the conference table. The glass top sparkled under the overhead recessed lights. A phone console sat at the head of the table next to a black leather portfolio. A Polycom voice station was positioned in the center, its cords running through a black flexible plastic tube that disappeared under the carpet. Next to it, a tray held a cut-crystal carafe of water and four matching glasses.

"I'm sorry I'm late," I said.

"No problem, Josie. Ana arrived a few minutes ago. I have her parked in an empty office. I wanted to talk to you first, see if there's anything new about Peter's threats I should be aware of."

"No. I just hope she isn't mad at me."

"Let's find out."

He pushed a button on the phone console, and his secretary opened the door and looked at him.

"Please bring Ms. Yartsin in, Marian."

She said she would and shut the door as she left.

"What happened to Gloria?" I asked.

"She took a four-month leave to go help her daughter Danni in Texas. Danni had a baby."

"Oh! That's wonderful. Wonderful for her, not so great for you. So Marian is a temp?"

"No, she's an admin shared by two of the firm's associates. She's terrific." He grinned. "They got the temp. I poached."

I laughed. "You devil, you."

He shook his head, his eyes twinkling. "The guilt weighs on me."

"I can tell."

He sat up straight, pressed his palm against his chest, and in an orator's voice said, "Uneasy lies the head that wears a crown."

I felt my brow furrow. "King Henry?"

"The Fourth. Shakespeare sure could write, couldn't he?"

"Like nobody's business."

Marian opened the door, and Ana stepped in. Max and I both stood up.

"Would either of you like some coffee or tea?" Marian asked.

We declined, and she backed out of the room. I introduced Ana, and Max pulled out a chair across from me. Max sat at the head of the table.

"I hope you haven't been waiting long," I said as they got settled.

Ana placed her purse on the chair next to her. Max slipped a yellow legal pad from the portfolio and took a fountain pen from his shirt pocket.

"Not at all." She looked at Max, then back at me.

I turned to Max, silently asking him to jump in.

"Josie was concerned that your brother was speaking on your behalf when he threatened to sue."

Ana's eyes flew open. "What are you talking about?"

"He called Wes Smith, the *Seacoast Star* reporter, early this morning."

She shifted her gaze to the wall, to a painting. "That must be why . . ." Her voice trailed off.

"Why what?" Max asked, making a note in his impossible-to-read scrawl.

She turned back to face him. "My brother is highly charged, but not highly disciplined when it comes to people he cares about. Please tell me what he said."

I repeated what Wes told me, then said, "I'm sor—"

Max jumped in. He patted my arm, gave me a kind, fatherly smile, then turned toward Ana. "Josie sent Wes those photos after discussing it with Police Chief Hunter. He hoped they might generate leads. Are you all right with that?"

"Of course! Why wouldn't I be?"

"It's possible you, like your brother, might have thought Josie should have asked permission."

"I appreciate your concern, but I gave those photos to Josie for her to use as she thinks best."

Max made a note. "Peter indicated something about privacy concerns."

Ana laughed, one unladylike snort. "Privacy concerns? I've been trying to get a reality TV show produced. I was going to feature the Fabergé egg on the show. What privacy concerns?" She flipped her hand backward in a derisive gesture of dismissal. "Besides which, my brother doesn't speak for me."

"What a relief," I said, leaning back. "I was so worried I'd upset you, and I wouldn't do that for the world."

"I'm plenty upset, but not at you." She shook her head. "Peter is misguided, but his heart is in the right place. He's so family-oriented. I'm certain he was only doing what he thought was best for me."

Max made another note, opened his portfolio, and extracted a single sheet of paper. He glanced at the paper, then slid it across the table toward Ana.

"Please read this," he said, "and if the language reflects your intent, please sign it."

Ana read through the document, signed her name, dated it, and slid it back toward him. "May I have a copy?"

"Certainly."

He pushed a button on the phone console, and Marian appeared at the door. He explained what he wanted. The three of us sat silently until she reappeared, copies in hand.

Max handed one to Ana, then the other to me. "For your files."

We all stood up, and Max shook hands with each of us.

Ana asked to use the restroom, and when Marian led her away, I whispered, "That went better than I expected."

Max smiled. "I agree."

"Why did you stop me from apologizing?"

"An apology implies wrongdoing."

"That isn't what I meant!"

"I know. People say 'I'm sorry' as a default, without thinking about the actual meaning or how it might be perceived."

I thought of Heather and how I'd questioned what was behind her repeated apologies. Perception. I stared at the three-sentence memo. Ana had just given me permission to use, publish, disseminate, or otherwise share her photographs of the Fabergé Spring Egg snow globe. I raised my eyes to his. "Thank you, Max."

"You're welcome. Good luck with your search."

I slipped the paper into my tote bag. "I have a feeling I'm going to need it."

Ana had never been to Ellie's Crêpes, one of my favorite restaurants.

Ellie's fronted on the village green. The seating area was long and narrow in what had been a chocolate manufactory. Mellowed bricks lined both walls. Every table was filled, and a line stretched out the door. No one made better crêpes than Ellie.

I left Ana looking at the menu and hurried into the single-unit, unisex restroom, and locked the door. I texted Ellis. "Any news re Drake?"

He replied within seconds. "No."

I returned to the table as the waitress, a tall young woman with earnest eyes, was pouring water from a stainless steel pitcher.

"I'm sorry you had to become involved in Peter's issues," Ana said. "Please add Max's bill to my invoice. There's no reason you should have to pay for my brother's bad behavior."

"That's very gracious of you, Ana, but completely unnecessary. I should have clients sign a release all the time. Now I have a template."

Ana sighed. "What a world we live in. Filled with suspicion."

"Suspicion and cynicism and litigation."

The waitress reappeared, and I ordered my regular, the chicken and asparagus crêpe with mornay sauce. Ana ordered the ratatouille crêpe.

She handed over her menu, waited for the waitress to walk away, then said, "Do you think there's any hope of finding the egg?"

"Yes, I do. I have lots of irons in the fire."

"Like what?"

"I can't tell you. Or rather, I have nothing to tell you yet. I promise I will as soon as I can."

"Need to know versus want to know. I dated an army officer once. He only told me things I needed to know." She smiled, head cocked, eyes dancing. "Made for limited chitchat."

I laughed, and it felt good, but then memories returned, and the mood passed. *Jason.* "Is Heather's family staying in town?"

"Most people have left already. The rest go tomorrow. For the funeral." Ana moved the salt shaker closer to its mate. "The church service is at nine, followed by the interment. I plan on driving back right away. I asked Heather if she wanted me to stay over and she said no, that she was being suffocated by love and caring and wanted everyone to leave her alone." She glanced over her shoulder to check out the tables in back of us. No one was paying us any attention. She swiveled back and met my eyes. "I'm scheduled to have a powwow with Maurice, Ray, and Suzanne tomorrow at three." She grimaced. "I'm in for a fun day, huh? First a funeral, then a talk with a madman."

"Do you think he's really mad?"

"I don't know. Everyone at the Blue Dolphin indulges him like he's the crown prince or something. I don't get it."

"Even Ray?"

"Especially Ray. I've known a lot of pastry chefs in my day. I went to school with scores of them. Heck, I am one. There's a lot of cockiness among us, God knows, but I've never seen anyone even half as arrogant or a quarter as rude as he is."

"Maybe he's just what he seems to be—a spoiled brat."

She shrugged. "I have no idea."

The waitress brought our plates. I watched as Ana tried her crêpe. "This is unbelievable," she said. "Luscious!"

"I know. And Ellie won't tell anyone how she does it."

"What do you think it is? It's not sugar. Could it be Grand Marnier?"

"In a savory crêpe? That would be a new one."

Ana lowered her fork to her plate and looked at me, a steady gaze. "I need to ask a favor." She paused. "Would you come with me to my meeting?"

"Me?" I asked, surprised.

"As a witness and a translator. To help me remember what's said and how people act, and to help me understand what I can do to make the situation work. I don't want to lose the Blue Dolphin account, and I don't want to get blamed if Maurice quits or flips out. To help me figure out how to avoid inflaming an already explosive situation." Ana laid her hand on top of mine and pressed down. "I know I have no right to ask, but I'd be so grateful."

"Let me check my schedule," I said, flattered to be asked and secretly glad to be offered an opportunity to see Maurice in action, to see if he was all hot air and bad attitude or whether there was some as yet unrecognized substance beneath his emotional meltdowns. I dug my phone out of my tote bag and checked my calendar. Nothing was scheduled. "I can go." I entered the meeting into the calendar.

"Thank you. I can't tell you how appreciative I am."

"Where are you meeting?"

"At the restaurant."

I added that info to the listing, then slipped the phone back into my bag. Ana picked up her fork and took a bite. "I should have thought of this earlier—having someone with me." She sighed. "Truthfully, I've been in such a funk, I haven't registered that Maurice might be out to derail me and my company and that this meeting really matters to my business. Between you, me, and this shaker of salt, I'm dreading it."

I understood some, at least, of the complexity she'd be walking into. Ana was in a tough spot. Her boyfriend, Chef Ray, would be there representing the Blue Dolphin, not her, and no matter what he wanted personally, his loyalty at work had to be to his job. His boss, Suzanne, wouldn't be concerned about Ana at all. Her responsibility was to her company, to her bottom line. And Maurice seemed out to get Ana regardless of what was best for the restaurant.

"I don't blame you," I said. "It's a pretty dreadful situation."

"I trust your judgment, Josie. It will be wonderful to have someone there who has no agenda."

I smiled and finished my crêpe, thinking that it was a good thing Ana couldn't read my mind. I did indeed have my own agenda, and it wasn't the same as hers.

CHAPTER TWENTY

Marianna Albert lived on Woodbridge Road in Durham, a university town about twenty miles inland from Rocky Point, about a half-hour drive. Ty and I had gone to a party at a house on that street a couple of years ago, so I knew the neighborhood was high-end, with large glass and stone contemporaries and sprawling Colonials set on five-plus-acre lots. I smiled to myself thinking about getting a gander at Marianna's husband's collection of eighty-seven gentleman's gadget canes.

"Fingers crossed," I said aloud. I glanced at the dash clock. It was only ten to two, so I had plenty of time to check in at work.

Before I started the drive, I called Ellis and got his voice mail.

"I'm calling just because I said I would. I have no news. Maybe Ana isn't involved after all—I don't know. She had no problem with my using the photos. She seems the same as always, except maybe a little preoccupied with business issues, which, given all she has going on, would be completely normal, if you ask me. Anyway, I guess no news is good news."

I ended the call and headed to my office. When I arrived, Fred was standing by the table doing a happy dance, half '70s disco, half modern-day hip-hop, his index fingers pointing to the ceiling. He dipped and spun and shook his hips, wiggling in time to Cara and Gretchen's rhythmic clapping.

Sasha's cheeks were rosy pink. She was smiling and clapping along, mostly off the beat.

"The happy dance!" I said, stepping inside. "What are we celebrating?"

Gretchen grinned, her emerald eyes sparkling. "Sasha's verification of the Victorian Christmas snow globe. It's authentic. And rare. And valuable."

I turned to Sasha. "Yay!"

She tucked her hair behind her ear, her smile widening, her cheeks reddening. She sounded proud when she said, "It's good."

Fred stopped dancing, and Cara and Gretchen stopped clapping. Everyone was looking at Sasha. I held up crossed fingers.

"You know how I spoke to the director of the Vienna Snow Globe Museum? He gave me a list of materials that would have been used by the company during various periods to help date ours. Silver and gold and certain kinds of wood for specific applications and different categories of embellishments and which was used when, and so on. The Victorian Christmas snow globe matches the materials lists perfectly. I thought we wouldn't be able to narrow the date any more than the early nineteen hundreds, but we can." She paused, and from the way her eyes shone, I could tell she was enjoying creating a little suspense. "The company no longer has any twentieth-century custom-order records, but they found a raw materials inventory listing from 1913—including exactly the kinds of greenery we see on the doors. It was the first and only year they used piece-made garlands. Before and after that year, they used lengths of garland material cut to fit." She leaned back and smiled as widely as I'd ever seen her smile. "I've just confirmed that it is a genuine Vienna Snow Globe company object. We have empirical evidence."

"And its value?" I asked.

"Based on past sales and current levels of interest in holiday-themed snow globes, I'm estimating that it would sell at auction for between twenty and twenty-five thousand dollars." She smiled. "It's in perfect condition."

I whistled, a two-toned brava. "And that, ladies and gentlemen, is how you do that. I want to join the happy dance!"

I leaped up and spun into a disco move, jiggling my right index finger up and down and up again toward an imaginary mirrored disco ball. Fred joined in, and Cara and Gretchen resumed their clapping. Sasha laughed, pressing her palms against her flushed cheeks. After about a minute, I flopped down at the guest table.

"Great job, Sasha. How about the other one, the one with two skaters?"

She smiled devilishly. "I think it might be even more valuable than the Victorian Christmas one." She walked it over and placed it carefully in front of me. She offered me a loupe, which I took and eased into place. "Look for a capital *G* in blue on the pond. It's hard to see because the pond is painted streaky blue to mimic ice. It's just to the left of the man."

I stared at the spot she indicated. "Well, looky, looky! Underglaze blue."

"Exactly."

I removed the loupe. "I don't know that mark. Whose is it?"

"It belongs to the Gardner factory, which was located in a suburb of Moscow called Verbilki. The Metropolitan Museum of Art has several examples of Gardner's work. This sculpture appears to date from around 1770, more than a hundred years before snow globes were invented."

"So it's just as you suspected. Someone placed it in a snow globe at a later date."

"It looks that way."

"Are you comfortable dating it based on the mark and style similarities to the ones in the Met?"

"Yes. The mark is telling. Francis Gardner was an Englishman who emigrated to Russia in 1746 to open a porcelain manufacturing company. The tsar had to okay all new manufacturing facilities, and it took him twenty years to get official permission to produce his wares." She shook her head. "Can you imagine? Twenty years."

Fred, leaning against the desk table, listening in, said, "And we think our bureaucracy is slow!"

"I know. It's amazing. He opened on the sly, but to hide what he was doing, he used the Meissen logo."

I laughed. "No way!" Meissen was a famous German porcelain manufacturer whose objects were popular and prevalent. Over the years, we'd appraised scores of them. "How can we have never known this?"

"It's only just come to light."

"This throws a real monkey wrench into the works," Fred said.

"I know," Sasha said. "He was super sneaky about it, too. He'd brought a Meissen craftsman with him to Russia, so re-creating Meissen's dual crossed-swords mark was easy."

Fred pushed up his glasses. "We'll need to look at materials."

"Agreed," Sasha said. She looked at the snow globe. "Gardner received authorization to open in 1766 and started using his own logo—a capital G—right away. So it's safe to assume that this sculpture was created after that."

Fred shook the snow globe and watched the silvery bits settle. "Any chance it was created earlier, right when he opened, before he learned he needed permission?"

"No. There's ample documentary evidence Gardner knew what he was doing, that he came because he recognized a market opportunity and was prepared for delays." She flipped open her hands. "Maybe not for twenty years, but still."

"Amazing," I said. "Now what?"

"Now I contact the State Hermitage Museum in Russia to see if they have any information about the kind of porcelain Gardner used."

I congratulated her again on her thorough work, then turned to Gretchen. "And you? How are you doing?"

"Fabulous! I've finished talking to all the carpet companies interested in bidding on the new carpet, and Jack and I finally picked colors for the baby's room—spring green and lemon yellow."

"Perfect spring colors for a baby born in spring," Cara said.

"They're happy colors, too," I said. "I'm going to run up to my office for a minute. I'll be leaving around three to meet the woman with the gadget canes." I smiled devilishly. "Eighty-seven of them."

Amid cheers and wishes of good luck and more applause, I pushed open the fire door and stepped into the warehouse. As I approached the spiral staircase, Hank came running up. He mewed, rubbing his jowl against my calf. I scooped him up, and he placed a paw on my cheek and tucked his head under my chin, purring.

"Hi, baby," I murmured. "Are you having a good afternoon?"

He purred louder.

"Good. I'm glad to hear that."

He repositioned his head against my chin, settling in. I sat on the bottom step and shifted him into a cradle position. I had an accounting report to read and e-mails to answer, and I decided to skip it all. Time spent with cats is never wasted.

"You're *such* a good boy, Hank. You're my little love bunny, aren't you, sweetheart?"

We sat like that, cuddling one another, until it was time for me to go.

The radio said that a storm they'd expected to go south of us had stalled and we were in for it. The flurries now falling were the front edge of a major storm; by midnight, snow would be falling heavily and steadily, and we could expect close to a foot by morning, with temperatures plunging to the single digits. I pushed the INFO button on my dashboard; the outside temperature was 18.

With the windshield wipers on low intermittent, I drove down Ocean

Boulevard to Cable Road and turned left onto the extension that dead-ended at the ocean. I got out of the car, turned up my coat collar, and watched frothy white waves crack like corn popping as they crashed against the rocky shore. I called Ty and got his voice mail.

"Hey, Ty . . . apparently we're in for a storm, as much as a foot of snow by morning. I'm thinking let's go to your place and make a big fire and I'll make us something warm and yummy for dinner. Okay? I love you. See you later."

I got back in the car, held my chilled hands over the heat vent for a minute, then headed west on Central Road to Love Lane. Ridges of snow lined the road, growing higher as I moved inland. The snow fell heavily for a few seconds, then backed off into sputtering flurries, then became more intense again, swirling down into a dense wall of white.

Just before Love Lane jigged to the left, past Bailey Brook, near Locke Pond, I spotted the kind of black marks left by a skidding car. I slowed to a crawl. The tire marks slithered for twenty feet, then cut hard to the right, slicing through the snowbank and disappearing. I rolled to a stop, edging as close to the snowy ridge as I could. I punched the button to activate my blinkers, stepped out, and looked around.

Love Lane ran along the west-most edge of Rocky Point, cutting through a multiacre patch of conservation land. Nothing but trees and water and the winding two-lane asphalt road was in sight. I shivered. The temperature was dropping as the clouds thickened. I followed the tire tracks to the precipice.

I gasped.

A car, a metallic gray Audi with Massachusetts plates, rested on its front end in the murky near-black water. The trunk was sticking into the air at a crazy angle. I started down the snowy incline, then stopped and scrambled back up the hill, ran for my car, and grabbed my phone. I dialed 911, reported what I'd seen, then called Ellis. I got his voice mail and left a message, only saying that I was at the scene of a car accident and needed him to join me as soon as he could.

I tossed my phone and the car keys on the front seat, ran back to the hill, and started down, stopping just short of the water. I squatted to plunge my hand into the icy water, testing whether wading in was a possibility. Immediately, my fingers went numb.

"Oh, God," I whispered and whipped my hand out of the water.

No way could I make it.

Shivering, I wiped my hand on my pants.

I pulled the retractable cord attached to the flashlight I wore on my belt and aimed the white light into the back window, but the car was canted in such a way that all I could see was the rear of the front seats.

Tears ran down my cheeks. Someone was in there, maybe still alive, and there was nothing I could do.

The falling snow was wetting my hair, freezing my head and neck. Flakes drifted down my collar, melting as they hit my back, sending chills running up and down my spine like spiders. I guessed it had been about ten minutes since I called for help. Ten minutes wasn't an unreasonable response time in such an isolated area, but it was too long for someone immersed in frigid water to live. It was also too long for someone—me—to be outside in a medium-weight coat, with no hat or gloves. I shivered again and flapped my elbows against my sides in a futile effort to generate warmth. My teeth chattered.

I needed to get out of the wind-driven bitter cold. I had to stop standing in knee-high snow.

I started up the incline. Three steps up, I tripped on a snow-covered something, a broken tree limb maybe, and spilled onto the ground. I rolled downhill toward the shore. Before I could stop myself, I hit a mogul and flew into the water face-first.

I sat up, breathless, disoriented, and terrified.

Pushing against the muddy bottom, I tried to stand, but my hands got sucked into a tangle of slippery algae. I waddled backward on my knees, each lumbering step a weighted nightmare, thrashing and dragging through the water-laden grasses that didn't want to let me go.

Finally, I made it to land. I sat on the snow, heaving for air, trembling uncontrollably.

I knew I shouldn't wait to catch my breath before making my way to my car, to warmth, to safety. It was dangerously cold. I crawled up the hill, one draggling step at a time, feeling my way around obstacles. When the road came into sight, I began to cry, I was so relieved. I made it to my car.

I reached over the driver's seat to start the motor and turn the heat on high, then found an old wool blanket I kept in the trunk for picnics. I stripped off my sodden clothes, leaving them in a heap on the road, wrapped myself in the dry blanket, and slid behind the wheel.

I hit the lever and the seat snapped back. I closed my eyes, waiting for the paralyzing cold to pass, waiting for help. Spiky needles pricked at my head and my back and my feet. I opened my eyes and looked out the window. The clouds were more gray than white, like a dove, I thought, flying freely. Earlier, I'd thought the sky was dove gray. Now I saw it was, in fact, an actual dove. I coughed, then coughed again. I was dry, but too tired to reach for the water bottle I kept in the console. I lay still and watched the dove swoop and soar and glide.

I heard sirens and sighed. I tried to sit up, to push the lever to raise the seat back, but I couldn't. My muscles seemed to have disappeared.

"I'm tired," I told the dove.

I hugged myself, rocking a little. I closed my eyes again, wishing I could fly like a dove, and waited to be rescued.

CHAPTER TWENTY-ONE

A t nine that night, I lay curled up on Ty's oversized sofa in front of a raging fire, wearing fuzzy, warm pale pink pajamas and a thick rose-colored chenille robe. I'd taken a hot shower, then sat in a hot bath, and was, oddly, ravenous. And desperately thirsty, craving, of all things, lemonade. I was on my last glass from the first pitcher and was relieved to hear Ty whisking up a fresh batch.

Ty was also making dinner. I could hear him rattling around the kitchen, reheating the chicken noodle soup I'd made two nights ago, with grilled cheese and tomato sandwiches to follow.

He came in with a folded-up plastic-coated tablecloth and shook it out. I'd bought it for us to use when we ate outside. The pattern was called Italian Kitchen and featured purple and green grapes and frilly bunches of herbs and ripe red tomatoes and jugs of red wine.

"I thought we'd have a picnic so we could stay near the fire. What do you think?"

"I think that's a fabulicious idea. This afghan is perfect. So is the fire. I may never move. For whatever reason, I'm dreading even the slightest prospect of being cold."

"Understood. Hot soup to follow."

He shook the tablecloth out, then spread it along the floor in front of the sofa.

I looked at him, tears welling in my eyes. "How did I get so lucky to find you?"

"I'm the lucky one." He touched my cheek. "Plus, you didn't find me. I found you. Let me get the soup."

"Good." I smiled, aware it was forced. I was tired to my bones. "Can I ask you something?"

Ty stopped at the doorway and turned to face me. "Sure."

"Was it Drake?" I asked, knowing the answer, dreading it nonetheless.

"I'm sorry, Josie. Yes."

Poor Drake. He arrived in New Hampshire a stranger and died alone. "Do the police know why he was at Locke Pond? I mean, talk about wandering off the beaten path."

Ty shook his head. "I haven't heard anything."

"I should call Ellis," I said.

"Why?"

"What do you mean, why? I can help—that's why."

"Not tonight, you can't." He smiled. "Don't fret." He left the way he'd come, through the butler's pantry that connected the dining room to the kitchen.

I stood, feeling shaky on my pins, clutching the blanket to my throat, not willing to relinquish any heat, not even for a moment. I found my tote bag by the front door and brought it back to the sofa. I rooted around until I located my phone. Wes had texted twice and left three voice mails, no surprise. I called Cara at home.

"I hope I'm not calling too late," I said when I had her.

"Not at all. Are you all right? I heard what happened on the news. They said you found him, the poor soul."

"It's awful. Unthinkable. I can't talk for long, Cara. I need you to do something for me. Would you call Marianna Albert and explain what happened? You'll find her contact info in my work calendar. Apologize for me, will you? And reschedule our appointment for anytime next week. I can go tomorrow, but what with the storm and a three o'clock appointment I already have—"

"Excuse me for interrupting, Josie. Of course I'll call Mrs. Albert first thing in the morning, and I'm sure she'll understand. But you shouldn't even think about going out tomorrow!"

"Thank you, Cara. I'm fine. No lasting damage. When you talk to Mrs. Albert, stress how disappointed I was not to get there. I don't want another dealer swooping in and stealing the deal. Do whatever you can to get her to promise to wait until we meet before making a decision."

"I'll explain everything. You just take care of yourself, and don't worry."

Ty told me not to fret. Cara told me not to worry. I was noticing a theme. "Call me as soon as you speak to her."

"I'll e-mail. I don't want to risk waking you in case you're sleeping."

I smiled and sighed. "Thank you, Cara." I punched the OFF button and leaned back, closing my eyes, relieved. I must have drifted off to sleep, because I woke up with a start as Ty placed a stack of three plastic trays on the coffee table, one for each of us and one to hold a plate of crackers.

"I fell asleep," I said, stretching.

"Do you want to sleep some more? I can keep the soup hot."

"No. I'm hungrier than I am sleepy. It smells great."

"No surprise. You made it."

"Thank my mom. It's her secret ingredient that makes the difference. Fresh thyme brined in stone-ground mustard and soy sauce. How did she even think of such a thing? For chicken soup? That's crazy."

"Crazy good."

"Crazy awesome."

We sat side by side leaning against the couch, facing the fire, eating soup, dipping crackers in the rich aromatic broth. I sipped lemonade. Ty had beer, Smuttynose. The fire spit and crackled; the flames that licked the wood were yellow and red. Outside, all was densely black except where the roof-mounted lights illuminated twirling, fast-falling snow.

"Lots of people from Massachusetts drive into New Hampshire for the scenery," I said.

"And the beaches."

"Not in March."

"And the cheap liquor."

"All year round for that one."

"Why did he get off the highway? How did he end up in Durham?"

"He was early and decided to take the scenic route."

"I wonder if his GPS was activated."

"The police can find that out."

"How long was he in the water?" I asked.

"I don't know. I don't know anything, Josie."

I finished my soup and shoved the tray a few inches away. "I'm frustrated. I want to know things."

"Tomorrow."

"I bet Drake was meeting someone."

"Who?"

"Someone who didn't want him talking to the police. He had no reason to be on Love Lane, Ty, but it's a great place to hold a secret meeting. There's almost no traffic there." I stared at the fire for a moment, watching as small peaks of blue flame teased the backside of a thick log. "The police need to let me look at his computer files. I can interpret the Fabergé egg appraisal."

Ty leaned over and kissed the top of my head, then picked up the tray and headed for the kitchen. "I'm sure they will," he said, "but not tonight."

I awoke to a loud boom. For a moment I couldn't remember where I was. I was so disoriented, I nearly rolled off the couch. It was the phone. Ty's phone. The landline. I lurched across the floor and grabbed the portable unit standing upright in its cradle.

"This is Josie," I answered from habit.

"It's Ellis. Are you all right? I've been calling your cell and you didn't answer."

I glanced at my tote bag. My phone was half visible, poking out from its pocket.

"Maybe I ran out of battery. Or maybe I just slept through it."

"How are you feeling?"

I took a survey. "Groggy. Fine. Hungry. How are you?"

Ellis laughed. "I'm okay. You don't sound like you had a near-death experience."

"I got lucky. As of this moment, I'm not even cold, a major improvement from yesterday."

I stumbled into the kitchen. Ty was long gone, but he'd filled the tea kettle with water and laid out tea bags. *What a guy*. A note on the counter read, "Call me when you're up. xxoo."

"That's great news," Ellis said. "And good for me. I need to talk to you."

I turned the burner on high and opened the refrigerator. Jars of stone-ground and Dijon mustard. Garlic pickles. Half a store-bought container of hummus. An almost empty quart of milk. One egg.

"What time is it?" I asked.

"Eleven. Two minutes to."

I snapped alert. "Really? That's unbelievable! I need to go."

"Why?"

The sun was summer bright, and rainbows glinted on the fast-melting snow.

"I don't know. 'Cause that's what you do. You get up and you go to work. By the time I'm dressed and ready to go, it will be noon. I've lost half a day."

"Throw some water on your face. I'll be there in twenty minutes."

"Make it thirty. And bring food."

I went to retrieve my phone. The battery was low but not depleted, which meant I had, in fact, slept through Ellis's calls. Checking messages, I realized I'd slept through eighteen voice calls, Wes's three from last night and fifteen others in addition to Ellis's two messages. Shelley had called from New York, wanting to make sure I was all right. So had my employees, Gretchen, Sasha, Fred, and Eric. Both Ana and her dad, Stefan, had called, Ana wanting to know if there was anything she could do, Stefan to tell me that he hoped I was fully recovered from my ordeal and wondering if I'd known the man who'd died. Zoë, my best buddy, had called twice, offering food, blankets, care, and love. Two longtime clients expressed concern; another expressed admiration at what he called my heroism. And Tim, the pastor of the Congregational church next door, asked if I wanted to talk. There was a text message, too, from Cara, saying Mrs. Albert would be glad to see me next week, and I should call her directly when I knew my schedule. Cara had also passed along Mrs. Albert's concern and assurances that Prescott's was still in the running.

"Good," I said aloud, then called Ty and got him. "Ellis is en route. He says he wants to talk to me."

"What about?"

"I don't know. I didn't ask. He's bringing food."

"Call me when he's gone. You can tell me what you want for dinner."

"Why don't we eat at the Blue Dolphin? I have a meeting there at three. I'll just stay, and you can join me whenever."

"You're not going out!"

"Why not? I'm fine."

I could hear him breathing, and I knew he was controlling himself. He was an innate caretaker, and protective.

"Sure," he said.

I told him I loved him and ran for the shower.

Wearing the comfy jeans, fisherman knit sweater, and warm woolly socks I stashed at Ty's, I was rinsing the teapot with boiling water when Ellis rang the doorbell. I took a few seconds to get the tea steeping, then hurried to the door.

"What did you bring?" I asked as I swung open the door.

Ellis held a large plastic bag from the best deli in Rocky Point shoulder high. "Everything. Sandwiches, salads, bagels."

"Thanks so much." I opened the bag and spread the options out across the counter, like a buffet. "Want some tea?"

"No, thanks."

He leaned against the counter watching me load up a plate. I started with half a bagel topped with salmon cream cheese spread, and half a turkey and Swiss sandwich on whole wheat.

"I'm meeting the Boston police to go through Milner's condo and office," he said. "I figure that I'll call or text you if there's anything I need help with."

"Sure. I've got a three o'clock appointment. Other than that, nothing."

"I'm due there at two. Keep your phone on, all right?"

"Will do. It's charging now." I spread a spoonful of coleslaw onto my sandwich. "Do you have any idea why Milner would be on Love Lane?"

"Do you?" he asked, avoiding answering, as usual.

"Maybe he was meeting someone."

"Who?"

"His client."

"You're still thinking Ana."

"It's hard not to."

"Why would they be meeting?"

"Because he screwed her over and she caught him."

"How?"

"The double cross we talked about. Once I examined the broken bits you gave me to look at, Milner's ruse was exposed. She met with him to give him a chance to make her whole."

"Why wouldn't she just go to the police?"

I paused, thinking. "Maybe she paid him to inflate the appraisal so she could qualify for a larger loan, and he threatened that if she exposed him, he'd expose her."

"Gotcha. It's complicated, all right. What should I be looking for?"

"The appraisal. A client list."

Ellis grinned as I reached for half a roast beef sandwich on a baguette. "You were hungry."

I smiled back. "Still am. You're a lifesaver, Ellis. Thank you."

"I'll be in touch."

Ellis let himself out. I finished eating standing at the counter. Without question Drake Milner knew more than he let on. I was willing to bet he knew who had replicated the Fabergé Spring Egg snow globe, and I wouldn't be a bit surprised to learn that he'd known who killed Jason.

CHAPTER TWENTY-TWO

I took a fresh cup of tea into Ty's living room, sat on the couch, and called Wes.

After a pointless two-minute conversation in which I refused to discuss anything about Drake Milner, Wes sighed to his toenails.

"I'll tell you what I found out—but I shouldn't. You're all take and no give."

"Don't be silly, Wes. I give you plenty."

He sighed again. "The ME is refusing to rule Milner's death an accident until she does more tests. The left side of his head is bashed in, maybe from hitting the doorframe when the car went into the pond. She's using imaging software to see if dents in the car match up."

My mouth opened, then closed. "Are you telling me she's thinking it might be murder?"

"Yes."

"Oh, my. Wes, this is incredible. Shocking. Horrific."

"*Now* will you tell me something I can print?"

I closed my eyes for a moment. "Here's a quote. 'I'm saddened that I couldn't do more.'"

After a two-second pause, Wes asked, "That's it?"

"That's it. What about the other questions we were thinking about . . . like how likely is it that Peter would go to the gym twice in one day. You remember, right—his alibi for Jason's murder? Any new insights?"

"The answer is very likely. He often works out twice a day. At home, he runs two to five miles each morning before work, rain or shine, then goes to the gym after work. He alternates working the machines with a Zumba class. Machines on Tuesday and Thursday. Zumba on Monday, Wednesday, and Friday. Weekends he rides his bike."

"Zumba? Peter?"

Wes chuckled. "I know. It's quite a picture, right? Usually, from what I hear, he's the only guy in the class. My source says he's great at it. He should be, right? He's a fitness junkie, for God's sake."

"But why Zumba?"

Wes chuckled. "Maybe he does it to meet girls."

"Maybe," I said, not convinced.

"From all accounts, he's pretty much a loner but good at the dance moves. Probably he does it because he likes it."

"What about his story that they showed the Fabergé egg to their neighbor? Toni, her name was, I think."

"Yeah, Toni and her friend Carly. I spoke to Toni myself. The story is confirmed. The egg was real at Christmas. Or she's lying for some reason. She insists she'd recognize shoddy workmanship a mile away. She's a master carpenter, very uppity about it. She fabricates wooden embellishments like missing drawer pulls for historical renovations."

"Get out. You talk to the most interesting people, Wes."

"I do, don't I? Anyway, I believed her."

"Which means we have a definite time frame when the theft occurred. The fact that Peter told the police about it doesn't eliminate him as a suspect."

"Just like everyone else."

I'd been in the manager's office in the Blue Dolphin once before, years earlier, back when the Blue Dolphin was owned by a man named Bobby Jordan.* Suzanne had redone the space completely. The walls were painted a pale cranberry with glossy white trim, and the drapes featured a cranberry and gold floral pattern. Her desk and credenza were made of mahogany. The guest chairs were upholstered in a dark cranberry nubby fabric. Lighting came from a crystal chandelier, her cut-glass desk lamp, and three matching cut-glass wall sconces. The overall feel was super luxe.

Suzanne sat behind her desk, with Chef Ray off to the side, using the end of her desk as his own. He had a sheaf of papers and kept flipping through them, stopping to read for a few seconds, then turning to another page and reading a bit there, as if he were a student cramming for a final. The rest of us sat in a line facing Suzanne. Maurice sat next to Ray, then me, then Ana.

*Please see *Deadly Threads*.

Suzanne smiled. "Thank you for coming, Ana. And of course, I'm always glad to see Josie. What a terrible experience, coming upon that accident. Are you all right?"

"Yes, thanks. I'm fine. I just wish I could have done more."

"I'm sure you did all you could." Suzanne turned to Ray and Maurice. "Ana asked Josie to join the meeting. As a new business owner, Ana felt the need to have some guidance. Since Josie's success with Prescott's could serve as an entrepreneurial tutorial, I'd say she made a good choice." Suzanne turned back to me. "Welcome."

Maurice crossed his arms and tightened his lips. I didn't know why Maurice was angry. Maybe it was that the meeting had been called in the first place. Possibly he was just an angry guy. Lots of people walked around with chips on their shoulders for no discernible reason. I tried hard to avoid them.

"I thought we might begin by—" Suzanne stopped talking midsentence as a knock sounded on the door.

Ray looked up, startled. Suzanne exhaled loudly, miffed at the interruption. Maurice looked down his nose. Ana looked at me, her eyes reflecting anxiety, I couldn't imagine why. I shrugged and made a "who knows—no biggie" face, hoping to reassure her.

"Come in," Suzanne called.

The door opened, and Stefan stepped into the room. "I'm sorry I'm late." He closed the door.

Ana swiveled to face her father but didn't speak. She looked stunned.

Ray frowned at Stefan, then resumed flipping through his papers. Maurice glanced at Stefan, then turned toward the window, communicating that none of this was of much interest or importance.

Suzanne smiled, despite her annoyance. "I don't believe we've met. I'm Suzanne Dyre, the Blue Dolphin's general manager."

"How do you do?" Stefan gave a little bow. "I'm Stefan Yartsin, Ana's father and an investor in her company. Ana mentioned you were going to have a conversation about partnering, and I thought I might be able to contribute something. May I join you?"

Suzanne's eyes moved to Ana's.

Ana took in a deep breath and sidled around to face her father. "Thanks, Dad, but no. I'm fine."

Stefan's eyes pierced mine, a sharp angry glare, then returned to Ana's for long enough to create an awkward moment.

"You're making a mistake," he said.

I glanced at Suzanne to gauge her reaction to whatever was occurring—a power struggle, perhaps, or a fight for autonomy. Suzanne's expression revealed nothing beyond polite interest.

"Perhaps," Ana said through clenched teeth, "but it's mine to make."

Stefan's smile faded. "Let me sit in."

"No."

His eyes remained fixed on Ana's face.

Ray stood up. "Ana?" he asked.

"It's all right, Ray," she said, her eyes holding steady on her father. "Dad's just trying to help." She smiled at her father. "I'll call when we're done."

Stefan glanced around the room. Everyone except Maurice was looking at him.

"You'll excuse me, then," he said to Suzanne with another half-bow.

"Of course."

He left, and Ray sat down again. Maurice shifted his gaze to Suzanne's face.

"So," Suzanne resumed, "let's jump in. We're here to discuss how we, the Blue Dolphin, can best do business with Ana's company. Let me begin with a brief statement describing where we are now and where I want us to end up. We all want the same thing. We want our guests to have the best desserts money can buy. To that end, Chef Ray hired Maurice as pastry chef. To this point, all our desserts have been made in-house, except for Ana's cakes." Suzanne leaned back in her maroon leather chair, her elbows on the arms, her hands folded together in her lap. She smiled. "I can officially report that Ana's creations sell like hotcakes. People love them. Therefore, we want to carry them." She turned to Maurice. "In other words, *whether* to carry them is no longer up for discussion." She paused, waiting to see if he'd flip out. He didn't speak or, as far as I could tell, react in any way. She let her eyes move, taking us all in. "The question on the table, the only question that matters, is how to best organize our relationship going forward. I'd like to hear your thoughts."

Ray tapped the stack of papers in front of him. "What we're doing now is working. I've been looking at our past orders. Not one has been missed. All the cakes have sold." He smiled. "If it ain't broke, don't fix it. Let's just keep ordering them."

Maurice slapped the desk. "And more and more people will buy them because they are a novelty. A child's gimmick. And soon there will be no orders for anything else. It is an insult!"

Suzanne tilted her head. "Perhaps you weren't listening, Maurice," she said, her tone icy. "We're keeping the cakes."

My phone began vibrating. "Sorry," I said softly. Ellis had texted, "Milner's computer is missing. Any thoughts?"

Maurice stood up and took two steps toward the door, rigidly stiff, like a soldier on parade. Chef Ray stood.

Maurice turned back to face Suzanne, raised his chin, and lowered his eyes, looking down at her. "Then I have no choice. I quit." He marched from the room, slamming the door.

"I'll go talk to him," Ray said, starting after him.

Suzanne held up her hand to stop him. "No. Don't try to talk him into something he doesn't want. Enough is enough. If you feel the need to say something, you can tell him how much you've enjoyed working with him, but that's it. Don't engage. Don't debrief. Don't let him rant. Make certain he only takes what belongs to him. Get his key and ID. Tell him he'll hear from corporate HR by the end of the day. If he won't go, or if he makes any trouble, buzz me immediately."

Ray looked incredulous. "I shouldn't try to smooth things out?"

"No. Let him go."

"Okay," Ray said, semishaking his head, as if he couldn't believe his ears.

Ray touched Ana's shoulder as he passed. Ana looked wary and worried. I needed to leave, to call Ellis, to think.

Suzanne smiled. "May I make a suggestion, Ana?"

"Of course."

"Expand your role. Become the go-to source for high-end desserts. If the dining establishment can support it, provide an on-site pastry chef who works under your supervision. If not, do what you've done for us—sell cakes. Do you have a pastry chef available? Someone who can create half a dozen desserts in addition to baking your cakes?"

"Yes."

"Can he or she start today?"

Ana's mouth opened, then closed. Her eyes were round. "Really?"

"Yes. If you like the idea, the Blue Dolphin will be your first customer."

After several seconds, Ana said, "I'm speechless."

"Say yes," I told her. "That's my official counsel."

Ana laughed and squeezed my arm. She looked at Suzanne. "Yes. Thank you. I'd love it."

"Good. Let's work out the pricing."

I stood up. "You don't need me for that, and I have a call I need to make." I smiled at Suzanne, then Ana. "Congratulations to you both. If you do need me for anything, I'll be in the lounge. I'm meeting Ty later, so I thought I'd just stick around."

Ana stood up and hugged me. Her eyes were fiery bright with, I was certain, equal parts excitement and relief and terror. "Thank you, Josie."

"You're welcome. Although all I did was sit here and look smart. When you're done negotiating, come to the lounge and I'll buy you a drink."

"Another time," Ana said. "I need to get a chef down here, meet with Ray to figure out what we need for tonight, and—well, you know."

Suzanne stood up. "Come to think of it, can we agree that we'll be fair with one another and negotiate the specifics tomorrow? I ought to go with you to explain our arrangement to Chef Ray and the kitchen staff. I'd also better check that Maurice isn't tearing up the kitchen."

Ana extended her hand. "Business on a handshake. That's how it ought to be."

They shook, and Suzanne opened the door and headed down the corridor that led to a small anteroom. One door led to the back of the kitchen; another opened into the dining room. Ana followed closely.

"I'll peel off here," I said.

"Good seeing you, Josie. Follow me, Ana. Let's get ready to rock and roll."

Ana paused at the threshold and impulsively kissed my cheek. "You're the best, Josie. Just the best friend."

I walked through the empty dining room to the lounge, wishing I could put my doubts about Ana aside. I liked her as much as anyone I'd met in a long, long time, but the questions surrounding her possible involvement in the theft of her Fabergé egg and Jason's murder—and maybe Milner's death—were like pebbles in my shoe. They simply couldn't be ignored.

CHAPTER TWENTY-THREE

Since it was still shy of four o'clock, I expected to be the Blue Dolphin lounge's only customer, but I wasn't. An older couple sat in a corner having an earnest discussion about something or other. They wore slacks and sweaters and sensible shoes. They were drinking highballs. A young man in a suit kept glancing at his watch. He sipped what looked like an iced tea. Jimmy was behind the bar slicing limes.

"Josie!" Jimmy said as I walked in. "Good to see ya. What can I getcha?"

"I'm in a tea mood, Jimmy. How about some Earl Grey?"

"You got it."

I took my favorite seat by the window and looked out over the river toward Maine.

A middle-aged man in jeans and a flannel shirt entered the lounge and looked around. He smiled at the young man who'd been looking at his watch and joined him at the table. The younger man looked relieved.

I pulled out my phone. Ty had texted that he thought he'd get to the Blue Dolphin by six. I responded *xxoo*. I called Ellis and got him in his car.

"Drake Milner's laptop is gone?" I said, half as a question, half incredulous.

"Yup," Ellis said. "The gal I spoke to, Julie, said it's not unusual for him to take his computer home with him, but it's not there. We checked."

"Does he have a girlfriend?"

"Evidently not. He's long divorced."

A small brown bird landed on a birch tree. It fluttered its wings for a moment, then grew still.

"Any chance he slipped it in a kitchen cabinet or something for safe-keeping?"

"Not likely. He lives in a condo by the State House. It's a high-end reno-vation of a classic town house. Two bedrooms, two baths, open concept liv-ing room/dining room/kitchen. There's only a few places he could have put it, and we searched them all—including the kitchen cabinets. The Boston police and techs are still going over it—and his office—but I don't expect them to find anything. Let me rephrase that: I don't expect them to find the laptop. You saw how many books Milner had in his office, right? When I left, three recruits were going through every one of them page by page. With any luck, Milner hid something in one of them."

"Like the combination to a safe. Did you look for a safe?"

"Yeah. We removed all the paintings on the walls, tapped for hollow spaces in closet floors, checked canned goods for fake bottoms. No safe."

"And you're certain the laptop wasn't in his car? Couldn't it have floated away?"

"The windows were up, so no."

Jimmy brought my tea, and I mouthed "thank you" to him. He gave me a thumbs-up and spun away.

"Where else would you look if you were me?" Ellis asked.

The little brown bird appeared to be resting, its head tucked under its wing.

I swished the tea bag around for a few seconds, then pulled it from the pot and set it aside.

"Milner went to meet someone," I said. "Whoever that was stole his lap-top. Milner was so upset, he got turned around and ended up in the pond."

"Who?"

"I don't know. Maybe the client who had him appraise the Fabergé egg, who may or may not be Ana."

"How can I identify that person?"

I laughed. "The irony of that question appeals to my sense of humor."

"I'm serious. I know that's what we've been trying to learn this whole time, but that doesn't make the question not worth asking again."

"Fair enough, but I still don't know the answer." I added sugar and a thimbleful of milk to the teapot and stirred. "What about the appraisal itself? Surely the client is named."

"Julie tells me they no longer keep hard copies of appraisal records. Everything is electronic."

"Makes sense. We do the same."

"What happens if your computer is stolen or lost?"

"We're networked, and everything is stored on an offsite server. In addition, everything is backed up once a day."

"At Marlborough Antiques, they're just talking about going to a cloud system. You know how that works, right? You think you're working on a computer, but you're not—your files and everything are stored somewhere on the Internet, not on a physical computer. Right now, though, each person is responsible for backing up his or her own work."

"That's crazy! I could never do that. People forget things. Computers crash. They get viruses. I'd never sleep, I'd be so worried." I looked back toward the river. The bird was gone. The water was dark, more blue than green, and running fast. "Do they use a file-sharing site of some sort? Graphics files—like appraisals because they always include a bunch of photographs—are huge, too big for e-mail. We upload ours to a site, then give each client a unique password so he or she can access it."

"I'll ask. What else?"

I poured tea, watching the mahogany brew swirl around the cup. I felt a memory tickling the edge of my consciousness. I knew something that would help, but I couldn't think of what it was. I looked around. The older woman was laughing, pressing her fingers into her cheeks, an expression of joyful shock on her face. Her companion was chuckling, looking pleased with himself, like he'd done a good job telling a joke. The two men had left. Jimmy was polishing wineglasses with a white cloth.

"Any chance he used an old-style appointment book?" I asked, thinking that was a good question but not what I'd been trying to recall.

"Yes. I have it with me. I'm hoping you'll look at it."

"Of course. Does anything stick out?"

"Not to me, but what do I know. What else?"

I looked out the window again. Wispy dark clouds were blowing in from the east. "Can you tell if he called someone right after I left his office?"

"We're getting the phone logs now. The shop owner is cooperating, so we don't need a subpoena. I should have them by the time I get back to Rocky Point."

"What about the stuff he was carrying in his pockets or in the car?" I knew Ellis wouldn't tell me what they'd recovered unless I could help with it. He never gossiped.

"We're still cataloguing his personal effects."

"Oh, my God!" The memory I'd been trying to recapture landed with a thud. "Ellis, I just remembered something. Drake Milner backed everything up onto a flash drive. Did you find it?"

"One. In a kitchen drawer. Nothing in his office. We checked it. It's loaded. Forms, docs, photos, everything nicely labeled, but all dates are three months ago, or earlier."

"When I was with him, he saved a document, removed the flash drive, and dropped it in his shirt pocket."

Ellis paused. I could hear him breathing. "Thanks, Josie." Another pause. "Any chance I can run this calendar by you as soon as I get back?"

Just before six, Zoë came running into the lounge. Ellis walked at a more leisurely pace, taking in the scene with cop's eyes, assessing the faces and attitudes. He carried a tawny brown leather briefcase.

Zoë swooped in and hugged me, then plunked down on the window seat. "Hey, cutie!" She swept aside her long black hair and patted my arm.

Ellis greeted me and sat next to Zoë, across from me. Under the dim amber lighting, I could barely see his scar.

Jimmy came over, and Zoë and I ordered watermelon martinis. Ellis opted for a Dewar's on the rocks with a twist. I asked about Zoë's kids and how her kitchen renovation was progressing. She asked about being on Ana's TV pilot and Fabergé eggs and Hank. When Jimmy delivered the drinks, Ellis reached for his briefcase.

"The lab hasn't worked on the calendar yet," Ellis explained, extracting a black leather day planner encased in a plastic evidence bag. "You can look all you want, but don't touch. I'll turn the pages for you. Zoë, would you move our drinks to that table? I don't want to risk an accident."

Zoë transferred the drinks one at a time, then sat back to watch.

"Why do you think he stayed with an old-fashioned calendar?" Ellis asked. "Everyone else at Marlborough uses an electronic one."

"Maybe to buy time to think. If your calendar is on your phone, people expect you to schedule appointments on the spot. If you use a paper diary of some sort, you can say you'll need to check it and get back to them. I've been tempted to go back to the old way for just that reason."

"Why don't you?" Zoë asked.

I smiled. "I decided the benefits of the technology outweigh the disadvantages—and I've learned to be more assertive. If I'm not ready to schedule an appointment or if I don't want to, I say so. Politely, tactfully, and directly."

"I'm impressed," Zoë said.

"Thanks. I only have so much time. I have to use it wisely."

Ellis took a brown leather pouch from his jacket pocket. He turned it upside down and jiggled it. Long-handled silver-colored tweezers fell onto the table. He snapped on plastic gloves, pulled the day planner from the evidence bag, and laid it on top of the plastic.

"It goes month by month," he said. "Where do you want to start? February? March?"

"March. Milner told me he worked on the appraisal the week before I saw him."

Ellis turned the pages one at a time until he reached March. I leaned forward and began at the beginning of the month. Milner's handwriting was as easy to read as print. He had two phone calls but no in-person appraisal appointments scheduled during the first week of the month. The phone calls listed a name, a phone number, and an object. The first object was a "kovsh b." The second one was a "boar's head c."

"I bet *b* stands for bowl and *c* for cup."

"Why?" Ellis asked. "Could it be, I don't know, 'box' and 'cabinet'?"

" 'Kovsh' is a boat-shaped vessel for serving punch or mead or the like. So 'bowl' is logical. A boar's head could decorate anything, including a cabinet, I suppose. Or a set of china." I grinned. "If we find his computer, we can check." I continued reading. "Look." I pointed to an entry on the Tuesday of the third week. It read: "F. e & d." I raised my eyes. "That's it. He appraised a Fabergé egg and dome."

"No name or phone number by that one," Ellis said.

"Someone wanted it very hush-hush."

"He had to have written the name somewhere."

"Maybe on the appraisal report."

Ellis sighed. "Which we don't have." He tapped the page with his tweezers. "We'll need to call all these folks and ask why they were in touch with Milner."

"Some of them will lie because they want to keep the appraisal a secret."

"And others will lie because they don't want to get involved in a police investigation. Still, we've got to make the calls."

"Want me to do it? I can call as an antiques expert asking if they have any additional questions about their objects, getting them to fill me in."

Ellis paused, thinking. "Let me run it by the DA, make sure it wouldn't screw up evidence. Personally, I like the idea."

He slid the tweezers into their pouch, sealed the planner in a new evidence bag, and placed both items in his briefcase. As soon as the table was clear, Zoë brought our drinks back.

Ten minutes later, Ty walked in, and my heart skipped a beat as it always did when I saw him. He smiled at me, and I smiled back, warmed by his presence. He took my hand as he sat and leaned in toward me. He brushed his lips against mine, a kiss and a promise.

CHAPTER TWENTY-FOUR

I was en route to work the next morning, Saturday, tag sale day, when my phone vibrated. Wes had texted, "Urgent. Call me. Now."

I pulled off to the side, set my blinkers, and called.

"All hell is breaking loose," he said, skipping a greeting, like always.

"What do you mean?"

"The cops have crushed Stefan's alibi!"

"No way!"

Wes chuckled. "Stefan only had a receipt for one hotel, a Holiday Inn in Binghamton, New York. He said he lost the other one. Yeah, right! Here's the thing. He left Detroit on Sunday in a rental car at eight in the morning. He checked into the Holiday Inn at nine that night. That's thirteen hours, give or take a few minutes. It's an eight-and-a-half hour drive. Add a couple of hours for pit stops—call it eleven hours, max. The police have been asking him to account for the other two hours, but he refuses, saying that he got off the highway and wandered for a while on back roads." Wes chucked again. "Wandered. *Pa-leeze.*"

"Why are you laughing, Wes? On long drives, I sometimes take back roads. Highways can be boring."

"Do you really? I don't. I'm a get-to-where-I'm-going-as-quickly-as-I-can sort of guy. Regardless, if you were being investigated about a murder, don't you think you'd tell the cops where you went? Stefan says he doesn't remember exactly where he 'wandered'"—Wes spoke the word with an exaggerated wink-wink in his voice—"and he's not going to try, since his wandering can't possibly be related to Jason's murder. What I want to know is why he'd stay in a hotel Monday night in the first place. He checked out of the Holiday Inn at nine Monday morning. It's only a five-and-a-half-hour drive from Binghamton to Rocky Point. Why wouldn't he just drive it on Monday? He's not answering that question either."

"Can't the police learn which hotel he stayed at by checking his credit card receipts?"

"He said he paid cash. Yeah, right. He used a credit card at the Holiday Inn on Monday, so it's logical to think he'd pay by credit card on Tuesday, right? Whatever . . . let's say he paid by cash for some reason. Every hotel makes you give them a credit or debit card when you check in, even if you pay cash in advance. None of his cards shows any activity. Which means Stefan told a wonker. The police are trying to figure out why. That's why I'm calling you. I know you've been working with the police. Any ideas?"

"He did something en route he doesn't want to talk about."

"Yeah, but what?"

"I have no idea," I said, wondering if Stefan could have stopped en route to have the egg replicated. I shook my head. Something like that took time and careful planning. There was some other reason why Stefan went off the grid.

"If you figure it out, call me. Okay?"

"I will. You, too."

"You got it. Catch ya later!"

I eased back into traffic and drove slowly to work. As I headed east, the sun was blindingly bright, a good omen, I thought, that the day would be warm and smell of spring.

I placed the no-name glass decanter I was appraising on the table in front of me. The woman sitting on the other side was in her twenties with shoulder-length dirty blond hair and brown eyes.

I was taking a stint in the free instant appraisal booth we ran each tag sale, and I was about to do one of the hardest things in the antiques appraisal business—burst someone's bubble.

"It's not valuable, I'm afraid."

"What are you talking about? It's been in my grandmother's china cabinet my entire life."

"That makes it special to you, which is the most important thing of all."

"No, it's not. Grandma said to sell it. That's why I'm here."

She'd said her name was Donna, and she was sounding a little whiny. I felt bad for her, and for her grandmother. Lots of people thought their objects had way more value than they did, and hearing otherwise, some of them got whiny.

"I'm sorry to be the bearer of bad news, but this would only retail for about ten dollars."

"How come? It's beautiful!"

"First, the stopper is loose and features a pleated design. The decanter has a floral pattern. Put those facts together and you can tell the stopper isn't the original." I laid the decanter on its side. "Second, look at this seam. That tells us the decanter was produced from a mold."

"What a gyp." She grabbed it by its neck, setting the stopper rattling, and stormed out.

I wondered who she was mad at. Me? Or her grandmother?

I was greeting an older man with a long white beard when Ellis entered the venue. I glanced at my phone. It read 10:12. He met my eyes and jerked his head sideways, toward the parking lot. I held up a finger. *Give me a minute.*

"Excuse me," I said to the man.

"Take your time, young lady," he said. "Everyone's in a hurry these days but me."

"Thanks." I stood and searched for Sasha. She was chatting with a customer near the art prints.

"I'll be right back," I told him.

"I'll be here."

I thanked him, walked quickly toward Sasha. I caught her eye and beckoned her with waggling fingers. She said something to the customer and hurried in my direction, her brow wrinkled with worry.

"Take over for me, okay? I need to step out."

She smiled, relieved that she wasn't in trouble, although I never knew why she thought she might be. Sasha was diligent, careful, honest, and kind. Sasha never got in trouble.

"Sure," she said.

Ellis was waiting for me outside, leaning against the building, his eyes closed, his face turned to the sun.

"Hey, good-looking," I said as I approached.

He straightened up, opening his eyes and smiling. "My great-aunt used to sing that song all the time. Hearing those words brings back memories."

"Good ones?"

"The best. Aunt Bea believed everything was possible. She ran a regional theater. That's where I met my wife, in one of her shows."

"And to think I was just saying hey."

His smile grew. He reached into an inner pocket and brought out an unsealed standard number 10 envelope, looked at it, then handed it to me.

"Regarding your offer to make the calls from Milner's diary, the DA says thank you. We accept. I have a tech coming to set up a recording system. The calls ought to be made from here so if anyone has phone ID, it's your number that shows, not a police department's. We want all the calls recorded. Detective Brownley will listen in and be available should someone want to talk to a police official. Okay?"

"Sure." I opened the envelope. The first sheet was a typed listing of eight names and phone numbers, the March phone call entries from Drake Milner's calendar. The second sheet was a letter on formal letterhead from Shirley Donovan, ADA, officially thanking me for my assistance while warning me not to say I was a police officer. I could say that the police asked me to help because of my antiques expertise. A paragraph included her recommended wording regarding the recording.

I refolded the papers and slipped them back into the envelope. "Got it."

The technician, a thin young man named Barry, with a scraggly mustache, sat in one of my guest chairs monitoring the recording device. Detective Claire Brownley sat next to Barry, a steno pad balanced on her knee. Both of them wore big black headphones. Barry kept his eyes on the display built into the front of the machine. Detective Brownley kept her eyes on me.

I felt awkward, as if I were onstage. I swiveled toward my window, so I wouldn't be distracted by them while I was on the phone.

I started with the first name on the list, Marni Gersten, from Atlanta.

"Hi," I said when she answered. "My name is Josie Prescott from Prescott's Antiques and Auctions in Rocky Point, New Hampshire. I'm hoping I can talk to you a little about a conversation I think you had with a man named Drake Milner from Marlborough Antiques in Boston. I'm trying to trace an antique."

"Oh, yes. Mr. Milner appraised my kovsh bowl."

"Great. If it's all right with you, I'm going to record this call for future reference."

"What future reference?" Ms. Gersten asked, sounding skeptical.

"Research, primarily."

"I guess so," she said, still skeptical.

"Thanks. Did you hire him to conduct an appraisal of the bowl?"

"Yes, and he did a wonderful job. Very thorough."

"That's great to hear. What was the outcome?"

"He tested the silver and all the rubies. There are nine of them." She lowered her voice confidentially. "Mr. Milner thought it would sell at auction for as much as twenty-five thousand dollars."

"That's great! Has Mr. Milner appraised anything else for you?"

"No."

"How about Marlborough Antiques?"

"No. Why?"

"Just checking. Thanks so much. You've been very helpful." I congratulated her on the bowl's high value, thanked her again, and went on to the next call.

Mel Smith's phone went to voice mail. I left a message saying I was an antiques dealer who'd heard about his Russian boar's head object and asking him to please call me as soon as he could.

Brian Vasquez, from Boston, was as happy to tell me about his Imperial Russian silver and enamel desk clock as Ms. Gersten had been and was even less concerned that I was recording the call.

"It's a fabulous piece—I'm getting ready to sell it. It's double signed, by both Fabergé in Cyrillic and by the work master, Perchin. Mr. Milner told me that's how he dated it. It was made somewhere from 1860 to 1903, during the years Perchin was on the job." He chuckled. "He thought it would sell for around forty thousand dollars. Can you believe it? Forty big ones." He chuckled louder. "I found it at a yard sale."

Cara IM'd that Mel Smith was on line two. I congratulated Mr. Vasquez on his find and ended the call, then punched the button for line two.

"I'm sorry you had to wait," I said to Mel Smith.

"No prob. You called about the boar's head cup?"

The caller was a young woman. Mel must be short for Melanie. I gave her my opening remarks, then asked, "Did you have it appraised?"

"Yeah, and it's worth biggo buckos. I inherited it from my grandfather and wanted to know what I had. Now I have an extra bill—insurance."

I laughed. "You're smart to get it insured. What did Mr. Milner say about it?"

"It's an Imperial Russian decorative object, probably only used in ceremonies. It's made of enameled silver and agate with cabochon rubies for the eyes—isn't that weird? Red eyes. Ick. It's by Fabergé. There's a double-headed eagle mark. More creepiness."

"It sounds like you don't like it much."

"I don't. But it's worth about seventy thousand dollars, so I'm learning to love it."

"Would you consider selling it?"

"I'd love to, but my mother would kill me."

"Did Mr. Milner appraise anything else for you?"

"No."

Neither did Marlborough's. I was learning that Drake Milner was a competent appraiser, respected by his clients, but not much else. I thanked her and ended the call. The next two callers were also pleased to tell me about their antiques and Milner's appraisals. Neither had an issue with my recording the calls. Both reported that Drake Milner was conscientious and personable. I found myself doubting my theory that Milner was somehow involved in replicating the egg. Yet a niggling feeling stayed with me that all was not as it appeared.

Some antiques appraisers found it hard working with spectacularly beautiful objects they adored and appreciated but couldn't afford. Especially when their clients were interested only in value, ignoring or disdaining an object's history, sentiment, and beauty. Year after year, looking at supremely magnificent objects, touching them, researching them, caring for them, while interacting with bored, avaricious, or mean-spirited clients, could eat away at a soul like acid. Doing the wrong thing was easy, and the chances of getting caught were slim. Jewelers could easily replace real stones with paste, and it might be years before a trusting client discovered the switch. Some art appraisers had ongoing relationships with talented artists who could reproduce masters' works so cleverly that only another expert would be able to uncover the fraud. Jealousy and envy combined with the prospect of easy money could wear a person down.

I picked up the sheet listing the names and dialed the next number. George McArthur, from Birmingham, New York, answered on the second ring. I rattled off my spiel.

"A recorded line," he said, his tone not quite making it a question.

"Yes."

"Drake Milner."

I waited for him to say something more, but he didn't. I counted to three, then asked, "Did you have an antique appraised by him?"

"No."

"Did you talk to him?"

"My business affairs are, as I'm certain you understand, Ms. Prescott, private."

I glanced at Detective Brownley. She sat forward, her eyes on my face. I could feel the increase in tension in the room. She nodded encouragingly.

"I'm not a police officer, Mr. McArthur, but I am helping the police."

"In what capacity?"

"A valuable antique has gone missing. We think Mr. Milner appraised it. Sadly, he has since died, so we can't ask him about it. Instead, we're asking people he listed in his diary."

"He died because of the antique?"

"I have no reason to think so."

"How did he die?"

"The ME hasn't finished her examination yet, but I think he drowned. In a car accident." I glanced at the detective again, and again she nodded at me.

"What's the antique?" he asked.

"A Fabergé egg encased in a snow globe."

"Sounds valuable."

"It is. Do you know anything about it?"

Detective Brownley's attention was unwavering—she was staring at me as if she could see through me.

"Yes," he said. "I spoke to Milner about a Fabergé egg he'd appraised. Someone approached me for a million-dollar loan using it as collateral. Before I accepted his appraisal as the basis of the loan, I wanted to speak to him, to confirm that everything was on the up-and-up. He assured me it was."

"You have the egg."

"Yes."

"It's intact. It's safe." I leaned back, as relieved as if I'd been the owner.

"Ms. Prescott, would you please tell me what's going on?"

"Who did you give the loan to?"

"I can't tell you that."

"Why not?"

"I signed a confidentiality agreement."

Detective Brownley waved at me to get my attention. When she had it, she raised her index finger and thumb to her ear, miming talking on a phone, then pointed to her chest.

"Detective Brownley from the Rocky Point police would like to talk to you," I said. "I'm going to hand her the phone."

"That's fine, but I can't tell her anything I haven't already told you. I take nondisclosure commitments very seriously."

"I understand. Here's Detective Brownley."

She removed her headphones and laid them on the desk. I handed her the receiver and put the headphones on. I didn't want to miss a word.

She introduced herself, then said, "The medical examiner is investigating whether Drake Milner died accidentally or whether he was murdered. We're trying to piece together Mr. Milner's last days. I respect confidentiality agreements, too, but there are times exceptions must be made. This is one of those times."

"I'm sorry, Detective. You'll need to compel my testimony. I have nothing to add."

"We can get that court order. Let's just save time."

"I don't mean to be rude, but I'm ending this call now."

He hung up.

Detective Brownley passed the phone to me, and I placed it in its cradle. I handed the headphones back to her. "The last time someone said he wouldn't talk without a court order, he died."

Her already obdurate expression grew more severe. "I'm going to call Chief Hunter. Then let's make the last calls."

"They're not going to be relevant."

"I know. But we need to make them anyway."

She was on the line with Ellis for less than two minutes. I would be willing to bet that by the time I dialed the seventh name on the list, Ellis would already have ADA Shirley Donovan working on the court order.

"Chief Hunter said to tell you we need to keep this development confidential," she said, "until we know what's what. Okay?"

"Sure," I said, understanding.

The next call was similar to the first ones; Frank Quinn had asked Milner to appraise a Russian painting, an Orthodox saint painted in oil on wood. Mr. Quinn was pleased with Milner's work but disappointed with the outcome—his painting was a modern repro, worth about five dollars. The last call, however, was different from all the rest.

Leigh Marlow's area code was 617, Boston. The letter following her name was *B*, another kovsh bowl, I assumed.

Before I finished my opening, Ms. Marlow started laughing.

"Boy, do you have it wrong! I wouldn't know a Russian antique from bok choy. Mr. Milner is a client of mine. I'm a travel agent."

Croatia, I thought. I was right all along. "A travel agent! I see. Was he planning a trip?"

"All booked and paid for. Bali. For two glorious weeks. How lucky is he?"

"When was he scheduled to leave?"

"May ninth. Returning the Saturday of Memorial Day weekend. He was smart, giving himself an extra day or two to get back in the swing of things." She laughed. "You gotta do laundry, right?"

"That's so true. It's how you know your vacation is over. Thanks, Ms. Marlow. You've been very helpful."

"I have? I don't see how—but thanks! And call me Leigh."

Leigh's peppy style drew a smile from me. I thanked her again and got off the phone.

"He made two replicas—one for his client and one for McArthur."

"Maybe," the detective said.

"I bet his return ticket was a sham, a ruse to avoid the red flags raised with Homeland Security when you buy a one-way ticket. If Milner sold the Fabergé egg, he could afford the round-trip fare even though he had no intention of using the return portion. Bali—you know that's in Indonesia, right?—has some of the world's best beaches and friendliest people. It's gorgeous—and Indonesia has no extradition treaty with the U.S." I smiled at Detective Brownley's surprised expression. "It's amazing the information you pick up in the antiques business."

"From what little I've seen, that's an understatement." She handed the headphones to Barry, who was busily disassembling the recording setup, and fluffed her hair. "Surely either the client or McArthur would have noticed that the egg was a phony."

"Not necessarily," I said. "McArthur wouldn't know what the original looked like. He accepted Milner's word. The client . . . that's a different can of worms." I paused, thinking. "Unless the client was in on it."

Officer Brownley cocked her head, considering my idea.

"Call the client X," I said. "X made a deal with Milner to pull off a double switch. X gets the original from the Yartsin house in Detroit. Milner has two replicas created, then sells the original, giving some or most of the proceeds to X. X then delivers a fake to McArthur and gets the loan. X sneaks the second fake back into the Yartsin house."

"Why would X need to get the loan if Milner shared the booty?"

"To account for the influx of cash. A way of laundering money."

The detective nodded slowly. "That's certainly possible. How can we prove it?"

"Find out who X is, and ask him—or her." I smiled. "Which isn't a new idea, I know. As a start, get McArthur to talk."

Detective Brownley smiled, a tight, businesslike smile. "Well, then, let's hope ADA Donovan can convince a judge to grant that court order."

CHAPTER TWENTY-FIVE

I was sitting in Ellis's office at the police station waiting to answer his questions about approaching McArthur once the court order was granted.

"I'll be right back," Ellis said as he hung up the phone. "I need to sit in on an interview. I shouldn't be more than five minutes or so. Are you all right to wait?"

"Sure," I said, thinking of the tag sale running full steam without me.

He used his foot to wedge a rubber doorstop under his office door, then left, heading down the corridor that led to Interrogation Rooms Three and Four.

I walked to the window. The tall grasses that lined the dunes shimmied in the light breeze.

"Where is he?" Peter asked, making his inquiry a demand, not idle curiosity.

I spun toward the open door in time to see Peter stomp to the front counter.

"Sir," Cathy said, "I need to ask you to lower your voice."

"Don't tell me what to do. Don't go there, lady. Just don't go there. Where's my father?"

Ana came running up to him and grabbed his arm, pulling him back. "Stop it, Peter. This won't help."

He shook her off like a flea, keeping his eyes on Cathy. "Now."

"Mr. Yartsin," Ellis said, coming into view. "Your father has been helping us out. He's just finishing up and should be coming out shortly." Ellis stepped into his office long enough to kick the doorstop aside. The door eased shut, moving slowly, guided by a hydraulic door closer. "If you'll just have a seat, I'll let him know—" The door closed, shutting off all sounds.

I waited a few seconds, then opened the door a crack, slipping a pencil between the door and the jamb about two inches above the ground. I tilted my head so I could see out. Ellis was nowhere in sight. Ana was standing in the middle of the lobby, her shoulders hunched. Peter stood close to the counter, his hands on his hips, ready for a fight. Officer Meade led Stefan out from the corridor.

"Thank you again, sir," she said.

"Ana," Stefan said. "Peter. What are you doing here?"

Peter took a step toward him. "That damn reporter said the police brought you in because they broke your alibi."

"He didn't say that, exactly," Ana corrected. "Wes said the police found inconsistencies in the timeline that might impact your alibi. We got worried, so we decided to come down here."

Stefan sat down on the hard wooden bench. He pressed his head against the backrest and closed his eyes for a moment. "Keeping secrets. Never a smart idea."

Ana sat beside him and took his hand. "What secret, Dad?"

"What are you talking about?" Peter asked. "They had no right to drag you down here."

"They didn't drag me. I came voluntarily." He sat forward and looked at Ana, sitting patiently, her eyes worried, her bearing stiff, then turned to Peter, looming over him. "Sit down, Peter. I'll tell you what's going on."

Peter sat on his other side and half-turned so he could face him full on.

"I've been seeing a woman, a lovely woman, for several months now. That's where I was the second night. She has a cottage in the Berkshires."

Ana blinked several times, then frowned. "Why would you keep it a secret?"

"I didn't want you to think I was disrespecting your mother."

"Oh, Dad, no! How could you think so after all these years?"

He glanced at Peter. "We Yartsin men are known for our fidelity. Even when there's no need. Even when the time for loyalty has long since passed." Peter lowered his gaze to his feet. "Your mother was an angel. No woman could ever replace her."

"Of course not," Ana said, rubbing the top of his hand with her thumb, small strokes, back and forth, back and forth. "I'm happy for you—I have no hesitation in saying that."

"And you, Peter? Are you happy for me, too?"

"Of course," he replied, his tone solemn, his gaze still on the floor. "Who is she?"

"Carly Summers. Toni's friend."

"We met her at Christmas!" Ana said.

"Yes. She lives in New York City and has a weekend place in Stockbridge, Massachusetts. We've been meeting there or in Rochester."

"Why Rochester?"

"She's a musician, a talented pianist. There's a fine music program in Rochester, the Eastman School of Music. She offers master classes there periodically."

"I understand why you didn't tell us right away, because of Mom and all, but when the police insisted on knowing where you were Monday night, why didn't you just tell them?"

Stefan patted Ana's hand, then placed it on her thigh. He stood up and stretched, arching his back. "Because I'm only human." He walked toward the front door. "Carly is married."

I pushed my fingers against my lips. *Oh my,* I thought.

"Oh, God," Ana said.

"Married?" Peter exclaimed as if he were unfamiliar with the word.

"The police called her to verify my story. She was upset—so upset. Understandable, of course. She dreads her husband finding out. There are children involved, and his elderly mother. Complications. Family complications. I must respect her need for privacy or I'd tell him myself." He looked at Ana, then Peter, then back to Ana. "This isn't some sordid affair. We love each other."

"What's going to happen?"

"She's gone to visit her daughter in Los Angeles. I begged her to come up here, to be with me through this difficult period." Stefan ran his fingers through his thick graying hair. "She says she needs time alone, time to think. I don't know why. She doesn't love him. She loves me."

He trudged to the door, pushed it open, and looked back over his shoulder. "I don't want to talk about it any more. It's a private situation."

He left, and Ana and Peter exchanged astonished glances, then followed him out.

I opened the door a tiny bit, and the pencil fell to the floor. I placed it back in Ellis's container and sat down to wait.

.   .   .

Ellis returned about ten minutes later.

"Sorry about the wait," he said, sitting behind his desk. "This thing's a real hairball, if you'll excuse my French."

"Excused. What in particular is wrong now?"

"We can't get a break. Those police recruits went through every book in Milner's office. Nothing. The search of his condo and office is now complete. Nothing. We checked whether Milner's GPS was working when he hit the water. He hadn't turned it on. And Judge Sandler just refused our request for a court order to compel McArthur to reveal who used the Fabergé egg as collateral with him."

"I'm surprised. How come?"

"She thought ADA Donovan's petition was specious."

"Specious. That's harsh."

"Yeah. She said that if we can connect the dots, showing that the Yartsin egg is the one McArthur has, she'll grant the petition."

"If you could do that, you wouldn't need the petition."

"Welcome to my world."

"But they're so rare."

"I know. What else can we try?"

Ellis and I brainstormed every which way, trying to find an unassailable connection between Ana's egg and George McArthur, without luck. Finally I stood up and told him I was going back to work.

After checking in with my staff working the tag sale, I scooped up Hank and went upstairs. My standing rule was when in doubt, do more research.

Hank curled into a tight ball in my lap, purring.

"Are you a good boy, Hank?"

He mewed.

"I know . . . you are *such* a good boy."

Google led me directly to George McArthur's company. McArthur was the founder and majority owner of McArthur Evergreen Technologies based in Birmingham, New York. The photo that accompanied his welcome-to-our-Web-site letter showed a man of about fifty with a professional grin and short brown hair. He was wearing a blue collared shirt, open at the neck. The letter was standard issue, saying everything that potential customers and investors wanted to hear. Business was booming. Patents were pending. The future was in sight and looking good.

McArthur Evergreen Technologies manufactured small cuplike vessels that captured wind, efficiently converting it to energy. The cups could be attached to any tall structure, like a cell tower or a roof. It was, according to the company's "about" page, the first time wind power didn't require a windmill. I was impressed. So were technology reviewers from major newspapers and magazines. One article in a 2008 *Technology Today* magazine roundup of up-and-coming firms to watch quoted McArthur Evergreen Technologies' director of marketing, Ana Yartsin.

I called Ellis and got him on his cell phone.

"I was just about to call you and pass along a little good news," he said, "but you go first."

"Ana got an MBA and worked in business for seven years before going back to culinary school. For five of them, she was the director of marketing for McArthur Evergreen Technologies."

"As in George McArthur."

"Yes."

"So we now have two breaks. The techs found the flash drive."

"That's great. Where?"

"Under one of the seats. They said it could have been in his shirt pocket, that as water rose, it got swept away. When the car pitched, it followed the tide, sliding under a mat."

"Can they read anything on it?"

"Not yet. It has to dry out. For days, probably. They talked about using a blow dryer, but they were afraid the extreme heat might fry it."

"Oh, God, Ellis. What a mess. The data's there, but we can't get to it."

"Not *yet.*"

"I hope you're right." I patted Hank's bottom, and he settled in tighter. "What should we do about Ana?"

"*You* should do nothing. I'll check it out."

I stroked Hank's chin, and he raised his head a little to offer better access.

"Okay," I said.

He told me he'd let me know when the data on the drive was available for me to look at, and I wished him luck. We hung up. I was tired of sitting and tired of thinking. I wanted to go dancing.

I texted Ty. "Dancing tonight?"

He replied right away. "I just made the rez."

I smiled. What a guy.

"I've got to go, Hank." I slid him down onto the floor. He meowed his objection and ambled away. "Sorry, baby."

I went to close the folder, then stopped. I cut-and-pasted the old magazine article, then printed it out. I had a feeling I'd want to consult it again.

CHAPTER TWENTY-SIX

M ost Sundays while Ty is working, I putter. I cook. I organize photos in albums. I polish silver. Today, I sat at my home computer researching everything I could think of that might possibly be related to Ana's relationship with McArthur Evergreen Technologies.

I read magazine articles, various interviews Ana conducted with the press, investor reports, annual reports, and archived internal company newsletters. At noon, I stood up and stretched. I knew a lot about the company, but if anything I'd learned was relevant, the link was beyond me.

"Time to cook," I said. I made my mother's recipe for Dijon chicken, letting the maple-syrup-infused sauce simmer as I made a tuna salad sandwich for my lunch.

The sun was veiled with a thin layer of wispy gray clouds. The temperature hovered in the high forties. A dreary day, a lonely day. I wished I had a hobby like whittling or knitting or jewelry making. A girl I'd known in college who'd majored in premed had made metal sculptures to relax. Her dad was a welder, and she'd learned to use a blowtorch in high school. I looked out over the meadow. *A metal worker,* I thought. My mouth opened. I ran for my computer.

Within ten minutes, I'd located four free ways to solicit metal workers for day work: a discussion forum, a free jobs-available site, an industry association job board, and a nationally organized, community-based job posting system for tradesmen. I called Ellis.

"We've been working to identify who brought the genuine Fabergé Spring Egg snow globe to Drake Milner. Maybe we can work it backward. Instead of issuing a call-for-sightings, what would you think of my issuing a statement saying, 'I've seen your work and I have a job for you'?"

"So he'll contact you," Ellis said, thinking aloud.

"Exactly."

"I like it. How would you work it?"

"I'd post an ad." I told him about the sites I'd found.

"You get any nibbles, you call me before you reply."

I promised I would. I wrote an ad, then revised it, trying to sound complimentary but not over the top, since a craftsman had to know the Fabergé Spring Egg snow globe replica was not, by any stretch of the imagination, stellar work.

The heading read: *You created a Fabergé egg snow globe replica.*

The text read: *I've seen it, and I want one, too! Will pay top dollar.*

I created a dedicated e-mail account on a free service and added response instructions to my ad: *E-mail with a time I can call you. Don't forget to include your phone number.* I listed the e-mail address, reread it carefully, and said, "Okay, then."

Twenty minutes later, all four ads were uploaded, and I went back to the kitchen to finish my sandwich.

At two, I called Wes.

"Do you know anything more?" I asked. "About anything?"

"Yup. I'm just heading out to Locke Pond. Meet me there in ten."

Before I could ask him why, he'd hung up.

Locke Pond looked as dark and dangerous as it had the day I'd discovered Drake Milner's car submerged in the water.

I rolled to a stop at a police barricade a hundred yards from where I'd parked before. Another barricade was positioned several hundred yards down the road. Officer F. Meade was standing with her back to me, watching for oncoming vehicles.

Wes's shiny red car was next to two marked police cars and an unmarked white van. The van's sliding side door was open. Inside, all the seats had been removed. A bench ran the length of the cargo hold. Blue mesh gear bags were scattered throughout.

Wes was standing at the barricade arguing with Griff.

"What's so secret?" Wes asked, sounding outraged.

"Nothing is secret, Wes," Griff replied, smiling tolerantly. "You can't make a conspiracy out of this, no matter how hard you try. A crime scene is what we have here, nothing more."

"And I'm the voice of the people demanding information."

"You're not allowed to traipse through an active crime scene. You know that, Wes."

"Hi, Wes," I said, joining him. "Hi, Griff."

"Josie." Griff touched his cap, old school. "You all right?"

"I'd be doing better if the temperature would catch up with the season, but I'm fine."

"It's cold, all right."

Wes, agitated, moved away, standing on tiptoes, trying to see through the trees.

"What's Wes trying to see?"

"Divers."

"Are they dredging the pond?" I asked, surprised. I couldn't imagine what they were looking for. "Is it confidential? Can you tell me what they're doing?"

Griff thought about it for half a minute, then shrugged. "They're not dredging. The medical examiner issued a statement to the press, which is why he's here." Griff nodded toward Wes. "So I guess I can fill you in." Wes saw Griff's motion toward him, and he hurried back to join us. "She's ruled Drake Milner's death a homicide. He was hit on the head with a rock. I guess she found some bits of mica embedded in his skull. Those divers, they're looking for the rock."

"How horrible," I said, wincing. "Gruesome." I paused. "Do they really think they can locate one rock in particular? The pond is huge!"

"They used this new imaging software and added animation and color enhancement and I don't know what-all else, so they have a picture of the rock they're looking for, or at least the part of it that did the damage. Then they calculated trajectory. It's amazing what they can calculate nowadays."

Wes rejoined us and listened in.

"From the angle of the blow," Griff continued, "they figured the killer hit Milner while he was behind the wheel, then chucked the stone into the water, lowered the windows a couple of inches so the water could get in, put the car in neutral, hit the auto-lock button, closed the door, and pushed the car in. Since they know where the car entered the pond from the tire tracks, they can approximate where the killer would have been standing when he threw the rock. It's like a slice of pizza with the killer at the pointy end. The arc of the wide end is the farthest a large, athletic man could reach. If the killer threw the stone like they think he did, it can't be outside that arc. That's the only area they need to search."

"Can I get copies of the animation?" Wes asked, making a note.

"Not from me."

Wes started arguing with him, moaning about freedom of the press and the public's right to know, like always, and I walked away.

The wooden sawhorse barricades ended about ten feet into the woods. While Griff was engaged with Wes, I sidestepped to the end, moving slowly, then trotted deeper into the woods toward the pond. When I reached the trees that lined the pond, I looked back. I couldn't see the street, which meant Griff couldn't see me.

It was hard going. The woods were thick and dark, with giant conifers creating a solid ceiling overhead and tangled vines and unseen roots underfoot. I pushed aside a low-hanging branch, ducked under another, stepped around a spiky bush, and crawled over an ancient tree trunk that had fallen diagonally across my path. I began to hear voices and speeded up.

"Whadja think?" a man asked. His accent was solidly Downeast, filled with the twang of upstate Maine.

"Who knows?" a woman said. "Just bag it." She sounded young.

"One more sector," the man said. "I'll go left."

A twig scraped my cheek about two inches below my right eye. I stopped and pressed my fingers against it, whispering, "Ouch." My fingers came away bloody. I wished I had a tissue, but I'd locked my tote bag in my car. All I was carrying was my key ring. I used a Boston fern frond to wipe my fingers and another as a makeshift gauze pad, and continued walking.

A minute later I had a view of the divers' launching vehicle, a kind of floating raft attached by long braces to a Jeep that had backed down the steep incline to the water's edge. Two pieces of what looked like nylon filament were attached to a four-foot-high stake someone had driven into the ground about five feet to the left of the Jeep. Each length of filament stretched out into the pond, one angling left, the other right, defining the search area, a pie shaped wedge, just like Griff described, a hundred feet across at its widest spot, about two hundred feet straight out. Neon orange plastic flags were tied onto the lines every yard or so.

A woman in her early twenties stood on the grassy shore holding a handful of plastic evidence bags. Her dark red-brown hair was cut as short as a man's. She wore hip-high gray rubber gaiters and an all-weather anorak. A clear deep plastic tub was half filled, not much output for an all-day dive.

A diver popped up out of the water, yanked off his mask and breathing apparatus, and held a rough roundish rock the size of a grapefruit high above his head, waving it like a trophy. Even from a distance and in gloomy light, I could see silvery specks glimmer as he moved the rock to and fro. *Mica*, I thought.

"Hey, Lottie," he called. "I got it! Mark the bag 'Marty's pick.'"

She shook open one of the evidence bags and waded into the water to meet him. He sidestroked toward her holding the rock about a foot above the waterline.

"It looks like all the others. What makes you think this is the one, Marty?"

"'Cause I'm all-seeing and all-knowing and I've been doing this for longer than you've been alive, sugar pie."

She giggled as she slogged farther in, pausing when the water was thigh-high and waiting for him to reach her. He tread water while she held the bag open, spreading her fingers to make the gap as large as possible. Marty dropped the stone in. She sealed it and headed for land.

"One more pass should do it," Marty said.

"Okay."

Marty grinned like he'd just won the lottery. "Don't forget—label it 'Marty's pick.'"

"Will do," she said, chuckling.

I watched him put his gear back on with unconscious confidence, check his gauges, and slide underwater with such effortless precision, the water barely rippled.

I sat on a boulder just behind the tree line and continued to watch. The scratch on my cheek had stopped bleeding, but it hurt, a kind of dull throbbing. Twenty minutes later, neither diver had resurfaced. Wet cold, the coldest kind, leached through my boots, turning my feet into frozen ice cubes and setting my teeth rattling. Five minutes later, I was shivering nonstop and I was tired of looking at nothing.

I headed back, veering inland as I walked. It was harder going up than down, not just because of the incline but because I was colder and it was darker. I stumbled on a rock, a big one, and fell, sprawling. I landed cheek down, and the scratch started bleeding again. I tore off another fern frond and held it tight against my cheek.

"Okay, then," I whispered after half a minute. "Let's not do that again."

I stood up and continued on, moving slowly now, testing the ground before carefully placing each foot. I made it up to more level ground without incident, then passed through a narrow passage with twigs snapping at my arms and face. As I neared the summit, I tripped over a slick patch of moss and fell again. I stayed down on all fours and negotiated a tricky pass. Finally, I popped out about ten feet beyond my car. *Perfect,* I thought.

Wes was standing at the end of the last barricade peering through binoculars. To the naked eye, all that was visible were trees. I wondered what he saw. Griff was tapping something into his smart phone.

I joined Wes, calling to him as I walked. "Hey, Wes. What do you say we get a cup of something warm?"

He lowered his binoculars and spun toward me. "What happened to your cheek?"

I touched the scratch. "A twig got me."

His eyes narrowed. "Where have you been?"

"Around. Want a cup of coffee?"

He glanced at Griff. "I'm not done here." He lowered his voice. "I'm about to slip into the woods without him noticing."

"Griff has eyes in the back of his head where you're concerned." Griff had put his phone away and was watching us. "Let's go to Sweet Treats," I said, adding in a whisper, "I'll tell you what I saw."

Wes grinned. "Coffee would be good."

CHAPTER TWENTY-SEVEN

I waved my hands over the steaming mug of tea, glad for the warmth. Wes was drinking coffee. We were sitting at a small table at the newly renovated Sweet Treats Bakery & Tea Shoppe enveloped in the aroma of cinnamon and vanilla. After my time navigating the rugged outside, I was thankful to be inside and warm.

After eliciting a promise not to quote me, I reported what I'd seen. "I can't believe Marty was certain he found the weapon."

"I can't believe you snuck down there and back without me or Griff spotting you."

"You had him occupied. He isn't suspicious of me like he is of you."

"He doesn't know you like I do. Very slick move, Joz."

I bowed, a mini-thank-you, then recupped my mug. "What do you know about Marty?"

"Martin Oilu. He's the lead diver on the cold-water rescue team. I researched them last year for a story. Those guys are pros, specially trained for cold-water searches. Mostly rescues, you know, when someone falls through the ice or there's a boat wreck or something, but they're the bomb when it comes to underwater anything."

"There's so much we don't know. Did you get any further with unraveling Jason's finances?"

"No, and the police are pretty pissed about it. His executor—some lawyer at a hula-hula Boston law firm—won't even officially acknowledge Jason had any trusts."

"I'm surprised a judge won't compel him to talk."

"Judges don't like to compel testimony about a victim. It doesn't look good. So first the police tried reasoning with the executor, requesting answers to certain specific questions, you know, limited scope, whatever. Then they gave up and filed the paperwork. So far, the judge says no. The judge says they know who inherits—his parents—and that's enough info, unless they can show that Jason was somehow involved in something illegal or related to a crime." Wes drank some coffee. "According to my police source, you asked them to check if Milner called anyone right after you left your meeting with him. How come?"

"I thought there was a chance I spooked him about the Fabergé egg. If so, he might well have called his client to warn him—or her."

"You were right. He called a 617 number, a disposable phone, you know the kind you buy at any big-box or electronics store. You can refill it anytime you want or throw it away. Untraceable. They spoke for fifteen minutes."

"That's long enough to plan a cover-up." I refilled my mug. "Can't they tell where and when that phone was sold by matching its serial number to the transaction? Everything is tracked electronically these days. That would let them examine security cameras."

"They tried. The unit was activated on February eighteenth at a mom-and-pop discount shop called Lucky Electronics, in Boston's Chinatown." Wes's tone changed from all-business to pals. "Have you ever been there—to Chinatown?"

"Lots of times. Our favorite restaurant there is the Mandarin Star. Why? Are you thinking of going?'

Wes flushed. "Yeah. Maybe. I booked a room at the Four Seasons in Boston next week—it's for our six-month anniversary, Maggie and me. I looked it up. It's not far from Chinatown. I want to take her to a really nice place for dinner. We both like Chinese food. Maybe that would be a good choice."

"I'm not sure the Mandarin Star is what you have in mind. It has great food, but it's pretty ordinary looking. I wouldn't describe it as romantic."

"Oh. How can I find a good place for dinner?"

"Call the concierge at the hotel."

"Thanks!" Wes said. "That's a great idea."

I smiled at him. "What do you have planned?"

"We're going to spend the day going to museums. The Fine Arts and the Isabella Stewart Gardner. Maggie likes museums." He looked down for a moment, then back up. "I just told her to take the day off, that I have a surprise for her." He swallowed hard. "I'm going to ask her to marry me."

Unexpected tears sprung to my eyes. "Oh, Wes. Congratulations."

"Don't congratulate me yet. She hasn't said yes."

"She will. How could she not? You're a catch. Do you have the ring yet?"

Concern clouded his eyes. "It's kind of old-fashioned looking. Traditional, you know? The diamond is round with little filigrees, or whatever you call them, in the setting. I'm a little scared the diamond is too small. It's a half karat. Do you think Maggie will think it's too small?"

"No, not at all!" I reached across the table and touched his hand. "I'm sure Maggie will love it, Wes."

He leaned back and took in a deep breath. "Thanks." He finished his coffee, pushed the mug aside, flipped through a few pages in his notebook, and said, "So, anyway . . . the police have already reviewed the security recording from that day. It's lucky Lucky Electronics keeps digital files for three months, huh?" We chuckled. "Get it? Lucky Lucky?"

"I get it."

He grinned. "That phone and another one were bought by a woman. For cash."

My heart gave an extra beat. "A woman?"

"Not Ana."

I sat back. "Really?"

"Yup. It's not Heather, either."

"Who is it?"

"No one knows. It's hard to tell much about her. She's wearing a hat, one of those furry ones with a big brim, and most of the time, she was looking down at the phones or counting out money. She paid in cash." He tapped on his phone. "Here. Take a look." He slid the unit across the table. "The police have asked me to publish this photo, hoping someone can ID her."

The woman wasn't just looking down, her head was angled away from the camera. The small bit of hair that showed from under the hat looked to be brown and shoulder-length, but it was hard to tell because her fuzzy fur or faux-fur coat collar was turned up. Her face seemed thin.

I handed back the phone. "You can barely see her. I doubt anyone would be able to recognize her."

"No one will tell regardless." Wes stared at the photo for a minute, then shrugged. "If she's a friend, you're not going to want to tell the police about her, and even if she's not a friend, who wants to get involved in a murder investigation, you know?"

"Why mention murder? Tell them she's needed to help find a missing antique." I smiled, my devilish one. "Use me as the contact person."

Wes grinned. "Good one, Josie! I'll do it. What kind of antique?"

I thought about it for a minute. "A Victorian-era European decorative object."

He wrote that down. "Very good. What is it?"

I raised my chin. "Given that the object in question was intended to be a gift, I'm sure you understand why I can't reveal any details. We don't want to lose the element of surprise."

Wes wrote quickly. "You're very good at this, aren't you?"

I smiled. "Yes."

"I'll get it posted to our news feed this afternoon and feature it in print tomorrow." He rat-a-tat-tatted his pen against his notebook. "As to whether there was any contact between the woman who bought the phone and Milner . . . he called that same number several times during the period he was appraising the Fabergé egg. After that, there were two other calls, one right after he saw you in his office and the other the morning he died, at seven thirty."

I paused, ideas rattling around in my head. "So during that last call, he was confirming his appointment with his client. They planned to meet before he saw the police, which suggests that the woman is from Rocky Point."

"Or that she lives close enough to get here easily."

"Were all those calls placed from Milner's office phone?" I asked.

"Yup. There were no calls from Milner's home or cell phones to that number."

"So the relationship was all business."

"Some business if it gets you killed."

"Yeah."

Wes put his notebook away. "I spoke to Julie, the woman who worked at Marlborough Antiques with Milner, and a gal in accounting. They both said it's absurd to think Milner was anything but on the up-and-up, that he was a complete straight arrow."

I waved it aside. "That's what people always say. 'Oh, he was such a nice, quiet young man.' You know that."

"You think Milner snowed them all?"

"Maybe." I shrugged. "Who knows? I'm just saying I don't take people's assessments of one another as gospel. Show me how they act; don't tell me what they say. I can paint a scenario of guilt for everyone as easily as they can deny it. Milner was in his early sixties—close to when many people start thinking about retirement—and alone. He'd been working his whole life, and what did he have to show for it? A small condo in Boston." I paused. "What else did he have? Do you know?"

"A modest 401(k) and a half-interest in a cottage in Wales he shared with his sister. She inherits everything."

"So he gets an opportunity of a lifetime, pulls a double cross, selling the Fabergé egg privately to a Russian mobster, and flies off to Bali, where he plans to live happily ever after on the proceeds. As I said, it's all speculation, but it fits."

"Do you think he did it?"

I drank some tea, then shook my head. "No. I think he was a good guy who never would have thought of such a thing."

"I don't know, Joz . . . you're pretty persuasive."

"I know. Beware the good talker."

"True. So what do you have for me?"

"A question. When Ana left McArthur Evergreen Technologies, did she take a chunk of money with her?"

"Huh?"

I filled him in about McArthur's loan and Ana's former role at the company, and Wes extracted his notebook again and jotted some notes.

"I'll check," he said. "Anything else?"

"No."

Wes pushed back his chair and shrugged into his down coat. "Catch ya later."

I finished my tea as I watched him stride across Bow Street heading for the Central Garage, a man with a purpose.

That afternoon, Hank curled up on the love seat while I settled in at my desk. Ty texted he'd be home around six, so I figured I might as well try to catch up at work. I read a good-news accounting report, revised catalogue copy for an upcoming auction, and got through enough e-mails to make my eyes blurry. One check of my new e-mail account, though, and I perked up. I had seven replies to my ad.

Three were from jewelers and four from metal workers; none had ever worked on a Fabergé egg snow globe replica, but all were eager to give it a whirl. I sighed, deleted them, got Hank organized for the night, and drove home.

The next morning, Monday, I was sitting at my kitchen table finishing a bowl of cereal when I checked the e-mail account I'd created for the ad.

Hello,
I'm Ralph Kovak. I made that Fabergé egg snow globe replica you asked about. I'll be at home after four if you want to call. 555.952.0852.
Sincerely,
Ralph Kovak

"Wow," I said aloud. I reached for my phone and called Ellis. I got him at his desk. "You're in early."

"Lots to do."

"My idea worked. I've got the guy."

"Tell me."

I read him the e-mail. I knew better than to expect any whoopin' or hollerin', since that was not Ellis's style, so I wasn't surprised when he said, "Can you come to the station around three?"

"Sure."

I drove to work through the rising sun thinking I couldn't wait to see how Ellis planned to play it.

CHAPTER TWENTY-EIGHT

I figured 8:30 A.M. was a decent hour, so at 8:31 I called Marianna Albert to ask if I could come look at her husband's gadget cane collection. She said she would be home all morning and I should come on ahead. I left a note for Cara and headed to Durham.

The Albert home was a traditional Colonial, painted white with cherry red trim. A long driveway curved to the right, ending at a two-car garage. I parked before the curve.

"This way," Marianna called. She was holding open the storm door.

"Hi!" I said. I reached into the back for my tote bag. I walked up the narrow pathway. "Thanks for seeing me on such short notice."

"Of course. Are you all right after your ordeal?"

"I'm fine. Thanks for asking. I just wish I could have done more to help that poor man."

She made a clucking sound and led me across a square entry hall to a large study. One wall was solid with built-in bookcases. Another showcased the canes and walking sticks. Each one was mounted horizontally, held in place by two brass rings. The arrangement was asymmetrical and awe-inspiring.

"What a remarkable display," I said. "I've never seen anything like it."

"Hearing you, Walter is beaming down on us."

"Did he arrange them by date of acquisition or value?"

She laughed. "He didn't have a system. He placed them in whatever order pleased him aesthetically. When he got a new one, he spent hours trying it here and there, until he found the spot he liked best."

"His care shows. It's a terrific arrangement." I extracted a video camera from my bag. "May I record the collection?"

"Certainly."

I followed Prescott's protocol, annotating what I saw as I created the video. When I was finished, I placed the camera back in the bag. "I'll be sending you a proposal, of course, but let me tell you what I recommend."

"Come into the kitchen. We can have some coffee while we talk."

Her kitchen was farmhouse contemporary, with butcher-block counters and antique white cabinets. I sat on one side of an old wood plank farm table. Marianna sat across from me. The coffee was strong, the steam soothing.

"If you select Prescott's, which of course I hope you do, we'll examine each cane looking for hidden cubbyholes, measuring and weighing each, confirming the accuracy of the catalogue entry. We'll then research each one, confirming or discovering all records of ownership, starting with the maker and the date of manufacture or fabrication and following the trail until we reach Walter. Once we've completed these two steps—ensuring we have an accurate and complete description of the object and confirming provenance—we move on to the final step, valuation. This step is part science and part artistry. We research sales records and consumer market trends, then use our experience and expertise to come up with an auction sales estimate. It's not an exact science, but we're right far more often than we're wrong."

"This is exactly the information I wanted. Thank you. Now all I need to know is the price."

"And that requires me thinking it through, estimating how long it would take us to conduct the appraisal, anticipating likely snags, and so on."

"How much would you charge to appraise one of them? I'd like to see what you do with one before I commit to letting you handle the entire collection."

"Interesting idea. You tell me which one, let me read the catalogue entry so I can see what is known about it, and I'll give you a price."

We returned to the study. Marianna faced the wall of canes, then began walking the length of the room and back again, considering her options.

"This one," she said, pointing to one close to the window at eye level. "That's one of the ones Walter didn't know much about."

"May I?" I asked, reaching for it.

"Sure."

I freed it by slipping it through the rings. It was heavy, made of dark burled wood, maybe walnut, possibly chestnut or maple. The elephant head handle was fashioned out of brass and fit my hand surprisingly comfortably. The bottom was protected by a three-inch-high brass plate.

While I looked at it, Marianna went to the desk, extracted an accordion file, and flipped through the pockets, wiggling out a half-page-sized sheet of white paper. She scanned the contents, then read it aloud. "Elephant head walking stick, circa 1820. Probably British, maybe East Asian. Burled maple and brass. Two openings. The entire head screws off to reveal an opening that held an umbrella (missing). The bottom tip also unscrews to reveal a small opening, perhaps to hold some folded money. Purchased in London at Mitchum's Haberdashery, 1987, for £140, roughly $215 then, or $440 now. No information about its history was available. The shop owner didn't typically deal in antiques; this was his deceased brother's cane, and his sister-in-law didn't know anything about it. He was selling it on her behalf." She looked up. "As I said, Walter didn't know much about it."

I lifted the walking stick up and studied it for a moment. I told her our hourly fee, estimating that it would take as many as ten hours to research it properly.

"How long will it take, do you think?"

"A week or more. I already know I'm going to want to contact several experts, and scheduling calls takes time."

"I appreciate your thoroughness. You've got a deal."

I took a photo with my phone and e-mailed it to Gretchen, asking her to prepare a receipt and an appraisal agreement and e-mail the documents to me. She IM'd to confirm receipt. While we waited, Marianna led me outside to the backyard.

"Walter's passion was his walking sticks. Mine is my garden. Come look."

Marianna had created a wonderland with eight-foot statues and a fountain reminiscent of the one in the Place de la Concorde in Paris. Ten-foot-high boxwoods wound through the yard, forming a private walkway.

"I'm speechless," I said. "All I can do is stand here and marvel."

She laughed. "Thank you. It's taken forty years of work for it to look like this."

My phone vibrated. Gretchen had sent the receipt and contract. "Let me read through these documents to be certain they're correct."

"Do you want to come inside?"

I smiled at her. "Something tells me that somewhere in this garden, there's a bench."

She laughed. "I knew you were a woman of discernment the first moment I met you." She started down the path, and I followed. "You won't be too chilly?"

"No, it's downright balmy today. What a difference a day makes."

The path curved to the left, then to the right, circling back on itself. An opening, marked by a latticed arched trellis, gave access to a secret garden. Four stone benches surrounded another, smaller fountain.

"Spectacular," I said. Ten minutes later, I asked for her e-mail address and forwarded the documents. "Everything is in order. If you can print them out, we can sign the forms and I can get started on the appraisal."

"Thank you, Josie."

She printed out a copy of Walter's notes; then we signed the documents and shook on the deal. I was back at work by eleven.

I carried the walking stick into the office and held it above my head. "We get to do a test appraisal. Who wants to get started?"

"Me," Fred said, before Sasha could reply.

"You all right with that?" I asked her.

She tucked her hair behind her ears. "Sure. I've got plenty to do."

I handed it and the paperwork over. "Let me know what you discover as you discover it, okay?"

"Sure," he said, his unerring focus already activated. He was running his index finger along the underside of the elephant's trunk.

I headed upstairs, white-hot curious about what Fred would learn.

CHAPTER TWENTY-NINE

A t five of four, I was sitting alone in Interrogation Room One waiting for Ellis to signal me, when my phone vibrated. It was a text from Fred.

"I found another opening. The elephant's trunk hides a trick latch."

I replied, "Wow."

"Double wow."

I smiled, put my phone back on the table, and glanced at the one-way mirror. Ellis was in the observation room talking with a technician, a different man than the one who'd come to my place. I couldn't decide which was worse, looking at myself in the one-way mirror or looking away. In either case, I felt conspicuous, and knowing people were watching me, or could be, was unsettling.

Ellis came in and sat across from me. He had a stack of blank index cards and a pen. He placed a metallic blue water bottle emblazoned with the Rocky Point Police Department logo beside the pen. The logo was fancy, a gold and black triangular shield with the words "integrity," "courtesy," and "service" running along the sides. A phone unit sat off to the left, with a set of headphones attached by a long black cable that snaked across the table and down the side.

He asked if I was ready, and when I said yes, he put on the headphones and used his index finger to shoot at the one-way mirror, signaling "Go."

I glanced at the printout of Ralph Kovak's e-mail and dialed. It rang four times, a hollow, echoing sound, before he answered.

"Mr. Kovak?"

"This is Ralph."

He sounded old.

"I'm Josie Prescott. I placed the ad about the Fabergé egg snow globe. Do you have a few minutes to chat?"

"Glad to. What can I tell you?"

"When did you make it?"

"Last month sometime." He made a hoarse sound, maybe a laugh, kind of a snort. *Hawn.* "Now that I'm retired, I don't keep work records. Never going to again, and that's the truth."

"I don't need work records, so that's not a problem. Who was your client?"

"Why are you asking?"

"References."

"I can give you plenty of solid references. Some going back sixty years. That's right, young lady. I'm seventy-eight now, and I've been working with metal since the war. The big one."

"That's great. Thanks. Have you been doing jewelry work that long, too?"

He made another *hawn* sound. "No, ma'am. That's only been fifteen years, since I retired."

"Fifteen years is a good amount of time."

"You liked my work, did you?"

"I had the sense you had to hurry some."

Hawn. "You got that right, young lady. That customer was going hell to leather. Didn't give me time for nothing beyond the minimum. I wasn't happy with that and I wasn't happy with what I did, but he said it was good enough, and here you are asking for another one, so I guess he was right."

"Where are you located?"

"Cleveland? You?"

"New Hampshire."

"Never been there."

Ellis flipped an index card toward me, using the same wrist-snapping move Jimmy used with cocktail napkins in the Blue Dolphin's lounge. I was so intent on my conversation with Kovak, I hadn't noticed him writing. The note read, "How did they meet?"

I read Ellis's question, then repeated it aloud. "Did this guy find you through an ad, too?"

"That's right. My son-in-law found his posting on an industry forum, same place he found yours."

"Which one?"

"With all respect, ma'am, you seem more interested in my client than in my work."

"Sorry, I'm just naturally curious." Ellis spun another card toward me. This one read, "Say you have an urgent call you need to take and ask to call him back."

I looked at Ellis. He shot his index finger at my chest. *Do it,* his manner stated. *Do it now.*

"Mr. Kovak, I apologize. There's a call I have to take. It's urgent. May I call you back?"

"Run that by me again?"

"May I call you back?"

"What's this about, young lady? I may be old, but I'm not stupid. Something fishy is going on."

"I promise it isn't. I'll call you back."

"Maybe I'll take your call, and maybe I won't." He hung up.

I replaced the receiver gently. "Well, that went well, don't you think?"

"I'm going to call the Cleveland police and ask them to bring him in and set up a Skype call. I need to see his eyes. I'll let you know the time. I hate to ask you to keep running back and forth like I am, but I need you."

"You know the way to my heart—tell me I'm needed."

Ellis leaned back and smiled. "Good to know."

"Any news on the flash drive?"

"Not yet. They tell me these things can't be hurried."

I stood up. "I'm not a patient person."

"That's one way of putting it."

I eyed him warily. "What's another?"

"You approach life with a strong sense of urgency."

I smiled. "One person's impatience is another person's urgent need."

He smiled and joined me at the door. "I'll call you when I have information about Skyping with Kovak."

Ana was chatting with Cara when I got back to my office.

"Real ginger?" Ana said. "I've never heard of that."

"Oh, yes, dear. Shave off a little bit and mince it. Sauté it in a tablespoon of olive oil and add it to the marinade."

"Can I use ginger powder?"

Cara smiled sweetly. "No."

"Ana," I said. "I'm so glad to see you. How are you doing?"

Ana turned and smiled. She was wearing a red cashmere turtleneck tunic cinched by a thick black leather belt with a large silver buckle, an above-the-knee black leather skirt, and ankle-high black leather boots with three-inch heels. Two rows of silver-colored spikes circled the back of each boot. Her hair was swept into a high ponytail.

"Honestly?" she said. "I'm reeling. Do you have a sec?"

"Sure," I said. "Just let me check in." I turned to my staff. "Talk to me."

"I'm updating the database," Cara said. "More than fifty people signed up for our newsletter at this week's tag sale."

"Nice!" I said.

Fred pushed up his glasses. "I'm working on the cane, doing a physical analysis first."

"Good."

"I'm working with Eric," Gretchen said, "to put together a will-call list of temps for Cara. I want to make it as easy as possible for her while I'm on maternity leave."

"Smart idea."

Sasha smiled and glanced at Ana, then back at me. "I'm writing up a conversation I just had with one of the curators at the State Hermitage Museum in St. Petersburg about Ana's skating snow globe."

"In Florida?" Ana asked, perplexed.

"In Russia."

Her eyes opened wide. "Oh." She smiled, a teasing one. "Can you tell me any early news?"

Sasha smiled again. "No . . . sorry. Appraising beautiful antiques takes time."

I gave Sasha a thumbs-up, then repeated the gesture for each of them in turn. "Thanks, everyone. Ana and I will be upstairs."

"Would either of you like something to drink?" Cara offered.

We both declined, and I led the way into the warehouse. We walked across the concrete floor, our footsteps loud in the cavernous space. Upstairs, Ana sat on one of my guest chairs and sighed. I tried to picture her in a brown wig and a big furry hat buying cell phones, but couldn't.

"I hired professional cleaners to deal with the mess in my house," she said, shuddering. "They worked around the clock with toothbrushes to get all the blood and so on out of every crevice. Just horrific." She wrapped her arms around her torso. "Then they sterilized everything."

I tried to think of something to say, something neutral, something polite. My dad taught me that the trick to diplomacy, an important business skill, is to talk about process, not content. After a moment, I said, "I once read that a return to normalcy is an important milestone in recovering from a traumatic shock."

"I can see that." She inhaled. "Dad and I are moving back in on Wednesday. Peter has gone back to Boston. He said he ran out of vacation time."

"You don't think that's true?"

"It may be true, but I think he went back to be with Heather."

"Be with? As in, Heather is seeing him?"

Ana shook her head. "No. Be with as in, keeping track of. That's Peter's normalcy."

"That sounds like stalking."

"To Peter, it sounds like care."

"What a situation."

Ana sighed. "Dad's not doing well, either. He was seeing a woman, and she left him."

"I'm sorry to hear that." I wondered if Ana would confide in me that the woman he'd been seeing was married.

"He's haunting the library, spending all his time reading those stupid investment papers and telling me what I'm doing wrong with my business. Peter's sarcastic. Dad is critical. No wonder I want to spend my time with Ray." She sighed again. "I can't believe that in the midst of such angst I feel like celebrating, but I do." She smiled radiantly. "I just got some good news. It's why I stopped by, actually. Timothy says the network remains excited about my show, can you believe it? They watched the parts we taped and loved it. We need to start filming again. They loved you, too."

"Me?" I asked, astonished. I felt as if I'd had two left feet walking up the driveway and barely knew the language talking to Ana.

"It's true. Timothy is more than happy with your performance. They're not going to use the footage of Heather and Jason, of course, which means we need another celebration." She took in a deep breath. "They're looking for a little schmaltz, to tell you the truth. What would you think of our filming Gretchen's baby shower? Timothy wants to catch her expression when she first sees the cake, then film a few people tasting it. You know the sort of thing they have in mind. You know Gretchen. Would she hate that idea?"

I laughed a little, then laughed harder. "This is right up her alley. She's completely starstruck. She'd love it. And her husband, Jack, will go along with the idea because (a) he's a good sport and (b) he loves making Gretchen happy."

Ana exhaled loudly and sank back against the cushion. "What a relief. I didn't know what we'd do if you thought it was a bad idea. Lots of people would find it offensively intrusive."

"Luckily, Gretchen isn't one of them."

"And the timing is perfect. Timothy wants to resume filming on Wednesday, including a shot of you approving the cake."

"The shower isn't until Sunday, so the cake will spoil."

"It's called poetic license. We'll make a new cake for the shower."

"You've thought of everything."

Ana smiled. "We share a methodical approach to life, you and I. I bet you're all organized for it—am I right?"

"Almost. I want to send an e-mail to everyone reminding them that it's a surprise. I guess I'll call the restaurant, too, to confirm the arrangements. Everything else is done."

"I knew it! Let me know if I can help with anything." She smiled and leaned forward, resting her elbows on her thighs. "Guess what I've done in my new role as the Blue Dolphin's executive pastry chef."

"Fired the entire staff?"

Ana laughed. "No. Rehired Maurice."

My mouth fell open. "He agreed to come back?"

"With only one condition—*my* pastry chef who'll be in *his* kitchen baking *my* cakes reports to him. He promised to do nothing to upset her or undermine my business. I promised to let him keep the title of executive pastry chef and leave him to rule the rest of the pastry team as he sees fit, unless, of course, it threatens my business."

"You negotiated a truce."

"A tentative truce, let's call it. I couldn't believe it either, but I had to do something. It became clear within a day that we needed him—or someone like him. Hard as it is to believe, some people prefer Maurice's desserts to mine. His peppermint twist, his chocolate tower, and his vanilla crème brûlée, for instance, are big sellers. I have no interest in creating a new menu or trying to replicate his recipes. He and I hammered out a deal privately, then I told Suzanne about it."

"I'm bedazzled. You ought to be secretary of state."

Ana waved it away. "Hardly. I'm just practical. The best way to deal with a bully is to befriend him. It doesn't always work, but when it does, it works well."

"How's Ray handling it?"

"With pride. I got his input before I approached Maurice, so he's taking credit for it all."

I started to laugh, but something in her tone and expression stopped me. There'd been no hint of laughter in her voice. Her eyes were flat. She wasn't joking. She was reporting. "That could be annoying."

She shrugged. "To some people, sure. I don't care who gets the credit. All that matters to me is that my ultimate goal gets reached."

"What does his attitude do to your personal relationship, though?"

She smiled. "Nothing."

I stood up. "You're a better woman than I."

She laughed. "Or a more foolish one." She stood up. "I'll call you later, if that's all right, once I know what time Timothy wants you on the set on Wednesday."

"Of course. Or e-mail, whatever is easiest for you."

"I'm not going to ask for news about my egg."

"I wish I had some to pass along."

"But you're still hopeful?" she asked.

"I am," I said, meaning it.

I walked her out, thinking that Ana had a definite Machiavellian streak in her. *Good to know,* I thought. As I waved good-bye, I found myself wondering just how good an actress she was. Maybe her calm, poised demeanor in front of the camera wasn't a reflection of who she was. Perhaps it was an act. Possibly her frank and open conversation with me was an act, too, a masterful performance staged to impress an audience of one—me.

I ran back upstairs to send the shower reminder, then called Jack. He reacted as expected—he was personally embarrassed, but on Gretchen's behalf, he was tickled pink. Ty called as I was hanging up to tell me he needed to stay overnight in Newport, close to the Canadian border; the training had uncovered some glitches, and he needed to meet with the team in the morning.

"I'll miss you," he said.

"Me, too. Maybe I'll call Zoë and see if she's around."

"If she's baked anything good, save me a piece."

I laughed. "Will do."

Zoë was home and planned to stay in all evening. I invited myself for dessert, and she eagerly started brainstorming what she should bake. I requested my favorite, Boston cream pie.

Downstairs, I fluffed the new pillow that Gretchen had made for Hank. She wanted his basket to be more cushy.

Cara's voice crackled over the PA system. "Josie, Chief Hunter on line one."

I ran for the phone.

"The police have brought Mr. Kovak to the station and are explaining Skype to him as we speak."

"When they're done, can they explain it to me?"

"I spoke to him briefly," he said, ignoring my joke. "He's eager to help. Can you come now?"

"I'm on my way."

CHAPTER THIRTY

A s soon as Mr. Kovak saw me on the police computer monitor, he chastised me. "You didn't need to try a sneak attack, young lady. I'm a good citizen. All you had to do is ask."

"I'm sorry," I said.

"Me, too," Ellis added.

"All this drama."

Ellis stared at the camera, his expression sober. "It's a serious situation, sir. We appreciate your cooperation."

"Glad to help. That's my point."

"Thank you. What can you tell us about your customer?"

Ralph Kovak looked his seventy-eight years. His face was deeply wrinkled, his hair blond-white, his blue eyes a little runny. Ellis and I sat side by side behind his desk, centered in front of his computer's built-in camera. Mr. Kovak sat in a standard-issue police office. A row of taupe metal four-drawer file cabinets was visible behind him. The walls were painted ivory and unadorned.

"Not much. What do you want to know?"

"His name."

"Didn't get it. I asked when he first called, and he just ignored my question."

"And you were okay with that?" Ellis asked, his tone curious, not confrontational.

"Hell, yes. It was a cash transaction, so I didn't care like I would if someone was going to be writing me a check."

"Do you have any security cameras installed?"

"No."

"We checked the neighborhood," one of the Cleveland police officers said, leaning into the frame so we could see who was speaking. He was young with lots of freckles and dark brown hair. "It's easy to get from the interstate into Mr. Kovak's neighborhood without passing a bank or other building likely to have security cameras."

"Thanks," Ellis said. The police officer backed away, and Ellis added, "What did he look like?"

Kovak scratched his cheek, then rubbed his nose. "I don't remember much beyond the Fabergé egg. You ever seen one close up?"

"No."

"How about you, young lady?"

"No. I bet it's something."

"It's like something I've never seen and don't expect to see again. The workmanship . . . the craft and techniques they used." He shook his head, remembering. "I wasn't looking at the man. I was looking at the egg."

"Understood," Ellis said. "Just one person came to your location, is that correct?"

"Right."

"A man?"

"Yup. He wore sunglasses, a leather jacket, a bomber jacket, they're called, and a cowboy hat. I liked that hat. Made him look like a real cowboy. Brown leather. Wide brim. Orange and blue pattern on the hatband. A dark blue feather. I asked about that hat, but he didn't tell me squat."

"Great," Ellis said, taking notes. "Was he white?"

"Yup. About six feet. I'm six-two, and he was a few inches shorter. I used to be six-three, but I've shrunk some."

"Did he have an accent?"

"Not to my ear."

"How old was he?"

"Younger than me." *Hawn.* "Which isn't saying much because at this point, pretty much everyone is younger than me. I'm not good at gauging people's ages. At a guess, he's about my son-in-law's age. Forty. Maybe older. Maybe younger. Somewhere in there."

"Eye color?"

"No idea."

"How about tattoos?"

"Not that I noticed. No scars, neither. Or moles or anything that I noticed. He was just a guy offering me one hell of a job."

"How many times did you see him?" Ellis asked.

"Twice. Once when he brought the egg for me to measure and so on. Once when he picked it up. When he picked it up, he made me remove both domes so he could compare the original egg directly with the replica. Made me mad. If he knew he was going to want to look at them so careful like, he should have told me before I put the domes on! He gave me double the work, but he didn't double the pay, oh, no." *Hawn.* "Served him right when the oil spilled all over and splashed some on the floor. Got on his pants and shoes, too. He told me not to worry about it, saying it was nothing. It wasn't nothing to me. Did he clean it up? Heck, no. He didn't even offer. I didn't have any extra oil, either. He was in a hurry, lucky for me, so he didn't make a big deal out of it, said filling them both with glycerin was fine."

"So he approved the work?"

"Yeah, but not after griping some. How can I get the veneer just right when he won't give me enough time for the glue to set?"

"Got it. Thanks so much, Mr. Kovak, for your cooperation. Before I let you go, I'm going to ask you to look at photographs of five men. I've e-mailed them to the police there in Cleveland, and they've printed them out. Would you take a careful look at each one?"

"Sure, but I told you, all I noticed was the hat and sunglasses."

"No harm in looking," Ellis said. "Officer?"

The same police officer who'd leaned into the camera earlier leaned in again. "Will do."

The police officer leaned back out of camera range and placed five photos on the table in front of Kovak, one at time, as if he were dealing cards. Ellis did the same for us. They were mug-shot-sized color printouts on glossy paper. The poses weren't staged, though; they were full-face candids, and I wondered when they'd been taken, and by whom. I picked up the first one in the lot, Jason, and turned it over. The numeral 1 was written in pencil. The five men shown in the photos were Jason, Stefan, Drake, Maurice, and Peter.

Ralph Kovak stared at each photo for several seconds before moving on to the next one. "I don't know." He continued looking. "Can I have a sheet of paper?"

"Sure," the officer said. "How come?"

"You'll see."

An 8½" × 11" sheet of standard white multiuse paper appeared on camera.

"Need a pen?"

"Nope."

Kovak laid the paper down over the top of Jason's head, sliding it down to cover his eyes. Once he'd positioned it to his satisfaction, he leaned back, tilted his head, and considered the result. He repeated the process with each photo.

"That helped," he said, looking straight into the camera. "If I was going to remember what he looked like, I needed to see only the parts of his face that I would have seen, not the whole thing."

"And?" Ellis prompted.

Kovak tapped Jason's photo. "I can't be sure, not by a long shot, but this is the closest to the picture in my head."

"I want to thank you again for your help," Ellis said.

"I have a question," I said. Ellis looked at me, but I stared into the camera. "Did you only make one replica?"

"Yup. No point in doing two bad jobs when one would serve." *Hawn.*

"Thanks," I said.

Ellis leaned into the camera. "Is there anywhere you can go for a few days, Mr. Kovak?"

"Are you saying I'm in danger?"

"I don't want to sugarcoat the situation. It's a possibility."

"I can go to my daughter's house. She lives in Cincinnati."

"Good. I mentioned this possibility to the police, and they agree that it would be prudent for you to stay out of sight for the time being. A police officer will see you home, help you pack, and drive you to your daughter's."

"I drive myself."

"That's fine. He'll tag along behind you, just to be safe."

"I do the right thing and look what happens."

"I know. Hopefully, there's nothing for you to be afraid of."

"I'm not afraid. I'm mad. No one's going to stop me from telling the truth. Never have. Never will."

"I wish all citizens were like you."

Hawn. "Me, too."

Ellis thanked him, made arrangements with the police officer to talk later in the day, and ended the call.

"Jason," I said.

"A surprise."

We walked to Ellis's office.

"There was no double switch," I said. "Milner's clean."

"Maybe."

"You don't think so?" I asked.

He shrugged.

"There seems to be a connection between Jason and the replica that was used as collateral. Let's see if there's a connection between Jason and McArthur. If so, we've just connected the dots and you should be able to get that court order forcing his executor to reveal his financial standing."

"How do you know we submitted a request for a court order?" he asked.

I opened my mouth to say that Wes told me, then shut it. "I don't remember. You listen, you hear things."

He stared at me, his expression stern. After several seconds, he said, "Any defense attorney worth his salt could get that ID thrown out."

"Sure, but do you have to tell that to the judge?"

Ellis shook his head, a half-smile twisting his lips. "You are some piece of work, Josie Prescott."

"Bring up Jason's company's Web site."

He entered Jason's name, and the search engine led us to his company's site. The home page was elegant and content-rich. The border was thick. The color scheme of hunter green, navy blue, and cranberry was evocative of luxury and substance. The font was solid and easy to read. The featured article was about managing risk in a volatile economic climate. It was dated today, and I wondered who was running Jason's company now that he was gone, and whether it would survive without him.

"Try typing 'McArthur' into the search bar," I suggested, pointing to the box at the top.

Ellis tapped the keys, checked his spelling, and hit ENTER.

Three matches appeared on the screen within seconds, all relating to McArthur Evergreen Technologies. Three years earlier, Jason's company labeled the start-up "One to watch." A year ago it was selected as a "Top Pick." Last September, Jason wrote, "Buy more."

"Wow," I whispered, staring at the monitor.

"Check the stock valuation over that period." I reached for the keyboard, then paused. "May I?"

"Be my guest."

Ellis rolled his chair back, and I moved in. I consulted one of the major stock-monitoring services, got the numbers, then asked the site to plot a trend graph. "Look at this." I pointed. "Anyone who bought shares in McArthur a year ago, then more last September, lost his shirt."

"Print that out for me, will you?"

"Sure. I'll e-mail you a screen shot, too." I held down the ALT and PRINT SCREEN buttons, then pasted the image into an e-mail. "That's probable cause, right? To get access to his financial records?"

"Looks that way to me."

"Let me take a look at McArthur Evergreen Technologies' Web site." I brought up the site and scanned the archived news releases starting last June. Three minutes later, I had an explanation for the drop in market value. "Here it is." I pointed to the screen. "McArthur sold his interest in the company last August. Part of the deal is he stays on as its CEO for a year, but investors weren't impressed. Evidently, people think the company's success is tied to the man, not the technology, so news of the sale caused the stock to plummet." I looked at Ellis. "The only person to make any money on the sale was McArthur."

I went back to my regular chair while Ellis read the release.

He wheeled his chair back three feet from his desk, toed open the bottom drawer, and used it as a footrest. He placed his hands behind his head, elbows out. "It would be interesting to see if anybody recognizes that cowboy hat. Kovak's description was pretty specific."

"Are you thinking of asking Wes to publish the description?"

He grinned. "No. I'm thinking of asking you to give Wes the description. You can tell the truth—you located the man who crafted the fake egg snow globe and need to know who his customer was. You don't need to say why you need to know. Leave it vague and antiques-related. Do you remember the description of the hat?"

"Yes."

"Tell Wes he can call me for a quote." He stood up. "Let me walk you out. I need to get going with this application if we're going to re-present it in the morning."

Ana called as I was driving back to the office. I pulled off to the side of the road to take the call.

"Timothy asked me to thank you for agreeing to film on Wednesday. He's setting up in the morning. He wants to film some intros and promos and I don't know what else starting at one, and hopes you'll come around two. He says it shouldn't take more than an hour, all told. Hair and makeup at two. Filming the scene at two forty-five-ish. Outta there by three."

"Let me get it in my calendar," I said. I opened the program on my netbook and entered the information. "Done."

"Great." She sighed, a deep, long one. "I'm tired. It's been a long day, and as happy as I am about the TV pilot, I'm all sad about this situation—Jason and Heather and my egg."

"I don't blame you a bit. How is Heather?"

"Back at work. Jason left a succession plan. His number two, Doug something or other, is taking over. He often subbed for Jason on the TV show. He specifically asked Heather to stay on as his chief researcher. I don't know that she'll stay long term, but it's good for her now."

"Work has always been my fallback position when life gets rocky."

"Me, too. My personal life can be in utter chaos, but if I'm working, I'm happy. Or at least happier."

"I have some news. I found the man who made the fake. He gave us a description of his client. It's pretty vague, but he remembered a lot about the guy's hat. I gave the info to Wes, the *Seacoast Star* reporter, so it will be all over the news in the morning."

"That's great, Josie. It sounds like real progress. How did he explain the poor-quality replica?"

"He had about a minute and a half to pull the whole thing together. His client was in a huge hurry."

"Do you think the client didn't notice the bad job or didn't care?"

"He cared enough to have the maker remove both domes so he could compare them side by side, although all he got for his trouble was oily pants and shoes."

"How come?"

"The guy spilled some when he opened them up."

"Oh, no! Won't that reduce the value?"

"It's not ideal," I said, "but as long as we find the egg intact, we're in good shape. In this case, it's the egg that matters. All the rest is gravy."

"Thank goodness for small favors." Ana sighed. "My fingers are crossed that Wes's article generates some leads. I try to put it out of mind. I have to if I'm going to be able to work, to live. But it's always there, like a fever."

"I understand completely. I'd feel the same."

We ended the call with a promise to talk soon, and as I pulled back into traffic, I found myself feeling conflicted on a deep emotional level. Ana felt like a friend, not a suspect.

I pulled into the lot. I should have realized that Jason was a likely candidate to be the person working with Milner and Kovak: He was ethically malleable and utterly narcissistic. If he lost his fortune investing in McArthur Evergreen Technologies, I could completely see him using Ana's Fabergé egg as a stopgap maneuver. He was wholly ignorant about the craftsmanship involved, so he might well have thought that Kovak's fake was adequate, noticing only the veneer.

I parked near the front door and lowered my head to the steering wheel. No matter what scenario I envisioned, the picture was sordid and sad and filled with anguish. I wanted to go home. I wanted a hot bath followed by a cool watermelon martini. I needed to wash away the stench of grim despair.

When I entered the office, Cara was standing by the photocopier, directing Eric. He was on his knees attaching a muslin skirt to the bottom of the machine. Hank sat nearby, watching.

"Yes, that's right," she said. "Now press hard to make certain the Velcro sticks."

"That looks great," I said. I turned toward Fred and Sasha. "Anything going on?"

"I have one more call to make about the skating snow globe," Sasha said.

Fred pushed up his glasses. "I'm deep in catalogue copy. How many ways can I call mahogany beautiful?"

I smiled. "Let's see . . . gleaming, rich, burnished . . ."

He grinned. "I see that you, too, have some experience in this field."

I laughed. "Just a touch."

I headed upstairs only long enough to check messages. Just as I was closing up, Cara forwarded an e-mail that had been sent to our general "info" mailbox. It came from someone called Phillippe LaBlanc and read, "I have a Picasso. I would like to sell it quickly. I'm on my way out of town in the morning. May I receive an offer right away?"

My trouble meter whirred onto high alert. There were Picasso fakes aplenty, and I didn't want to buy one of them.

I e-mailed, "We'd love to take a look at it. How's 9 A.M. tomorrow?"

His reply came in seconds. "I'm sorry. I must be on the road early. This painting, it is beautiful. From the Blue Period. I will tell you how I come to own it and why I need to sell it. How is 7:30?"

I stared at my monitor and shrugged. "Sure," I wrote. "See you then."

An unknown man e-mailing our generic address with a genuine Picasso and a story. Stranger things had been known to happen, but rarely.

CHAPTER THIRTY-ONE

I helped Jake, Zoë's thirteen-year-old son, set up a new professional-quality Winmau dart board in their basement rec room, then lost four games in a row.

"You're a shark," I said as I relinquished the javelins.

"Nah. You're just bad."

I laughed and promised to practice so I could give him a decent game next time.

"Although I'm not sure that will help any," I told Zoë upstairs. "Practice doesn't make perfect. Practice only perfects what you're doing, and if I'm doing it wrong, I'm going to get really, really good at doing it wrong."

She smiled empathetically. "You may not be as bad as he's implying. He's really good."

"Go, Jake."

I drank a watermelon martini and ate a slice of Boston cream pie and listened as Zoë told me all about how ten-year-old Emma had dropped out of ballet, choosing to pursue gymnastics instead, and how Jake wasn't merely good at darts, he was good at anything requiring hand-eye coordination, and how she was thinking about taking an online class in computer security, since maybe she'd want to go back to work part-time now that the kids were older, and I didn't think about fraud or murder at all. Instead, I had fun.

Tuesday morning around six thirty, I poured myself a cup of coffee and booted up my computer. Wes had found a series of line-art sketches showing wide-brimmed cowboy hats with patterned hatbands and feathers to illustrate his story. Overall, I thought it read well, as Wes's articles always did.

I called him, unconcerned about the hour. If Wes didn't want to take the call, he'd turn off his phone. He answered on the first ring.

"Good article, Wes. Love the art."

"Thanks. Do any of those look like what Kovac described?"

I scanned the illustrations. "I don't know." I walked back into the kitchen. "Any nibbles so far?"

"No, but it just hit. It's early."

"True. How about on the woman who bought the phones?"

"Nope. But did you hear what Chief Hunter did? It's amazing, like a movie. You know, the emergency-haul-the-judge-out-of-bed scene. He amended his petition requesting access to Jason's financial records and presented it to the judge overnight, and—wait for it—he got it. He's driving down to the executor's office now with a forensic accountant on loan from the DA's office."

"Jeez, Wes. You know too much."

"As if. I don't hear my readers complaining. I don't hear you complaining."

"What happens next?" I asked, skipping over his too-close-for-comfort comment.

"We see what the chief learns. We hope for nibbles. We keep pushing."

I sighed. "I'm going into work, and I'm not going to think of theft or murder at all."

"Right," Wes said, chuckling. His tone made it clear that he didn't believe me and he didn't think I believed me either. "Catch ya later."

I got into work at ten after seven and made a beeline for our walk-in safe. I couldn't wait to see the super-secret opening Fred had found in Marianna's elephant-head cane firsthand.

Hank meowed good morning.

"Hi, baby. Did you sleep well?" I reached down to pet him, stroking his back, adding a little pat to his bottom.

He mewed and rubbed my leg.

"You're right. Let me change your water before I get the walking stick."

I refreshed his food, too, then walked to the safe. I signed out the cane, hurried back to the front office, and sat at the guest table to wait for Phillippe LaBlanc. I turned the walking stick upside down to view the elephant's head from the bottom up. Even knowing I was looking for a hinge, I couldn't see it. Hank jumped into the chair next to me and mewed. He wanted face petties. I rubbed his jowl and he purred.

"How on earth did Fred find it? Do you know, baby?"

I used my free hand to try to raise the elephant's trunk. Nothing. I pushed it to the left, then to the right, and the trunk didn't wiggle. I tapped the trunk lightly where it joined the face, and it opened outward a hair, just enough for me to see a tiny latch. I used my fingernail to spring it, and the trunk swung aside as smoothly as a well-fit door.

"Look at that, Hank."

The abditory was small, about 3" × 4". I opened the bottom one. It was even smaller.

"Given that this is an umbrella cane, what are these openings for? Any ideas, Hank?"

He was too busy purring to answer me.

"A cane that held cigarettes might have another opening for matches. One that hid a whiskey flask might also hold a glass. But what would go with an umbrella?"

I ran my index finger along the abditory's inside walls, looking for a second, deeper, inner opening, but the brass siding was smooth, without ridges, indentations, or hinges, any of which might indicate another hidden cubby. I shrugged and closed it up.

"It's a mystery, Hank. I'll tell you one thing, though. We need to examine every inch of this cane. There may well be additional openings."

Gretchen's wind chimes tinkled. I looked up, ready to greet Mr. LaBlanc. A man wearing a black ski mask stepped inside and strode toward me, swinging a baseball bat like a hitter warming up. I gasped and stood up, slipping into crisis mode. My attention was concentrated, my focus absolute. I registered every detail.

The bat was made of blond wood, ash maybe. The man was taller than me but not as tall as Ty. Perhaps it was a man; possibly I only assumed it was. *Forget that,* I thought. The mask was wool, too hot for today, too hot for spring. He wore black leather gloves, black jeans, a black long-sleeved turtleneck, black socks, and black sneakers. The only skin that showed was near the eye and nose holes. He was white. He didn't make a sound. With the bat held shoulder high, like a cleanup man, he aimed for my head. I dropped the walking stick. It clattered across the table and rolled onto the floor.

Time slowed.

I dove for the floor, crawling to the side, away from him, scuttling toward Sasha's desk.

The bat missed me and connected with the table, shattering its edge. Bits of wood sprayed over me. I closed my eyes for a moment, avoiding sawdust and splinters, then crab-walked backward, into the narrow space between Sasha's desk and the inside wall. When I opened my eyes, I saw him moving toward me, circling the desk, holding the bat over his head like a hammer. I was trapped, my back to the wall, my knees drawn up to my chin.

The silence was terrifying, oppressive, overwhelming. I looked around wildly. There was nowhere to go. *Get away. Get out. Do it now.* I lunged forward back under the guest table, scurrying toward the front door. He swung the bat low, like a golf club, and connected with my thigh.

I screamed, a harrowing sound, as the pain shot up my leg to my spine to my neck, and into my jaw. Gold flecks danced in front of my eyes. They drifted away as the pain subsided. The bat swung up as he prepared to deliver another blow. I dragged my injured leg out of his line of fire.

Fight back, I told myself. If I couldn't hide, if I couldn't run, I had to fight.

My eyes lit on the cane. I grabbed it and swung at his ankles, my only target. The brass elephant head connected as if I'd rehearsed it for a year, but with such a limited range, the blow lacked the oomph to do much damage. Still, he grunted, which fueled my confidence, and I swung a second time, and again I connected. He grunted again, louder this time, but I hadn't stopped him. I hadn't even slowed him down. I was annoying him, nothing more. I needed more power, and that required a more open area.

He stooped over to better his aim at me and swung at my head as if he were trying for the big green wall at Fenway. I scooted farther away, and he missed me, thudding on carpet instead.

I crawled another few feet, trying to reach the front door. Clear of the table, I stood up, but my timing was bad. He swung with the fury of a cyclone. I jumped away, but not far enough to avoid it completely, and I landed on my gimpy leg, sending shock waves of pain raging up my spine. The blow glanced off my shoulder, slamming me against the wall, leaving me dizzy and breathless from the pain.

Then I got mad.

I used the cane like he used the bat, swinging the elephant head at his stomach, and the blow landed perfectly. He grunted again but recovered quickly and took another swing, again aiming at my head. I saw it coming in time to duck aside. His bat crashed into the wall three inches from my head, leaving a deep gash in the plaster. I swung again, aiming at his right wrist, hitting his right arm. His bat fell to the floor. He clutched his arm to his stomach protectively, grunting loudly. I pulled back, ready to aim for his head, and he ran. He charged at the front door and ripped it open, and he was gone.

I lunged for the door and locked it, then fell back against the table, shaking. I grabbed Gretchen's phone, the closest unit, and punched 911. Out the window, I saw him running in a zigzag pattern across the parking lot, stumbling, recovering his footing, stumbling again. His ankles had to hurt. He made it to the woods, heading toward the church.

The operator answered, "What's your emergency?"

"A man in a ski mask," I said, gasping for air as if I'd run a marathon. "I've been attacked. He tried to kill me." I reported his route, then pressed the END CALL button. I waited two seconds, got a dial tone, and called Ted at the church. I knew he'd be there. His wife, a nurse, dropped him off each morning en route to her 7:00 A.M. shift at Rocky Point Hospital. He didn't answer. I made a fist and pounded the desk, terrified that my attacker might take Ted hostage or worse.

"Ted," I said, as steadily as I could into the church's general voice mail, "it's Josie. I've just been attacked. I scared him off, but he's running your way through the woods. Lock your doors." I heard sirens, a welcome sound. "The police are en route."

I hung up, then sank to the floor. I pressed my right hand against my left shoulder in a futile effort to stop it from throbbing. I rubbed it a little, which also didn't help. A bitter taste made me swallow hard. Adrenaline. I couldn't think of what I should do next, so I did nothing.

The sirens grew louder.

I got up, using a guest chair for support, and peeked through the window in the door, I watched as a Rocky Point patrol car roared into my lot. I unlocked the door and stepped out. I swayed and grabbed the frame.

Griff was alone and walking toward me. I didn't see him get out of his vehicle, but there he was, approaching.

"Are you okay?"

The question seemed too complicated to answer simply, so I stayed quiet, holding my shoulder, waiting for him to come up with an easier one.

He took a few more steps toward me. "What's going on, Josie?"

His tone was gentle, caring, but the question was still too complex.

"I'm worried about Ted," I said. "At the church."

"We've got someone there. What's going on with you?"

"I think maybe he broke my shoulder."

He lifted his collar to talk into his microphone and called for an ambulance.

"I don't need an ambulance. I can walk. Not quickly, though. He got my leg, too."

"Just in case," he said. "Who attacked you?"

"I don't know."

"What did he want?"

"I don't know. He didn't say a word. He left his weapon behind, though. Want me to show you?"

Griff approached the door. I pointed to the bat.

"How'd you get away?"

"I didn't. He ran off." I smiled, a shaky one. "I made him. I used the cane to fight back."

He looked at me, surprised, it seemed, that I could fight my way out of trouble.

"Okay, then. I want to get you into the patrol car until the ambulance gets here. Go ahead and lean on me.

We set off at a turtle pace.

"I want to talk to Ty. I need to call him."

"I'll call for you," Griff said.

I sat sideways on the backseat, my feet on the asphalt. I called out Ty's number, and Griff punched it into his phone.

"It's going to voice mail," he said. "I'll leave a message."

"I should."

"Let me."

I nodded and closed my eyes, willing the sharp barbs of pain to stop stabbing me. When I opened them, Griff was beside the car, talking to someone through his collar mic. Moments later, the ambulance turned into the lot, its lights flashing. Two men jumped out of the cab, one young, one older.

"I'm fine," I said.

They hauled a gurney out of the back.

"My staff. I can't leave the place open. The man may come back."

"I'll wait for them," Griff said. "You're safe now, Josie. Go."

Griff left me with nothing to worry about, and as soon as I realized that, I collapsed onto the stretcher and let the men do their jobs. They took my blood pressure, timed my respiration, and checked my pulse, calling in the numbers to someone far away. Moving hurt more than staying still, so I closed my eyes and didn't move. With Griff taking care of my worldly responsibilities and paramedics taking care of me, I was fearless and free to feel the pain.

CHAPTER THIRTY-TWO

N othing is broken," the doctor said. I'd already forgotten his name. "But you're going to have some pretty colorful bruises."

"That's great news," I said. "I can't believe I got so lucky."

He gave me instructions about painkillers and rest and ice and heat and told me I could go. "I understand Chief Hunter plans on driving you home."

Ellis and Zoë were waiting for me in the emergency room lobby. A big round clock read 1:20. I'd been in the hospital for more than five hours. I thanked the aide who'd wheeled me out into bright sunshine, then watched him disappear down a hallway.

"Can I hug you?" Zoë asked.

"Sure—if you want to hear a grown woman scream. I've got major bruises."

Ellis stood nearby. "Let me pull the car up."

"Okay."

Zoë sat on a thigh-high stone wall. I leaned against it. I would have liked to sit, but I didn't have the strength to hoist myself up.

"Ty is driving down," she said. "He expects to be here by four."

"Good."

Ellis drove under the overhang. Walking was work, and every step hurt. I managed to get into the backseat and latch my seat belt, but barely.

"Your place or Ty's?" Ellis asked.

"Mine, I think. I want to go home."

"I'm assigning an officer twenty-four/seven until this is sorted out."

My throat closed for a moment, and I couldn't speak. I coughed. "Thanks."

When we got there, Ellis walked inside ahead of me and cleared each room. Zoë took my hand and patted it. I leaned my head against her shoulder.

"All clear," he said. "Let's be prudent, though, and close all the drapes."

"You sit," Zoë said to me. "Ellis and I can do it."

I felt too battered to argue. I sank into my favorite chair, a blue velvet club chair. The pain was constant but dull. Zoë turned on lamps, then pulled down the blackout blinds and drew the velvet panels together. The living room looked cozy in the incandescent light.

Ellis came into the living room. "You look like you're ready for a nap. Can I ask a few questions before we help you get settled?"

"I take it that means you haven't caught him?"

"Not yet. My guess is that he parked on Dover Street, on the far side of the church. No one who lives in the area noticed him—or a car. Why were you at work so early?"

I told him about the e-mail and how I was certain it would be a dead end, a message sent from an account set up for the purpose from a public computer in some location without security cameras, like a mom and pop Internet café.

"You're probably right. We'll check it out anyway. How about a physical description?"

"I don't know. He was tall, but in the normal range. Ditto, his weight."

"How sure are you it was a man?"

I met his eyes. "Not very."

"No outstanding features?"

"No."

Zoë came up beside me and squeezed my arm. "Do you want something to eat, Josie? I have chicken soup."

"You're a wonder woman. Boston cream pie last night and chicken soup today. I'd love some. Thanks."

Zoë headed out. "I'll bring the pot."

I closed my eyes for a moment, then opened them. "Would you get my tote bag, Ellis? I should check messages and e-mails."

"Let them wait."

I tried to smile. "That's a sensible idea." I closed my eyes for a moment, then opened them. "Will you call my office and let them know I'm okay?"

"Sure."

I felt disassociated, strangely unconnected to what was happening around me. I could hear Zoë and Ellis chatting, not their words but the pace and tone of their comfortable companionship, yet it was as if I were dreaming it, not living it.

"She's going to be stiff as a board when she wakes up," Ty whispered. "I'm going to carry her up to bed."

I opened my eyes and smiled. "Ty. You're here."

He stretched his left arm under my knees and slipped his right arm around my back.

"I'm too heavy."

"No, you're not. Put your arms around my neck."

I did as he said and pressed my cheek against his chest. He stood up, lifting me as if I weighed nothing.

"I didn't have my soup."

"I'll bring it to you in bed."

"You don't need to do that. I can sit at the table."

He kissed the top of my head. "Let me take care of you."

I smiled again and closed my eyes, and for the first time since Phillippe LaBlanc had burst into my office, I relaxed.

I slept for ten hours. It was dark. I turned to see the time, rolled onto my bruised shoulder, and groaned, then glanced at Ty, hoping I hadn't awakened him. He was on his side, facing away from me, solidly asleep. I reached for the old-fashioned clock, a relic from my childhood. The green luminescence glowed brightly: 4:03. I was hungry and achy and stiff. I dragged myself to a sitting position and stood up, holding on to the bedside table. I made it downstairs by taking one stair at a time and leaning on the banister in between steps. The bottle of painkillers was near the sink. I took one with a glass of apple juice, then put Zoë's soup pot on low.

While I waited for the soup to warm up, I went through my "are you okay" voice mails and e-mails. Wes had left three messages. The first one wanted details of my attack, including pictures of my bruises. I shook my head at Wes's moxie. His second message came at eleven last night. He told me that the police had already located the sales record for the phone Phillippe LaBlanc had used to call me. It was another disposable, this one purchased from a big-box store in Rocky Point by a white man last week for cash. The store's security cameras showed a tall man wearing a Red Sox baseball cap and big sunglasses. I downloaded the photo. The man's chin was tucked in close to his chest, his head angled down. I couldn't see any distinguishing marks. He was of normal weight. It could be anyone. Wes's last call delivered what he described as an info bomb: Ellis got the information he sought from Jason's executor. Jason had died a wealthy man. In addition to various trusts and real estate worth more than $10 million, he had $554,318 in his checking account.

"What?"

How can that be? It didn't make any sense. If Jason didn't need the money, he didn't get a loan from McArthur. Jason didn't hire Ralph Kovak. Which meant Kovak's identification of Jason was wrong.

I e-mailed Wes thanking him for the update, telling him I would not be sending him photos of my bruises, and confessing that I was mystified.

I had two bowls of soup, thinking about why someone would attack me. My father once said that when you face a problem that seems to have no solution, do more research. When you can't think of anything else to research, make a decision. To stay in limbo was always counterproductive. To delay making a decision was, in fact, a decision by default, and usually a bad one. Once your research was done—act. I tried to think of something to research. I couldn't, but neither was I ready to act. *Tomorrow,* I thought. Thinking productively was beyond my current capabilities.

Ty came down about six thirty, yawning for coffee, offering to scramble eggs. I accepted. Zoë's soup was delicious but not enough.

"I don't know why that man attacked me," I said, watching Ty wield the whisk.

"You know something. Or he thinks you do."

"I can't imagine what."

"Something no one else knows or something you don't know you know."

"Or something only I know the significance of, even though I don't realize it."

Ty paused and looked at me, his intelligence radiating from his dark eyes. "So what do you know?"

I shook my head. "I have no idea."

"Don't think about it now. It will come to you later."

"I feel pretty punky."

"You should. You got beat up."

I grinned. "I bet he feels worse than me."

Ty added diced honey-baked ham and shredded Emmentaler into the eggs. He stirred constantly, adjusting the heat periodically, a little lower, then higher, then lower again.

He toasted hearty white bread and sprinkled it with cinnamon sugar, then spread some of the blueberry preserves Zoë had put up last summer.

I ate it all. "This is maybe the best breakfast ever."

"You're forgetting Zoë's French toast."

"True. This is one of the best breakfasts ever."

"Is this enough? I can make you something else or more of this."

"This is perfect. I need a bath and more rest. Then I'll be good as new."

"In other words, the painkiller has kicked in."

I smiled and faux-primped my hair, giving little pushes against my scalp. "I'm going on TV later today. I need to get my beauty rest so I'm ready for my close-up."

"You're beautiful, Josie. Rest or no rest. You're always ready for a close-up."

"Wow. That's nice."

"Let me get you upstairs."

"I can do it. Don't you have to go to work?"

"No. I can stay for as long as I need to."

"Did you straighten out those training glitches?"

"It's a process."

"In other words, no."

"In other words, it's a process."

I limped over to him. I touched his chin, drawing my finger along his jawline. "I love you with all my heart."

He leaned down and kissed me, and I kissed him back.

CHAPTER THIRTY-THREE

O fficer Meade knocked on my door around ten, shortly after I came downstairs again. Ty had left at seven. Yes, he could stay, but I assured him there was no need to do so, not with Ellis's promise of police protection, and after a little pull and tug, he went to work.

"You doing all right?" she asked.

"Better than I expected." I raised my arms above my head, elbows out, and arched my back. "Bruised but not stiff."

"Glad to hear it. I've just come on duty. The overnight officer said all was quiet. Do you know your plans for the day?"

I told her about my participation in Timothy's TV pilot. "I can drive myself, with you following if you think you should, but you don't need to stay."

"I'm fine with staying."

I felt myself blush. "To tell you the truth, I'd feel pretty awkward with you there."

"How come?"

I laughed, embarrassed. "I don't like to be the center of attention. I freeze and get all stupid. With you there, everyone will wonder what's going on and I'll feel even more conspicuous."

She smiled. "They'll think you're important."

"They'll think I'm pretentious."

"We can't risk your being on your own."

"What risk? The place is crawling with people, including an armed guard."

"Why do you want your own car?"

"If I get bored waiting, I can use it like an office. I do it all the time."

She tilted her head and scanned my face, trying to decide if she believed me. "You don't have plans to ditch us, do you?"

I laughed, a real one. "No way."

"I'll check." She stepped into an oblong of yellow sunshine on the porch and made a phone call. Two minutes later she came back inside. "Chief Hunter said okay on one condition. I follow you there, and when you're ready to leave, you call and let one of us follow you to your next stop."

"Perfect. Thanks."

"I'll be outside in my car if you need anything."

I got into work before eleven and spent the rest of the morning working with Fred researching Mrs. Albert's umbrella cane. While he tested the materials, I researched umbrella canes.

I contacted a New Orleans–based antiques dealer, one of the world's leading experts on system canes, the formal name for gadget canes. His name was Bo Givens and he e-mailed me photos of two canes he thought might be similar to ours. One was an umbrella cane from 1805 that looked nothing like ours; the other, a painter's walking stick from 1815 that could have been a twin.

"Look at that," I said aloud.

The painter's walking stick was thicker than many nongadget canes, but not conspicuously so. It contained everything a plein air artist needed to work outside: brushes, paints, rags, water canisters, and pencils. According to Mr. Givens, the shaft of the walking stick converted into a portable easel.

I called Fred. "You need to talk to Bo Givens." I explained why. "Even without the cane's contents, I think we're looking at twenty thousand dollars." I smiled, thinking how happy Walter Albert would be knowing his $440 investment had paid off big-time.

"We're not going to be able to film me walking up the driveway this time," I said to Timothy. "I got pretty bruised up the other day. When I walk, I wobble."

"You poor thing," he said, sounding truly concerned. "Are you all right to be here?"

"It's better to move around," I said. "Otherwise, I'll stiffen up."

"We'll figure it out, then. What happened?"

"It's a long story—one you can read about in the paper."

His eyes grew round. "Oh, my." He patted my arm. "As to your wobbling, don't fret at all. We'll skip you walking completely. It's better to have a variety of shots anyway, and we already have you coming up the drive when you placed the cake order. Maybe we'll start with you knocking on the door, then cut to Ana, then film you already seated for the cake presentation. How does that sound?"

Awed at the speed with which his director's eye recalibrated the shot sequences, I said, "Your brain is fully charged, I see."

"All in a day's work." He squeezed my hand. "You let us know if you need anything, all right?" He scanned the grounds, spotted the young man with the spiky yellow hair, and waved him over. "Nevie! Come here a sec."

Ana spotted me and came running up. "Josie! I heard what happened on the news. Are you all right?"

"Better than expected. Thanks. Good enough to do the show."

"Are you sure?"

I smiled at her. "Thanks for your concern."

Nevie trotted over. He wore black jeans and a black crewneck sweater with the arms pushed up to his elbows. A scuffed black leather pouch attached to his belt hung over his right hip.

"This is Josie Prescott, today's costar. She's a little bruised up. No way can she hop into a director's chair. Get her something comfy, will you, and keep an eye on her."

"Will do." Nevie pulled a small walkie-talkie from his pouch.

"Whatever she wants, she gets."

"You got it."

"That's so nice," I said, giggling a bit at the unaccustomed attention, "but completely unnecessary."

Timothy squeezed my hand again. "Let us fuss. We're very good at it."

I laughed and turned to Nevie. "A low chair would be good."

Timothy beamed at me, then turned to Ana. "As for you—back to makeup!"

Ana grinned. "He's such a tyrant." She gave an airy wave and headed off to the tent.

Nevie spoke into the walkie-talkie. "Get me a low dirch."

I looked at Timothy.

"Low director's chair," he whispered.

"Of course," I whispered back. "That would have been my fourth guess."

He laughed. Nevie ran to the 18-wheeler as a tall, wiry man with a fringe of gray hair jumped down with a folded-up, short-legged director's chair.

"Can you give me a little time after we're done shooting?" Timothy asked. "To talk?"

His expression was guileless, but I didn't for a minute believe he had nothing important on his mind. Over the years I'd learned that when people said they wanted to talk, it was generally because they needed to deliver bad news and knew enough to do it in private.

"Sure," I said.

"Put your smile on, honey! It's all good. I promise. Date?"

His charm was irresistible. I smiled. "Date!"

He waved, then walked quickly toward Ana.

"Where would you like to perch?" Nevie asked.

"Somewhere I can watch what's going on while you're filming outside."

Nevie did a 360, considering the options. "How about the gazebo? Is that too far for you to walk?"

"Not at all. Getting there won't be pretty, but I'll be fine."

I followed Nevie as he crossed the driveway and set off down the field-stone path that circled the house and led to the porch. The stones were rounded and uneven, and with my gimpy leg, it made for hard going.

The security guard stood on the porch, surveying the scene. He was a new one, new to me, younger than the last one. Nevie called hello, and the guard gave a little salute. Nevie cut across the lawn toward the gazebo, with me limping along, trying hard to keep up.

Nevie ran up the three steps, unfolded the chair, and got it situated under the crossbeam roof. Thigh-high latticework walls created an illusion of privacy. I climbed the steps, moving gingerly, and took a look around. Dappled sun streamed in through the semiopen roof. To my left, past the rose-bushes, waves crashed against the boulders below. The stand of birch ran to my right. From where I sat, I had a clear view of the lawn, the trees, the porch, the top of the driveway, and the entrance to Ana's converted garage. No one could approach me without my seeing him unless he could scale the hundred-foot-high craggy cliff. It was a perfect spot.

"This is great, Nevie. Thank you."

He smiled and patted the bone-colored canvas chairback. "Come give it a test drive."

I sat, using the wooden arms to lower myself gently, favoring my hurt leg, wishing I were back to normal, hating feeling weak, hating being weak.

"Thanks, Nevie. It's comfy. Easy in, easy out."

"Good. What else can I get you? A cup of coffee? Water? Anything?"

"I'm all set. Thanks, though."

"You need something, you holler."

I promised I would, and he jogged off to join the crew hovering around Ana. The security guard set off on his rounds, heading toward the back of the cottage. The sun was warming, more May than March. I took off my sweater, glad I was wearing short sleeves. Nevie said something to the man I recognized as Mack. I recognized Vinnie, too, and the makeup girl with the pink hair whose job was de-shining. It felt good to recognize people, as if I belonged.

I glanced at the time display on my phone. It was noon, time for more pain meds. I swallowed a big white pill with water I took from my tote and leaned back. I'd come early on purpose to watch the fun, and I was glad I had, but now I was glad to sit. A light breeze fluffed my hair. Early violets were showing near Ana's commercial kitchen, their deep purple petals still furled. Timothy was lucky with the weather. In New Hampshire, March was typically a snowy month.

Ana came out of the makeup tent, glowing in a gold sheath and gold and black fleur-de-lis-patterned blazer. She waved at me, and I waved back. She looked fabulous. Nevie led her to the tall grass. Behind her, the ocean shimmered in gilt-tipped blue.

Timothy shouted, "Rolling!" He followed that with "Action!"

I couldn't hear Ana speak, but I could see her smile. In front of the camera she transformed herself from everywoman to wanna-be-that-woman. It was as if she were talking to her best friend, an all-knowing, all-safe confidant. Her love for her work and her respect for her viewers was apparent.

A glint to my right caught my eye. Peter was glancing at his watch as he climbed the porch steps, and the sun flicked off the silver metal, creating minibolts of fluorescent-bright white light. He didn't notice me. He must have noticed Ana, but he didn't pay any attention to her, or to anything. She continued talking to the camera, smiling, gesturing, laughing. Peter disappeared into the house. Last I'd heard, Peter was back at work in Boston. I wondered what he was doing here.

Five minutes later, Peter came out grasping a kitchen-sized plastic garbage bag by the twirled top. The bag was white but not opaque. Through the semitransparent plastic, I could make out hints of colors. Something reddish brown was at the bottom. A larger, bulkier item, whitish, like the bag, was crumpled up in the middle. Another brown item was on top. He walked quickly, almost running, down the path to the driveway and turned the corner.

I grabbed my tote bag and limped after him, looking around for the security guard. He wasn't in sight.

I got to the driveway in time to see Peter pull out from the curb in a dark blue Toyota Camry. I memorized two digits of his license plate before he took off, heading south.

I eased myself behind the wheel and set off after him. I peered down each side street as I drove. Three streets down from Ana's house, on Turner Road, I saw his car in the far distance and turned. Turner led to I-95. I slipped in my earpiece and called Ellis. The call went to voice mail.

"I'm following Peter. It's weird. He showed up at Ana's, went inside empty-handed, and came out with a plastic bag." I described the bag's contents and his car and repeated the part of his license plate number I'd memorized. "He didn't say hello to her or anyone. Now he's hot-tailing it somewhere, probably back to Boston. I'm on Turner. I'll keep you posted."

I turned onto I-95 south. Peter's car wasn't in sight. I speeded up to seventy, then seventy-five, but I didn't see him.

Ellis called, and I slipped in my earpiece.

"Where are you now?" he asked.

"Heading south on I-95. Passing exit six."

"I've dispatched Officer Meade to find you and escort you to home or work, wherever you want to go. Pull off into the breakdown lane and set your flashers. Don't make me regret canceling your protection."

"Don't be silly, Ellis. I'm hanging up now."

I squinted, seeking any sign of a blue car. I didn't see one, but ten minutes later, I saw Ellis's SUV pulled off to the side. Peter's car was in front of him. I rolled to a stop a hundred yards behind Ellis's vehicle. I didn't want to interfere, but I wanted to see.

My earpiece still in place, I called Wes. The call went to voice mail. "The police have just pulled Peter over. We're on I-95, about a quarter mile before exit three. Hurry."

A marked patrol car appeared in my rearview mirror, its red and blue lights spinning, its siren blaring, traveling far faster than the flow of traffic. As he flew by, I recognized the driver, the young police officer named Daryl. He veered sharply to the right and pulled up two car lengths ahead of

Peter's car. He cut the siren but left the lights flashing as he backed up, closing the gap between the vehicles. Peter was surrounded.

Peter stood by his trunk, his arms hanging by his sides, his hands forming loose fists. His eyes stayed on Ellis. His chin jutted out pugnaciously. I saw flashing lights in back of me. Officer Meade had found me.

My phone vibrated. Wes texted, "In Boston w/ Maggie. Get pics for me."

I thought about it for a moment. *Why not?*

I raised my phone and started taking photos.

Officer Meade walked up as I stepped partway out of the car. I banged my thigh against the door jamb and nearly collapsed from the pain. I moaned, then took in a deep breath, and in a few seconds, the pain subsided into a dull thud.

"Chief Hunter told me to escort you to safety. Do you want to go home?"

"In a minute," I said, thinking only about photographs. I turned the phone sideways and zoomed in for a close-up of Peter's angry profile and another of Ellis, wearing blue plastic gloves, looking inside the trash bag he was holding open.

"Now, Josie," Officer Meade said.

"Okay." I got a good one of Peter being placed inside the back of Daryl's car, turned to her, and smiled apologetically. "I'll go to work, if that's all right."

"Sure. Let's go."

Ellis approached Daryl and said something, then listened for a moment. He double-tapped the roof and stepped back.

"Josie?"

I ignored Officer Meade for just another moment. Daryl pulled out into traffic. Ellis turned toward his vehicle, spotted me, and marched in my direction.

"If you're well enough to be here, you're well enough to give a formal statement," he said coldly.

I glanced at the dash clock. I was due to be on camera in ten minutes. "Okay."

"Officer Meade will escort you to the station." He stomped off toward his SUV.

"Is the flash drive dry yet?"

He spun back to face me, his expression fierce.

"I'm sure Milner kept his client list on it," I added. "It's the only place left. The murderer's name will be on it. That will confirm what I know." I took in a breath. "It's just so awful, Ellis."

His expression changed from annoyed to curious. "What's going on, Josie?"

"I know what happened, and I know why. I can help you get a confession."

"Tell me."

"The only physical evidence is the mineral-oil-stained pants and shoes and the cowboy hat you just confiscated. Aren't I right? Isn't that what was in the bag?"

"Assume it was. What's your point?"

"Any good defense attorney will have a field day with that. You can't prove that the mineral oil on the clothes is the same as that which came from the snow globe, nor can you prove that it got on the clothes during the commission of a felony. The hat is not unique." I paused, thinking. "I might be able to get him to acknowledge that he killed Jason."

"I won't let you put yourself in harm's way. He's already tried to kill you once."

"He won't try to hurt me if he thinks I can get him three million dollars."

A slow grin came over Ellis's face. "You've got a plan."

I smiled. "A good one."

CHAPTER THIRTY-FOUR

I had a double escort to the police station, with Officer Meade in front and Ellis close behind. When we got there, I explained my plan. Ellis approved it and printed out an authorization letter. I faxed it to Max for his review. The gist was that I was to do my best and that I wouldn't be liable for anything, no matter what.

While Ellis went to get Peter situated, I made some calls and sent some texts. I asked Cara to let Timothy know that I was called away on police business and that I looked forward to rescheduling. From Gretchen, I learned that everything at work was fine, except that Hank was a bad boy— he'd lost his new felt mouse. Not under the photocopier, obviously, since it now had a skirt. Probably under a shelf in the warehouse.

"We need to attach some kind of homing device to them," I said.

She giggled. "Maybe we can LoJack them."

"It's probably easier to buy him some new ones."

"Already done. I ran out at lunch. We don't want Hank upset."

"Of course not."

"On a separate subject, Jason's executor, a Boston lawyer, called about appraising Jason's chess set collection. When I told him that we didn't have it, he said he'd arrange for shipment." Gretchen paused, and when she spoke again, I sensed concern. "He said we were to report only to him. Is that all right?"

"Probably. Go ahead and call him back and ask him to send the paperwork documenting his authority."

"Good," Gretchen said, sounding relieved. "Sasha is waving at me. She'd like to talk to you."

"Good job with the lawyer. You can put Sasha on."

"I've finished my report on Ana's Russian skating snow globe," Sasha said. "Do you want me to e-mail it to you?"

"Yes. What's your estimate?"

"Only a few thousand. Three to four, maybe, if we get lucky. It turns out that these ice-skating sculptures were strong sellers for Gardner."

"So it's not rare," I said.

"Or scarce."

"Too bad, but this is excellent work, Sasha."

"Thanks," she said shyly.

I leaned back for a moment, resting, then followed up on Cara's message by texting Timothy with my apologies, saying I'd explain why I'd run out when I saw him and suggesting that he call or text when he was ready to talk. I reached Ty and asked him to pick up dinner on his way home, which he said he was glad to do. I e-mailed the photos to Wes.

Wes called, and I let it go to voice mail. "Wicked cool photos, Joz. Thanks. Maggie and I should be back within half an hour or so. What's going on? The police radio is crickets, and my contacts aren't telling me Jack."

Detective Brownley entered. "Chief Hunter is ready for you."

"Sure." I limped toward her.

She opened the first door we passed, the one that led to the observation room. I stepped in, but she didn't. She closed the door behind me. Daryl was punching buttons and twirling dials, getting everything set. Ellis stood watching him.

"I'm letting you sit in on this for your antiques expertise. Text me as needed. Also, I heard from the lab. Letting the flash drive air-dry worked. You were right. Milner's client list is there."

"And the name I expected is on it?"

"Yup. Along with that disposable cell number. Two dots connected."

"Is it okay that you confiscated that trash bag? Is Peter going to say it's an illegal search?"

"Probably. But he won't succeed. I pulled him over for speeding, which he was. The bag was in plain sight."

"So what? You can't go around opening plastic bags just because they're in plain sight."

"The legal term is exigent circumstances. He's a suspect in a murder case. You're a reliable witness. You reported he entered Ana's house empty-handed and left almost immediately with a plastic bag. We couldn't let him leave the state with potential evidence. I'm not sure we'll need it, but juries like tangible evidence, so I'm glad we have it. I think we have a strong evidence chain leading from the Fabergé egg snow globe to Milner to Kovak to McArthur Evergreen Technologies to Jason to you. The contents of the plastic bag are the cherry on top." He rubbed his chin. "What's your sense? Do you think Milner was pulling a fast one?"

"No. I think he was just what he seemed to be, an expert antiques appraiser planning an exotic vacation. I think he got killed because he actually saw the killer, so he could provide an ID. Kovak didn't. You should ask the travel agent if this was his first big vacation."

"I already did. Last year he went to the Seychelles, an island chain in the Indian Ocean. The year before, he went to Barbuda, a resort with nine suites. It's supposed to be one of the most luxurious in the world."

"Alone?"

"Both times."

"That clinches it, doesn't it? Milner's not involved."

"All set, sir," Daryl said.

"Thanks." Ellis took a step toward the door, then paused. "Do you think Jason was killed because of money?"

I shook my head. "Money was merely the symptom. The disease was pride. This entire nightmare sprang from Jason's cynically given advice. Can you get his newsletter subscriber list?"

"Good idea." He picked up the receiver from a wall-mounted phone. "Cathy, get me Heather Walker at *Ferris Investor News*. The number is in the Jason Ferris case file. I'll take the call in my office." He hung up the receiver and turned to me. "Thanks for the idea." He headed out, adding, "Get yourself settled. I won't be long."

I sat down and closed my eyes. I was weary, worn out, and worn down.

Ellis came back, his expression hard to read. He looked solemn, not like he was going to a funeral, more like the guy who told the family a loved one had died.

"You were right," he said.

"Another dot connected."

Peter sat on the long side of the table facing the one-way mirror. Ellis was at the head, so I had him in profile. Detective Brownley sat behind Peter. Ellis had Peter sign a form indicating that he understood his rights and explained that the interviews would be recorded.

Ellis stated the date and time and the names of everyone present, then turned to Peter. "The DA is drawing up the paperwork charging you with tampering with evidence, obstructing justice, and maybe accessory after the fact. That one is pending. It's tricky because it depends on prior knowledge."

"Are you trying to frighten me by listing trumped-up charges?" Peter asked, looking amused. "Give me a break."

"Name-calling won't help you now. Just because you call them trumped up doesn't mean they are."

"Please. Hauling me in here because I have a bag of laundry in my car."

"Not a bag of laundry," Ellis said pleasantly. "A bag of evidence. Why did you remove the dirty pants, stained shoes, and the hat from Ana's house?"

"They needed cleaning. I'm a helpful sort of guy."

Ellis remained unperturbed. "You know the truth about your father, don't you, Peter?"

Peter didn't reply.

"It was Wes Smith's article that got you thinking," Ellis continued. "As soon as you heard about the cowboy hat, you knew. What made you think about the pants and shoes?"

My heart leaped into my throat and I grabbed my phone and texted, "I mentioned mineral oil to Ana."

Ellis read the message. "I can see trying to protect your dad. You're a family-first kinda guy. You read about the hat, and Ana told you about the mineral oil spill. To her, it was just an interesting tidbit. To you, it meant your dad was in trouble, that you needed to act."

"I'm not saying a word. Nothing."

Ellis stood. "I'll be back with the arrest warrants."

Peter glowered at him.

CHAPTER THIRTY-FIVE

T he technician, a beautiful blonde named Katie I'd met before, had us wired up within minutes. Her eyes opened wide when she saw my purple, yellow, and brown bruises, but she didn't comment.

Ellis arranged for two plainclothes police officers to be on-scene with me. Stan was a newcomer to the force, a middle-aged man I was meeting for the first time. He had pleasant enough features, but his was the kind of face that was hard to describe. Everything was proportional. Nothing stood out. He wore a black sweatshirt and jeans. The other officer was a woman named Dawn, on loan from a neighboring department. She and I had worked together before.* Dawn was about my height and sturdy-looking, with shaggy brown hair, cut shorter than I remembered, and a dusting of freckles on her cheeks and nose. She wore brown slacks with a red sweater. Ellis told me he'd be outside in the communications van.

While Ellis walked me through what I should say, and what I should avoid, Stan and Dawn set out ahead of me to get in position.

I stood up. "I hope I don't screw up."

"Me, too," Ellis said.

Rocky Point library was 110 years old. It was a huge building constructed of gray granite blocks. A turret housed the children's section. Every time I saw the building I smiled. I love libraries and have haunted them since I was a kid.

I parked in the side lot and walked to the front, swaying a bit as I dragged my leg. The pain was constant but blunted by the medication. On a scale of one to ten, it was a two.

---

*Please see *Deadly Threads* and *Dolled Up for Murder*.

. . .

Stefan was sitting in a green-patterned armchair positioned to capture the view of Old Mill Pond, an idyllic location. He was wearing a white cotton sweater, green shorts, and brown leather sandals, a bold move in early spring. He held the *Financial Times* open wide, his sleeves pushed up, his elbows resting on the chair arms. Dawn sat three chairs away, apparently texting. Stan stood at a nearby bookshelf, a book in his hands, flipping pages.

"Hi, Stefan," I whispered, sitting next to him.

"Josie," he said, surprised, starting to rise.

"Don't get up. I was hoping I'd find you here. Do you have a few minutes to chat?"

"Of course."

I looked around as if I wanted to be certain that no one was eavesdropping. When I spoke, I kept my voice low. "I have a proposition for you."

He looked startled.

A woman walked by holding a toddler's hand, and I waited for them to pass before continuing. I leaned in close to Stefan's ear. "About the Fabergé egg."

He folded the newspaper and placed it on the table next to his chair. "I don't understand."

"I figured it out, Stefan. You had the Fabergé Spring Egg snow globe appraised, then used it for collateral. You got a million-dollar loan. I have a firm offer of three million for you. I'll front you a million so you can redeem the egg plus whatever more you need for the interest."

He looked ill. "I don't know what you're talking about."

"I'm not judging you, Stefan." I smiled, one friend to another. "I know what happened, and you shouldn't blame yourself. You lost money. It happens. Three million dollars would solve a lot of money problems."

"Three million dollars."

"Cash."

"Who would pay such an amount?"

"A Russian businessman."

Stefan lowered his eyes to his hands. He rubbed his left index finger with his right thumb.

I sat back, in no hurry. "It's because you followed Jason's newsletter's instructions, right? What a jerk he was. Arrogant. Narcissistic. Mean-spirited."

He raised his eyes and looked at me straight on. "Add in uncaring. He never thought about the people he hurt."

"Hiding behind his education-not-advice mantra," I agreed, "like a banker hides behind small print."

"He was a charlatan," Stefan said.

"And you got taken."

"A fool and his money are quickly parted."

I titch-titched softly and shook my head sympathetically. "How did you happen to subscribe to Jason's newsletter, anyway?"

"At first, I signed up because of Heather, to support her in her new job, but I renewed because of its quality. Or what at the time appeared to be its quality. Jason didn't follow the pack. He seemed to have a more holistic view of investing."

I sighed and shook my head again. "That makes perfect sense. He used words well. He was persuasive. Did you get hurt by the recession?"

"No. I got hurt by my reaction to the recession. I followed Jason's advice about silver and family restaurants." He paused, looking again at his hands. "Timing is all, certainly when it comes to investing. In October 2007, Jason recommended getting ahead of the coming recession. He was right about the recession but wrong about the advice. He recommended buying silver and selling family restaurants. He said a metal like silver was a tried-and-true hedge during economic downturns, and in a recession middle-class families, the ones who frequent family restaurants, can't afford to eat out." Stefan raised his eyes to the window and stared out over the pond for several seconds. "He never told us when to sell. The market for silver plunged as consumer confidence rose, and when Mom and Dad feel more hopeful about the future, they take the kids out to dinner."

"How about now? Has your luck turned?"

"It's not luck we're talking about. We're talking about smarts. And no, I haven't grown any smarter."

"How bad is it? Three million bad?"

"No, thank God. Even paying off my mortgage . . . three million would put me on solid ground again. I'd be left with enough, and I'd stop this foolishness."

"You mortgaged your house?"

"I had no other option. That was last fall. I mortgaged the house I'd worked thirty years to pay off to get cash to live on, then stupidly followed

Jason's advice to buy a pharma company's stock. He said it was about to receive FDA approval on a new drug. Except it didn't receive the approval, and I lost that money, too. I was busted flat."

"Oh, Stefan. I'm so sorry." I sighed again. "That explains why you drove to Rocky Point—you couldn't afford the plane fare. Why did you rent a car? Why not drive your own?"

"I've cut back on everything. Including maintenance on my own car. I was afraid it wouldn't make the trip." He snorted, a self-deprecating sound. "It's humiliating. You must promise me you'll never let Ana or Peter know."

I sighed empathetically. "I guarantee you they won't learn about your situation from me."

"Thank you, Josie." He stared out the window. "I can't believe we're having this conversation. How did you find out about my loan?"

I shrugged, faux-embarrassed on his behalf. "I know about McArthur. I spoke to him."

Stefan slapped the chair arm. "What!"

"Don't get mad at him. He didn't give you up."

He stared at me. "What are you saying?"

"Let's see what we can work out. You had the snow globe copied. How did you choose an appraiser?"

Stefan leaned back and closed his eyes. I glanced at Dawn. She was smiling, looking at her phone. After a moment, she felt my eyes on hers and flicked me a glance. I turned toward where I'd last seen Stan. He wasn't there. I looked around and spotted him sitting about ten feet away, still flipping through a book. I looked back at Stefan. His eyes remained closed. After a few more seconds, he sighed deeply and opened them.

"You got to McArthur through Ana, right?" I asked.

"Through Ana and Jason. Ana worked for McArthur. Jason recommended his company as a buy. Another loser. McArthur sells out and gets rich while all his investors lose their shirts."

"How did you find Drake Milner?"

Stefan rubbed his forehead as if he had a headache. "Why?"

"My client is willing to pay top dollar for an antique that lacks provenance. One of his concerns is that Milner inflated his appraisal. Of course I'll be appraising the egg, too, but my client has rightly observed that I'm hardly objective. I'm hoping you'll give me some information I can use to reassure my client."

"Reassurance is a mirage, since people believe what they want to believe. It's astonishing the deluded narratives we humans weave to satisfy our need for stability." He shrugged. "You can only imagine the hoopla if I'd gone to one of the big outfits. So I didn't. I consulted an industry association to find a Russian decorative objects expert. Milner headed the list."

"What did you think of Kovak's work?"

He gave a little snort. "It was atrocious, but I had no time. I had to use it. When I devised the plan, I had no expectation that Ana would reclaim the egg. Why would I? She never wanted it in her possession before. I was certain I could make a recovery, pay off the loan, and get the egg back safe and sound, with no one the wiser. That damn television show—don't get me wrong. I'm happy for her, of course I am, but the timing couldn't have been worse." He paused, shaking his head. "I had to get the replica made quickly. I had no choice."

"And when you picked it up, mineral oil spilled."

"That old fool."

"You brought the original to McArthur and the replica to Ana."

He stared out over the pond for several seconds, then turned back to face me. "How does it work? This sale?"

I leaned in close and lowered my voice even further. "We launder the egg in addition to the money. You sign a bill of sale to a company in Panama. They sell it to a London gallery. That gallery does research and finds previously undiscovered documentation authenticating the egg. They then sell it to the Russian client, openly."

"So he pays twice. Three million to me and who knows how much to the London gallery."

"Three times, actually. Three million to you. Five million to the Panamanian company. And twenty million to the London gallery. Everybody's happy because what was merely a beautiful artifact without provenance, worth at most eight million dollars, is now transformed into a priceless possession, worth anything, more than a hundred million dollars, certainly, on the open market."

"How do you make money?"

"I charge a buyer's premium. Nineteen percent."

Stefan nodded. "Of course. And the Panamanian company will do the same. And the London gallery."

"Yes."

"Someone has twenty-eight million dollars to spend on this egg?"

"Between you and me, I think he's a mobster."

"I'll need time to have a proper replica created. Ana can't ever know about it."

"I can help you arrange that." I opened my tote bag and pulled out my phone. "What number should I call you on?"

Stefan gave me the number of the disposable phone with a 617 area code, the one that had been purchased at Lucky Electronics.

"Got it," I said. "Did your girlfriend Carly buy this for you?"

He sighed again. "Yes, she got one for each of us." He blinked. "How on earth did you know that?"

I stared at him, the red-hot anger I'd been quashing bubbling to the surface. "I know everything. I know how and why you killed Jason. I know why you killed Milner. I even know why you tried to kill me. Your goose is cooked."

Stefan stood up.

Dawn came hurrying across the open area. "That's enough, Josie."

Stan stood behind Stefan.

"What's going on?" Stefan asked, looking around wildly.

I stepped back, nearly panting with pent-up emotion. I was both enraged and outraged.

Stan identified himself and showed his badge. He kept his voice low. "I need you to come to the station, sir. Your son is already there."

Stefan blanched, stricken. "Peter. I must go to him."

Stan and Stefan walked quickly across the floor and out the door. I stood, still breathing hard, hoping I hadn't ruined everything with my outburst, knowing I couldn't have keep quiet if I'd tried. Dawn came and patted my back.

"It's okay," she said.

"No, it's not. I lost control. I messed up."

"Hard to see it that way from where I sit." She pressed her earpiece. "Let's go. The powers that be want us pronto."

I girded myself, certain I was about to get yelled at.

CHAPTER THIRTY-SIX

e'll talk later," Ellis said as the technician removed the wires that ran along my spine. "I don't want to lose any momentum. You'll go back into the observation room. Text me if you think of anything or if I'm wrong about anything."

"Okay."

"Ana's here, too. She came as soon as she saw the photos Wes published, the ones you sent him of Peter getting arrested."

I raised my chin. "I figured she would."

Ellis held the door for me. "Let's go." He shook his head, a rueful expression on his face. "A Panamanian company? A Russian collector who's in the mob?"

I smiled, my saucy one. "I told you I had a good plan."

I got settled in the observation room, sitting next to Daryl, who was wearing headphones and concentrating on sound levels. I was tired and achy and still fuming. I wanted to go to work. I wanted to go home. I wanted this to be over.

Ana sat at the foot of the long table, her hands primly folded, her shoulders hunched forward. She looked as tired as I felt. Peter sat to her right, tapping his foot. Detective Brownley and Griff sat in back of Peter on metal folding chairs they'd positioned against the wall.

Stefan stepped into the room and froze. "What's going on here?"

"Daddy," Ana said, sitting up.

"Don't say a word," Peter said.

Ellis, coming in behind Stefan, pointed to the chair next to Peter and closed the door. Stefan sat down. Ellis took his usual chair at the head of the table. He slid the sheet containing the Miranda warning across the table to Stefan.

"Please take a minute and read this," Ellis said.

Stefan signed it without reading it and slid it back.

Ellis smiled at him, man to man. "I'm hoping you'll decide to help your son."

"Of course. Always."

"No, Dad," Peter said. "Don't say a word. It's all a trick to squeeze me for a confession."

"A confession?" Stefan asked, bewildered. He faced Ellis. "What do you think my son needs to confess?"

"You need to know that arrest warrants have arrived. For Peter. The charges are serious, obstructing justice and tampering with evidence. The DA is still considering whether to add a charge of accessory to murder after the fact. What I need to ask you about now is laundry, your laundry." Ellis explained how and why Peter had been arrested. "The charges, while serious, are ancillary to the main issue, of course. I don't need his confession. What I need is yours—I need you to tell me about killing Jason Ferris, which, of course, may well have been an accident."

Peter fist-pounded the table. "Don't fall for it, Dad. They can't charge me with anything if we don't talk."

"The charges have already been filed. The paperwork is in my office. If I have to execute the warrants, I will." Ellis turned to Stefan. "If you tell us what happened to Jason, honestly and completely, I'm sure the DA will drop these charges."

"Forget it," Peter said.

"It's the only thing you can do to help him," Ellis said. "It's also the right thing to do. Tell me what happened. Tell the truth."

"It was an accident," Stefan said, his eyes down.

Ana gasped and pressed her hands to her mouth.

"No!" Peter shouted. "Not another word."

Ellis touched Stefan's arm, and when he looked up, he met his eyes. "You have my word, Stefan. I'll do everything I can to ensure that your son is not arrested on these charges."

Stefan bowed his head. "Thank you."

Ellis nodded at Griff and Detective Brownley. They stood up. Griff approached Ana.

"Let me walk you out," he said.

"Daddy?"

"Go," Stefan said.

She kept his eyes on his for a moment, then followed Griff from the room.

Detective Brownley touched Peter's upper arm. "Sir?"

"Forget it," he said, brushing her hand aside. "Feel lucky you got Ana out. I'm staying."

"No, you're not," Stefan said. "I don't want you here."

"Too bad. I'm staying."

Ellis joined Detective Brownley beside his chair.

"If I have to haul you out of the chair," Ellis said, "you might get hurt. It's better to leave upright, under your own steam."

Peter looked up at him. "Tough guy, huh?"

"Tough has nothing to do with it. You can go easy or you can go hard, just so long as you're clear on one thing—you're going."

"Peter," Stefan said softly, "you have no part in this. Go comfort your sister."

Peter stared at his father for ten seconds, maybe longer, then stood up and walked out, slamming the door behind him.

The interrogation room was quiet as we waited for Detective Brownley to return.

From outside, I heard a lawn mower rev up, then shut down. A dog barked. A car door shut.

Griff stuck his head in and asked Ellis if he wanted anything.

"Would you like some water?" Ellis asked Stefan.

"Yes, please."

Ellis glanced at Griff, and he backed out of the room. I had to stop myself from laughing at their mannerly conversation, so polite, so gentlemanly, so bizarre.

Detective Brownley came into the room and spoke to Stefan. "Your children asked me to tell you they'll wait in the lobby."

"They should leave. There's nothing for them to do."

"I told them the same thing," she said, "but they want to stay."

"They love you," Ellis said.

Griff returned carrying a clear plastic pitcher in one hand and a stack of white plastic cups in the other. He poured a cup for Stefan and placed it in front of him. Stefan thanked him. Griff asked if anyone else wanted any, and when Ellis and Detective Brownley said no, he placed the pitcher and cups on the table and left the room.

Ellis glanced at the video cameras to confirm that the red lights were on, indicating the machines were running.

"Thank you for agreeing to talk to us."

"Josie was a plant," Stefan said. "There is no Russian collector."

"That's right," Ellis said. "She was wearing a wire. We have the recording. Two undercover police officers were on the scene as well, also listening in."

Stefan paused, thinking. "If I recall correctly, the only crime I admitted to was replicating the Fabergé egg without telling the owner. I doubt you can charge me with fraud. It would require that my daughter testify against me, and I don't think she will."

"I agree with you. That's why I asked to talk to you privately. The charges against your son are not a put-up job. They're serious. He'll be convicted and he'll do hard time. You need to tell me the truth. Start with Jason. You said killing him was an accident."

Stefan sipped water. He seemed oddly calm. "Jason was in Ana's house when I got there. I'd never met him before, but of course I'd heard of him from Ana and Heather, and I recognized him from his photo." He raised and then lowered his shoulders, trying to relax, perhaps. "Can you imagine how I felt walking in with the reproduction egg in my hand? Here he was, the cause of my downfall, the man that drove me to crime." Stefan shook his head, trying to rid himself of the memory. "He was insufferable."

"What happened?"

"I told him I'd lost some money on his recommendations. He was derisive, joking that only a fool takes a newsletter's advice. I asked if he was serious, and he laughed in my face."

"So you knocked him down."

"No. I told him to get some manners, to show a little class, but he just kept laughing." Stefan took in a deep breath. "I pushed him, and he stumbled. He hit his head."

"Then what happened?"

"I ran to him, and I tripped. That's when the snow globe and egg broke. I could see right away that Jason was dead. I'm not proud of what I did next." He took in a breath. "I left and went to the library."

"You pushed him. He fell and hit his head. That's it?"

Stefan looked puzzled. "What else?"

"Did you hit him after he was down?"

"Hit him? What are you talking about?"

Ellis paused, keeping his eyes on Stefan's. "Why did you kill Milner?"

He met Ellis's eyes. "I didn't."

"Why did you attack Josie Prescott?"

He shook his head. "Attack Josie? I didn't."

"You need to tell me the whole truth, Stefan. A deal's a deal."

Stefan finished his water and slid the cup aside. "I have."

"Who do you think killed Milner?"

"I assume it was a tragic accident."

"It wasn't. It was murder. The dive team found the weapon, a rock. The ME uses imaging technology to match weapons to wounds."

Stefan stared at Ellis. "I didn't know."

"Did you meet him that morning?"

Stefan refilled his cup, then sipped some water.

"We know you called him," Ellis said.

"I met him, yes."

"Where?"

"By Bailey Brook. It's deserted, a good place to have a private conversation."

"Not by Locke Pond?"

"No. When we were finished, I drove back to Rocky Point. Milner headed the other way, toward Durham." Stefan leaned forward. "When I left him, he was alive and well."

Ellis tilted his head and leaned back. "What did you talk about?"

"I asked him to keep the appraisal confidential. He said he'd tried, but you got a court order, so he was going to have to answer your questions and he wouldn't perjure himself. I told him I understood, and I did. I was prepared to face Ana, to tell her what I'd done."

"And then Milner died. Quite a fortuitous coincidence."

"I didn't kill him."

"Who did?"

"I don't know."

"Who did you tell that you were going to meet Milner?" Ellis asked.

Stefan rubbed his head again as he had in the library. His headache must have worsened.

"You told someone," Ellis said. "You must have."

Stefan shook his head.

"Tell me."

"I feel terrible about Jason," Stefan said. "Just awful. I'm glad I told you about it. It's been a terrible weight to bear."

"I don't think you set Milner up on purpose, but whoever you told killed him. We'll check your phone log. See who you called directly after you called him."

Stefan stared at him for several seconds. "I speak to my children frequently. It means nothing."

"Peter was in on it."

"No!" Stefan protested. "Of course not."

"It was Ana?"

"Don't be absurd."

"I know how hard it is," Ellis said. "Implicating your own flesh and blood."

"Family above all." Stefan raised his chin. "I won't do it."

I texted Ellis, "He's wearing sandals."

Ellis stared at his phone display for a moment, then pushed back his chair and stood up.

"I'll be back in a minute," he told Stefan. "Detective Brownley will be here, and we'll leave the recorder rolling. If you have anything to add while I'm gone, don't hesitate."

Ellis stuck his head into the observation room, pointed at me, and said, "Follow me."

"What's going on?"

"Your role is over. Let's get you out of here."

"I know what happened," I said.

"Yeah. Me, too. Which means all that's left is the paperwork."

llis and I walked into the lobby side by side. As soon as we rounded the corner, Peter leaped to his feet. Ana, sitting beside him on the long wooden bench, scooched forward. Her eyes were moist. Her teeth were clamped on her bottom lip.

"Where's my father?" Peter demanded, turning the words into a threat.

Griff came into the open area from behind the counter. Stan walked out from the hallway that led to the other side of the station house. Two other uniformed officers who'd been working at desks near Cathy stood up and approached the counter. Cathy kept on typing.

Peter took in the posse and crossed his arms. Ellis put out his arm like a blockade, signaling me to stop. I moved aside and leaned against the wall. He continued walking until he stood directly in front of Peter.

"I'm going to ask you to do something," Ellis said, "and you're not going to like it."

"I already don't like it and you haven't asked."

"Take off your sweater."

Peter stared at him. "You're nuts."

"Let's see your right arm."

Peter swung around to talk to Ana. "This is bull. Let's get out of here."

Ana looked toward the hallway that led to Interrogation Room One. "What about Dad?"

Peter didn't reply; instead, he marched toward the heavy front door.

Ellis pointed both index fingers toward Peter, and Griff and Stan got in front of him, blocking the exit.

"You can't leave," Ellis said. "I have a warrant for your arrest."

"Peter," Ana said, walking slowly toward him. "What have you done?"

"Whatever I could to help Dad."

Tears sprang to her eyes. "Oh, Peter."

Peter swung back to face Ellis. "Am I under arrest?"

Ellis met his gaze and held it. "Yes."

The sun had disappeared behind fast-moving clouds, yet the temperature had risen. I stood with Ana in the parking lot, waiting for Ray to come get her. I'd offered to drive her wherever she wanted to go, but she declined, asking me to keep her company instead.

"Did you tell Peter about the mineral oil?" I asked.

She didn't reply. She didn't look at me. Her gaze was steady on the ocean. The water had turned a dull dark green.

"I mentioned it to you," I said. "You told him, didn't you? Not for a bad reason, just because it was an interesting little detail."

She still didn't comment. I turned toward the water. Rows of striated waves thundered to shore fueled by a steady northeast wind.

"Ana?"

"I'm all alone," she said.

I didn't know how to reply.

"My husband left me for an older woman."

"I'm sorry," I said.

"No one liked him but me. My dad thought he was an idiot. My friends thought he was a complete loser. I loved him, and he left me for a woman old enough to be his mother."

"I had a boyfriend leave me because I was a downer, his word. I'd lost my job, my friends, and then my dad died, all within the space of a month or so. Two weeks later, he walked."

"How did you cope?" Ana asked.

"I moved to New Hampshire to start a new life."

"Did it work?"

"Yes."

"Maybe there's hope for me."

"Is there something I can do?" I asked.

"No."

I kept my eyes on the ocean. Two minutes later Ray pulled into the lot and Ana hurled herself into his arms.

· · ·

Wes and I met in the Blue Dolphin lounge at five. Ty texted that he expected to arrive earlier than expected.

I got there first and sank into my usual spot by the window. Wes walked in with an unexpected bounce to his step. He was wearing pressed navy blue slacks that fit nicely and a blue and pale pink pin-striped Oxford shirt.

"You look sharp," I said.

He grinned. "Maggie took me shopping in Boston." He laughed, half awkward, half proud. "I spent like a month's pay."

"You look great, Wes."

"Thanks."

He looked over his shoulder until he caught Jimmy's eye. He ordered a coffee. I got a watermelon martini.

He waggled his fingers. "So . . . talk to me."

"It looks like your article helped motivate Peter to act. Seeing those cowboy hat designs got him going."

"Good to know." He grinned. "I'll tell my editor." His grin faded. "I heard from my police source that you were there. How come the cops let you stay the whole time?"

"I was just-in-case protection. You know . . . just in case an antiques question came up. Just in case Stefan said something that didn't gel with a fact I knew. Just in case Ellis needed to talk to McArthur about the Fabergé egg. Just in case."

He grinned. "And you figured it out. Bonzo, Josie! Completely bonzo."

"I can't believe it took me so long. It was obvious that Stefan couldn't be my attacker. He was wearing shorts and sandals, and his sleeves were pushed up. No bruises anywhere, and I'm telling you, Wes, from the whacks I got in on his ankles and arm, I'm surprised I didn't break bones." I shrugged. "If it wasn't Stefan, it had to be Peter."

"Or Ana."

I shook my head. "She wasn't the person who attacked me."

Wes tilted his head. "Do you think Jason's death was really an accident?"

"Yes. What does Stefan do when Jason falls and dies? He flees to the library and buries himself in journals and newspapers. That's perfectly consistent with his character. What happens when Peter shows up and finds Jason's body? Some kind of jealous-like-a-madman blood thirst comes over him, and he pounds Jason's head against those stones over and over again. It's logical."

"You think?" Wes asked, sounding skeptical. "Do you think Peter is loony tunes?"

"I don't think so, but I don't know the official terminology. I know he's obsessed with Heather. She's the sun around which his world revolves. No joke. It's his be-all and end-all. He covers it up pretty well, but he's a stalker, just like in the movies, except it's real. It's terrifying, but whether that means he's crazy?" I shrugged. "If it ever gets to a trial, it's certain to be a case of dueling experts. The prosecutor will prove that Peter is rational and understands the difference between right and wrong. The defense will prove that when it comes to Heather, Peter operates in the ether."

"What makes you think Stefan didn't do the pounding? He's aggressive, too."

"Not like Peter. According to Heather's mom, Allison, Stefan's wife mellowed him, and when she died, he got into a confrontational funk that didn't go away until Carly came along all these years later. Allison didn't know about Carly, of course, but she definitely noticed the difference in him. That's why Stefan seemed to be calmer, warmer, nicer in the last few months."

"This is all sounding pretty touchy-feely, Joz. Fluffy. Like you're trying to tie up a pretty package. A dedicated son protecting a much-loved father. Please. Facts are facts. Stefan confessed to pushing Jason, to watching him fall, and to leaving him, a gravely injured man, while he tootled off to the library. Does that sound 'warmer' and 'nicer' to you? It sure doesn't to me. It sounds pretty darn callous."

"I know." I looked out the window into Maine. A ragged line of wispy clouds hung low over the river. To a sailor, it would look like fog. I turned back to Wes. "I suspect Stefan's warmer side was largely lost in his anxiety about money. But in terms of Stefan—if you'd heard him, Wes, you'd understand. We knew that there were multiple blows because we were privy to the ME's imaging, but he didn't. The police never released the report, remember? You told me it was all hush-hush. When Ellis asked if he hit Jason after he was down, Stefan looked at him like he was speaking in tongues. It wasn't an act, Wes. Stefan didn't have a clue what Ellis was talking about."

Wes shrugged. "I'm not convinced, but whatever." He extracted his notebook, flipped to a fresh page, and made a note. "Let's say you're right. Peter saw Jason and went postal. Why did he kill Milner?"

"Because Milner was going to testify against his dad. Stefan was reconciled—faux noble, if you ask me, but that's a separate conversation. Stefan was confident that Ana wouldn't press charges, so he could take the high road, admit his wrongdoing, and announce that he was ready to accept the consequences." I scrunched up my nose as if a distasteful odor enveloped me. "To me, it seems pretty self-serving. Regardless, Peter knew about Milner's testimony because Stefan confided in him—he called Peter right after he made the appointment to see Milner." I held up a hand to stop Wes from interrupting. "Stefan didn't admit it, but it's the only explanation. Ellis will check Stefan's phone logs and confirm it." I waved it aside. "In any event, Peter was afraid there would be a domino effect, that if Milner testified that his dad hired him to appraise the Fabergé egg, Stefan would be found out as a liar and would therefore become a viable suspect in Jason's murder. You know how it goes. If you lie about one thing, everything you say is suspect. Stefan's insistence that Jason died as a result of an accidental fall, if and when it came to pass that he had to acknowledge his role in Jason's death, would no longer be credible." I shrugged. "He was protecting his dad. Family above all." I sipped some martini, watching Wes write in his notebook. "Was Marty right? About the rock."

"Oh, yeah. Bang on."

"I knew it. Experts are rarely wrong."

"Do you think that's true?"

I grinned. "Probably not."

"Except you. You're never wrong."

I flipped a palm and spoke in a haughty tone. "But of course, my dear. That goes without saying."

He chuckled. "Now that we've put that puppy to bed . . . why do you think Peter attacked you?"

I sighed and looked aside. "I told Ana about snow globes and mineral oil, and she told Peter. He knew right away what it meant, and he knew that I knew, even if the significance hadn't yet occurred to me. He thought that my expertise was the only thing between his dad and clear sailing. With me out of the way, he was certain no one would ever think of it again, especially not the police with six thousand two hundred and twelve other things to worry about."

"None of this would have happened if Stefan had just washed his pants and shined his shoes in the first place. Why didn't he?"

"He would have. Remember that he got chased out of Ana's house the first night he was in town because Jason got killed. No one takes dirty clothes to a hotel. I'm sure he would have cleaned up everything as soon as they got home." I shrugged. "Plus, it probably never occurred to him that there was any big deal. He thought he'd covered his tracks way better than he did. He didn't expect anyone to connect him with the fake egg."

"Same with the cowboy hat, right? He should have chucked it."

"And he would have, if he'd had a glimmer of a hint of a thought that we were closing in on him. That news story had to have rattled him to his core."

"So why didn't he throw it away?" Wes asked.

"By the time Stefan saw the paper, Timothy's crew was setting up at Ana's. I guarantee he would have tossed it as soon as he thought it was safe."

"I don't know . . . if Peter was determined to help him, he should have done the cleanup then and there, right? I mean, why not just pop the pants in the washer and grab a sponge for the shoes?"

"Same issue. There were people all around, and he didn't want to be connected to a cover-up. He thought he could get in and out of Ana's house and never be noticed. If I hadn't seen him, he would have pulled it off, too."

"And he tried to kill you because you understood the importance of the mineral oil spill. That still seems like a huge stretch to me. Attacking you seems like swatting at a fly with a sledge hammer."

"Peter is a fool. By the time he attacked me, he'd lost all perspective. He'd brutalized Jason's corpse and killed Milner in cold blood. In his warped view, I was his new enemy."

"So we're back to whether he's crazy-crazy or just nuts? Which do you think it is??"

"I think he's crazy like a shark—territorial, aggressive, heartless, and indiscriminate."

"Good point—sometimes things are just what they seem to be. Peter's crazy aggressive, and sure enough, he's a killer." He made a note. "You don't think Stefan confided in him, asked him for help?"

"God, no. Stefan did everything he could to keep the truth from both Peter and Ana. Peter figured it out on his own. First, if he'd had any intimation that his dad was involved, he never would have told the police how certain he was that the Fabregé egg was intact at Christmas. It was only later, when he started thinking about it, that he realized that, realistically, no one but his dad could have pulled off the switch. A dinner guest? Please. Once Peter realized that it had to be his dad, he kept close tabs on him, maybe checking his phone calls on that disposable cell, perhaps following him. When Stefan called him after he met with Drake, well, that confirmed everything."

"Do you think Ana's just an innocent victim in all this?"

"It looks that way."

"But you're not sure. How come?"

I looked out over the river for a moment. "It's hard to tell what's real with her."

"Like she's acting all the time?"

"Or that she's simply chameleon-like. I can't tell."

Ty walked in, filling the doorway with his tall, well-built presence. He wore khakis and a collared blue shirt with the sleeves rolled up. He spotted me in the corner and smiled, drawing me to him as if he were magnetized. I smiled back, sending out some magnetism of my own.

"Wes," he said, extending his hand for a shake. "Good to see you."

Wes stood, and the two men shook. "Hey, Ty. Any news from on high you want to share?"

"No."

"I didn't think so." Wes swallowed the last of his coffee. "I've got to go."

"Wait!" I said. "Did you pop the question?"

Wes grinned. "Maggie said yes."

I squealed and clapped.

"Way to go," Ty said, offering his hand for a low five.

Wes laughed and slapped it.

"Any plans yet?" I asked.

"That's why I have to go. We're having dinner at Maggie's folks' house. Her mom is pretty excited."

"Oh, Wes. I'm so pleased."

"Me, too," he said, grinning as broadly as I'd ever seen, and made for the door.

"Will Peter confess?" Ty asked.

He used his fork to scrape the last frosting-coated crumbs from the plate. This time we'd shared Maurice's chocolate tower. He took my hand in his and squeezed a little, a love-squeeze.

"No." I squeezed back. "What do you think will happen?"

"They'll make him a deal. His dad walks if he cops to Milner."

I shook my head. "He'll think his dad will walk regardless. Ana won't press charges about the theft, and there's nothing to suggest that Jason's death didn't happen exactly as he says it did." I used my finger to pick up one last crumb. "This is like the best dessert ever."

"Except for Ana's Fabergé egg cake."

"True. If you were still police chief, would you have played it the same as Ellis?"

"Probably." He grinned. "What do you think of being on camera?"

"Embarrassing. Silly. Fun."

"I bet you're terrific."

"I'm not even close to terrific. I'm shy and awkward."

"You're not shy. You're reserved. You're not awkward. You're genuine."

I shook my head, discomforted, as always, in the face of praise. "Thanks. I'm doing my best, that's for sure."

Ty looked down at the dessert plate. It looked spic-and-span. "Maybe we should have gotten two."

"I can't imagine why we didn't. Thankfully, it's not too late to remedy our mistake."

"An astute observation," he said and signaled our waiter.

Heather stopped by Thursday morning at nine. She looked the same. Her skin was still pale, but not paler. Her black hair was still held off her face, this time by a bubble-gum pink plastic headband. She'd moved her engagement ring to her right hand. She wore a long-sleeved black wrap dress with a pink and black blazer and knee-high boots. She asked to talk to me for a moment, and with some trepidation, I agreed and led the way upstairs.

Her mood was different from before, more subdued.

"I want to apologize for my behavior when I was at your place. I was out of control."

"Apology accepted, although none is due. Grief is tricky."

"Thanks for understanding." She looked around. "I came up for Peter's arraignment. Are you going?"

"No."

"Even though one of the charges involves you? Attempted murder?"

"I've had enough of Peter. I hope I never see him again."

"I've said that a lot of times over the years. I hope today is the last time I see him, ever."

"Why did you come?"

"To let him know I know what he did."

"Did they charge him with something related to Jason?"

"Murder. Jason was still alive when he began pounding his head on the stones."

I shook my head. "That's horrible—just horrific. Peter is an awful man."

"So was Jason."

I gawked.

"I know, I know," she said. "It's unseemly to speak ill of the dead, but it's true. I've just begun to find out how horrible he was. I bought into his caveat emptor routine until I started hearing individual investors' stories, how they trusted him, how he laughed at their losses, how he called them fools." She smoothed her dress over her thighs. "He sheltered me from it all. Doug, the new CEO, doesn't. Some lawyer is starting a class-action lawsuit. The firm may go under." She shrugged. "Maybe it should." She stood up. "I'm not like Jason. That's one reason I wanted to see you. I didn't want you to think I was."

"I understand. What a situation." I walked her out. "Have you decided what you're going to do next?"

"Move. I need a fresh start, new people, new things. I like to hike. I like the cold. I want a real change. I'm thinking Boise. I've applied for a job as a research assistant at a consulting firm there."

"It's supposed to be beautiful."

"We'll see. Lots of things are supposed to be something they're not."

I thanked her for stopping by and watched as she walked slowly across the parking lot.

If you change your environment, do you change? I wondered. Or does who you are follow you forever, like your shadow? Had Heather really not known what Jason was up to? Or had she merely looked the other way? No one consorting with evil is innocent. My dad used to quote the Irish statesman Edmund Burke: "All it takes for evil to succeed is for a few good men to do nothing." From where I sat, Heather was a silent partner in Jason's machinations, and I wasn't sure which was worse—to openly try to trick people or to stand by and do nothing.

•   •   •

Timothy wedged me into his otherwise packed Friday afternoon shooting schedule, and my approval of Gretchen's cake went perfectly. Knocking on the garage/kitchen door, I felt as awkward as I had when I'd placed the order, but seeing the cake changed everything.

"Would you look at this!" I exclaimed, forgetting a camera was recording my every word. I gleefully pointed out each delicate detail. I was excited, astonished, and thrilled.

"You're fabulous!" Timothy told me, giving me a butterfly kiss and whispering that we'd talk more on Sunday, after Gretchen's shower. "More than fabulous!"

I felt a little glowy as I drove home. There is no substitute for affirmation.

CHAPTER THIRTY-EIGHT

T he shower was called for one thirty that Sunday, with Gretchen and Jack due to arrive at two, but Timothy needed access beginning at nine, so Ty and I started decorating at seven. We were in the River View Room at the Rocky Point Café, a popular bistro known for its eggs Benedict and salads. Timothy had marked off positions for cameras and light poles, so we were working around his big masking-tape X's.

We hung Japanese lanterns, positioned the dozen palm trees I'd rented, distributed the leis and place cards at every seat, placed the orchid centerpieces on every table, and set up the 10' × 7' backdrop of a sunset off Waikiki.

That was the photographer's idea. He'd take photos of everyone, both candids throughout the event and posed shots in front of the backdrop, and use the best to put together an online photo album. I planned to give the backdrop to Gretchen and Jack after the party. If I knew Gretchen, it would be on permanent display in their den.

I'd hired a three-piece band from Boston to play Hawaiian tunes, and we had a low riser brought in and placed kitty-corner near the window so they could be visible yet out of the way. A cocktail table festooned with orchid garlands was set aside for Ana's cake. I'd placed a six-foot-long table, also festooned with orchid garlands, next to it for presents.

I stretched and looked around, assessing what we missed.

"It doesn't hurt to stretch," I said.

"That's good. Your bruises still look bad, though."

I lifted my skirt to examine my thigh. The worst of the bruises had faded to yellowish purple. I poked it a little. "It's still tender."

"Another week and you'll be as good as new."

"I think we're done. Want some coffee?"

We were standing by the window sipping coffee and admiring the view when Jack stopped in. It was ten to nine.

"Wow," Jack said, looking around. "This place looks great. Gretchen is going to be knocked out."

"I hope so," I said. "You don't think she has any idea?"

"Not a clue."

"Where does she think you are now?"

"Getting bagels." He grinned. "We're having a light breakfast because we're coming here for brunch with my folks." He winked. "We have a two o'clock reservation."

I was uncharacteristically anxious. I wanted everything to go perfectly, and I didn't see how it could. It was five minutes till two, and all thirty-two of us were standing around in silent anticipation. The door was closed. All I could think of was what might go wrong. Gretchen was familiar with the restaurant, which meant she knew this was a private room. When the hostess led them here, she'd know something was up. I didn't know why I hadn't thought of it until now. She might see someone she knew in the restaurant, or Jack's parents might, someone who would invite them to join their table, and how could Jack navigate around that without giving everything away? What if there was an accident on the highway and they were delayed for hours?

The door opened and we all yelled "Surprise!" and Gretchen screamed and threw up her arms and burst into tears and everyone applauded.

It was perfect.

"I can't believe you pulled this off!" Gretchen told me at the end, hugging me. "Thank you."

"You're welcome."

She hugged me again and whispered, "You're like a sister to me. Thank you."

My eyes filled and I closed them, aware that Timothy's unerring instinct for drama would ensure he got the shot.

"I feel the same," I whispered back. "Lucky us."

Wes and Maggie held hands the whole time.

I went to chat with them as Maggie was shrugging into her camel-hair coat. "I can't believe I haven't had a minute to say hello. Before you leave, may I see your ring?"

She held up her left hand with unabashed delight.

"It's beautiful!"

"Thanks," Maggie said, patting Wes's arm. "I love it."

Gretchen came running up to say good-bye, to thank them for coming, to thank them for the oh-so-cute swaddling blanket.

Wes leaned in toward my ear and whispered, "Did you hear what Ana did?"

"No. What?"

He grinned. "She got her Fabergé egg out of hock. Stefan hadn't spent much of the loan proceeds, and she was able to make up the rest herself. Turns out she had plenty of money—her checking account was empty because she moved all her cash into a corporate account."

"That's great news. I wonder if she'll still want me to appraise it."

"From what I hear, no. She's satisfied with Milner's appraisal."

"Fair enough. Too bad for me, though."

"Something else. It looks like Stefan is going to cop a plea. He's negotiated a sweet deal—leaving the scene of an accident, down from involuntary manslaughter."

"I can't believe that!"

"Peter's still playing hardball, though. Looks like we might get to see those dueling experts after all."

I shook my head, picturing him as I last saw him—defiant. "How's Ana?" I asked.

"Good. She's hired a COO, someone Timothy recommended. The new guy is going to take care of the day-to-day operations while she focuses on the TV show and bringing in new business."

"No one said she wasn't smart."

"Anything for me?" Wes asked.

"No."

He nodded toward Maggie, still chatting to Gretchen, and lowered his voice. "Isn't Maggie great?"

"More than great . . . she's great and she's perfect for you. You're perfect for one another."

Wes smiled, and they left, hand in hand.

Timothy flitted up as soon as they left. "Was that the newly engaged couple you told me about?"

"Yes."

"You're right—they are cute as bugs."

The crew wheeled out the last of the crates as Ty and I finished folding and packing all the garlands.

Timothy turned to me. "Got a minute?"

"You bet. As long as we can do it sitting. I'm beat."

"Let's do it over a cocktail."

"Not a mai tai. I'm done with Hawaiian drinks for a while. Is it all right if Ty joins us?"

"Up to you. I need to discuss a bit of business about your performance."

"What we shot Friday? Didn't it go well?"

"Let's get those drinks."

I turned to Ty. "I need to talk to Timothy for a few minutes. Are you all right finishing packing up everything without me?"

Ty shot Timothy a look, trying to get a read on the situation. Timothy's expression revealed nothing except mild pleasantness.

"Sure."

We headed for the bar. Timothy ordered Jack neat in a rocks glass. I had my regular, a watermelon martini.

"So," he said once we'd clinked glasses, "New York is happy."

"New York," I now knew, was euphemistic for his bosses, the industry executives who could green-light his projects.

"That's good news."

He made a "you have no idea" expression and took a sip. "Very. They're happy with Ana, and it looks good that we'll get a full season out of the deal." He sighed. "I put together a montage of vignettes for Heather. We won't be using any of those scenes, of course."

"That's lovely of you. I'm sure she'll cherish it." I wondered if that was true or if, in her newfound efforts to start fresh, she'd toss it in a drawer, unwatched.

"It was the least I could do." He cupped his drink, staring into the amber liquid for a moment. "But that isn't what I want to talk to you about."

I braced myself for what I was certain would be constructive feedback. Timothy was a gentleman and an experienced professional. It might be hard to hear, but I was determined to listen like a reporter, taking it in like a sponge, without judgment, to be evaluated later, alone.

"What do you think of *Josie's Antiques*?"

"Huh?"

"When I said New York loved you, I meant it. They super-loved you. They want to do a pilot of a new show featuring you and your world. I like *Josie's Antiques*, don't you? It's simple, clear, and friendly."

"Me?" I asked, stunned. "You want to do a show about me?" I laughed. "That's insane. I get all tongue-tied on camera."

"No, you don't. You're you. Earnest and sweet. You're the girl next door, except you know way more about antiques than the girl next door."

I laughed until I howled. Tears streamed down my cheeks. When I was finally able to stop, I patted my eyes with a cocktail napkin and sipped some water Timothy thoughtfully asked the bartender to provide.

"That's the funniest thing I've ever heard," I said.

"I'm serious, Josie. I have contracts in my car ready for your review. What do you say?"

I stopped laughing and started thinking. The publicity potential was indescribable. This show had the ability to catapult my company into the big leagues. The very, very big leagues. I'd been thinking that if Ty got a promotion at Homeland Security, we might need to relocate to Washington, D.C., and I could open a second location, Prescott's Capital Antiques and Auctions, commuting back and forth from D.C. to Rocky Point. I could learn to be comfortable in front of the camera. And even if I never felt comfortable, I could learn to do a good job anyway.

"I'm astonished and honored, and I accept." I raised my martini glass. "To *Josie's Antiques*."

Timothy clinked my glass. "We're going to make beautiful TV together, Josie." His phone vibrated, and he read a text. "Oh, God! They can't do anything without me." He clinked my glass again. "I'll go get those contracts."

He flitted away, and I texted Ty to come join me. I started laughing again, and I was still chuckling when Ty swung onto the stool next to me and ordered a Smuttynose.

"Timothy wants to do a reality TV show starring me. The network executives love me. They want to call it *Josie's Antiques*."

Ty smiled. "You're joking, right? You hate being the center of attention."

"I know. Isn't it absurd?"

"What did you say?"

"What do you think I said?"

Ty took a long drink, then squared up his cocktail napkin before placing the bottle dead center. He reached over and tucked my hair behind my ear, then outlined my lips with his finger. He smiled, just him to me.

"I think you said yes. I think you'll be wonderful."

I smiled back, just me to him. "Ah, shucks, you're just saying that."

"No, I'm not. I've always known you were a star."

I touched his cheek. "I love you, Ty."

"I love you, too, Josie."

I started laughing again. "Can you imagine? Me on TV?"

Timothy reappeared, a legal-sized envelope in hand. "Yes, darlin'! I can."

Timothy and I shook on the deal; then Ty and I started exchanging ideas for the show. A perfect end to a perfect day.

ACKNOWLEDGMENTS

Thanks to G. D. Peters and Steve Shulman for their assistance with this novel.

Special thanks go to my literary agent, Cristina Concepcion, of Don Congdon Associates, Inc. Thanks also go to Michael Congdon, Katie Kotchman, and Katie Grimm.

The Minotaur Books team also gets special thanks, especially those I work with most closely, including executive editor Hope Dellon; assistant editor Silissa Kenney; publicist Sarah Melnyk; director of library marketing and national accounts manager (Macmillan) Talia Ross; copyeditor India Cooper; and jacket designer David Baldeosingh Rotstein.